HOTSHOT
DOC

USA TODAY BESTSELLING AUTHOR
R.S. GREY

Published: R.S. Grey 2018
authorrsgrey@gmail.com
Editing: Editing by C. Marie
Proofreading: JaVa Editing, Red Leaf Proofing
Cover Design: R.S. Grey
ISBN: 9781790867233

CHAPTER ONE
B A I L E Y

I WONDER WHAT other people my age are doing at this very moment.

Scrolling through Tinder?

Hitting the town with their squad?

I don't have a squad.

I have a little sister. She's squashed against me on the couch so we can both see my computer screen. Reruns of *Grey's Anatomy* play out in high definition. Dr. McDreamy's hair is thick and shiny. I want to run my finger across the screen and try to feel it.

On my face is green sludge. It's supposed to be a homemade face mask. Josie whipped it up a few minutes ago and swore to me that when we wipe it off, we'll look like movie stars. I'm pretty sure she's wrong, and worse, she might have wasted our last avocado. I was going to slice it onto some rice and call that a well-balanced dinner. Looks like I'll have to get creative.

Two doctors start tearing off each other's scrubs on my computer screen. They're about to get it on, and I hold up my hand to cover Josie's eyes.

"You're too young to be watching this."

It's a joke. We've already watched a million episodes and at least two million raunchy sex scenes.

Josie swats my hand away and turns up the volume. Our living room is now filled with moans and groans. Maybe I'm not such a good guardian.

"Are your friends at school allowed to watch shows

like this?" I ask, suddenly racked with guilt. We should be watching nature documentaries on PBS, penguins waddling around on snow accompanied by the soothing sound of Morgan Freeman's voice.

"Are you kidding?" she asks, not taking her eyes off the screen. "People at my school are *doing* stuff like this."

I'm horrified by the idea of fourteen-year-olds partaking in any physical activity beyond holding hands.

"Promise me you won't touch a boy until you're eighteen."

She rolls her eyes and holds up her pinky. I wrap my own around it, and just like that, we have a pact. I can breathe easier now.

Once the credits roll, I stand up to wash my face, hoping at the very least this weird concoction hasn't caused me to break out in an angry rash. I have work in the morning and I'd rather not be the laughing stock of the hospital.

Josie trails after me and hogs half the sink.

"Is it really like that? Are doctors all over each other in the on-call room?"

"I've already told you—that stuff never happens."

I meet her gaze in the mirror and pass her the towel after I pat my face dry. No angry boils yet. That's a good sign.

"Right, okay, maybe not the really crazy stuff, but I bet you've caught people making out in the supply closet once or twice."

"Never."

"What about having sex in the locker room?"

"No."

"Stolen glances in the operating room?" she asks, her tone growing desperate.

"Josie, *Grey's Anatomy* is a television show—scripted drama, pretend love. Don't read too much into it."

She sighs, deeply annoyed. "What about the surgeons?" She drops the towel and turns toward me. Her hands grip my arms and I can't break free. She's surprisingly strong for someone so scrawny. "Are any of them even half as cute as Dr. McDreamy?"

"Most of them are old men. Gray hair, mustaches, bellies like Santa Claus. You've seen my boss."

I pry her hands off me and then head to the kitchen. We're low on pretty much everything, but I don't get paid until Tuesday. Tuna fish sandwiches it is...*again*.

"Ugh, seriously? No one is even remotely good-looking?!"

I'm distracted because I'm currently in a fight with the can opener, so I don't think before I answer her. "There is one..."

She leaps across the kitchen, yanks the can of tuna out of my hand, and stares up at me with wide, expectant eyes. "Who?"

"I don't know his name."

Lie.

"What does he look like?"

"Tall. Brown hair." I shrug.

Devastatingly handsome is the key phrase I'm leaving out. *Arrogant* and *jerk* are another two words I'm better off not saying.

I'm being evasive on purpose because my sister is a little precocious and a whole lot scary. Within three seconds, she has my computer open on the couch and is scrolling through the *Staff* tab on the hospital's website. I know from late-night stalking that it's organized alphabetically, which is why she yells from the other room,

"What's his last name?"

I cough to cover up another lie. "I can't recall."

"What department?"

I pop two pieces of bread in the toaster and get out the mayonnaise, wondering how long it will take her to find him without my help.

"*BAILEY*, what department?!"

I continue ignoring her. Her fingers are really flying in there. The keys are probably popping off my laptop.

The toast pops up just as I hear her audible intake of breath.

"I FOUND HIM!"

My stomach drops.

"Dr. Matthew C. Russell!" She starts scrolling through his bio quickly. "Medical school at UT Southwestern. Residency at UCLA. Fellowship in complex spine and another in pediatric scoliosis, yada yada. Who cares?! I don't know what half those words mean. Are there more pictures of him other than this headshot? Maybe ones from a beach vacation?"

"I don't know. That name doesn't ring a bell. Dr. Russell, you said? That might be him. Who cares." I'm utilizing my very best acting skills to throw her off the scent. Then, I try a second method: distraction. "Your sandwich is ready!"

She drags the laptop into the kitchen and takes a spot at the table across from me, a small smirk in place. I eat on my own, munching in silence. Meanwhile, Josie's sandwich goes untouched. Her eyes are narrowed at the screen as she scrolls and types away. She's a private detective desperate for a new lead. I half-expect her to whip out a magnifying glass and grow a mustache.

"He doesn't have any social media accounts, which is

extremely annoying. I checked the UT Southwestern alumni page, but they don't post pictures."

"Why does it matter? Eat your food."

She levels me with an annoyed glare, holding eye contact as she takes a massive bite of her sandwich, and then she gets back to the mission at hand with her cheeks puffed up like a chipmunk.

I know why my sister has latched onto Dr. Russell like this. In the six years since I've taken guardianship of her, I haven't been on many dates. I haven't been interested in guys in general. Romance has taken the back seat in my life—no, worse: romance has become those aluminum cans trailing by strings behind my car. My lips have not felt human contact in so long I can't quite remember how kissing works. Do you just stick your tongue in and go for it? Hopefully it's like riding a bike or I'm screwed.

Josie has been worried about me for a while.

Just last week she told me she felt bad that I've had to give up so much of my life for her.

Of course, I protested.

"I have no idea what you're talking about. I love having you here. You know that."

"You've sacrificed a lot for me."

"Oh c'mon. No I haven't."

"You don't have any friends."

"I have Ms. Murphy next door."

"She's an old coot who wears crystals around her neck."

"I don't appreciate you calling my very best friend an old coot."

She doesn't pause to laugh. "You had to quit college because of me."

"Big deal. I love the job I have now."

"And you never go out."

"Not true."

"The last time you went on a date, I was still a preteen."

"Surely that can't be…"

I didn't finish my thought because she wasn't kidding. It really has been that long.

The truth is I *have* had to sacrifice a lot of things to take care of Josie. For all intents and purposes, I live the life of a single mom. My days are consumed with tasks like laundry, cooking, and cleaning. I have to make sure Josie is staying on top of her grades and getting to school on time while also not growing out of her jeans so quickly she has to walk down the halls at school in high-waters. I don't go out to bars on Friday nights. I don't give myself the opportunity to meet people. I work and I save every penny I earn so one day I'll be able to afford a down payment on a house and move us out of this hovel we've squeezed into for the last few years.

Still, lack of romantic relationships aside, it's not a bad life. In fact, it's a pretty great one.

Josie just doesn't see it that way.

She turns the computer around so I'm forced to see the image of Dr. Russell she's blown up to epic proportions. I refuse to give in to her demands to acknowledge his hotness. Instead, I go cross-eyed and stick out my tongue in the hopes of making her laugh.

Her sigh tells me she thinks I'm deeply hopeless. "If you had an ounce of courage you would march up to this doctor and ask him out on a date tomorrow morning."

Ha ha ha. I laugh at that idea all the way through the rest of dinner, and while I do the dishes, and after as I drag a canvas bag filled with our dirty clothes to the laundromat down the street, and as I sit in front of those ancient machines watching them swirl around and around.

Josie has no idea what she's talking about.

Dr. Russell doesn't know I exist. We've never talked. He's the youngest, most hotshot surgeon at the hospital, and he has a reputation for being the most aggressive, rude doctor in all the land.

I'd be better off trying to pin down Dr. McDreamy than attempting to date him.

CHAPTER TWO
MATT

"I'D LIKE TO put in my two weeks' notice."

I glance up from the mountain of paperwork on my desk to see Kirt, my brand-new surgical assistant, standing at the door of my office. He's wringing out his hands. A bead of sweat rolls down his forehead.

"Why?"

His gaze jerks to me and his eyes widen in fear. "*Why?*"

He didn't think he'd have to explain himself. He's about to lose his bowels on my carpet.

I toss my pen onto my desk and lean back in my chair. This is the last thing I was expecting him to say. I thought we had a good thing going. I've only made him cry twice.

"I know you're a great surgeon." My expression must harden because he amends his statement. "The *best* surgeon! Truly! It's why I took this job. I figured if I stuck it out with you for a few months, you'd give me a good letter of recommendation for my next job. Honestly, I thought this was a *Devil Wears Prada* situation—"

"A what?"

His cheeks redden. "*The Devil Wears Prada*...the movie?" My face doesn't change. "Sorry, my girlfriend made me watch it the other day and it really helped me put some things into perspective." His hands start waving as he explains the plot. "There's this terrible boss who basically terrorizes the whole office. The main character thinks if she toughs it out as her assistant long enough, she'll be able to work anywhere she wants."

He's too stupid to realize he's just implied I'm a "terrible boss" who "terrorizes" people. If he wasn't already quitting, I'd fire him.

"Get to the point."

"Oh, well, yeah. The point is…I can't do this. The stress of this job is more than I can handle. I have a stomach ulcer. I've started to develop nervous bowels." I'm now more concerned than ever that he's going to soil my carpet. "I'm not sleeping. My girlfriend gave me an ultimatum: either I leave New England Medical Center or she leaves me. I thought I'd be able to make it until the new year, but that's still a few months away. So…" He pauses and glances down at the ground. "I'm giving my two weeks' notice."

My secretary appears behind him, holding a file, which means my next patient is here: a seven-year-old girl named Fiona. In a few minutes, I'll join her and her parents in the conference room for a consultation about a complex procedure that will relieve the pain and suffering she's endured from being born with a severe curvature of her spine.

I don't have time for Kirt and his stomach ulcer.

I stand to receive the file.

"They're already in the conference room," she says with a no-nonsense tone.

"Thank you, Patricia."

She straightens the glasses on the bridge of her nose and aims daggers at the back of Kirt's head, which tells me she likely heard part of his speech and she didn't like it. Unlike him, she's loyal. She's been working for me since I first started here.

Kirt scrambles as I leave him standing there and head

14

for the conference room. "Dr. Russell. *Dr. Russell*! You'll still give me a good rec letter, right?" he shouts down the hallway. "I've been a good surgical assistant, haven't I?!"

I don't answer him because I'm already flipping through Fiona's file, reacquainting myself with the x-rays and CT scans I've been studying for the last few days. She's been turned away from four other doctors. The curvature in her back is severe enough that the procedure would prove difficult even for the top pediatric spinal surgeons in the world. Fortunately for her and her parents, I'm one of them.

I push the door open and see Fiona's parents sitting at a table wearing expressions of fear and apprehension. Her mother has dark circles under her eyes. Her father's hand is clasped over his wife's on top of the table and he squeezes twice in an act of reassurance as I walk in. Fiona sits beside her mom, tucked in the oversized leather chair, making a little doll dance on her lap. At first, she leans awkwardly against one of the chair's armrests, but when she sees me, she tries and fails to sit up straight. A deep frown cuts across her chubby-cheeked face. Seeing that small struggle ensures I'll go through with this procedure even if it kills me. She deserves to have someone fighting for her, and if Kirt is too much of a pansy to do it with me, I'll find someone new.

I'VE BEEN AT New England Medical Center for five years now. When I first started, I'd just come off of not one, but two fellowships—one in complex spine and the other in pediatric scoliosis. Even after all that training, I had a lot to learn. Some would say I still do. Most of my colleagues think I'm naive to take the kind of cases I do. There are four other spine doctors in our department, and I'm the only one who specializes in peds. The rest of them—the ones sitting together at a table in the doctors' lounge as I walk in for lunch—do routine adult spinal fusions, the kind of cases that take two hours, the kind that allow for a four-day work week and extra time on the golf course.

They wave me down and I inwardly groan. I know what this is going to be about, and I don't have the energy to deal with their boys' club bullshit today.

"Hear you're losing another assistant, Matt," Dr. Goddard says. In his late thirties, he's the closest to me in age, but that's where our similarities stop. He's in surgery for the money and the reputation. He wears monogrammed polos. He drives a cherry red Porsche. His wife looks like an inflated sex doll.

"How'd your fusion case go this morning, Jeff? Break any nails?"

His eyes narrow on me.

"At ease, boys." Dr. Lopez chuckles and then leans toward me. "I heard you might be taking on that seven-year-old. I took a look at her x-rays and they're not pretty."

I shrug. In my hand, I have a stack of files containing surgical details from cases I've successfully executed in the past that are similar to Fiona's. If Dr. Lopez weren't sitting with Dr. Goddard and the rest of them, I'd ask him for his input.

"How are you going to do the case without a surgical assistant?" Dr. Goddard asks, needling me again.

I want to ask him how he manages to look in the mirror in the mornings without punching the glass. We all have our unanswered questions.

"You know they have a picture of Dr. Russell up in the staff lounge?" he continues, turning to the group with a shit-eating smirk on his face. "They added devil horns and a red tail. I'm thinking of asking one of them to give it to me so I can have it framed."

I offer a wry smile. "As always, gentlemen, it's been a pleasure."

I wouldn't bother with the doctors' lounge at all, but the gourmet catering is usually pretty good and it saves me from having to worry about lunch. I pile up a plate with grilled salmon, sautéed vegetables, and a cheesy potato dish that has my mouth watering, and then I find a quiet table in the corner.

The lounge operates a lot like a high school cafeteria. NEMC is a private hospital that consists of fifty-four surgeons covering fifteen specialties. Each specialty has its own quirks.

Here's how to tell them apart:

The beer-drinking sports fans? Those are the general orthopedic surgeons. They do their fellowship in sports medicine and they've never met a protein supplement they didn't love.

The masochists, the men and women who enjoy being woken up at all hours so they can rush in and save the day? Those are the transplant surgeons.

If they like to hit on the nurses and tell everyone they make the most money, it's a good chance they're cardiothoracic surgeons.

The Ferrari drivers who want to be popular with the local celebrities, wear shiny suits, and do what we all refer to as "fake surgery"—plastic surgeons.

You catch my drift. We all have our idiosyncrasies, even me. I'm one part masochist, one part perfectionist. I have a little hero complex of my own and an ego that could fill this entire room, but it's necessary. Who wants to put their kid's spine in the hands of a simpering fool who buckles under pressure?

"Mind if I take a look?" Dr. Lopez asks.

I glance up from my plate to see him pointing to the files laid out in front of me.

I nod. "Go for it." Then I think better of it and reach for the third one down—one from a particularly trying case I tackled last year. "Start with that one."

He pulls out a chair opposite mine and sits down. "You intimidate Dr. Goddard. That's why he acts like that." I don't reply. I didn't sign up for a therapy session. "I probably shouldn't be telling you, but he interviewed for the same fellowship as you and the program directors didn't pick him."

I muster up a half-interested hum then shove another bite of salmon in my mouth. He won't succeed in convincing me that Dr. Goddard deserves my pity.

Dr. Lopez chuckles. "All right, I can see that you two won't ever reach an understanding, so let's focus on a different problem. How many surgical assistants have you run into the ground in the last year? Two? *Three*?"

Five, but I don't correct him.

"I've had the same assistant for years and she's great. She anticipates what I need in the operating room, she's timely, and she's sharp as a tack. She makes me a better surgeon. Do you catch my drift?"

I level him with a bored stare. He's dangerously close to getting asked to leave my table. He might be one of the senior surgeons in this hospital, but he's not my boss.

He trudges on, unmoved by the daggers I'm aiming at him. "You're wasting your time training new assistants every few months. Your surgeries are hard enough without having someone green by your side. Think of how much more you could do with a team you trust."

I'm annoyed to realize he does have a valid point, but it's nothing new. I've come to this same conclusion myself. The problem is, I've yet to find an assistant who could last longer than a few weeks.

CHAPTER THREE
BAILEY

JOSIE DOESN'T BELIEVE me when I say it, but I actually love my job as a surgical assistant. It feels like the path I would have chosen even if life hadn't forced my hand. Sure, some parts get tedious—pulling instruments, prepping sterile fields, cleaning the OR—but the rest of it is awesome.

This work isn't for the faint of heart. I'm Dr. Lopez's right-hand woman during his surgeries. I've seen more blood and guts than a medic on a Civil War battlefield. I've watched patients code, surgeons breakdown, device reps faint, and instruments go missing.

The case we have this morning starts as they usually do, with Dr. Lopez and me fighting over which playlist we should stream over the speakers.

"You're seriously going to pick oldies again?" I groan. "Don't you see you're walking right into a cliché?"

He grins. "I operate better when I'm listening to The Eagles."

"Uh huh, so it's just my imagination that I saw you shaking your hips to Maroon 5 last week?"

The anesthesiologist clears his throat as a gentle way of forcing Dr. Lopez's hand.

"Fine. Why don't we just let the rep decide?"

All eyes shift to a young guy standing in the corner of the operating room. His eyes widen in fear. He exudes nervous energy from every pore. He doesn't want this responsibility. He's here because he's a glorified salesman.

He wants Dr. Lopez to continue using his company's insanely expensive spinal implants, and from the look of sheer terror on his face, he assumes one wrong song choice will get him kicked out of the OR.

"Uhh, I like The Eagles too," he says, his voice wobbly.

Dr. Lopez throws me a conspiratorial wink. He really shouldn't mess with them like that, but I know it's too hard for him to resist.

It's truly his only fault.

He's a rare gem, and I fully realize how good I have it with this job. Surgeons are notoriously difficult to work for. They tend to have egos, attitudes, or god complexes— sometimes all three. *Shiver.* Dr. Lopez isn't like that. His default mood is jovial. His scrub cap is adorned with smiling cartoon dogs. He takes a vested interest in his staff. He's also old enough to be my grandfather, something he routinely tells me when I give him a hard time.

"I need the eight-millimeter spreader," he says to me later, during the surgery.

I shake my head. "You always have me start with the eight on cases like this, but then you end up using the six, so I'm handing you the six. Let me know if you still want the eight."

I catch the audible intake of breath from the device rep. No doubt he's expecting Dr. Lopez to blow up at me for having the gall to question him. Any other surgeon might, but Dr. Lopez nods and takes the instrument.

I'm left with a big, cheesy smile hidden under my mask.

I'm good at my job.

I love my job.

I love my boss.

"Oh," Dr. Lopez continues offhandedly, "would you mind coming to talk to me in my office this afternoon? After lunch?"

I HAVE A good feeling about my meeting with Dr. Lopez. After I finish eating my sandwich, I dab, dab, dab my face with a napkin, swish around a little mouthwash, and then fire my finger guns straight at my reflection with a wink.

"This is it," I say aloud, eyes aglow with possibilities. "Dr. Lopez is going to give you the raise you've been waiting for. He's going to make it rain hundred-dollar bills, and Josie isn't going to have to eat a tuna sandwich tonight. Nope. This calls for something fancy. STEAK. Okay, we aren't *that* rich. Maybe some chicken that's in the bargain bin because it's one day shy of going bad."

"Lady, are you almost done?"

Oh, right. I move aside and let the custodian push her mop past me. I want to ask how long she's been standing there, but then she tells me the supermarket down the street is running a sale on beef. I should feel embarrassed, but who cares?! A RAISE is in my imminent future.

When I arrive outside Dr. Lopez's door, I rap my knuckles across the thick oak in a cheerful cadence and then wait for his cue to enter.

"Come on in, Bailey!"

"How was your lunch?" I ask as I walk in, prepared to dabble in a little bit of small talk in the event that it will pad my raise just a teensy bit more. Hell, I'll sit here and listen to him painstakingly describe his last round of golf if it means I don't have to crack another can of shredded fish in this lifetime.

"Lunch was good." He smiles at me from behind his desk and tells me to have a seat.

I have such a strong urge to flail with excitement that I have to stuff my hands under my butt. Dollar signs float in the dead space between the top of his head and the bottom of his fancy diplomas. He starts talking and I can barely pay attention as I start to rack up future purchases in my head.

I'm going to buy a new pair of tennis shoes. Josie is finally going to get a new winter coat. Maybe, *maybe* I can swing for a washer and dryer so I can stop carting our clothes to the laundromat.

"I hope this doesn't come as too much of a surprise," Dr. Lopez says, tugging me out of a vivid daydream in which I was smooching the front of a newly delivered washing machine.

"What? I'm sorry, I missed that last part."

He chuckles and shakes his head. "I don't think you caught any of that, did you? Bailey, I'm retiring."

Retiring.

I sound it out slowly in my mind. *Reeeetttiiiirrriiinnnggg.*

The word spins me around like a whirlpool, which makes sense because that was the brand of washer and dryer I was considering.

"Retiring? From what, golf?" I sound hopeful. It's a possibility. He sometimes complains about his lower back after he plays too many rounds.

"No. No." He stands and walks to his window so he can stare out at the sprawling metropolis below. I swear I hear his bones creak as he walks. He's always been old, but since when is he *old?* "I've been due to retire for a few years now and I've put it off, but Laurie has had enough.

She wants to spend more time with our grandchildren and travel while we still can. What's the use of socking away all this savings if we aren't even going to use it?" he jokes, reciting the argument he's probably heard on repeat for the last few years.

"Can't you delay it just a little longer?" I ask, pleading. "You've only been practicing for what, thirty years?"

"It'll be forty next month."

FORTY?! Jesus. Get the man a cane already.

I'm shaking my head and my hands aren't under my butt anymore—they're tugging at the collar of my scrubs, trying to give my airway an easier go of it.

This can't happen. I just need him to stay long enough for me to grow my nest egg into a nest chicken. I need that down payment for a house, dammit—and if not that, at least enough for Josie and me to move into a slightly bigger, nicer hovel, one with a reliable dishwasher and a shower that doesn't spurt brown poop water onto my head after a hard rain.

He sighs and turns back to face me. "I knew you'd react this way. We're a good team, Bailey, and rest assured, I'm not going to leave you without options."

I perk up, my panic attack momentarily taking a back seat. "Options?"

Maybe he's going to write me a check. Maybe he feels bad for abandoning me like this. Maybe he's always thought of me as the daughter he's never had (he has three very lovely daughters) and he's going to name me as a beneficiary in his will. That's when I remind myself that he's retiring, not *dying*. Jesus.

He nods. "Yes. Options. There are four other spinal surgeons at this hospital."

"Yes…" I confirm slowly, my brain still having a hard

time catching up.

"So all we need to do is hook you up with one of them. I've put in a good word around the office. They'd be crazy to turn you away."

Images of each of the four other physicians pop up like little thought bubbles. There's Dr. Goddard, who is perpetually red-faced and puffy. He only hires young, pretty females. His nurses look like they've all competed in the Miss USA pageant. I pop his bubble.

Dr. Richards is okay, a little stuffy and boring, but I wouldn't have to worry about him hitting on me. He's closest to Dr. Lopez in age and has a good reputation around the hospital. He's a definite possibility.

Dr. Smoot (yes, that's his real name) is another good choice, though I've never once heard him speak. He's extremely thin, skeletal even, and apparently only listens to classical music while he operates. He also only takes on geriatric cases. Talk about a good time. Old geezers splayed out on the operating table while Beethoven blasts overhead. Still, I can't be picky, because the last remaining surgeon, Dr. Russell, is not an option at all.

I know his current surgical assistant, Kirt, and I knew the last one he had too. Oh, and the one before that and the one before that. I ate with every single one of them in the employee lounge. I became friendly with them, listened to their woes, nodded and frowned as they described the horrors of working for a surgeon like Dr. Russell. I watched them cry, grown men and women blubbering like their lives were ending all because of something he said to them during surgery.

I won't do it. I will never work for him.

"Let's start with Dr. Richards and go from there," I say reluctantly. He nods and moves away from the window, and I finally work up the courage to ask the question I've been avoiding. "How long until you leave?"

"A few weeks."

"*Weeks*?!"

I was prepared for him to say months. He's worked here for forty years and he's going to try to phase himself out in a few short weeks?

"What about your cases?" I ask incredulously.

"Haven't you noticed I've stopped taking on new patients? I only have a handful of surgeries left."

No, I've been busy crumbling under the weight of life.

"Laurie wants me out by Halloween at the latest. She wants to travel a bit and go see the grandkids over the holidays."

How wonderful. Dr. Lopez will be carving pumpkins and decorating gingerbread houses, and I'll be left here alone, without a new washer and dryer set.

"What if none of them want me on their team?" I ask, embarrassed that my bottom lip is wobbling just a little.

He shakes his head and rounds his desk. "Not possible. Let's go. Dr. Richards should be in his office. No time like the present."

DR. RICHARDS HAS a big coffee stain on the lapel of his white coat. His office is decorated with furniture from the 70s. Fitting, because I think that era was the last time he had a full head of hair.

We plead my case and he grimaces.

"Oh, wish I could help out, but I already have Marlene and Chris. They've been with me for nearly a year now, and Dr. Lopez, you know more than anyone that I can't overlook that kind of loyalty."

That's what Dr. Richards says.

A big, fat no.

So we try Dr. Smoot. He's playing classical music in his office while he finishes paperwork. His skin is so pale and his office is so dark, I'm not totally convinced he's not a vampire.

After we lay out the situation for him, he slides off his glasses, folds them carefully in his hands, and then looks at us with a thin-lipped sneer. "Unfortunately, I'm not in need of a surgical assistant right now. Have you tried Dr. Richards?"

Yes, we've tried Dr. Richards, you pale, pale man!

I want to storm out of his office, but instead I thank him for his time and tell him I'm available if he is ever looking for an assistant. He smiles and I swear to God the man has overdeveloped canines. A shiver runs down my spine and I'm actually glad he doesn't need me because I'm not sure I'd feel comfortable working for the undead.

"All right then," I say, mock cheer clouding my face as I turn to Dr. Lopez in the hallway. My smile feels so tight, I know I'm not doing it right. My teeth are showing, but my lips aren't tilted up. "Last one, right? Should we try Dr. Goddard?"

At first, he wasn't even an option, but the pickings are getting slim, and it's either him or…

I refuse to finish that thought.

Dr. Goddard's office is filled with a chrome coffee table and fancy leather armchairs. There's a large framed photo of him and the rest of his platinum blond brood smiling on a beach in coordinating white outfits. It would seem wholesome if not for the equally large framed photo of a red Porsche hanging beside it.

Dr. Goddard gives me a casual once-over when we walk in, and upon realizing I am A) female and B) under 75, his eyes light up.

"Dr. Lopez, what can I do for you?"

Nothing.

He can do nothing.

"Aw man, wish I could help," he groans. "But I'm all set with my staff at the moment."

Not even my boobs (the ones he keeps staring at) can convince him to give me a position. The fact is: none of the other surgeons are hiring. They have employees they like and a good team around them. I get it. A good, trained team makes for seamless, successful surgeries.

I was a part of a team like that just this morning. Now? I'm on the outside looking in, just a lowly surgical assistant without a surgeon.

"There's still one last option, Bailey," Dr. Lopez says after we leave Dr. Goddard's office.

His tone betrays his lack of hope.

I hold up my hand.

"Not today. Let's not discuss that one. Okay? Let me just wrap my head around the fact that you're retiring and I'll likely be out of a job, and then tomorrow, we can keep coming up with ideas."

"I'm sorry."

His words stab me in the gut. Poor Dr. Lopez. It's not his fault this is happening. What is he supposed to do, work himself into the grave just so I can have a steady job? (Yes.) No. I don't want that for him.

I shake my head. "Don't worry about it. Tomorrow things will look better. I know it." I start to walk away. "And hey, thanks for trying. It was worth a shot, right?"

I BREAK THE news that we'll be living on the streets to Josie over dinner. We're eating peanut butter and jelly sandwiches and baby carrots, a pitiful dinner by anyone's standards. It's not that I don't make good money as a surgical assistant, it's just not great money. Twice a month, my paycheck hits my bank account, and as soon as the money goes in, it goes right back out thanks to credit card payments and rent and health insurance and cell phone bills and groceries and, and, and…it's not easy, but we're making do. I regret having to use credit cards to get us through the lean years back when I was getting certified, but I didn't have any other option. Josie's with me because our parents passed away in a car accident.

Their death was sudden and unplanned. No life insurance policies. No wills. I finished paying off their funeral costs two years after we buried them. Side note: funeral homes don't appreciate you suggesting you'll just make the caskets yourself. (Those things are expensive!)

The reality that they are *gone* gone, not just at-work gone or out-of-town gone still sinks into me like a sharp dagger whenever I think about it, but guess who doesn't have the luxury of grief? *Raises hand.*

It's just me and Josie. All that matters now is that we have each other and I won't let her down.

"I'll find another position," I promise. "I was totally kidding about living on the streets."

She shrugs. "I think it'd be fun to be homeless. I've always wanted to live under a bridge like a troll."

"Hilarious."

"I mean it." Her brown eyes are wide with wonder. "Think of how cool I'll be at school when I tell everyone

I'm a vagabond!" Then she tilts her head to the side and frowns as if realizing something. "It really does suck that you sold your car a while back. It was a clunker, but we could have lived in it if times got tough."

I set my sandwich down and lean forward to ensure she's really listening.

"Josie, we aren't going to get kicked out of here. That was a bad joke. I'm going to find another doctor to work for. Now eat your dinner or no *Grey's Anatomy* tonight."

She stuffs the rest of her sandwich in her mouth in one fell swoop. Then she chugs her milk and sticks her tongue out like a mental patient proving they swallowed their medicine.

"Am I excused now?"

She doesn't wait for me to reply, just scoots back and leaves me there to finish my meal by myself. I take a bite of the stale bread and convince myself I'm eating at a Michelin-starred restaurant. That's not water, it's champagne, and that line of ants trailing along the baseboard over there in perfect formation? That's called having dinner *and a show*.

My brain breaks down my current predicament while I finish eating. I honestly have no clue what to do. If none of the spine surgeons want me, I could switch specialties, but retraining would take months, if not years, and I happen to like spine. I could switch to another hospital or move to another city, but I don't want to have to pull Josie out of school and away from her friends unless it's absolutely necessary.

I could potentially go back and grovel at the feet of Dr. Goddard, Dr. Richards, or Dr. Smoot, but honestly, I know they aren't going to change their minds. If they turned me down with Dr. Lopez there to vouch for me, they really don't need me.

I do the dishes, wipe down the counter, tuck away the loaf of bread, and set out ant bait. Then, as I'm walking out of the kitchen, I flip the light off, and there in the darkness, I finally allow myself to consider my last, desperate, really-not-an-option option:

Working for Dr. Russell.

The devil incarnate.

Everyone at the practice calls him that, but *I* was the one to draw that hilarious picture of him in the lounge. Kirt was crying and I felt bad for him because he's 6' 3'' and built like a linebacker and I honestly had no idea so many tears could come out of a man that size. He was blowing his nose into a tissue I'd passed him and crying so hard I couldn't understand him, so I added the devil horns and red tail to Dr. Russell's headshot as a distraction. Everyone laughed and Kirt stopped crying, but I instantly regretted it.

Just the thought of Dr. Russell ever finding out about that picture sends a shiver down my spine.

No.

There's no way I can work for him.

Maybe Josie's right—would living on the streets really be so bad?

CHAPTER FOUR
MATT

I'VE BEEN ACCUSED of being set in my ways by a few people in my life, and they're right. I rely on routine. I eat the same breakfast every morning: protein smoothie, four egg whites scrambled with freshly cracked pepper, turkey sausage, and two cups of coffee (one right when I wake up and one when I arrive at work). After breakfast, I work out. That routine stays the same every day too. Cardio. Weights—not so much that I'm an over-engorged beast, but enough that I can stand over an operating table for nine hours and torque a spine without breaking a sweat. Core work is vital.

I wake up at 4:00 AM Monday through Friday, and I'm in my office by 5:30. If there's a resident or a fellow on my team, I prefer for them to meet me at this time so we can go over the case schedule before we start rounding. During rounds, I check that post-op patients are recovering and go over any final questions with my pre-op patients and their guardians. I've learned to pad this time. Parents are always nervous, and children always come up with the most random, curious questions. Often, it's about the anesthesia.

"You mean I won't remember anything? It'll feel like I'm sleeping? Will I dream?"

Today, I'm in the office at 5:00 AM, even earlier than usual. I have a routine procedure scheduled in a few hours, but I wanted to spend some time looking over Fiona's file. Her parents aren't sure they want to go through with the surgery. They're confused why so many doctors turned her away and yet I'm willing to try. They don't want to put their daughter in danger, which is understandable, but still, my gut tells me they'll be back. Her case is severe and they're going to be completely out of options soon. When that time comes, I want to be ready.

Unfortunately, when I arrive at my desk, I discover I won't have the thirty minutes of uninterrupted time I was craving. My voicemail announces thirteen unheard messages, and there are a few dozen emails demanding responses. Two doctors are requesting a surgical visit in the upcoming week. Another one is asking for my assistance on a case on the west coast. It's not unusual as there are so few of us who specialize in complex pediatric scoliosis.

Before I reply to the emails, the blinking red light from my office phone demands my attention. I press play and listen while I tidy up my desk. Three of the messages are from Victoria, telling me "it's nothing urgent" but asking me to call her back as soon as possible. I wonder why she didn't just call my cell phone, and then I remember I forgot to give her my new number. It wasn't intentional, but now I wonder if it's not better this way.

I have no idea what she'd want to talk to me about, but since it's not urgent, I skip past her message and make a mental note to get back to her when I have the time.

"Knock knock!" Dr. Lopez says from the hallway as he opens the door and waltzes into my office without a care in the world. "Do you have a second?"

I don't look up. "No."

Undeterred, he walks in to take a seat across from me. I think he's half-tempted to prop his feet up and interlace his fingers behind his head, but he knows that'd be pushing it too far.

"I like what you've done with the place. It's homey in

here."

He's staring pointedly at my framed diplomas stacked against the wall behind my desk, still waiting to be hung. Beside them, there's a mountain of issues of *European Spine Journal* and old textbooks. Spinal hardware litters most of my couch. Admittedly, it's a mess. It's why I meet my patients in the conference room for consultations.

"It's like stepping into the laboratory of a mad scientist," he notes with a teasing smile. "I wouldn't be surprised to find the secrets of the universe in here."

He's wasting my precious time. "What can I do for you, Dr. Lopez?"

"Oh right—busy busy. We doctors never have enough time, do we? Well, I'm about to get a lot more of it actually. You've heard I'm retiring, haven't you?" A rumor has been circulating for months, but I never thought he'd actually go through with it so soon. He has another five years of surgery left in him, ten if he pushed himself. "Yup. Laurie's pretty excited. She has all sorts of plans for us for the coming months—a Caribbean cruise, holidays with the grandkids. Your parents live here, right?"

I nod as I start sorting through my emails, triaging the most important ones and deleting the ones from medical device reps I don't care to entertain.

"Lucky for them. They'll be close by when you have kids. All the better to spoil them rotten."

Kids. My gut clenches. Right. I tense and finally glance up at him.

"Congratulations on your retirement," I say, my voice professional and unfriendly. "Is that what you wanted to talk to me about?"

He grins and threads his fingers together on his lap. He looks mighty comfortable in my office, like he plans on staying here for quite some time.

"Sort of. You've probably heard me mention my surgical assistant a time or two?"

I rack my brain but nothing comes to mind. "If you have, I wasn't listening."

He laughs. "Never one to bullshit are you, Dr. Russell? Anyway, Bailey is great, one of the best damn surgical assistants I've ever had, but unfortunately, I'm going to leave her high and dry in a few weeks when I retire."

"Why is that my problem?"

He shakes his head, and then wags a *Let me teach you something* finger at me. "Bailey isn't your problem, but she could be your salvation. Kirt put in his two weeks' notice—"

"Kirt was never going to last. He doesn't have the stomach for surgery."

Literally.

"Bailey does."

I arch a brow and give him my best bored expression. "Just say what you're hinting at or get out of my office. I have shit to do before my resident arrives."

He stands and leans over, pressing the button on my office phone that connects me to my secretary.

"Patricia, are you at your desk yet?"

A second later, her words bite through the line. "What do you want? It's too damn early. I haven't even had my coffee yet."

"I understand and I apologize for the inconvenience," Dr. Lopez says, his voice full of deference for the woman who actually wears the pants in this place. "But would you mind checking real quick to see how many surgical assistants have applied to replace Kirt?"

I get his point even before there's a long silence,

followed by a chuckle from Patricia. "No one yet, but I only put the ad out a couple of days ago."

Dr. Lopez is wearing a shit-eating grin. "That's what I thought. Thank you, Patricia. Now you can go enjoy that cup of coffee and I won't bother you again."

His finger lifts up off the intercom button and silence fills my office. We stare at each other across my desk. He couldn't be making his point any clearer if he was waving his hands wildly overhead, pointing to a marquee that spelled out, *Matt, you insufferable asshole, no one wants to work with you!*

I look away first and clear my throat. "I get it. You can get out of my office now."

He fails to hide a big victorious smile before he turns for the door and I think he's finally going to leave me in peace, but then he throws out one last piece of advice over his shoulder. "I know you like to operate as a lone wolf, but the best surgeons know how to be team players. You'd be an idiot to let Bailey slip through your fingers. She's been my right hand for the last four years, and if circumstances in her life had been different, she would have made a damn good surgeon herself. Take my advice and hire her before it's too late."

CHAPTER FIVE
B A I L E Y

THE TIME HAS come: Dr. Lopez's last week with the practice. He's taken to wearing Hawaiian shirts under his white coat. Vacation brochures litter his desk. Movers will be here on Friday to pack up his office. He has one foot out the door, and I still don't have a new job. He agreed it was best for me to contact a headhunter, and she found a few open positions. Unfortunately, none of them quite fit the bill. Most are too far away. Some are even across the country, not to mention the salaries weren't as high as what I make here. I'd be taking a major gamble, moving Josie, and earning less, all in the hopes that the surgeon I end up working for is half as decent as Dr. Lopez.

At this point, it almost makes more sense to switch specialties. I tell this to Dr. Lopez on Monday while we're eating lunch in his office, printed emails from the headhunter spread out on his desk between us. We've already found something wrong with every single one of them.

He acts deeply affronted by the idea of me moving out of spine.

"You'd be bored out of your mind on another floor," he says, sipping on coconut water while luau music plays from his computer.

I shrug, trying to come up with another specialty that would interest me. "General ortho wouldn't be so bad."

He narrows his eyes as if I just said I wouldn't mind dabbling in prostitution. "Remind me again why you don't

39

want to just take the position with Dr. Russell?"

"Well, first off, he hasn't offered it to me."

"Because you haven't applied."

"And also, I've heard the horror stories."

"Can I offer you some insight?"

I tip my head to the side and present a knowing half-smile. "You're going to anyway. Why ask?"

He cuts the music and leans forward in his chair. The tone of our conversation changes in an instant. "We all know simple, successful surgeries are lucrative. There are enough routine fusions to keep this practice afloat for the next decade. Dr. Russell doesn't see it that way, though. To him, the second a procedure becomes routine, it means he's not pushing himself hard enough. He's high-strung and intense in the operating room because he's striving to do better, to *be* better. Why do you think the gallery in his OR is standing-room only? Why do you think people travel from all around the world to observe him while he operates? It's not because he's playing it safe, and it's not because he's a mild-mannered surgeon. I completely understand if you don't want to work with him. Hell, I wouldn't. Give it some thought, though, kid. Worst-case scenario, we reassess and try to place you with a surgeon down on two."

He knows what he's doing. The second floor is where the hand surgeons operate. I'd be assisting on outpatient carpal tunnel procedures day in and day out, and I would bash my head against a hard object within the first few days.

As the day progresses and the deadline to make my decision looms closer and closer, I try to mostly ignore his words of wisdom, but I can't. *He's striving to do better, to be better.* Right. That's all well and good, but Kirt had to pop TUMS like they were candy while he was working for him. Word on the street is the guy's currently in therapy for PTSD.

Still, a small part of me wonders if Kirt might have been exaggerating. It occurs to me that I've let the rumors about Dr. Russell taint my perception of him past the point of logic. I mean, most of them aren't even believable. Making device reps cry? Firing surgical assistants in the middle of a procedure? That one time he was supposedly so mean to a nurse she sued the company for subjecting her to a hostile work environment and won the case? According to urban legend, she lives on a private island near St. Barts. Even I can admit that's probably unlikely.

So, I decide to do some investigating of my own and carve out time to watch Dr. Russell operate. That way, I'll know exactly what I could be dealing with—except, when I arrive at his surgery after I wrap things up with Dr. Lopez on Monday, the viewing gallery is so packed I can't even make it past the door. The next day, I try to shove my way in, and one particularly overzealous fellow elbows me in the ribs and rudely suggests I should get there earlier if I want a good view. I resist the urge to stomp on his foot.

On Wednesday, I finally catch a break. Dr. Lopez's case gets canceled so I take advantage of the opportunity and show up to Dr. Russell's gallery as early as possible. I'm the first one there. I have snacks and a front-row seat. I also have mace in my purse just in case some stupid medical student thinks they deserve this spot more than I do.

Within a few minutes, the gallery fills around me. There are conversations about the planned case and idle chatter about some party they were all at last night, but I sit quietly, talking to no one, waiting for the show to begin.

The viewing window stretches from one side of the room to the other, almost like a movie screen. We're up on the second floor looking down on the auxiliary staff trickling into the operating room.

Exactly on schedule, down to the minute, the patient—a young boy—is wheeled in and transferred to the operating table. After the anesthesia kicks in, there's a flurry of activity as nurses and scrub techs unpack the instrument sets. Sterile trays are arranged and placed around the operating table and then, once the drape is covering everything but the center of the patient's back, Hotshot makes his entrance.

The swinging door is pushed open and Dr. Russell steps in, arms bent at ninety degrees as water drips to the floor.

A hush falls around me.

My gut clenches as if I'm watching an Olympic athlete enter the arena. Everyone in the gallery and everyone in the operating room is laser-focused on him. His presence is larger than life. *He's* larger than life. It's not necessarily because of his size, though he is tall and broad-shouldered. It's more in the way he carries himself, the defiant tilt of his chin.

With his surgical mask and protective glasses on, his chiseled jaw, intriguing mouth, and piercing blue gaze are all out of sight. If I'm honest, though, I could close my eyes and easily visualize them.

A nurse rushes over with a sterile towel so he can dry his hands off. Then she holds up a gown so he can push his arms through. It's tied behind his back and his gloves are carefully added next. It's funny, really—with all the surgical gear on, he should look like an amorphous blob, but in reality, he's as formidable as I've ever seen him.

It's the hair. Just like with Dr. McDreamy, a lot of his power lies in those short, slightly curly brown locks. Their allure cannot be dulled by that light blue scrub cap.

The beginning of every surgery always starts with a roll call—or as we call it, a time-out. It's a way to ensure everyone in the room is on the same page and surgeons don't accidentally operate on the wrong limb—or worse, the wrong person. Scary, but…it happens.

The neuromonitoring tech sitting at a computer in the corner of the room checks in, then the circulating nurse and the device rep. They continue to go around, and I try to imagine myself standing there beside him, proudly proclaiming to be Bailey Jennings, Dr. Russell's surgical assistant, and a shiver runs down my spine. I'm not convinced I'm up to the task.

Today, he has a resident beside him at the operating table. Kirt's two weeks has expired and apparently Dr. Russell has yet to find a replacement.

The anesthesiologist stands up and speaks confidently. "We're doing a general with an endotracheal tube. Antibiotics have been administered. We have two units of blood available."

Then all eyes fall back on Dr. Russell as it's his turn to address the room. His booming voice easily reaches us in the gallery and, like everything else, it inspires awe. Also, if I'm honest, a teensy bit of fear.

"Our patient is Jeffrey Lewis. Eleven years old. He's here today for a hemivertebra excision. He also has hardware placed in L3 and L4 from a previous procedure. We'll be removing and replacing that hardware. Does everyone agree?"

They do.

The anesthesiologist declares the surgical start time.

Then, without a moment's hesitation, Dr. Russell is handed a ten blade. It glints under the bright lights of the operating room. He takes a deep breath and then, determinedly, he begins. Scalpel meets skin.

For the next few hours, I don't move a muscle. I don't fidget. I doubt I take a single deep breath. People filter in and out of the gallery, but I pay them no attention.

Someone new fills the seat behind me and leans over my shoulder.

"How long has he been at it?"

I don't take my eyes away from Dr. Russell as I reply, "Three hours, last time I checked."

Now, it's probably been four, five, ten—who knows?

"What's taking him so long? It should have been a simple excision, right?"

"The patient had failing hardware and Dr. Russell's having a hell of a time getting it out."

"Who's that guy in the corner looking like he's about to have a nervous breakdown?"

"The device rep for Newton Corp. The one gloating across the room is here with the new hardware from SpineTech."

It's a complete disaster. Everyone in the operating room holds their breath. Long, tense minutes pass as we listen to Dr. Russell shred the device rep from Newton for endangering his patient.

The rep tries in vain to defend himself. "The engineers are the ones in control of the design flaws."

I inwardly groan. He's better off keeping his mouth shut. At this point, he should break out in tears and plead for forgiveness. Although, maybe not, as Dr. Russell doesn't seem like the type of guy who handles grown men weeping very well.

"Do you not also work for the company?" Dr. Russell barks as he adjusts his stance and asks the nurse to angle his light source so he has a better view of the surgical field. He continues to struggle to remove all the broken fragments of the malfunctioning hardware from the patient's spine while the rep blubbers on. I want to jump to my feet, press the gallery's intercom button, and shout at him to shut up. He's only digging himself into a bigger hole. Soon, he'll have himself six feet under.

"Even with its faults, the patient was interested in the system—"

"The patient is also interested in fucking fire trucks!" Dr. Russell booms. "And don't you try to pin it on the parents either. These devices were banned by the FDA two years ago and they never should have been on the market in the first place. Your company knew they were faulty." Then he turns to the resident assisting him and asks for suction.

I sit there completely speechless, not quite sure why I have the urge to run down and scrub in so I can assist.

I've never endured a surgery with Dr. Lopez that was half this traumatic. Every person in that operating room is fidgeting and nervous, careful to keep Dr. Russell's anger from shifting onto them.

I'm on the edge of my seat. Even though I'm as annoyed with the Newton rep as he is, I don't agree with how Dr. Russell is handling it. His temper is fierce. I can see how he would be a nightmare to work with, and yet I stay until the final stitch, until Dr. Russell turns from the operating table, yanks his gown and gloves off, and slams his hand against the swinging door. The patient gets wheeled out of the room and I'm still sitting there, alone in the gallery, awestruck.

DR. LOPEZ'S RETIREMENT party is tonight. NEMC went all out and rented a ballroom at a fancy hotel. They're going to open the dinner buffet soon, and I've already surreptitiously scoped it out. I have a plan of attack: I'm getting the truffle mac n cheese *and* the mashed potatoes.

In the meantime, waiters are passing around tiny decadent appetizers. I accept one of everything and wonder if I made a mistake wearing a dress with no pockets. If I could do it inconspicuously, I'd tuck a few of these bacon-wrapped dates in my purse for Josie. We've been subsisting on the bare minimum lately since I still haven't found another position. My meager savings might have to support us for a few weeks, though I really hope it doesn't come to that.

I push the thought aside. All I've been doing is worrying and applying for jobs and counting every penny that leaves my pocket. Tonight, I'm going to have fun! I'm going to pluck one of these coconut shrimps from a passing tray, let it melt in my mouth, and pretend life is going to work out. Okay, wow. That is *good*. I've really got to cram one of those down my bra for Josie. It's the most delicious thing I've ever eaten.

I turn to catch the waiter before he gets too far. "Sir—"

"Kiddo!" Dr. Lopez grins and steps between me and my end goal: pilfering every last shrimp on that silver tray.

"Oh, hey, Dr. Lopez." I try not to sound as dejected as I feel as the waiter disappears into the crowd. "I didn't realize you'd arrived."

He chuckles and knocks me gently on the shoulder. "You don't have to look so sad. You'll find another boss like me one day."

That's not why I was sad, but *now* it's why I'm sad.

"At least we still have one last surgery in the morning," I say with a half-hearted smile.

"I'll even let you pick the playlist."

Oh jeez. Tears are welling up in the corners of my eyes. I'd use my crumpled napkin to dab them away but it's covered in shrimp juice.

"Let's change the subject or we'll both be crying." He chuckles. "Have I already told you that you clean up nice? I'm not sure I've ever seen you in anything but scrubs—and your hair's down."

At work, it's all high ponytails and scrub city. Tonight, I probably look like a different human. Thanks to Josie, my eyeshadow is smoky and blended flawlessly like I'm a YouTube beauty influencer. I feel good.

"You look sharp too, Dr. Lopez."

It's weird seeing everyone from the practice in their street clothes, albeit nice street clothes. The invitation demanded we dress up, so I had to pull something out of the back of my closet, a cocktail dress I purchased a few years back for a college formal. It's black and simple, and thankfully, timeless. Unfortunately, it's slightly tighter in the chest area than it used to be, but hopefully it's not completely indecent. Josie's eyes widened when she saw me as I was leaving the house.

"WHOA! Who knew you were so hot?!"

"It's not too much?" I asked, trying to tug down the hemline.

"Are you kidding? If I had boobs like that, I'd never wear clothes."

"It's scary because I don't even think you're kidding. Also, I didn't have these when I was your age either.

There's still hope for you."

Now, of course, I feel weird thinking about my boobs while in a conversation with my soon-to-be-retired boss, but that's just life.

"I'd like to introduce you to Dr. Russell tonight when he gets here."

"He's not here yet?" I ask the question innocently enough even though I know damn well he's not here. I stationed myself by the door when I first arrived for two reasons. One, because I think that's where the buffet line will start, and two, because I wanted to see Dr. Russell as soon as he arrived.

I'm still waiting.

I'm worried he won't show up. He doesn't seem like the kind of guy to make cheesy company parties a priority, even for a colleague like Dr. Russell.

"No, but he told me he'd be here."

"I watched him operate this morning," I mention, sounding way more cavalier than I feel.

His brow arches with interest. "And?"

"And it was a really intense surgery. It took a few hours longer than it should have because of faulty hardware. Everyone in the OR was peeing their pants."

He shrugs as if that's nothing to worry about. "I heard the surgery was a success."

"It was but...maybe I have enough stress in my life without going to work for someone like him."

"Maybe so." He looks away, claps the back of a guy passing by, and then nods hello to another guest. "Like I said, floor two is still an option."

I roll my eyes. "C'mon, be serious."

His eyes glance back to me and he shakes his head. "I am being serious. Believe in yourself. You're exactly the

48

kind of surgical assistant Dr. Russell needs—and look here, he's walking in right behind you."

My stomach drops.

My eyes widen, and even though I want to, I can't make myself turn around.

A chill runs down my spine knowing he's behind me. My hand tightens around my balled-up napkin. This feels more ominous than it should. *He's just a surgeon*, I remind myself. *Just a man! You've seen men before!*

I slowly venture a glance over my left shoulder, fully prepared to be knocked off my feet by the sight of him, but nope. *Jesus.* I was not prepared enough.

Midnight suit. Midnight hair. Tall, built frame. Dr. Russell is standing at the threshold of the ballroom, scanning the crowd coolly and deciding if anyone or anything is worth his notice. I wonder if I'd make the cut if Dr. Lopez didn't take it upon himself to draw his attention. He raises his arm and waves it back and forth, flagging his colleague down. "Dr. Russell!"

His blue gaze cuts to us and my gut clenches. It's fitting that his eyes are the color of ice. I bat at my arm for an imaginary jacket I can pull closed around myself. It's a reflex. For some reason, I want to cower. If I could get away with it, I'd step behind Dr. Lopez. Instead, I lift my chin and steel myself against the arctic blast of his approach.

"You're late," Dr. Lopez teases.

Dr. Russell shrugs, his eyes still scanning. He still hasn't really looked at me. "Paperwork called."

"Don't worry, you didn't miss dinner."

"Good. I didn't eat lunch and I'm starving."

Then I realize why he was scanning the room: he was looking for food. A waitress passes and he stops her, taking two little puffed pastries. Meanwhile, the waitress' eyes widen. Her tongue wets her bottom lip. It's all probably subconscious on her part. I want to lean in close and tell her I get it. *Boy*, do I get it. He's taken the time to shave, and there's beauty in the sharp contours of his jaw. I think if I ran my finger across it, it'd feel as smooth as silk.

"I was worried you'd miss my party," Dr. Lopez quips.

The edge of Dr. Russell's mouth tips up and the waitress finally realizes her presence here is no longer necessary. She reluctantly moves on.

"How could I? You had Patricia leave about forty notes on my desk reminding me."

They talk without me. Dr. Russell doesn't seem to notice me standing there, but that doesn't stop me from studying him. We've never had a reason to be this close. I've seen him from across conference rooms. I've seen the back of his tall figure as he disappeared down a hallway. Once, I nearly bumped into him getting onto the elevator at work. He was too preoccupied reading a file, so I was the one who had to sidestep and veer out of his way. There was no apology, no acknowledgment from him. I had to suppress the urge to utter a bitter, *Excuse me!*

This proximity is new and heady. After watching him operate this morning, I've come to admire (or fear) him even more.

"That's because I've been eager for you to meet Bailey."

Shit.

That's me!

Dr. Lopez's hand hits my shoulder and he pushes me gently in Dr. Russell's direction like I'm an offering. Dr. Russell's eyes finally fall on me, and I'm assessed with a look of cool indifference. Blue eyes meet mine for only a

50

moment. He doesn't even do a once-over. The expression on his face is unreadable and austere. I might as well be gum on the bottom of his shoe.

"She's the surgical assistant I've been raving about," Dr. Lopez says, looking down at me proudly.

My cheeks flush and I extend a hand. "Nice to meet you, Dr. Russell."

He accepts my handshake and for a few seconds, my palm is completely enveloped by the warmth of his grasp. I'm shaking the hand that operated flawlessly this morning. This is the hand that changed that little boy's life. This is the hand that inspires awe in so many.

My breath catches in my throat as I try to keep my wits about me. Wow, I think he and I might be having a real moment…then another waiter passes and Dr. Russell drops my hand and steps toward her so he can ask for a water. *Welp*, *scratch that.*

Then, silence.

I'm aware that this is where conversation should take place. Dr. Russell ought to ask questions in the hopes of getting to know me: where I'm from, how long I've been working at NEMC, if I'd be willing to accept a job with him.

Instead, crickets.

Dr. Lopez clears his throat.

"Bailey had the chance to watch your surgery this morning."

His eyes narrow at something over Dr. Lopez's shoulder. "What a fucking mess. I've permanently banned Newton reps from my OR."

"And the patient?" I ask. "How is he doing?"

A glimmer of surprise hits Dr. Russell's pale eyes, and when he glances back toward me, it feels like he's actually seeing me for the first time. "He's fine, recovering quickly, but then that's the good thing about kids—their bodies are resilient."

This is something, an actual conversation, but it's over before it even begins when Dr. Goddard walks up behind Dr. Russell and grasps his shoulders tightly, trying to shake him off balance.

"Matty boy, I didn't think we'd see you here tonight. No drink?"

Dr. Russell shakes him off and rolls out his neck. If he had them, his hackles would be raised.

Dr. Goddard doesn't seem to care that none of us are happy to have him here. He reaches out and rudely tugs on the arm of a passing waiter. "Get my pal a Jack and Coke, will you?"

The waiter nods. "Right away, sir."

Dr. Goddard turns back to us, his slimy gaze landing on me. What I'm sure he assumes is a seductive smile unfurls across his mouth. "And who is this delicate creature?"

Delicate creature?

What. The. Hell.

I lift my chin and narrow my gaze. "Bailey Jennings. I'm a surgical assistant at the hospital."

His eyes widen with recognition and then he does a slow perusal of my dress. Dammit, I knew it was too tight. Appreciation colors his eyes as he finally makes his way back to my face. "Pity that position on my team didn't end up working out, though maybe I could shuffle some things around…"

The end of his sentence is left unsaid: *now that I realize I'd like to sleep with you.*

The waiter scurries back over with a Jack and Coke

and the water Dr. Russell originally requested. He accepts both with a thank you, keeps the water, and drops the Jack and Coke on a nearby cocktail table. A little bit of the drink laps over the edge.

"Aw, c'mon. We were going to make a toast for our pal here," Dr. Goddard groans.

Dr. Russell tucks his hand in his pocket and sips his water with all the confidence in the world. "I don't drink the night before surgeries."

Dr. Goddard throws me a teasing wink. "My colleague here is such a bore, but I assure you, I'm no bore. What do you think, Bailey? Still looking for a new position?"

His words make it clear that the position is in fact *underneath* him.

If I were closer, I'd oh-so-subtly dig my heel into his foot.

I'm about to tell him I'd rather clean toilets at a truck stop for a living but Dr. Lopez clears his throat and steps forward, nearly cutting off Dr. Goddard's view of me. "Actually, Bailey here is going to be working with Dr. Russell starting on Monday."

"I'm going to—"

"She's *what*?"

We speak simultaneously, and then Dr. Russell snaps his attention to me, his eyes filled with accusation as if I was the one who just announced we'd be working together.

My mouth drops open. "I—*no*. I'm not sure—"

Dr. Lopez is quick to continue. "The minor details haven't been quite hammered out. It's a new development. Dr. Goddard, would you mind coming with me? My wife has been asking about you all night and I know she'll be sad if she doesn't get to say hello."

Dr. Goddard lights up at the idea that someone actually

requested his presence, and he's all too glad to be led away.

I'm left standing with Dr. Russell and cursing Dr. Lopez in my head.

"I don't know why he said that," I say, fidgeting on my heels and wishing a waiter would pass by so I could grab a glass of champagne and drown myself in it.

His dark brows are furrowed in confusion. "Have I unknowingly offered you a position?"

"No. *No.*" I rub my hand up and down my forearm. "Dr. Lopez is just trying to ensure I find a new position before he leaves, and for some reason, he thinks we would work well together."

He grunts and looks away. "That'd be a first."

He's no doubt referring to the scores of surgical assistants that have come before me.

"Believe me, I'm not convinced it's a good idea. Like Dr. Lopez said, I watched your surgery—you were brutal to that device rep."

"You think I should have let him off easier?" He lets out a bitter laugh. "The toxicology report showed my patient had lethal levels of cobalt in his blood. He was being poisoned by the very thing that was supposed to be healing him. You think *I* was brutal?"

His eyes are two hot flames.

I take a small step back.

I didn't know it was that bad. I didn't know the hardware was *poisoning* him.

"Brutal wasn't the right word," I admit, voice quivering.

He shakes his head, clearly done with me. "Do me a favor and tell Dr. Lopez this won't work out. You'll need to find another surgeon to work for."

He turns and is about to walk away when I reach out

and grab his arm to stop him. In an instant, my fear is doused with a nice, healthy dose of rage at the idea of him rejecting me. *ME!*

I'd laugh if I weren't seeing red.

"Are you *kidding*? Do you realize I'm the best surgical assistant Dr. Lopez has ever had? You'd be *lucky* to have me working for you, and yes, maybe I misspoke a moment ago, but that doesn't mean I was wrong. You ARE brutal, and you know it. You can't keep a good team around you because you stomp around like you're the second coming of Christ. I've had to listen to all your surgical assistants as they wallowed and wept, and I always thought they were embellishing just how terrible you are, but it turns out they were right." I realize I'm still gripping his arm, and I jerk back as if he's a hot stove. His suit jacket is rumpled from my hand, but he doesn't care. His attention is riveted on me like it's never been before. My tone turns hard and unyielding. "And don't worry, I'll tell Dr. Lopez this won't work out, but come Monday morning when you walk into that operating room, you're going to look to your left and *wish* you had a surgical assistant as good as me standing beside you." I laugh and shake my head like he's the biggest disappointment I've ever seen. "Have a good night, Dr. Russell."

Then I curve around and accidentally (on purpose) bump my shoulder into him before seeing myself out.

"Hey, you," I snap at a waiter on his phone just outside the door. "Are those the coconut shrimp?"

He nods dumbly, eyes wide at being caught slacking on the job.

"Give them to me."

"What?"

He's scared. He looks around for a manager, but it's

just us.

"You heard me. Stuff them in my purse—now!"

And that's how I leave Dr. Lopez's retirement party toting two dozen coconut shrimp. Josie and I devour every last one in our pajamas while *Grey's* reruns play in succession.

CHAPTER SIX
MATT

NO ONE HAS ever talked to me like Bailey did last night, not a colleague, not another attending at the hospital, and definitely not a surgical assistant. Admittedly, at first, I was blown away that she'd have the nerve to use that tone with me, but shock and embarrassment gave way to a healthy dose of interest, and oddly enough, a small dose of respect. I can't get her speech out of my head. I should have paid more attention to her before she stormed out. I remember her being small compared to Dr. Lopez. I remember the feel of her delicate hand clenched on my bicep. Most importantly, I remember her sharp words.

I always thought they were embellishing just how terrible you are, but it turns out they were right.

She doesn't lack boldness. I'll give her that.

The next morning, I find Patricia at her desk perusing a knitting magazine, and I ask her for Bailey's employee file. She pauses, mid-page-flip, and then she stares up at me over the brim of her reading glasses.

"What do you want it for?" she asks with barely concealed trepidation. "I like that girl. Don't go making her quit."

I roll my eyes. "Just give it to me."

It's rare that Patricia likes someone. If she feels the need to defend Bailey, it speaks volumes about her character.

She grumbles a bit more and then reluctantly stands to retrieve the file from HR. When she brings it to my office a

57

few minutes later, I have to tug hard to pry it from her hand.

I thank her then lay the file open flat across my desk. I don't know what I'm hoping to find—a dossier outlining her life? Details about her likes and dislikes? There are just a few pages. I learn her full name: Bailey Anne Jennings, and her age: 26. From what little I remember, she seemed younger last night.

I scan over her address and suddenly feel like I'm stalking her, but in reality, any employer would do this. I want to know more about the person I'm considering hiring. Under education, it says she finished a few years of college before quitting and opting to complete a surgical assistant program. I flip to the last page and at the bottom, I notice there's no one listed as her emergency contact. There are just a few letters scratched out like she began writing someone down before thinking better of it.

That blank line is a shot to my cold, unfeeling heart.

I flip the file closed and shove it aside. Sip my coffee, browse emails. Open it again, reread her address, and type it into Google Maps. She doesn't live in a great area of town, but it's not exactly the slums either. I delete my browsing history and snap at Patricia over the intercom to get me another cup of coffee. She tells me if I ever talk to her like that again, I'll be getting a healthy dose of rat poison in my next cup of joe.

I can't meet her eyes when she brings it to me. I can't explain this unnerving feeling. It's like someone's pressing their full weight down on my chest and making it hard to breathe.

My resident arrives soon after and I shove Bailey's file in the top drawer of my desk like I'm hiding a dirty secret. He brought me coffee, but I can't drink it. I've already had one cup too many this morning and I feel jittery. I'll have to take a piss midway through my surgery if I'm not careful.

"Did you have a good night, Dr. Russell?" he asks with a cheerful pep in his step.

"You're not here to be my friend," I say. "Did you review the case for today?"

He's visibly shaken at my outburst. I can see in his eyes that he wants to call me a prick, but he won't. He doesn't have the courage. Unlike Bailey.

BY THE TIME I'm finished with my surgery, it's lunchtime. My stomach is growling, but there's something I need to take care of before I eat.

I have a hard time finding the staff lounge. I assumed it was on the same floor as the doctors' lounge, but it's up on seven. I feel like an idiot for having wandered aimlessly for fifteen minutes.

I can hear the noise and chatter from down the hall. The door is wide open, but I don't step inside. I hover on the precipice and scan the room for her. Part of me wonders if I'll even be able to pick her out from amongst the masses, and then I freeze.

There.

She's sitting at the center table, surrounded by people. The popular girl. She's smiling and dipping a baby carrot into peanut butter, which seems utterly disgusting to me. Someone nudges her in the side to get her attention and she glances up at me at the exact moment my face betrays my disapproval of her culinary choice. Baby carrots should be dipped in ranch and hummus, nothing else.

Her eyes narrow. She thinks I'm looking disapprovingly at her, and well...I am.

I nod my head toward the hallway, giving her an unspoken command: *Come here.*

She doesn't budge.

I could go in, but there are rules against it. No doctors are allowed in the staff lounge, and no auxiliary staff are allowed in the doctors' lounge. Rules are rules. If I step inside, I'm liable to get a soup can thrown at my head.

A hush has fallen over the lounge as everyone's gazes ping back and forth between us.

Her eyes flicker to the side wall and I follow. Ah, yes: the devil picture. I smirk. I'd assumed Dr. Goddard was lying about it, but there I am, up on the bulletin board with devil horns and a tail. On top of my head someone's written: *Hotshot.*

It's actually pretty funny.

I look back over at her and speak loud and clear, ensuring everyone in the lounge hears me. "Bailey, I need to speak with you for a moment."

Someone has the gall to gasp.

Finally, she sighs and stands up, leaving her lunch right where it is. She doesn't think this is going to take long. I bet she thinks she's going to call the shots like she tried to do last night. Adorable.

She's a tortoise as she makes her way toward me.

"Sometime today would be nice."

Her pale brown eyes sear into me as she passes by, walks out into the hallway, and keeps right on going. She doesn't stop until she's a few yards away, and though I appreciate the fact that she's putting distance between us and the prying ears in the lounge, I'm annoyed that it's now *me* following *her.*

Once she feels like she's gone far enough, she turns back to me, crosses her arms, and tilts her chin up. "Whatever you want to say, do it quickly. I only have fifteen minutes left of my lunch break."

There she goes again with her demands. How did she manage to stay on Dr. Lopez's team for years? She won't last a week on mine.

I step closer and stare down at her, quickly taking in the details I failed to notice last night. Young is the first word that comes to mind. She's almost childlike, fresh-faced and freckled just across the bridge of her nose and the top of her defined cheekbones. She has a button nose and pink lips tugged into an angry line. Her light blonde hair is pulled up in a high ponytail. Soft unruly wisps frame her face. Menacing frown aside, she looks like she should be playing the lead in a children's movie instead of standing in this hospital wearing scrubs.

I'm curious.

"Where do you even find scrubs that small?"

She rears back, confused. I've never seen a shade of brown eyes quite like hers. They're such a vivid color as she glares up at me like she'd like to sink a dagger into my heart. Ah *right*…the color of rage.

"*What*?"

I laugh as I rub my hand back and forth across my forehead. Am I sick? Dreaming? Having a psychotic break?

"Did you interrupt my lunch just to ask me that?"

I get it together and ask, "How long have you been with Dr. Lopez?"

She crosses her arms and shifts her gaze over my shoulders, taking a second to collect herself. When she answers, her tone is sharp but cool. "Nearly four years."

"He speaks highly of you."

61

She shrugs. "We had a good thing going."

"Would you like to continue working in spine?"

"Preferably."

"Have you ever assisted on a pediatric scoliosis case?"

"No. Dr. Lopez only operates on adults, fusions mainly."

That's exactly my concern.

"Those take two or three hours max. My surgeries can last three times that long."

She forces herself to meet my eyes, and I'm shocked. A moment ago, she seemed ready to burst, but now she looks bored, almost as if she's about to dismiss me. It's a ruse. I wish I could press two fingers to the porcelain skin just below her neck and feel for her pulse. I bet it's racing. There's no way she's as calm as she's pretending to be.

"I'm confused," she says, her tone betraying nothing but curiosity. "Are you offering me a job or trying to warn me away?"

That's the question of the morning it seems. Half of me is convinced working with her would be a complete disaster. My job is stressful enough. Unfortunately, I'm also in need of a decent surgical assistant, someone up to the task.

I think Bailey could be that person.

I sigh and step back. "Your first case is Monday morning. Ask Patricia for the information and learn the steps of a pedicle subtraction osteotomy like a child's life depends on it—because it does. I'm giving you one chance."

Then, I turn and walk away.

It feels slightly unnerving turning my back on the enemy. I think she's going to shout something at me in an effort to get the last word, but there's nothing but silence as

I head to the stairwell. I yank the heavy metal door open and disappear inside.

I know without a shadow of a doubt she'll be there on Monday morning.

I smile as I take the stairs two at a time.

I just got myself a shiny new surgical assistant.

CHAPTER SEVEN
BAILEY

I ARRIVE AT work on Monday bright-eyed and bushy-tailed. My hair and makeup look flawless. My scrubs are starched and fit to a T. My coffee thermos is in hand and I sip from it until I have just enough caffeine to keep me alert, but not so much that I'll have to run to the bathroom every five seconds. I make the kind of first impression people dream about. Dr. Russell pulls me aside after surgery to commend me on my work ethic, and his eyes look especially blue. What's that? He's going to give me a little smooch to show me his appreciation? This is totally unexpected, but oddly...thrilling. I want this kiss. I might hate his guts, but I don't hate his lips, or his face, or his hair.

That arguing we did in the hallway on Friday was foreplay if I've ever felt it.

I want this kiss so badly. I press up onto my tiptoes, and when that's not enough, I wrap my hand around his neck and tug down, down, down, then I pucker up and hold on for dear life.

Just before our lips meet, a loud pounding starts reverberating through the hospital hallway. I flinch and the dream disappears

Josie's banging on my door. "Wake up, you idiot! You're going to be late!"

NO.

NO!

My eyes jerk open and I reach for my phone on the

bedside table. It's 7:27 AM.

Dr. Russell's surgery is scheduled for eight o'clock, sharp.

I shove my blanket aside and leap out of bed.

"WHY DIDN'T YOU WAKE ME UP?!"

"Because I thought you were already at work! You're never here at this time!"

"Shit! Shit! Shiiiiiit!"

I scramble.

I want to weep and stamp my feet and curse the gods for this injustice, but I really just curse Dr. Russell. This is all his fault. He got into my head on Friday, scaring me about being prepared. *Learn the steps of a pedicle subtraction osteotomy like a child's life depends on it—because it does.* Oh, okay, no pressure or anything!

I had every step of the procedure memorized by Saturday night, but even still, I studied all day yesterday too. I stayed up late, reviewing the patient's file and committing every detail to memory. The procedure is going to be difficult, ten times more so than anything I've done with Dr. Lopez. My nerves were getting to me, so I pushed through and kept studying until my sight went fuzzy and the lines of text on the page turned into inky blobs. I wanted to know the surgery forward and backward. I wanted to be able to identify every piece of hardware with my eyes closed.

By the time I finally went to bed, it was well into the early morning hours, and now look at me—I'M GOING TO BE LATE! I hop around on one foot while I tug on my pants. I put my jeans on backward. Only half my hair makes it into my ponytail.

I dart around for things I think I'll need: keys, purse, phone, shoe. *Where's the other one?!*

This isn't happening. This is another dream. I've never been late. I'm not a late person. In all my years working with Dr. Lopez, this has never happened. I'm so totally screwed.

Josie chucks a wrapped-up muffin at my head as I run for the door. I catch it before it falls to the floor and stuff it in my purse.

"Don't worry, I'll start looking into other jobs for you!" she shouts at my back, and instead of rolling my eyes and thinking, *That Josie is going to send me to an early grave*, I think, *Great! That'd actually be wonderful because I am 110% going to need it.* Even knowing I'll be jobless soon, I decide to splurge on an Uber and skip the bus, knowing I don't have time for public transportation today. I'm shaking and on the verge of tears as we hit traffic.

Today of all days, the city streets are pure gridlock.

"Maybe you could just hop up on the sidewalk for a mile or two? Just to get around this wreck?"

The driver thinks I'm kidding and laughs heartily. I want to climb over the seat and shove him out of the way so I can get behind the wheel, *Grand Theft Auto* style.

I wonder how many years in prison you get for hijacking someone's car.

My knees are bouncing like I'm ready to run, and I do as soon as the Uber pulls up to the hospital. I leap out of the back seat, dart through the lobby, run up the never-ending flights of stairs, and slide onto the fifth floor like I'm on ice. I'm so close to the finish line. I can see the operating room at the end of the hall, the one I should have started to prep about thirty minutes ago.

I'm breathing like an old geezer at the finish line of a marathon.

People unknowingly step into my path and I shout at

them to get out of my way.

"Move! Watch it!"

I have time to recover, I tell myself. I won't let this late start ruin my one chance to impress Dr. Russell. I've set up an OR quickly before, and I know how to kick it into high gear. I check the surgical board as I sprint past and confirm that yes, the surgery has been delayed by twenty minutes *(Don't panic!),* but it's still going to happen.

In room four, I'm expecting the worst: a messy, disorganized OR that needs to be completely overhauled, but fortunately, my luck turns. Dr. Russell's nurse is already inside prepping the room. She's tall, with extremely short hair and round, navy glasses. She's older than most of the surgical nurses on the floor and when she sees me enter the room, I am fully prepared for her to chew me out for being late.

"Oh my god, I'm so sor—"

She holds up her hand and cuts me off. "If you want to survive your first day, you'll stop right there, turn around, and go get changed into scrubs. I've got this. Dr. Russell knows you're late. I couldn't help that when he came in here and saw you were missing, but we can salvage this. Go. *Hurry!*"

My mouth drops open in shock.

I think…I think she's my fairy godmother.

I bolt and do as she says, running straight for the scrub vending machine. It's a hulking beast of a contraption at the very end of the hallway. It's where we all grab our scrubs before every surgery, and it's where we turn them back in when we're done so they can be sanitized. I think of Dr. Russell's stupid comment on Friday: *Where do you even find scrubs that small?*

Right here, you jerk.

Though, I do have to roll the elastic band a few times so they'll fit snugly, but he'll never know that.

I'm changed and looking the part when I rush back into the room, adjusting my ponytail so it sits a little higher on my head before I cover it with a surgical cap. I puff out a breath and prop my hands on my hips. I have dried tears on my cheeks and shaky hands, but I am so close to pulling this off.

"Where do you want me?"

The nurse nods toward the back door of the OR, the one that leads to the room where the hospital stores its clean instrument sets. "Go in and check that they have everything ready to go. The autoclaves were backed up earlier and I don't want anything else delaying this case."

I do exactly as she says and I don't declare my love for her like I want to. There'll be time for that later, like after this surgery goes off without a hitch. Ha. I'm going to buy her a gift, something epic, something with melted chocolate.

That is…if I survive the morning.

CHAPTER EIGHT
MATT

"WE'RE LOOKING AT a thirty-minute delay, nothing more."

Mrs. Valdez is wringing her hands. Her husband is pacing. They're both worried. Fiona should have been taken back to the OR already, but the surgical team hasn't moved her. I understand their concern. They've traveled 1400 miles to be here today. Their daughter is about to have a major operation. Any number of things could go wrong. They won't, of course—I won't allow it—but her parents don't know that.

They don't trust me, and now this delay is giving them even more cause for concern.

"Back home, the doctors weren't sure about this procedure," Mrs. Valdez says, turning to her husband and shaking her head quickly. She's about to pull the plug on this whole thing.

I step forward and try to catch her eyes. I need her to listen to what I'm about to say. "I understand, but that's because those doctors don't have the skills I do. I've spent my entire career working on complex pediatric spine cases. This surgery is exactly what I've been trained to do. I promise your daughter is in good hands."

There's movement behind them, at the door of the room. It's my nurse, Kendra.

"We're ready," she mouths while winding up her finger as if to say, *Let's get this show on the road.*

I nod and inwardly sigh.

That means Bailey has finally arrived. Late on her first day.

I have another surgeon assisting me today, Dr. Collins. He's a colleague I've worked with in the past. It's a hassle coordinating our schedules, but he's good, and for this case, I need all the hands I can get.

Unfortunately, that means Bailey has not only wasted my time, the patient's time, and my staff's time, but also Dr. Collins'. The operating room is booked up for the rest of the day. If this case runs late, that means the hospital is shitting money and we have an entire surgical crew pissed that we've eaten into their schedule.

I want to dismiss her on the spot, but I can't. Right now, I have a seven-year-old girl who needs my full attention, so I compartmentalize my annoyance, reassure the family one last time, and then excuse myself from the room so I can find my colleague. He's in a conference room, taking calls, and when I let him know we're ready, he's relieved.

"I have a flight booked at 3:00 PM, so I hope your staff won't cause any more delays," he says with a shake of his head as he stands to follow me to the OR.

"We'll get you out of here in time."

That's all I'll say. I like Dr. Collins because he's a good surgeon, but he's kind of a prick. We aren't friends, and though he has the right to be upset, I won't indulge him.

We scrub in side by side, and I watch through the window as they roll Fiona into the room and transition her onto the operating table. She looks tiny up there. They always do.

I can see the fear in her eyes. One of the nurses tries to make her laugh, but she won't. Her eyes scan the room, trying to peek at the tools we'll use on her, but they're hidden on purpose.

She's still looking around, trying to spot anything menacing, when the anesthesia takes effect. One second she's awake, counting backward from ten, and the next she's out cold.

It's time to roll.

I press my back to the swinging door and enter the operating room to join the flurry of activity. In an effort to shield the patient from the worst of it, the instrument sets and tools aren't arranged until after they're asleep, but we're also on a time crunch because we want her to be under for as little time as possible. This give and take means everyone is running around like a chicken with its head cut off. It's a dance, one my staff is usually pretty good at, and today is no different—except for our new team member.

I see her across the room, assisting the device rep. He's holding the instrument box while she carefully lifts the sterile set out. I scan her quickly, looking for blood or a newly placed cast—a legitimate reason for her tardiness—but unfortunately for her, she looks fresh as a daisy.

"Which one of you is to blame for holding up this surgery?" Dr. Collins asks the room.

Everyone freezes and then their gazes sweep to Bailey as she slowly turns around, steeling herself. With her mask on, all I can see are her worried brown eyes.

"I'm sorry about the delay," she says, voice stronger than I expected it to be.

He points his finger at her. "You'll be the one paying for my flight if I have to book a new one."

Her eyes widen. He's not being serious; it's a threat in name only. He wants to let her know he's pissed, but now

I'm pissed. This is my goddamn OR and we have a patient who needs our full attention.

"I've already assured you you'll catch your flight."

With a wave of my arm as if to say, *Let's get on with it*, my staff jumps back into action. There's a rush of movement as everyone finishes setting up. Kendra hands Dr. Collins and me sterile towels to dry our hands then makes quick work of helping him with his gown. Meanwhile, Bailey's taking too damn long with the instrument sets. I'm still standing here waiting for her help.

She leans in close to whisper something to the device rep.

I clear my throat. "Any day now, Bailey."

She jumps out of her skin and twirls around to face me. "Dr. Lopez usually had his nurse help him with this gown."

"Yes, well, my assistant helps me."

She rushes over to take the gown out of the pack Kendra's holding open for her. She holds it up. I step forward and slide my arms into it then turn so she can get to the top back button. She clears her throat and I bend my knees a smidge so she can actually reach it. I barely hear a quiet "Thank you" before she finishes. Then her hand skims inside the gown, along my waist so she can grab for the first of two strings that tie the sides closed. Her hand feels along the fabric of my scrubs and I inhale, hyperaware of her movements. I've never paid this much attention to a surgical assistant while they tied my gown. Her hand is small and it's taking her thirty fucking minutes to find the damn thing.

"Do I need to have someone else do this?"

Without a word, she finds the string and its mate quickly, twirls them around one another, and pulls—*tight*, like she's trying to punish me.

"Oops," she says, docile as a lamb as she loosens it a bit and ties it in a bow.

The ridiculous holdups don't stop there. When I move to the operating table, Bailey scurries over to stand at my side...and by my side, I mean halfway down the table. I'll have to extend my arm and lean over just to reach the instruments she'll be passing to me. On top of that, she's short, too short for the height the table's currently set at, and she realizes that fact at the same time I do.

"Dr. Lopez usually kept his table a little lower..."

Dr. Collins murmurs impatiently under his breath.

I turn over my shoulder and nod to a tech. "Grab some of those stepstools."

A few moments later, they're dropped next to Bailey's feet and I sigh, trying hard to keep my cool after a hellacious morning.

"Bring them closer," I bite out impatiently.

The tech scoots them right beside me and Bailey steps up and clears her throat. Now she's closer to my height and not so far away.

Not wanting to waste any more time, I start the time-out, and each member of my team confirms they're ready for the procedure to begin. The roll call circles back to the operating table, Dr. Collins introduces himself, and then it's Bailey's turn.

Part of me expects her to turn on the spot and walk right out of the room. Dr. Collins just publicly shamed her. She's single-handedly wasted everyone's time this morning. If she's half the surgical assistant Dr. Lopez claimed she is, she's likely beating herself up right now.

She looks over at me and so much of her is concealed beneath her scrub cap and mask—the freckles, the smile, the pale blonde hair. All I have are her eyes, and they're staring up at me, revealing a mixture of emotion I can't quite name. To the world, our exchange might be a millisecond, but between us, it feels like a long, contemplative pause.

My eyebrow quirks as if I'm asking, *Well? What'll it be?*

She jerks her attention back to the table, and I stare at her masked profile as she says for the entire OR to hear, "Bailey Jennings, Dr. Russell's surgical assistant. Everything's set."

Well then.

Dr. Collins clears his throat, clearly annoyed he didn't get a better chance to lay into her. Then I speak up, my voice booming over the quiet room. "This morning we're operating on a seven-year-old female named Fiona Valdez. She and her family have traveled a long way to be here in our operating room. We'll be performing a pedicle subtraction osteotomy in an effort to remedy and delay further curvature. We'll take a posterior approach. Does everyone agree?"

A chorus of voices speak at once and then I hold out my gloved palm.

"Bailey, ten blade."

CHAPTER NINE
BAILEY

THIS IS RIDICULOUS. I knew I'd suffer consequences because of my tardiness, but it must be my lucky day because I have to endure not only one crabby surgeon, but two. I thought Dr. Russell was bad, but he doesn't compare to Dr. Collins.

Older, tall, in shape. In the five minutes I've stood at the operating table with him, he's already mentioned the fact that he "cycles" twice.

I decide to ignore him as much as possible, mostly because I'm still reeling from the public scolding he gave me when he first entered the OR, but apparently my lack of interest needles him because right after the first incision, he meets my eyes over the operating table and sneers. "Y'know, Dr. Russell, I don't know if I would put up with my surgical assistant holding up a quarter-million-dollar case like this."

He says it just like that, while looking me in the eyes! My cheeks grow hot. I want to snap at him to drop it. *Yes, I was late, but I've apologized and there's nothing more I can do about it.* Instead, I jerk my gaze back to the patient, knowing better than to respond.

"Well then it's a good thing this surgery is coming out of the hospital's pro bono budget," Dr. Russell replies, his voice even colder than usual. "Bailey, pay attention. I need you to suction more."

I jerk forward and shout at myself to stay focused.

A few minutes later, Dr. Collins decides to turn his

attention back to me once again. Like a grade-school bully, he just can't seem to get enough. "How long have you been on Dr. Russell's team?"

Why, oh why did he have to ask that question?

"This is my first day," I say, voice barely above a whisper. With my mask on, I doubt he can hear me, but he must, because he laughs like I've just said the most ridiculous thing in the world—and, well, I have.

"Not making a great first impression, are you?"

I want to tell him to fuck off, but I can't. It's not how this works. I have to sit quietly and stay focused. He can basically say or do whatever the hell he wants. *Oh, the privilege that comes with a white coat.*

Dr. Russell could speak up and come to my defense. He could tell Dr. Collins to shut his trap, but he doesn't. He's focused on the case. He doesn't say a word unless he's asking for an instrument or giving an order.

On the Worst Surgery Ever scale, I'm hovering somewhere near a 9.5, and then fate decides to ramp it all the way up to a perfect 10 when my stomach starts to growl. We're only halfway through. I realize I completely forgot to eat the muffin Josie threw at me when I left the house.

For a second, I think no one heard it.

Thank God.

"Is that your stomach, Bailey?" Dr. Russell asks, accepting the pedical screwdriver I hand to him.

I swallow and am careful to avoid eye contact. "Yes."

"Did you eat breakfast?"

I consider lying, but there's no denying the very loud, angry noises coming from my stomach, so I sort of veer around the question. "I was in a hurry to leave the house."

He nods and then with an even, hard tone that sends

chills down my spine, he says, "Don't ever step into my operating room without eating again. It's careless. This is grueling work. You're standing over a table for hours, retracting and cauterizing. If you pass out, you endanger my patient. Do you understand?"

"Yes sir."

"What is that, the second or third strike against you, Bailey?" Dr. Collins asks with a chuckle that slices straight through me. "Looks like you might be in the market for a new surgical assistant sooner than you thought, Dr. Russell."

It's not the worst thing a surgeon has said to me, I know that, but it's the straw that breaks the camel's back. I'm not good at taking criticism. I thrive on positive feedback and try my hardest to be a good employee. I don't like getting in trouble, and I definitely don't like being scolded in front of my peers.

It's too much. Maybe I can take one shot or even two, but I can't stand in front of a freaking firing squad and pretend like I'm not getting destroyed. Worse, every person in this operating room has a front-row seat to my humiliation. I feel everyone's eyes on me, judging. I know they feel bad for me, and then, because my brain loves me, it chirps up and reminds me there's a whole slew of people up in the viewing gallery too. *Wonderful.*

I think of all the effort I put into preparing for this case. I didn't want to let Dr. Russell down. I wanted to be better than all the failed assistants who came before me, but it turns out I'm worse.

I'm grateful for my protective glasses as a tear works its way down my cheek. It soaks into the corner of the blue mask covering my mouth and I scream at myself to get it together. Just like with baseball, there's no crying in surgery.

Stop! Stop! STOP!

Except, the floodgates are now open, and sure, I'm not sobbing, but my eyes are welling with tears enough that I have to blink quickly to clear them away so they don't obscure my vision. That's just what I need: a tear dripping from my face onto the surgical field. I would melt into the floor.

In all, I think I'm doing an okay job of hiding my distress by spacing out a few necessary sniffs so they can be chalked up to nothing more than allergies, but I'm not.

"Do I need to have someone relieve you?" Dr. Russell asks.

I shake my head, knowing if I speak, an errant sob will sneak out. I won't give either of them the satisfaction.

Dr. Collins is staring at me. He knows I'm crying, and his opinion of me has hit an all-time low. My eyes narrow on him, *daring* him to call me out.

"I need you to communicate," Dr. Russell says harshly. "My attention is on my patient. If you need to be excused then say so."

I want to scream at him to leave me alone, but I can't. Instead, I take his angry, sharp words and use them to evaporate my remaining tears.

"I'm fine," I bite out with a shockingly steady voice. "Would you like me to ask Kendra to start preparing tray three?"

"Yes."

That's all. No *Thank you for being efficient and attentive even as two overbearing surgeons berate you in front of all of your coworkers.* No *Thank you for salvaging this situation as best you could even though I've put so much pressure on you that you're liable to have a nervous breakdown.*

Though they're both treating me like I am, I'm *not* an idiot. Just like Dr. Russell requested on Friday, I memorized every step of this surgery. I know every detail of Fiona's case. I know her spine curves in a particularly difficult way, which is likely why Dr. Collins flew in to assist. I know why he's chosen to shave off that specific section of vertebrae in her lumbar spine and why it's imperative that Dr. Russell gets it exactly right, down to the millimeter. I know that even though this has been the most trying, worst day I've ever had in the operating room, difficulties aside, I'm enjoying the case. I'm completely enthralled by Dr. Russell's skill and expertise, the detail with which he performs this surgery. It's like I'm standing right beside Einstein as he works through an equation or Muhammad Ali as he prepares to enter the ring.

Dr. Collins is completely unnecessary.

Dr. Russell is single-handedly repairing this girl's spine, and in a few hours, when she wakes up and asks her parents how the surgery went, they'll be able to look her in the eye and tell her Dr. Russell did it. He gave her the very thing she wants the most: a normal childhood.

It's unfortunate I screwed up so badly.

I overslept. I ruined my one shot. Then I cried at the operating table. CRIED. I might as well pack my metaphorical bags; I get that.

Near the end of the surgery, I glance up at the clock and see that it's not yet noon. Dr. Collins will make his flight. Dr. Russell made up for the lost time. I've never been more relieved. He tells me to close and dress the sutures and then leaves the room with Dr. Collins on his tail.

I'm the only one left at the operating table. I have

81

never taken such a deep, clearing breath in my life.

I love this part. I'm good at it. My hand is steady and my work is clean. Every suture is placed with care and attention to minimize Fiona's scar.

When I'm done, Kendra compliments my technique, placing her hand on my shoulder as I strip off my gloves and toss them in the trash.

"Usually Dr. Russell is picky about sutures. You did a good job."

I half-laugh, half-grunt. "Yeah? And what about the rest of it?"

She laughs. "Let's just say it was fun while it lasted, right?"

I'M EATING ALONE in the lounge like a loser. I have an untouched bag of pretzels and an apple. I'm trying to force a sandwich into my mouth, but it's too dry. My body is using all my fluids for tear production. Every bite is a struggle. What I really want to do is sling the stupid sandwich against the wall—or better yet, at Dr. Russell's head.

"There she is!" someone calls from the doorway, and I glance up to see a group of surgical assistants walk into the lunchroom. We always eat lunch together. They're my work friends, the people who laughed when I drew the devil horns on Dr. Russell.

"You survived your first day!" Erika says with a big smile and two thumbs up.

Before I can protest, she and the rest of the group gather around and claim the remaining spots at my table. They think this is a celebration when it's actually a pity party. If there were a record playing, I'd scratch it.

"Yup, and I won't survive another," I say, all gloom and doom.

"Oh, c'mon, don't be dramatic!" Megan says, shoving my shoulder playfully. Megan and Erika work on the dermatology floor, assisting their doctors with mole biopsies and laser hair removal. They are both moisturized and cheerful, and they routinely leave the hospital by 3:00 PM. Megan told me last week that she felt *too* well-rested. I hate them more than I like them.

"We're taking you out for a celebratory drink tonight!" Erika declares like it's a done deal.

"No." I shake my head. "Honestly, I'm not in the mood, not after the morning I've had."

"Aw, c'mon. It can't be that bad. You knew Dr. Russell was going to be tough, but if anyone can handle him, it's you—"

My hand shoots up, displaying the universal sign for *Shut the hell up*, but then I spot Patricia in the doorway, scanning the room. She doesn't eat in here; she eats at her desk so she can flip through her knitting magazines. I know this because I pay careful attention to her. It's important to be on Patricia's good side.

When she sees me across the room, she nods and cuts a path straight for me.

I imagine what she's about to say. Most likely, Dr. Russell has given her a note he'd like her to read in front of the entire lunchroom. *Yes, it says here you're incompetent and a huge disappointment.*

I push my sandwich away and squeeze my eyes closed.

"I've been looking for you everywhere," Patricia says, puffing out an annoyed breath.

Then there's a loud splat. I blink my eyes open and

realize it was the sound of a manila folder hitting the table in front of me.

"This is for Dr. Russell's surgery on Wednesday."

I release a bitter, sad laugh then attempt to hand it back to her. "Oh, I won't need this."

She doesn't accept it. "I know Dr. Lopez didn't have you go over patient files like this, but Dr. Russell insists his surgical assistants know his cases as well as he does."

She misunderstands. "It's not that. I just don't think I'm going to be on his team come Wednesday."

Her wise gray eyes assess me over the rims of her glasses. It's clear she thinks I have a few screws loose. "Well, *he* was the one who just asked me to pass this along to you. If you're planning on quitting, better go let him know now so he can arrange to have a resident assist him on Wednesday."

My mouth is a fly trap.

WHAT?

"He gave you this file just now?"

She nods slowly.

"This file?"

"Yes."

"After the surgery?"

"Yes."

"Now? And he said to hand it to *me*? Bailey Jennings?"

She reaches forward and thumps me on the forehead. "Yes. Now stop asking stupid questions."

Then she turns and walks out of the lunchroom, muttering under her breath.

My tablemates stare at me in shock.

Erika throws her hands up. "SEE! YOU DID IT!"

Megan claps. "This is cause for celebration! Drinks tonight, on me!"

I'm so shocked, I don't even have enough sense to turn them down.

JOSIE, UNSURPRISINGLY, SCREAMS into the phone when I tell her I'm going out with friends and I'll be home a little later than usual.

"What are you going to wear?" Her voice carries clear across the locker room. People shoot me strange looks.

"Uh…" I look down at the clothes I wore to work this morning. "Nothing fancy. That black blouse you hate."

She groans. "Just please don't button it all the way to your neck. I swear to God—"

"I didn't, *jeez*!" I hurry and undo the top two buttons, glad she can't see me through the phone. "Do you think I'm a *total* loser?"

"And the jeans?"

"They're the tight ones you bought me with my credit card without my permission."

"Oh thank God. Shoes?"

"Tennis shoes," I murmur shamefully. "With thick wool socks."

She sighs deeply. "Why do you insist on sabotaging yourself?"

I glance down and clap my heels together like Dorothy.

"They're comfortable."

"They're also obnoxious. I'm going to burn them when you get home."

"Hey! They aren't that bad. And you better be asleep when I get home. It might be late."

She marches on, ignoring me. "Your hair is in a ponytail, isn't it?"

"Of course."

"Can you take it down?"

"Nope."

"Makeup? Please tell me you put some mascara on this morning."

"No. I was rushed, but I keep some stuff in my locker. I'll put it on if it'll make you feel better."

"*PLEASE.*"

"Bailey!" Erika calls my name from across the locker room. "Are you almost ready? We want to try to catch the end of happy hour."

I shoot her a thumbs-up. "Josie, I gotta go."

"Okay, fine, but you better talk to a guy! *Any guy*! The bartender! The bus boy—"

I hang up on her and grab for my makeup bag, telling Erika I just need a few minutes. I swipe on mascara, blend a little blush onto my cheeks, and dab on some Chapstick. I look remarkably more human when we walk into the bar across the street from New England Medical Center.

Smooth Tony's is an institution around the hospital. It has stood the test of time, a small faded bungalow shoved in the middle of skyscrapers, and best of all, Smooth Tony himself still mans the bar every night. Erika and Megan are on a first-name basis with him, and he knows their preferred drinks without them having to order.

"What about you, blondie?" he asks me as he slides full cocktails their way.

I stare at the bottles of liquor lined up behind him, trying to remember the name of a drink…*any* drink.

"Uh, I think I need a second."

"We're going to go snag a booth before they're all taken!" Erika says, and I'm left alone, searching in vain for a drink menu.

"Still thinking it over?" Tony asks after he helps another customer.

I frown. "What'd you make my friends? Maybe I'll just have one of those."

"Vodka sodas."

I scrunch my nose. "Sounds boring."

He laughs, and it's deep and hearty. "Tell you what: why don't I just make you something and if you don't like it, we'll try something else."

I climb up onto a stool and shoot him an appreciative smile. "Yes. Thank you. That sounds perfect."

So, that's how I come to be sitting by myself at the bar, sampling a drink that actually tastes really good.

"What'd he end up making you?"

The question comes from the guy sitting to my right. I turn, and my eyebrows shoot up. This isn't just a guy. This is a blond hunk with dimples and a winning smile. This is a guy worth a double take—a third take, even.

I smile and tilt my glass toward him. "Oh, uh…actually, I'm not sure."

I look up to ask Tony, but he's already moved on to another customer down at the other end of the bar.

The hunk laughs. "Looks like an Old Fashioned. Does it taste like it's got bourbon in it?"

"Maybe." I narrow my eyes. "But just for clarification, what does bourbon taste like?"

He laughs and shakes his head. "First time at a bar?"

"*No* " My cheeks redden. "It's my *third* time."

He unleashes a heart-stopping grin and reaches his hand out toward me. "I'm Cooper."

I'm pleased to find he has one of those manly, strong handshakes, one that would impress any discerning judge. "Bailey."

"Bailey," he repeats, testing it out before he nods as if coming to a conclusion. "You look like a Bailey."

My brows rise curiously. "Oh yeah? Why's that?"

"It's a sweet name." He shrugs. "Cute. Cheerful."

His eyes scan down me quickly, and I think I spot a hint of interest in his light blue eyes, which seem oddly familiar.

"Well thanks, Cooper. You have a good name too. I think my best friend growing up had a dog named Cooper."

He laughs and turns back to the bar. "Was it a cute dog at least?"

He's fishing and I can practically hear Josie screaming at me to flirt with him, to not let this moment slip through my fingers.

"Very cute. A little French bulldog," I reveal with a big cheesy smile.

He groans playfully. "Oh, c'mon—couldn't you have told me it was a massive Rottweiler? Maybe a German shepherd?"

I laugh. "Nope. He was a tiny thing." I hold my hands up about half a foot apart, winking one eye closed like I'm trying to get the measurement just right. "About this big."

"Ha ha." He tips the neck of his beer toward me. "You know what? Maybe I got it wrong. Maybe you don't fit your name after all."

I can't believe how quickly we hit it off. He's funny and nice. I'm supposed to join my group over in the corner, but when I glance over my shoulder, Erika claps like she's proud of me and Megan shouts, "Yes girl!"

Thankfully I don't think Cooper hears her over the music. He does follow my gaze, though, and Erika and Megan make quick work of trying and failing to appear normal. Erika takes a big swig of her drink and then chokes. Megan has to clap her on the back.

"Do you need to go join your friends?"

I frown. What am I supposed to say? No, I'd rather talk to you? What kind of person ditches their friends for a cute guy? SOMEONE WHO HASN'T BEEN ON A DATE IN A MILLENIA.

I frown. "I don't know. Probably. I don't want to be a bad friend."

He smiles and nods. "I get it. It's cool. I'm actually waiting for someone myself."

My heart shatters. "Oh, yeah? A girl?"

Wow. So subtle. So cool.

"No." He looks down at his watch and shakes his head. "Just some prick with no regard for people's time."

"Oh." I slide off my stool. "Well…if you're left hanging, you're welcome to join me and my friends."

He smiles. "Thanks, but I'll probably call it soon. I have an early flight tomorrow."

NO. That means he's leaving the city. My chances of ever seeing him again are decreasing by the second.

"But if you give me your number, maybe I could call you sometime?"

MAYBE HE COULD CALL ME SOMETIME?

I don't think I've ever smiled so wide. My cheeks are liable to split right down the middle. My face betrays every ounce of my excitement, which means Cooper sees it too. Maybe my excitement is infectious because soon enough, we're two smiling fiends.

He tugs out his cell phone, I type in my number, and just like that, I have the possibility of love on the horizon.

Josie is going to pee her pants.

CHAPTER TEN
MATT

"AH, THERE HE is, the man of the hour."

My pen stills and I pinch my eyes closed.

Cooper.

Shit. I completely forgot I was supposed to have drinks with him tonight.

I look up and my little brother is standing at the doorway of my office with his arms crossed. He looks pissed, which is a rare expression for him. His factory setting is easygoing nice guy. His feathers don't get ruffled very often, but then, if I'd been stood up by my asshole brother, I'd be pissed too.

I glance at the clock and cringe. An hour. I made him sit there for an hour. I push away from my desk and stand.

"There's no excuse. I'm sorry. C'mon, we can still go. I'll finish this later."

He shakes his head and cuts me off before I can reach for my coat. "Don't bother. I already had two beers while I was waiting. If I have another, I'll feel like shit in the morning."

He walks to my leather couch and pushes a mess of hardware out of the way, clearing a spot so he can sit down. I would snap at anyone else for moving my shit, but not Cooper.

"Paperwork keep you?" he asks.

I roll my desk chair over toward him, take a seat, and lean back. "Always."

"Must have been a busy day if you're still in your

scrubs."

He's right. Usually, I change after surgery.

I rub the nape of my neck, massaging the tired muscles. "The day got away from me. It was hectic to say the least."

He holds up his hand. "Spare me the details."

I get it. Cooper's in this world too, just in a different realm. He works in sales for Hasting Biosciences, the largest medical devices company in the country. We were both jocks in high school, stars on the baseball team, but he amplified his popularity and I ran from mine, more comfortable concentrating on my grades while he ruled the lunchroom. That outgoing personality has paid off for him; he's the leading salesman in the northeast region.

"You missed a good opportunity to hang out and bond with your dear brother," he says, pushing to stand and passing me by to head to my desk. "I leave tomorrow for Cincinnati. I'll be gone for a while."

He opens my topmost desk drawer and roots around until he finds what he's looking for: a small toy basketball.

"What's in Cincinnati?"

"A prospective doctor."

"Big fish?"

He walks back around the desk and inspects the floor until he finds the small X made out of duct tape. I've had to redo it a few times, but it's more or less in the same spot it was when we placed it there a few years back.

"Biggest fish I've ever seen."

He lines up his shot, aims the ball at the hoop hanging on the back of my door, shoots, and misses by a hair.

I hiss and stand to retrieve the ball. "Will you be back in time for Molly's wedding?"

"When is that again?"

"Mid-November, I think."

It's my turn now, so I head back to the X, aim, and sink the ball into the net.

"Pfft." He shakes his head. "Luck, nothing else."

I smirk and hold the ball out to him. It's the least I can do after standing him up for a drink. "You better fly back for it. Aunts, uncles, cousins—everyone'll be there. I won't last without you. Besides, they like you better anyway. They only ever tolerate me."

"Aw c'mon, you're going to make me blush." He swats the ball out of my hand, shoots, and scores. "Oh hey, I forgot to ask—did you submit that grant proposal you've been working on?"

I laugh. "Yeah, like six months ago."

"When do you hear back?"

"Before the holidays."

My heart races thinking about it…the possibilities, the lives it would affect.

His brow arches with interest. "Think you'll be able to give up this cushy life if the committee picks you?"

"I'll manage," I reply sarcastically.

We continue like that for a little while, taking the toy basketball game more seriously than we should, but we get like that with each other. I'm concentrating so hard on landing the perfect shot that I don't really pay attention as he starts describing the girl he just picked up at the bar across the street.

"—total babe. So you see, it wasn't all bad. I'm actually glad you didn't show. She's sweet. Blonde, just like I prefer. A little short, but on her, it works. She put her name in my phone as Bailey, Girl from the Bar, like I wouldn't remember her."

I jerk forward, throw, and end up missing the net by a good two feet as I turn to face him. "Wait—what'd you say she looked like again?"

He frowns, confused by my sudden interest.

"Blonde, perky, freckles." He shrugs. "Not your type, don't worry."

I grunt. "Yeah, you'd be correct in assessing that she's not my type considering she works for me as of this morning."

"No way. Not this girl."

I roll my eyes. "Were her eyes a really light brown? Almost hazel?"

"I don't know. The bar was hazy."

"Did she have high cheekbones? Dimples when she smiled?"

"Shit. Bailey? Blonde, happy-go-lucky Bailey works for you? What does she do? Is she a nurse?"

"She's my surgical assistant."

He cracks up. Eyes-closed, knee-slapped levels of laughter spill out of him.

"No," he says, wiping tears from the corners of his eyes. "No fucking way."

I thrust the ball against his chest. "Are you going to take your shot or what?"

He tosses the basketball over the arm of the couch with total disregard for where it'll end up. It pings off the wall, collides with my chair, and makes a final sad descent beside my trashcan. "Tell me exactly how that came to be because the last time I heard from you, you didn't have a surgical assistant. According to you, no one could keep up."

"Dr. Lopez foisted her onto me."

He shakes his head and steps closer, pressing his hand against my chest. "No, no, no. Don't bullshit me. You hired her."

I shrug and try to move around him but he blocks my path. I let him. I've got a few inches on him. I could easily go around, but I don't want to make this seem like it's more than it is, because in fact, it's nothing. My little brother, the golden boy, tried to pick up Bailey. Big deal.

"Why?"

"She was in the right place at the right time. I was out a surgical assistant and she was out a surgeon. It works."

A slow, sly smile unravels across his face, and I have the sudden urge to hurt him.

"Well, will it be awkward for you when we start dating?"

I step back, brows furrowed as my annoyance morphs into something a little more sinister. "Dating? What do you mean? Didn't you just meet her five minutes ago?"

He shrugs and moves away. Suddenly he's a sly punk running his hand along my desk, touching things that don't belong to him. "Yeah, but we hit it off. There was this instant connection. You get it. You probably feel the same way when you get a new medical device, this sort of excitement down in your loins."

His eyebrows are wagging suggestively.

"That's really funny, Coop," I tease, reaching out for his shoulder and squeezing it a little too tight. "I wonder if that doctor up in Cincinnati would be put off by a black eye?"

His brows shoot up. "Black eye?" His tone is feigned innocence. "What? I thought we were just discussing my new lady friend and now suddenly you're threatening bodily harm. This just isn't like you, Matthew."

He never calls me Matthew. He thinks he's onto something. It'll be awkward to have to explain to my parents that I accidentally murdered their favorite son.

"I'm warning you," I say menacingly. "Drop it."

"Drop what, exactly? You'll have to be specific since I'm clearly confused."

I let go of his shoulder and round my desk, starting to straighten up my shit so I can get the hell out of here. "You're doing this because you want to rile me up. You want to punish me for making you sit at that bar. Well, it's done. You did it. Now leave her out of it."

He laughs and shakes his head. "No, actually that's not it at all. I met a beautiful woman tonight and she gave me her number. I told you about it and instead of being happy for me, you went apeshit. Kind of interesting, don't you think? Would you care if I dated Patricia?"

I level him with a *Don't fuck with me* glare.

"You're right." He nods. "She's too good for me. What about Kendra?"

"Drop it, Coop."

"No, I need to know—do you not want me dating *any* of your employees or do you not want me dating Bailey?"

"You're being an asshole. Drop it."

He holds up his hands in surrender. "You're right. Fine. Lesson learned: anything having to do with Bailey, I'll keep to myself."

I DON'T LET Cooper's little game get to me. He's my younger brother. He was put on this earth to torment me. He thinks he's really got a good thing going, but honestly, it's not much. Date Bailey. I don't care.

He texts me the next day with a screenshot of their conversation.

Cooper: Hey! This is Cooper.

96

Cooper: Oh, let me clarify: the guy from the bar, not your friend's dog.

Bailey: Ha! I was confused there for a second...thanks for clarifying. How are you?

Cooper: Good, just landed in Cincinnati for work. It's cold AF here.

Then he sent a stupid-ass selfie of him standing outside with his hood pulled up and his teeth chattering. She replied a few hours later.

Bailey: Oh my gosh! You poor thing.

Cooper seemed to think that was promising.

Aw she feels sorry for me. ;) was his exact text to me.

My response: *Apparently not considering how long it took her to reply to you. Odd since she doesn't work on Tuesdays. What was her excuse?*

Cooper: Maybe she just isn't a slave to her phone like the rest of society...

I didn't reply, opting instead to get back to work, but he texted again.

Cooper: Just to be clear, of the two of us, I know way more about women than you do.

Matt: All right.

Cooper: I've had three successful long-term relationships. You've had one divorce.

Matt: K

My short replies must have been pissing him off because then he replied: *In fact, I really feel like Bailey and I will hit it off. I'm going to ask her out on a date when I get back from Cincinnati.*

I didn't reply.

The following morning, I have my second surgery scheduled with Bailey. It's up on the board for 8:00 AM, but when I arrive at six, she's already there, leaning against the wall outside my office with a thermos of coffee in one hand and a Tupperware container in the other. I glance back and forth past my door, wondering if she's confused.

"Are you waiting for me?" I ask once I'm in earshot.

She jerks forward and nods, her demeanor shifting from relaxed to professional just like that. "Yes. Hi. Good morning."

Her cheeks are flushed, nearly the same shade as her lips. Her jacket is still zipped up to her neck. I wonder where she parked to get that cold on her way into the hospital. Then the thought dissipates as the distinct aroma of baked goods distracts me. My mouth waters like I'm one of Pavlov's dogs as I come to stand in front of her.

My key is in hand, ready to be used.

She doesn't move. Her eyes scan up across my suit jacket, over my chest and neck, and then higher until her light brown eyes meet mine. She has to tip her head back quite a bit to meet my eyes, and maybe I was inspecting her as much as she was inspecting me because she asks, "Are you waiting for something?" and I swear her voice is a little breathy.

I resist the urge to smirk. "You're blocking my door. I can't unlock it."

Her high cheekbones are doused with even more color and then she shifts quickly to get out of my way. "Oh god, sorry. Clearly, I haven't had my coffee yet."

"What's in there?" I ask, motioning to the Tupperware. "It smells good."

"This? Oh, well…" She holds it up, pauses, and then looks back at me as she shrugs. "It's a bribe."

I finish unlocking the door then stand back and arch a brow in her direction. "A bribe?"

She chews on the corner of her bottom lip to keep from

smiling. "Yes. Banana bread. Patricia said it was your favorite, so I made some for you on my day off."

Huh.

Interesting.

She should have been texting with Cooper, but instead, she was baking for me.

"Are you trying to make up for Monday?" I ask, no hint of humor in my tone.

I open my door and step inside, leaving it ajar so she can follow me in if she wants to. She does.

"Yes. Exactly." She looks down at the container as if considering something and then glances back up, her gaze meeting mine. "I'm sorry for being late. There's really no excuse, but you should know I've never been late before and I don't intend on being late ever again. I figure an apology isn't good enough, though, so my plan is to ply you with sweets."

Then, for emphasis, she cracks the lid.

Damn, that smells good. Inside-of-a-bakery good. Grandma's-kitchen good.

My stomach growls.

It occurs to me how different this exchange is from my previous encounters with surgical assistants. When Kirt stepped into my office, his knees shook. He avoided eye contact and hovered near the door as if to ensure a quick getaway. By contrast, Bailey seems confident—so confident, in fact, that she's looking around the space, perusing it leisurely. She smiles at something and I follow her gaze to the toy basketball sitting by my couch. I forgot to put it back in my desk the other night.

I start to rummage through a few files for no other reason than to have an excuse to look away from her. She's not in her scrubs yet. Her jeans are cute. Her puffer jacket is pink. Her hair is golden blonde, angelic.

Cooper was right: she's not my usual type.

The fact that I have to remind myself of that annoys me.

"The bribe is unnecessary," I declare suddenly, wanting to make things perfectly clear to her. Her brows furrow and I continue, "For you to work for me, for us to be a good team, I don't need to like you. You don't have to bake for me. Just show up on time and do a good job. How about that?"

"But I want you to like me," she says, sounding baffled at the idea that she has to explain herself.

I shrug like it's not a big deal. "If it helps, I don't really like anyone who works here save for Patricia, and I think that's actually just mutual respect."

"So for you, it's better to respect someone than to like them?"

I look up to see her head tilted to the side. She's studying me with furrowed brows. This wisp of a girl is putting me under a microscope in *my* own office and I don't like it.

"Yeah, I guess so."

The edge of her mouth softens and then tilts up into an alluring smile. "So, there's no hope for us? As friends?"

She's teasing me and right here, in this moment, there's a hopeful feeling blooming in my chest. My cold dead heart might not be completely out of commission after all.

Then, I do the only logical thing: I shove that feeling aside.

"No. There's no hope."

Not as friends, and not as anything more, though I feel stupid even having to clarify that to myself. I would never even consider Bailey attractive if Cooper hadn't shifted her into the category for me. These errant thoughts are his fault.

She nods, and I'm surprised to see she doesn't look upset. In fact, she looks relieved. She snaps the lid back on the Tupperware. "Then I'll just take this bread to the break room. No point in it going to waste. See you in surgery!"

Then she saunters out.

She leaves my office and takes my damn banana bread with her.

CHAPTER ELEVEN
BAILEY

WHAT A COLOSSAL waste of my time. I cringe thinking of how carefully I measured out those ingredients yesterday. I hovered near our ancient stove, face inches from the glass, sweat beading down my forehead from how much heat that sucker was putting off, just to ensure the loaf didn't burn.

Baking was my way of trying to gain control of the situation. I'd already memorized the procedural steps for today's surgery and I was still a ball of anxiety. As proof: my alarm clock went off at 5:15 AM this morning. Then, my ancient clock radio started blaring pop music, and seconds later, my sister's fist started pounding against my door.

"HEY! Did you set my alarm?! The sun isn't even up, you psycho. Let me sleep! I'm an adolescent! My brain is still growing!"

I had no choice. I needed to be sure I didn't oversleep again so I took every necessary precaution, including waking up my sister. My clothes were already laid out on the floor as if I'd been raptured right out of them the night before. My shoes were untied and ready to go. My toothbrush was pre-loaded. I was outside, shivering at my bus stop fifteen minutes after waking up.

I was going to make a stellar second impression, and I was confident of this right up until I arrived outside of Dr. Russell's office and found it empty. The hallway was quiet. I grew nervous. I stared down at my Tupperware, wondering if maybe it wasn't such a good idea after all. *What if he's allergic to nuts?*

Oh right, I didn't use any nuts.

I was seconds away from bolting when I heard his deep, unwelcoming voice down the hall.

"Are you waiting for me?"

I glanced up and nearly swallowed my tongue. My gut clenched as I blinked a comical number of times, trying to comprehend how a robot could be so beautiful. He was wearing a navy suit that set off his dark, thick hair. His camel coat was tossed over his forearm. His hard jaw was locked tight as he assessed me suspiciously upon his approach.

I suddenly felt silly and adolescent standing there waiting for him. I cursed my outfit, wishing I'd already changed into my scrubs. My tennis shoes were scuffed. His brown oxfords looked as if they'd been shined mere seconds before. My jacket had been purchased at a thrift store. His looked bespoke.

He kept walking until he was standing right in front of me, and my neck craned back and back some more until that blue gaze knocked the air right out of my lungs. *Oof.*

I haven't been around many men like Dr. Russell in my life. Standing close to him in a quiet hallway was thrilling in the same way a death-defying rollercoaster is thrilling…maybe one that hasn't been inspected in a while, made of rickety wood and squeaky iron bars. I was fairly sure I wouldn't survive the ride, but something made me want to step right up anyway.

He was studying me, too, and I wish I could have known what was going on in that microprocessor of his.

"Are you waiting for something?" I asked.

"You're blocking my door. I can't unlock it."

Mortification drenched me from head to toe. I wanted to toss the bread at him and sprint down the hall. I forced myself to try to save face as I followed him into his office, but that was a stupid idea. *Oh, you're already feeling nervous? Step into the lion's den.* The first thing I noticed was that the room smelled like him. I hadn't realized he had a distinct scent until that moment—crisp and woodsy. I had a weird, sudden urge to rub myself across his leather couch in the hopes that it'd linger on me after I left.

Scent aside, his office was a total mess, which I found oddly charming. There were no old food containers lying around, no trash overflowing the bin. Rather, it was messy in the way a well-loved kitchen is messy. Medical devices strewn about. Files stacked on his desk. His bookshelves were stuffed to the brim with medical texts, the overflow piled on the floor nearby. If I had a photographic memory, I would have memorized every spine.

At least I had fun encroaching on his space because the rest of the experience sucked *mucho*. Let's just say it wasn't my best showing (I told him I was trying to bribe him!) and then he made matters worse by turning down said bribe on all fronts. No bread, no friendship, no nothing. Apparently, my banana bread wasn't as tempting as I'd hoped it'd be. I really thought Dr. Russell would go for it. What sane gluten-eating American turns down homemade baked goods?

I toss the banana bread onto the counter in the break room and resist the urge to stab it with a knife.

"*Oh*! Did someone make banana bread?" Shelly asks from the doorway. She turns and shouts down the hall. "Hey, Larry, there's banana bread in here!"

Within minutes, coworkers are crowded around me like vultures. I watch them eat my bread, soaking in every emphatic moan and groan.

"Bailey, this is something *else*," Larry says with a little shimmy of his shoulders.

Their praise is nice, but it's not what I wanted. Dr. Russell should be licking his chops right now but instead he turned the tables around on me.

I don't need to like you.

Who says that to someone?!

A psychopath, that's who. Everyone wants to be liked. Including him.

I know it.

I DON'T SEE Dr. Russell again until he walks into the operating room. He confers with the anesthesiologist, checks in with the device rep, and then heads straight for me. I'm already holding up his gown, waiting for him, sterile gloves and mask in place. Every strand of my hair is tucked beneath my pink scrub cap—the one I didn't have time to grab on Monday.

He notices it and shakes his head as he steps into the gown.

"What?" I ask.

"Nothing."

I don't think he's a fan of pink. He better pray he doesn't have a princess-loving daughter someday.

I reach in to tie the gown at his back. Just like the last time, it feels slightly more intimate than it should. It's the proximity. I'm inches away from his butt, and though I'm not proud of myself, I do glance down. It's great. Firm.

It's just him and me today—no secondary surgeon making me cry—so I stand across from him at the operating table. I can't decide which position is better. On Monday, I was keenly aware of his every move, careful not to accidently bump into him as I worked. Now, I have a better view of the parts of him that could easily soften a heart: his startling blue eyes, tall frame, and black hair just *barely* visible beneath his navy scrub cap. His olive skin tone looks nice even under the harsh glare of these fluorescent lights. I think to myself that he could be *such* a heartbreaker at the exact moment he snaps an order at the device rep. Oh right, that isn't a Casanova standing across from me; it's Dr. Beep Boop Robot. I'm not even sure there's a heart beating beneath those scrubs.

His gaze shoots up to me. Apparently, I'm not observing him as surreptitiously as I thought. "Are you paying attention to the surgery?" he asks, annoyed.

"Yes."

It's technically not a lie. Sure, I was kind of ogling him, but it was in the context of the surgery itself. I'm still getting used to the fact that I get to observe someone like him from this proximity. It's a heady experience.

"Tell me what instrument I'll need next."

I smirk under my mask. "The prism lumbar curette, 13.75 inches."

He's too practiced to reveal any note of surprise, but I swear I just gained a tiny modicum of his respect. I want to run around the room with my hand outstretched, collecting high fives. Instead, I check to confirm the retractor is still placed correctly, remembering his speech in his office. *Just show up on time and do a good job.* It's more important to gain his respect than his affection, and if that's the case, at least I know where I stand.

Except there's still one thing gnawing at me.

I hand him the curette and then speak gently. "I have to

know—why'd you give me a second chance after I was late on Monday? I seem to remember you saying very sternly that I would only get one shot at this."

For a moment, he's quiet as he continues working. The sounds of surgery surround us: the rhythmic beeps from the pulse oximeter, the dull hum of the Bair Hugger blowing warm air on the patient's legs, the conversations taking place around us.

"You're reading too much into it," he says, pausing. "I need a slightly larger curette. Is there one in the kit?"

I find one and swap it with the one he's holding.

"Am I? Reading too much into it?"

"You came highly recommended," he continues, satisfied with the new tool. "I didn't have any other options. Now if you're done with the chitchat, I need to focus."

It's a tactic; he doesn't need to focus any more than he already is. Dr. Lopez chatted his way through every procedure he ever did, and I know Dr. Russell is a better surgeon than most. He could probably operate with his eyes closed, so if he says he needs to focus, in reality, he just doesn't want to finish the conversation.

Fine.

I spend the rest of the surgery thinking over what I learned in his office earlier. If Dr. Russell would rather respect someone than like them, it's obvious he would prefer the same for himself, as if he were a king choosing to be feared rather than loved. There's something sad about that. It's got to be a lonely existence to walk around terrifying everyone, not to mention, a part of me wonders if it's a defense mechanism.

I know it shouldn't matter. I should leave well enough alone. He was very clear with me in his office…but I can't seem to drop it. I want to know more. Maybe before I wouldn't have cared, but he turned down my banana bread, dammit. He said he didn't want to be my friend! I need answers.

I decide the best person to ask is Patricia. She's worked for him for years. She has to know more about him than anyone else in the hospital. I find her sitting at her desk at lunch. There's a mug of tea, a small Caesar salad, and a fresh edition of *Creative Knitting* spread out in front of her. She doesn't even bother looking up from the pages as we skate through the usual small talk: *hi, how are you, how's your day going.* Finally, I get to the heart of the conversation.

"So you're pretty close with Dr. Russell, huh?" I ask, lifting my leg to sit on the edge of her desk.

She clears her throat in distaste and I immediately move. Okay, we aren't there yet. Noted.

"I mean, you've been with him since he started here, right?"

She snorts. "I'm the only one who could put up with him."

"So you admit he's difficult to work for?"

"Damn near impossible."

"But that has to be an act. He's not actually that mean in real life, is he?"

How can he be? Who has the energy to tackle world domination every single day of their life?

"I'll just say this…" She flips a page of her magazine and points down. "The harder the shell, the softer the heart."

Wow. *Patricia.* Who knew she had such a way with words? It sounds like something that should be printed on an inspirational poster or something. Then I glance down and see she has, in fact, stolen the phrase right off an embroidered pillow in her magazine.

Whatever.

"So you think he's a softie deep down?"

She glances up at me over the brim of her glasses. "He's gotta be, don't you think? To do what he does for these kids day in and day out? Not to mention the stuff he's got going on with that grant."

"What grant?"

She shakes her head. "You'll have to ask him about it. I don't know all the details."

Then she pointedly returns her attention to her magazine and goes right back to reading, so I thank her and make myself scarce.

I can't stop thinking about her assessment as I eat lunch. It's true: Dr. Russell usually operates on three children a week, which means he's already impacted hundreds of lives in his short career.

He can't be all bad.

He can't be the villain everyone thinks he is.

THERE'S A TEXT from Cooper waiting for me when I check my phone in the locker room after work.

Cooper: Hey Bailey! What's up?

He sent it hours ago when I was still in surgery. I feel bad for making him wait so long for a reply.

Bailey: Just getting off work, sorry! I'm good, just exhausted, ha.

Cooper: Yeah, I bet. Those surgeons run you guys into the ground.

Bailey: It's not so bad :) I like my job.

110

Cooper: What about your doctor? Is he nice? I've worked with some terrible ones.

Since my fingers would fall off if I attempted to explain the entire portfolio of emotions I feel for Dr. Russell, I condense it.

Bailey: I'm still deciding. My old doctor just retired and I really liked him. I think this new guy will be okay once we find our rhythm.

He and I text back and forth into the evening. It feels good that he seems to be pursuing me, but I'm not really all there yet. I have no idea how long he'll be in Cincinnati, not to mention, I'm not sure I'm even in a good place to be dating someone right now. I explain this to Josie after she sees my phone light up with his name while we're folding laundry and demands to know every detail of our relationship.

"I'm confused—how could you be any more available? You've had zero dates lately. ZERO."

I nod. "Yeah, I know that. It's just…" I let my sentence linger because I'm not sure how to explain. Cooper is really cute and nice and wants to get to know me. But, my heart doesn't flutter when I think about him. I don't turn into a ball of nervous energy when I see an incoming text with his name on it. "I don't know." I push up off the couch. "I need to start making dinner."

"But Cooper is still waiting for a reply!"

Ugh, this whole texting-with-a-hot-guy thing isn't all it's cracked up to be.

"Can you reply for me? Just don't make me sound too eager," I say as I start grabbing ingredients from the refrigerator for taco night.

"So I shouldn't send half a dozen kissy-face emojis?" She smiles and tilts her head to the side like an adorable puppy when I glare at her over my shoulder. "Kidding."

They go back and forth texting while I chop up onions. Cooper asks about my plans for the night and I tell her to be vague. He doesn't need to know how embarrassingly nonexistent my social life is.

"I told him you were going to 'hit the town with your girls and do body shots.' What are body shots again?"

"Josie!"

She ignores me. "Aw, poor guy. He says he's eating room service alone in his hotel room."

Someone else cooking and cleaning? Sounds pretty great to me.

A few minutes later, my phone chimes with an incoming email and Josie asks, "Who's Dr. Russell?"

My stomach falls out of my butt and I drop the block of cheese I was halfway through shredding. "WHAT?!"

Her eyes widen in shock. "Oh my god! It's *him*! The hot guy from the website!"

I have never moved so fast in my life. I'm up and over the kitchen island and yanking that phone out of Josie's hand before she has time to blink.

"Jesus," she cries. "You nearly tore my finger off!"

My heart drums hard against my ribcage as I unlock my phone and open the email app. My fingers are covered in cheese, making my phone screen blurry, but I don't care. He emailed me! *Why?* I could vomit or scream. My emotions have gone off the rails.

He's never contacted me outside of work. This could be a small step in the right direction. My finger is shaky as I tap to open his email, and I know Josie sees it.

Then I actually read the dang thing and I'm a sad, deflating balloon. It's just a last-minute time change for the surgery we have on Friday. He didn't even address me

112

personally. Three other people on our surgical team were CCed.

"What does it say?" Josie asks, grabbing a bag of cold peas out of the freezer to apply to her finger. "And why is the hot doctor emailing you?!"

"Oh...um..." I look down. "I kind of work for him now." The bag of peas hits my chest and I stumble back like I've been shot. "Ow!"

"You work for him?!" she asks incredulously. "Since when?"

She picks up the peas and is about to throw them at me again when I try to wrestle them out of her hand. The bag splits and tiny green spheres spray out around us like confetti.

The two of us freeze. Her head cocks to the side as she waits for me to cave.

"Since this week," I finally offer, sounding nonchalant. "It's new. It might not work out."

We both drop to our knees to start collecting peas.

She narrows her eyes in disbelief. "What is he emailing you about?"

"Boring work stuff."

"Oh." She's sad about that too. "You acted like it was something else." Her eyes jump back to mine. "Did you *want* it to be something else?"

"I don't know." I stand to toss a handful of peas into the trash so she can't see my face. "I guess."

"Like something personal?"

My phone pings again with an incoming text from Cooper and I jump on the opportunity to redirect Josie. While she responds to him, I continue cleaning and face the fact that there is a major difference between how I feel when I get a text from Cooper and how I felt when I thought Dr. Russell might have been emailing me about something other than work.

My excitement was through the roof. I mean, Jesus, I nearly broke my sister's finger. I sprayed frozen vegetables across my kitchen.

I know I only care this much because of the way things are between him and me. Our working relationship feels like a volcano liable to explode at any minute. It's like he can hardly stand me. Not only that, he's put up a wall between us, which only makes me want to get to know him even more. It's silly. He's just my boss. I never cared if Dr. Lopez emailed me, but then that was a different situation entirely.

Dr. Lopez liked me. He was nice to me. He talked to me during surgery and asked me about my life.

I can't imagine a day in which Dr. Russell tries to dabble in idle small talk. In fact, the very idea is ludicrous.

"Cooper really seems into you," Josie notes from the ground as she sweeps up the last of the peas, her voice taking on a hopeful tone. She's trying to lighten my mood, and it makes me angry that my mood even needs to be lightened. What business do I have worrying about Dr. Russell? It makes no sense. The last time I checked, I couldn't really stand him, and now suddenly I'm upset he hasn't noticed me and turned down my offer of friendship.

It doesn't make sense. I don't want to be his friend!

The only logical explanation is that I just want him to like me. That's all. I want to take a pickaxe to his defenses and chip away slowly until one day he looks up and realizes, *Huh, that Bailey, she's not half bad.*

It sounds like a good enough plan, so I vow to put my nose to the grindstone and get to work.

FOR THE NEXT two weeks, I am a model employee. I am early, I am focused, I am respectful and polite and eager to learn. Dr. Russell and I have six more cases together in which I assist him flawlessly. The nurses notice, the anesthesiologist compliments me, and the device reps confide in me that Dr. Russell has never had such seamless surgeries.

I am preparing a spot in my locker where my Employee of the Month certificate will hang. I practice in front of the mirror, trying to look the exact right combination of shocked and appreciative, but in the end, it's laughable. I bend over backward to try to earn Dr. Russell's respect, and everyone notices—except for Dr. Russell.

If anything, his attitude toward me has only worsened.

He's snippy with me for no reason, angry if I make even the slightest mistake. For instance, if I take too long arranging an instrument on the device tray, or if I don't answer him quickly enough when he asks a question, or if I have the audacity to ask for a bathroom break during an eight-hour procedure. Most surgeons would allow their assistants to take a break or even—*God forbid*—swap out with someone new. I thought I was making a point by sticking by him, but I guess not.

I never see him outside of the OR. He's gone by the time I scrub out. I try to catch him in the hallways, but if he's not in surgery, he's locked away in his office. Patricia warns me not to bother him.

"I've never seen him like this. Something must be going on outside of work," she tells me on Wednesday. "If I were you, I'd steer clear."

I don't take her advice.

I can't steer clear of him. We stand across from each other at an operating table for hours on end and I've done nothing to warrant this sort of attitude on his part.

My work has been flawless. I've been a model employee. He is allowed to be quiet and professional. He's allowed to not want to be my friend, but he is not allowed to be rude!

So, I brush past her desk and knock on his office door, cross my arms, and wait for him to let me in.

He doesn't.

I press my ear to the door and listen for a phone conversation. There isn't one.

"Dr. Russell, could I have a word please?"

I ensure my tone is even and calm, but still, I hear an annoyed groan followed by the creaking of a chair, footsteps, and then the door is yanked open.

He stares down at me with cool, calculating eyes. His scrubs have been replaced with a sharp gray suit. His hair is perfectly tousled. I ignore these details and focus on the important part: how much I despise him.

"What do you need?" he asks.

Right. What a lovely tone to take with your hardworking new employee.

I resist the urge to cower, and instead, I lift my chin and meet his gaze head-on. My hands are on my hips in what I hope is a power pose.

"I'd like to speak with you about my job performance."

His brows furrow. "Job performance?"

"Yes. Is there something more you'd like from me? An even earlier start time? An even faster response time? A larger bladder?"

He doesn't find my sarcasm amusing.

"Your work is fine." He steps back and starts to close his door, but I block it with my foot.

"If my work is fine, why are you being so rude to me? Have you not forgiven me for being late on the first day? Because I think my work since then has shown how seriously I'm taking this opportunity."

He looks down at my foot and then back up at me, patronizing expression firmly in place.

"Bailey, do you enjoy filing paperwork with HR? Because if you don't move, they're going to have a lot of questions for the both of us—namely, why I felt compelled to close your foot in my office door."

"Oh good," I say, throwing my hands up in defeat. "Now you're threatening bodily harm."

I swear there's *almost* amusement shining in his gaze before he toes my foot out of the path of his door with his fancy oxford then shuts it in my face.

"What a show of professionalism, Dr. Russell," I shout to the closed door.

As I walk away, as furious as ever, Patricia shakes her head. "I warned you."

Things only escalate on Friday.

Dr. Russell seems more short-tempered than usual. His blue eyes are icy and hard, glaring at me from across the operating table. I have no idea what his problem is, but I'm determined to push through, to brush off his antagonizing energy and do the job he's paying me to do—but it's not that easy.

"Bailey, if you're determined to take forever with the curette, I'll hire someone else to hand it to me."

I bite my tongue and resist the urge to sling the instrument at his face.

"I wanted to make sure it was the right size," I say,

117

handing it off carefully and returning my attention to my cauterization forceps.

"Well your effort was in vain. This isn't the right one."

YES IT IS, YOU EGOMANIACAL JERK.

"Would you like a different one?" I ask, my voice so gentle it nearly verges on being passive-aggressive.

"Yes, Bailey," he drawls out slowly, like he's worried I can't comprehend simple words. "I'd like the *correct* one."

The operating room is absolutely still. Sure, everyone makes a show of pretending to work, but in reality, their ears are trained on us, waiting to see just how much of his bullshit I'm willing to take.

No doubt they're anticipating an imminent blowup, but I harness what can only be described as the patience of a saint, take a deep, yoga-worthy breath, and reply sweetly, "Of course. Let me get that for you right away."

I think I have it. I've beat him at his own game by keeping my cool, right up until I turn and my elbow collides with the sterile instrument tray that was resting precariously beside me. In a flash, it crashes to the ground and metal pings in every direction. Implants scatter. Pedical screws disappear beneath the operating table.

My mouth hangs agape behind my mask.

One of the nurses gasps.

The anesthesiologist peeks out from behind his curtain and his eyes widen in shock.

Dr. Russell turns quickly to the device rep. "Do we have another sterile set?"

I swear the man's chin quivers as he shakes his head. "Not a complete one."

My eyes pinch closed and I brace myself for the impact. Biting words from Dr. Russell are about to rain down on me like an enemy siege. I will not make it out alive.

"Pick everything up and get it in the autoclave. Now."

His voice is cool and precise, like the blade of a knife sinking into my gut. I yank off my gloves, fall to my knees, and start crawling around the operating room floor as quickly as possible.

Dr. Russell barks at Kendra to help him cover the patient.

This is bad. This is cry-and-plead-for-forgiveness bad.

Accidents like this happened once or twice during one of Dr. Lopez's surgeries, but *I* was never the cause, and we always had a backup instrument set prepared just in case.

I really want to give in to the urge to cry, but it would only make things worse.

There is no way I will survive this. He'll give me the axe as soon as this surgery is finished. This has to be a new record. Kirt—the sobbing giant—lasted at least a couple months. I've lasted a paltry few weeks.

I'm shaking as I hurry to collect all the equipment on the ground. Dr. Russell growls at the techs to help. There are half a dozen of us crawling around the operating room, and I swear if a single tear falls from my eyes I will never forgive myself. Everyone is waiting for me to crumble, but I refuse to let it happen.

I keep it together through a feat of superhuman strength. I compartmentalize my feelings and stay focused. I count the instruments and confirm with the device rep that we've collected everything The autoclave only takes 45 minutes. We're hardly delayed. The surgery finishes with flawless results, and I'm still completely numb as Dr. Russell tells me to close, pulls off his gloves and gown, and leaves the room.

I watch him go, heaving a sigh as soon as the swinging

door shuts behind him.

I can't believe how unlucky I've been. I've tried my hardest and worked my butt off, but in the end, the universe and Dr. Russell seem to be in cahoots against me.

"Bailey?" Kendra asks gently. "Are you okay to close?"

I nod. Of course.

It might be the last thing I ever do at New England Medical Center.

CHAPTER TWELVE
MATT

I DIP MY hands under the faucet, letting the warm water rinse away the suds from my skin as the door to the OR swings open. Kendra peeks her head around it and grimaces.

"Do you have a minute, Dr. Russell?"

There's a mountain of work standing between me and my weekend. I've got a lot to do and not enough time to do it. I'm usually in the office as much on Saturday and Sunday as I am Monday through Friday, but I'm less efficient. Patricia's gone. There's no resident rushing in with Starbucks, and I usually have to contend with the cleaning staff. They skitter past when they see me walking down the hall, and they don't even bother knocking on my door anymore. I don't want anyone in my office rearranging things. There's a method to my madness and I'm perfectly capable of taking out my own trash.

This weekend is different, though. Tomorrow is Molly's wedding, and I actually have to make it out of the office at a decent hour if I want to grab my suit from the tailor before he closes his shop.

I wouldn't have to rush if my surgery hadn't run over time thanks to Bailey's mistake.

"What do you need?"

I turn and grab a towel.

She steps out and lets the door swing closed behind her. "It really could have happened to anyone." She's talking about Bailey's accident. "And I don't think you should punish her for it. You might not have noticed, but she's good. These last few weeks have been paradise compared to when you were working with Kirt."

I toss my towel into the laundry bin, and she must sense that I'm about to run out of patience because she scrambles to continue.

"Okay, yes, that mistake delayed your surgery today, but usually with Bailey by your side, you drastically cut down on your procedure times."

I'm aware.

"So today aside, she's the best assistant you've had. Please don't go hard on her."

"What do you think I'm going to do? Fire her?"

Her eyes widen in fear. "Please don't. She makes my job easier too. I'm not run ragged anymore."

I sigh and brush past her. "Thank you for the insight, Kendra, but Bailey isn't going anywhere. I assure you. Have a good weekend."

As I work through some emails at my desk, I'm annoyed to find the cold front the newscasters were droning on about this morning finally makes an appearance. It's raining cats and dogs, which means Friday after-work traffic will be more hellish than usual. I'll have to take my paperwork and finish it at home so I can pick up my suit in time.

I use my personal bathroom to change out of my scrubs, grab my coat, and gather the files I want to take with me. The elevator is crowded, but everyone gives me a healthy berth—one perk of being universally disliked is I never have people encroaching on my personal space.

The elevator doors slide open and I'm about to take a sharp left toward the parking garage when I spot Bailey standing just inside the front entrance to our building with her arms wrapped around her middle. She changed out of her scrubs and she's wearing jeans and that same pink, puffy coat that completely drowns her. I wonder if she's waiting for someone to pick her up. Why else would she be hovering near the front door? Then she wipes furiously at her cheek and I realize she's crying.

Fuck.

I eye the parking garage door. I'm seconds away from freedom.

I glance back at her in time to see her shake her head at her phone, stuff it in her pocket, and then reach down for her backpack like she's about to march right out the front door. Except, there are no cars out front, just sheets of rain and rumbling, dark skies.

Aw hell.

"Bailey," I say, my voice carrying easily across the marble floor. "Wait."

She turns back and rolls her eyes, clearly annoyed to see me coming her way. She quickly wipes at her cheeks then holds up her hand to wave me off. "I'm off the clock. I don't want to talk to you right now. If you want to chew me out for what happened back there, you'll have to do it on Monday. I'm going home."

"How?"

Her pretty brown eyes, full of tears, narrow up at me in confusion. "How what?"

"How are you getting home? Did you park on the street or something?"

Her brows relax as she realizes I'm not about to scold her. "Oh." She turns to the window. "I'm going to catch the bus." *The bus?* "The stop is just down the street a little bit."

"Don't you have a car?"

She steels her spine. "No. I don't."

I'll have to look into what we're paying her—surely she should have no problem affording a car to get her to and from work.

"Okay, well then what about an Uber or something?"

Her tone doesn't lighten as she replies, "I usually take the bus. It's fine."

I look for an umbrella and frown when I see her hands are empty. "You're going to get drenched and it's freezing out there."

She laughs and starts to step back. "It's not your concern. Don't worry about me."

Yes, well unfortunately, I do worry about her. For the last three weeks, all I've done is *worry* about her.

Cooper is to blame. He fuels my annoyance on a daily basis, updating me about their texts and bragging to me about how their relationship is developing. *Relationship*—I find that laughable. They haven't gone on a date. They haven't even spoken on the phone. If the metric for a "relationship" lies solely in the number of text messages exchanged then as of this week, I'm in a relationship with my tailor, my UberEats delivery guy, and my housekeeper. I've got my hands fucking full.

"Well I'm not going to let you wait out at the bus stop in this weather. C'mon, I'll drive you."

Her soft feminine laugh echoes around the lobby.

"Thank you, but I'd rather walk."

What she really means is, *Thank you, but I'd rather die.*

"It's really not a request. You're no good to me if you have to call in sick on Monday because you caught pneumonia."

Her gaze sheens with a new layer of hatred. "You of all people know you don't catch pneumonia just from being cold and wet."

She tries to step around me, but I catch her backpack and tug it off her shoulder. I can't put it on because she has the shoulder straps set to fit a toddler, so I hold it in my hand and start walking. She can either follow me or not. I tell myself I don't care either way.

"Dr. Russell—" she says behind me, her feet lightly tap-tap-tapping on the marble as she hurries to keep up.

"You're clocked out, aren't you? Call me Matt."

"*Doctor*," she says pointedly. "Please give me my backpack before I call security."

I laugh because really, she's hilarious. No one has ever threatened to call security on me before.

"It's Matt, and if you're going to call security, make sure you ask for Tommy. He's younger and stands a decent chance of catching me before I hightail it out of here with your *pink* JanSport backpack. What do you have in here anyway?"

It weighs nothing.

"My lunchbox. A water bottle. Some empty Tupperware."

Tupperware.

I glance behind me to check on her. She's fast-walking as she trails behind me. Am I really that much taller than her?

"Did you bring more banana bread?"

She nods and nearly breaks out in a jog. "Patricia didn't get any last time and I felt bad."

"I didn't get any last time either," I point out.

She snorts. "Yeah well, I don't feel bad about that."

I face forward again so she can't see my smile. There she goes again with that brutal honesty. In the operating room, she's perfectly compliant. Everywhere else, she's not.

We take the stairs down to the first level of the parking garage and I lead us toward the area reserved for doctors. She makes her way toward a black Audi, turns, and waits for me to join her.

I smirk. "That's not my car."

She nods. "Right, of course. I see it now."

She goes to a bright yellow Ferrari that belongs to one of the plastic surgeons. The vanity license plate reads: SXY DOC88. "Here we are."

"Not even close."

"Oh, okay. I get it. You aren't flashy. Maybe that gray Range Rover over there?"

I press the unlock button on my key fob and my rear lights flash. There she is, the car I've driven since I was in medical school.

"You're kidding. *A Prius*?! Satan himself drives a Prius?!" She turns around as if hoping to find someone else she can share this moment with. All she's got is me.

I shrug. "It gets good gas mileage."

She blinks exaggeratedly. "I couldn't be more shocked if you'd hitched a horse to a buggy."

I chuckle and open the back door to toss in her backpack. "Get in. Traffic is going to be hell."

We buckle up in silence, back up and leave the parking garage in silence, pull out into traffic in silence.

Finally, I ask, "Where do you live?"

"On the west side. Right across from Franklin Park."

"Good. I have an errand I need to run that's right by there. Mind if I do that before I drop you off?"

"Well seeing as how you stole my backpack and forced me into your car, I don't really think it matters what I want."

I see. She's still pouting. That's fine. "Good. Glad we're on the same page."

She doesn't think I'm funny.

I drum my thumb against the steering wheel and try to keep my attention on the road and off of her.

It's been a long time since I've had anyone in this car besides me, a longer time since it was someone I found as interesting as I find Bailey Jennings. I try to study her surreptitiously. She seems smaller now when she's sitting still. I could fit two of her on that seat. I look down and smirk when I see there's no phone in her lap. Doesn't she need to text Cooper and let him know about her day? She ought to tell him she's currently in hell being driven home by her crotchety boss—the boss who made her cry.

I loosen my tie, uncomfortable with how tight it feels all of sudden.

We're a few miles away from the hospital by the time she finally works up the courage to speak. "Not including what happened today, have I done something to offend you?" *Oh good, deep conversation.* "You've seemed annoyed with me over the last few weeks and I haven't been able to work out why."

"You know, actually, I was hoping we could just sit in amiable silence for the entire trip." Her gaze tries to bore through my skull, so I relent. "Have you considered that it has nothing to do with you?"

"Yes," she replies right away, "but that doesn't make sense because you seem to only get snappy and aggravated with me. It's not like you're shouting at Kendra when she takes more than one second to get you something in the OR. You practically snarl when you look at me."

Truly, that can't be the case. If it is, I haven't noticed.

"I have a few things going on right now," I admit,

giving her an inch.

"Work related?" she presses.

"Some of it is, yes. I'm supposed to have heard back about a grant proposal but the committee is delayed."

"Patricia mentioned something about it."

"It's been stressful, not to mention I've taken on more cases recently. With more cases comes more consults, paperwork, pre-ops, post-ops."

"I get it, you're a busy guy—but that still doesn't quite explain why you seem to want to take your stress and anger out on *me*. Can't you go to the gym or something? Punch a beanbag?"

I smile. "I think you mean a punching bag."

"That's what I said. Now, what else? You said some of your stress is work related. Is the other stuff personal?"

I put my blinker on and change lanes, not sure I want to go down this path with her. A part of me wants to admit I'm annoyed she's texting and flirting with my brother, except she doesn't know Cooper's my brother. I asked him about it the other day and he said it hasn't come up organically in conversation. What the hell does that mean? I told him to work it into conversation *artificially*. Simple as that. He said he'd do it soon but didn't want to scare her off. Like being my sibling means he's tainted by association. Honestly, his logic made absolutely no sense to me, but I've kept my word not to bring it up with Bailey. Besides, there's never been a chance to talk about it. I only ever see her in the operating room.

Until now. Until I put her in the passenger seat of my car and pretended like it was normal. I can smell her perfume. I notice every time she shifts in her seat, trying to get comfortable—or is she trying to get as far away from me as possible?

Her cheek is about to be squashed against the window.

It shouldn't bother me that they're texting, so I tell myself it doesn't, as if I'll change my stance on the subject by sheer willpower alone.

Cooper can do whatever the hell he wants and I'll carry on with my life as normal. That's been my plan, except I guess it hasn't really been working. Apparently, I've been a real asshole to work with. Imagine that.

"Let's change the subject," I say, reaching forward and turning on the radio as if that will help matters. This is nothing today's top hits can't solve.

She swats my hand away and turns it down. "No, we're going to get down to the real reason you hate me."

I scowl. "I don't hate you."

"Oh, okay, I'm sorry, you just don't *like* me. What's the difference?"

I don't say anything and the car is filled with tense silence. I change lanes and exit the freeway as the song ends and another one starts up. She crosses her arms on a heavy sigh.

"I think I should just quit. This isn't working out."

It feels like someone just sucker-punched me.

"What? Why?" I flick quick glances in her direction while also trying to keep my eyes on the road. I don't want to miss my turn. "Because of what happened in the OR today?"

"Yes—well, no. I mean, it's part of it. I just feel like your presence in the operating room is too intimidating. My every move is magnified and judged. You make me feel like I'm not quick enough or smart enough to keep up with you." She throws up her hands in defeat. "Maybe we just aren't a good match. I thought I could handle pressure, but I realize now that working with Dr. Lopez was nothing compared to being on your team. Dr. Lopez was sunshine and rainbows and playlists filled with The Beach Boys, and you're…"

"I'm what?" I demand.

I think she whispers, "Scary," but I'm not sure I hear her right.

I take a left then pull into a lot and now we're outside my tailor's shop. I need to get out, but it's still storming and I can't just leave her in here after that speech. I put the car in park and turn to face her.

She's staring straight ahead though I know she can't see a thing with the rain beating down on the windshield.

"Okay. All right." I clear my throat. "It's come to my attention that I might be the problem."

She throws her head back and laughs and laughs and laughs. Her blonde hair spills down her back. Her long dark lashes fan out across her pronounced cheekbones. I sit perfectly still watching her, hands clenched because for some inane reason, I have the urge to reach out and touch her, to brush the freckles across the bridge of her nose, to run the pad of my finger along her bottom lip—the one currently stretched into a smile at my expense.

Jesus, the power she wields.

Finally, she gathers herself and turns to me, tears of laughter collected along the bottom rows of her lashes. "'I might be the problem.' Uh, *ya think*?" Her words drip with sarcasm.

I shake my head and force myself to look away. Damn the rain. I need to get out of this car.

"Wait here. I won't be long."

I don't bother with an umbrella as I dart outside and into the shop. I have my suit in hand a few minutes later, glad the tailor took the time to wrap the garment bag in plastic to ensure it stayed dry. I, however, did not. I'm a wet dog when I slam my door and turn to hang the suit up in my back seat.

"You're soaked," Bailey says, stating the obvious.

She must have composed herself while I was inside because there's no hint of laughter in her eyes anymore. Her golden brown gaze skims across me quickly and I glance in the rearview mirror to see what she sees. Soaked hair falling across my forehead, annoyed scowl paired with a grimace—I look like an emotional vampire. With a grunt, I shrug out of my suit jacket and toss it in the back before rolling my sleeves up to my elbows. My white button-up is just as wet as my jacket, but with the heat blasting in the car, it should dry out soon enough.

"What's your address?" I ask bluntly.

"I'd like to finish our conversation."

"No. You see, I picked up my suit and now I'm going to take you home. That's how this works."

Her hand reaches out to touch my forearm, and it's delicate and warm and porcelain white. I stare down at it, half-expecting her to jerk it away, but she doesn't.

"I shouldn't have laughed when you admitted you might be the problem."

Oh, I get it. She thinks she wounded my pride, like I'm a fragile, temperamental creature.

I hate that I might be.

"If you want me to continue working for you, you're going to have to talk to me."

"I don't give two shits if you stay." I'm annoyed that she thinks she has me figured out. With a gentle touch and a sweet tone, she thinks she'll crack open my shell and I'll spill some deep dark secrets to her.

Her hand squeezes my arm painfully and then she

tosses it away, crosses her arms, and stares out the passenger window. "8745 Oak Drive. Take me home. Now."

I'm at a crossroads. I want to come out on top, preserve what's left of my dignity, and get Bailey the hell out of my car, but then I think of how annoying it will be to walk into work on Monday and admit to Patricia and Kendra that Bailey quit because I couldn't put my ego aside.

"Take. Me. Home," she says again, each word bitten out.

"I'll never be the nice guy in the operating room," I say suddenly, words spilling out of me before I've even decided I want to say them. "I won't put on a Beach Boys playlist and joke around. With pediatric scoliosis surgery, you aren't making the spine straight again. You're taking a spine that operates like a slinky and turning it into a rock. It's a preventive measure, not a cure. There's no definitive reason why this happens to some people and not to others. Through no fault of their own, my patients are given a life sentence of pain and suffering."

She doesn't budge, so I continue talking to the back of her head.

"I'm passionate about what I do, and sometimes that carries over into how I treat my staff."

"Not everyone. Just me," she clarifies.

"I hold you to a higher standard."

She snorts and shakes her head. I want to yank her ponytail and force her to turn around and look at me. I want her to meet my gaze and see for herself that I'm trying as hard as I can. I can't touch her while I'm this worked up, though. So, instead, I focus on the storm brewing outside her window and try to ignore the painful tightening in my chest. This is hard for me. I don't like to dwell in the dark underbelly of my job, but she dragged me here, and she doesn't get to turn back now.

"Tell me, have you ever held a child's life in your hands, Bailey?" My voice is cold and unfeeling. "Have you ever had to walk into a waiting room after a ten-hour surgery, look a mother in the eyes, and explain to her that there's nothing more you can do for her child? That if you keep trying, you'll shred her daughter's spine? That she won't be able to walk no matter how many surgeries or rounds of physical therapy she endures?

"Have you ever had a ten-year-old code on your table? Ever accidently nicked a nerve and nearly paralyzed someone? You think I'm a cold bastard. You want me to be polite and gentle with you. You want me to pat your head and give you a gold star for doing your job. I won't." I pause briefly. "Grow up."

CHAPTER THIRTEEN
BAILEY

IF I COULD roll out of Dr. Russell's car on the highway without sustaining any major injuries, I would. As it is, I sit beside him silently, shaking with untold emotions until we pull up in front of my house. There are no words exchanged as I reach into the back seat for my backpack and brace it against my chest so it doesn't get completely drenched. We don't look at each other. We barely breathe. I clutch the door handle, consider thanking him for driving me home or apologizing for whatever it was that just happened, but in the end, I say nothing before I dart out into the rain. I'm running because it's raining, but I'm also running because I want to get away from him as fast as I possibly can.

I push open the front door to our house with too much force and slam it closed behind me even harder, peeking past the window shade in time to see him peel away. I watch him go and my heart pounds in my chest like a stampede of wild horses.

"You're not going to believe it!" Josie shouts behind me.

I jump out of my skin and whirl around to see her holding up the laptop we share. The messenger app is open and when I step closer, I see that she's been having a conversation with Cooper without me knowing.

Shit. I haven't checked our texts all day.

"Josie!"

She waves her hand to cut me off. "Yes, okay, *technically* I've been texting him without your explicit permission, but he's back in town and he invited you on a date tomorrow!"

My stomach fills with dread. "Please tell me you—"

"Told him yes?! Duh! And you aren't going to believe it! You're going to a *wedding*!"

Her eyes—the same light brown shade as mine—fill with stars as if a wedding is on par with the Oscars.

Oh my god. How many times am I going to feel panicky and weepy in one day? I can't believe she did this. Sure, Cooper is nice, but I'm not sure I would have agreed to go on a date with him, and definitely not to a wedding!

I grab the computer and scroll furiously through the texts, trying to catch up. Their conversation is innocuous and kind of boring. They talk about the weather (*So cold, right? Brrr!*) and his flight back from Cincinnati (*The guy next to me is snoring so loud!*). Josie uses way more emojis than I would. Pretty much every sentence is dotted with three or four. Jesus, if I were him, I would never text me back, but Cooper isn't deterred.

Unfortunately.

There, at the bottom, I see with my own eyes that he did invite me to be his date for a wedding, and Josie stupidly accepted on my behalf—with four hearts-in-my-eyes smiley faces. I look like a desperate weirdo.

Worse, Cooper goes on to explain that it won't be a big, fun, eat-cake-and-blend-into-the-wall sort of affair.

I jerk my attention back to her. "It's his cousin's wedding! That means his entire family will be there!"

Her brows scrunch together like she doesn't see the problem.

"He said it would be small," she argues. "See there? 'Just fifty people or so, nothing too crazy'."

"That's worse, Josie! It means there's no way I can just

136

fly under the radar!"

"Ooooh, yeah." She nods, lip starting to quiver. "Now I see your point."

I drop the computer onto the couch and start pacing. On a good day, this would stress me out. Today, I can barely stop from pulling my hair out.

"How do we undo this?"

"We don't!" she says, trying to cut into my path and grab ahold of my shoulders, but I don't let her. I need to keep moving or I might spontaneously combust. "He's really nice and you said yourself you thought he was cute! So it's kind of an awkward first date—so what? It could be really fun!"

I stop suddenly, drop my hands to my knees, and force down the urge to throw up.

Her hand hits my lower back. "Do you want me to get you out of it?"

"Yes! *Please*!"

She groans. "You were supposed to say no! It's too late. I accepted the date on your behalf and now he's all excited. Are you really going to let the poor guy go to a wedding by himself? Only losers do that!"

This is a mess, and unfortunately, it's not entirely Josie's fault. I'm the idiot who asked her to start messaging him in the first place. I look up at her and she's standing before me, blonde hair tied up in a bun, cheeks stained red with embarrassment. She's wringing out her hands and trying very hard not to cry.

"I don't have a dress, Josie." I sigh with defeat.

"The thrift shop a few streets over is still open for another two hours," she says softly, the edge of her mouth curving with the start of a smile.

"And what about…"

I trail off, realizing I don't actually have another excuse.

She rushes forward and wraps her arms around my middle. "We'll get you a dress! I'll do your hair and makeup. I've been practicing on myself all day." Well that explains the heavy eyeshadow; I thought it was a little much for a weekday afternoon. "You'll look like Cinderella going to the ball!"

References like that remind me that in some ways, Josie is still so young. She wants to believe in fairy tales so badly, and I know I have no choice. I'll go to the wedding even if the experience leaves me permanently scarred.

THE NEXT DAY, I sit dutifully in front of our bathroom mirror while my sister does my hair. I have a face full of fancy makeup I could have never done myself. My eyes have never seemed so bright thanks to the combination of eyeshadows she's painstakingly applied over the last hour. It's subtle and pretty. I should feel like a million bucks, but I feel nothing beyond the knot of tension in the pit of my stomach.

"Why does it seem like you don't trust me?" she says, waving the curling iron over my head haphazardly. I cower to avoid getting burned. *Oh, I don't know, maybe because you're about to sear my forehead.* "I've been practicing these curls for weeks and you're going to look amazing!"

I try to relax my features, but it's no use. I've felt anxious ever since Dr. Russell dropped me off yesterday. I barely slept. I kept replaying his words, and I've come to two conclusions. One, he was right. I have no idea the kind of stress he deals with all day, every day. I can put my head down and focus on work a little more, but—two, he also has to admit fault. He can't keep using me as a punching bag.

I have no clue what I'll do come Monday morning. Should I address what happened in the car and apologize for my part of it? And if he's unwilling to change, do I want to keep working for him?

Josie thinks I'm quiet and anxious because of the wedding. That's why she's taking extra care with my hair and makeup. It looks really good. Her obsession with beauty videos on YouTube has clearly paid off.

"There!" She sets down the curling iron. "Now we just need to brush out the curls so they look soft, like you're an Old Hollywood movie star!"

I have exactly enough energy to give her a feeble thumbs-up.

Dress shopping yesterday took a lot out of me. The thrift shop we walked to in the rain is in a nicer area of town so it was filled with designer castoffs. I thought we'd just go in and grab the first thing we saw, but Josie turned it into a mini fashion show. In the end, after a lot of suffering on my part, *she* settled on a formfitting ice blue cocktail dress with an elegant floral lace overlay. The long sleeves cling to my arms all the way to my wrists, and the flowy skirt hits halfway down my thighs. An open back adds a touch of sexiness without seeming indecent.

I'll be absolutely freezing if the wedding is outside.

She puts the finishing touches on my hair then steps back with a proud smile. "Gorgeous." I smile at my reflection more for her sake than my own. My heart's not in it tonight, no matter how hard I try. "Too bad we couldn't afford a new coat. Your pink one doesn't go with this at all."

She's right. It's too casual, but it's all I have at the moment.

"I'll take it off right when we get inside," I promise her. "Don't worry, I won't ruin all your hard work."

The doorbell rings a few minutes later while I'm in the bathroom alone, giving myself a pep talk that centers more on trying to put Dr. Russell out of my mind than it does on my impending date. I close my eyes and see his dark, wet hair, the way his damp shirt clung to his biceps when he got back into the car, his large hands gripping the steering wheel as he drove me home in silence, and the disdain in his voice when he told me to grow up.

If I concentrate, I swear I can still smell him. His car held the same intoxicating scent as his office, but in the smaller space, it was magnified. The scent clings to my memory like those drops of rain were clinging to him.

"Bailey! Are you ready?" Josie shouts from the living room. "Cooper's here!"

I blink my eyes open and meet my gaze in the mirror, trying on a weak, awkward smile before shaking my head and giving up. "Yes! *Coming!*"

Cooper is waiting for me by the door, and I'm surprised to see how handsome he looks. It's been weeks since we met in the bar, and Smooth Tony's was hazy and dark. My memory didn't quite do him justice. His hair is a dark, ashy blond, thick and styled well. His suit is navy blue, and his light blue tie is clipped in place with a slice of silver metal. He's put together and debonair in a way that makes me feel like a child in comparison.

His eyes glide down me and apparently I merit his approval, even with my pink coat, because he smiles wide and steps forward to kiss my cheek.

"You look great. When you told me you were wearing

blue, I wanted to match."

I'm slightly confused until I realize Josie must have texted him a hint about my outfit. I slice my gaze to her and she winks before shooing us out the door.

"Don't hurry home! I have everything I need. I'm going to bury myself in Netflix and popcorn."

"Don't stay up too late," I warn.

She laughs. "Of course. In bed by 10:00, you got it. Hey, it was nice to meet you, Cooper!"

"You too, Josie."

He smiles back at her and I'm not surprised to see genuine affection in his eyes. Josie wins everyone over. She could walk into peace negotiations in the Middle East and have that situation buttoned up in no time.

"Your sister looks like you," he notes as he leads me down the driveway toward a shiny black BMW purring at the curb.

I hum.

"She's sweet."

"Don't let her guise fool you. She's sly," I warn with a shake of my head.

As he opens my door and takes my hand to help me step off the curb, Cooper informs me we're running a little late.

I'm immediately worried. "How late are we talking?"

"Oh, just a few minutes. Nothing to worry about."

He's lying of course. Once I insist upon seeing the invitation, I realize we're extremely late, only a few minutes shy of the bride making her descent down the aisle. Hell, there's a chance we'll walk in right as the preacher asks if anyone objects.

"My flight back from Cincinnati was delayed. Everyone will understand," he promises after we park. He takes my hand and leads me toward the small church.

I hate being late. I especially hate being late to an event like this, and my worst fears are realized when Cooper opens the door to the chapel and every person in attendance turns in their pews to look back at us. Eyes blink expectantly. A small child asks if we're the ones getting married. And yes, it really does feel like we're the bride and groom making our way toward the altar. My cheeks burn. I want to yank my hand out of his, spin around, and walk right back outside, but of course, I can't. I swallow and glance down to the floor, willing the color to drain from my face. It's no use. I'm Rudolph.

The situation doesn't bother Cooper in the least. I peer up to see that he's smiling wide, waving and patting shoulders as we walk down the aisle at an annoyingly leisurely pace. He's Prince Harry waving at his people.

I want to sit in the back, in the first pew we pass.

"What about here?" I say quickly, tugging him to the left. Bride's side, groom's side, floor, pew—who the hell cares. I just want to sit!

"My family's up front. It looks like they saved us seats."

Oh good. Next, he'll tell me we're actually going to stand up at the altar during the ceremony. *You've officiated a wedding before, right?*

I can't make eye contact with anyone we pass because not only am I late, I'm also walking into a small, intimate wedding on the arm of a guy I barely know. Hell, I don't even know his last name. Everyone is definitely judging me from head to toe, and now I wish I'd ditched my puffy jacket back in the foyer when Cooper offered to hang it up, but I didn't want to delay us further.

"Cooper, there you are! I was worried you wouldn't

make it," says a polite, feminine voice. It belongs to the woman standing up and waving us over. She has the same ashy blonde hair and easygoing smile as my date. She's wearing a dark plum dress with a cashmere scarf tied stylishly around her shoulders. She is, of course, Cooper's mother.

I wish we were meeting each other under different circumstances, but I aim a smile at her all the same. Her own smile widens in response and a small sense of relief rushes through me just before the world slips out from beneath my feet.

We're turning into the pew when I freeze.

Cooper runs into me from behind and I nearly topple forward like a domino. He grabs my elbow to right me, but I can't feel his touch because I'm staring at a figment of my imagination, or maybe it's just my worst nightmare.

"Dr. Russell?" I ask, voice barely above a whisper.

My boss shoots to his feet, all six-plus feet of him. My mouth hangs agape. My heart sputters to a screeching halt in my chest. He's nothing but darkness—his hair, his suit, his demeanor—everything except for his blue eyes, which are the exact shade of my dress.

His gaze slices over to Cooper. "Are you kidding me? You brought her?"

He talks to him like they know each other.

Wait.

My gaze snaps back to Cooper.

Do they know each other?!

A heavy organ starts to echo around the chapel, announcing the start of the ceremony. Cooper ushers me forward and tugs me down so the backs of my thighs hit the hard wood of the pew.

His mom leans forward and narrows her eyes on Dr.

Russell. "Do you know Cooper's date?"

At the same time, Cooper's hand hits my shoulder. "Here, let me get your coat."

I lean forward and let him tug it off.

Everything is happening so fast.

"Yes, Mom. We work together," Dr. Russell answers simply, turning back to me.

"How is this—"

My sentence trails off at the exact moment I lay eyes on the man on the other side of Cooper's mom, the last person in their group. His black hair might be sprinkled with salt and the glasses perched on the end of his nose detract from the similarities, but there's no doubt I'm staring at Dr. Russell's father.

Equations swirl in my head. So, if that woman is Cooper's mom...and that man is Dr. Russell's dad then...$E = mc^2$?

"Matt's my brother," Cooper whispers quickly in my ear before he lays my coat on the pew on the other side of him.

The word collides into me with the subtlety of a Mack truck.

BROTHER. As in related, as in I'm sandwiched between my date and my boss. Brothers. The man I'm supposed to be into and the man I can't get out of my head. This makes absolutely no sense. I have so many questions and I can't ask them because there is a freaking wedding ceremony taking place around us. The mother of the bride and the mother of the groom are gushing and pink and sparkly and they're being ushered down the aisle so they can take their seats two pews in front of ours.

It'd be rude to talk now, so I bite my tongue and try to stare straight ahead. *Good. There. Focus on Jesus.*

It doesn't work.

I'm well aware I'm shaking while the men around me sit perfectly still. This isn't as shocking to them as it is to me. *What did Dr. Russell say when he first saw me?*

"You brought her?"

So he was surprised to see me here, but not surprised to see that I knew Cooper.

What the hell does that mean?

I can feel Dr. Russell's gaze on me. He wants me to turn toward him, but I won't. I shift a little in my seat and now his thigh presses against mine. He doesn't move away, and I don't know what to do. The lacy fabric of my dress bunches up between us, but it doesn't matter. His suit pants are searing my skin all the same, and it's so hot we're fused now, because no matter how much I scream at myself to move away, I can't. It's just not possible.

Cooper's hand wraps around mine on the other side and he squeezes reassuringly.

A moment later, Dr. Russell's hand clenches around his wedding program.

I frown and he must catch it because he offers the program to me, like that's what I wanted—his stupid program. The backs of our fingers barely touch as I take it and yet the contact zips across my heart like he just hauled me up against a wall and kissed me.

Kissed me.

I stifle a laugh.

Grow up.

I might not be able to move my leg from his, but I turn my body so I'm angled toward the aisle, toward Cooper. My long hair falls over my shoulder and I can feel Dr. Russell's gaze on the back of my neck and my bare back. Why did I pick this dress? Oh right, it wasn't my choice.

I can't believe this is happening. Yesterday's car ride was intense to say the least. I thought I'd have another 24 hours to work up what I wanted to say to him. Now here we are, thigh to thigh at a wedding. And there's that smell again, his cologne. I want to buy up every bottle in existence and pour them down a toilet.

Cooper catches my eye, smiles, and mouths, "Sorry."

I don't say a word.

There'll be plenty of time for explanations after the ceremony when I don't have a million pairs of curious eyes focused on me.

CHAPTER FOURTEEN
MATT

IT'S THE COCKTAIL hour between the ceremony and the reception, an hour in which I plan on drinking my body weight in alcohol in the hopes that it will distract me from the fact that Bailey is here at this wedding with my brother.

She's standing right beside me, listening to Cooper try to explain his way out of this situation. I take another sip of my drink and am already trying to flag down a passing waiter so I can order another.

Bailey's angry, though I'm not surprised. My brother handled the situation deplorably and now somehow, I'm in the middle of what feels dangerously close to a love triangle I want nothing to do with.

"So you see, it's pretty simple. Bailey, you came into the bar with a few of your friends. I was there waiting for Matt. He never showed and I couldn't pass up the opportunity to meet you."

Cooper's standing in front of me like a dog with his tail between his legs. Bailey's eyes could burn a hole through his head if he's not careful. "Okay, fine, but did you know at the time that I worked for Dr. Russell?"

Again with the Dr. Russell bullshit. We're off the clock.

"Matt," I correct.

She shoots me a quick, searing glare that leaves me with third-degree burns.

Cooper adjusts his shirt collar, clearly uncomfortable. "I figured it out later that night."

"So then why didn't you just tell me? We've been texting for weeks." She shakes her head. "This just feels weird now."

Cooper steps forward, his tone taking on a pleading lilt. "I was going to tell you, but then I got busy with work, and tonight seemed like as good an opportunity as any."

Honestly, I don't mind standing here. It's like watching a slow-moving train wreck. I kind of like watching him squirm. I move to take another sip of my drink but stall when Bailey's eyes slice over to me again.

"And you knew too? Why didn't *you* tell me?"

I chuckle and shake my head. "I don't think so. This isn't my fight. If you're going to be mad at someone, it should be your date."

She crosses her arms, clearly in disagreement. "Yesterday when you were driving me home, you could have told me about Cooper. There was plenty of time."

I finish bringing my glass to my mouth in lieu of replying. The drink burns just a little on the way down, but it's nothing compared to her gaze raking over me, taking in the suit I picked up yesterday while she waited in the car. It seems to offend her as much as my brother and I have.

"Wait, what do you mean?" Coop asks indignantly. "Driving her home?"

Oh, this is rich.

Cooper's the angry one now, and I can't help but laugh. "Relax, Coop. It was raining and I didn't want your precious date to walk home. You can stop looking at me like you want to kill me."

"This is a mess." Bailey tosses her hands up and walks away. "You two can sort it out. I'm getting a drink."

When she's out of earshot, I step toward Cooper so we're toe to toe and he can't look away. "What the fuck were you thinking bringing her here as your date? Is this a game to you?"

He squares his shoulders and cocks his jaw. "Not a game—an *experiment*. I knew it would make you mad if I brought her, so I couldn't resist. You've acted so weird about me talking to her. I wanted to see for myself how you'd act if she came tonight, and my suspicions were correct."

I arch a brow. "Oh yeah? Please, enlighten me."

He smiles smugly. "You like Bailey. When I showed up, you weren't upset that she was here. You were upset that she was here *with me*."

I push him hard. He loses his footing and stumbles back.

My reaction surprises us both. Sure, we roughhoused as teenagers, but we've never gotten into anything physical as adults.

"You're acting like an idiot," I say, stepping forward again. I'm starting to get pissed.

He meets me halfway and gets right up in my face, finger hitting my chest. "Maybe so, but at least I'm not a miserable asshole. You're so used to being alone, you don't even recognize an opportunity to be happy when it's staring you in the face."

One of our uncles suddenly steps between us, laughing awkwardly. "Everything okay over here, boys?"

"Peachy," Cooper says, holding his hands up in innocence. "Now if you'll excuse me, I'm going to go find my date."

I let him walk away, run a hand down my suit jacket, and try to shove aside Cooper's brand of pop psych trying to take root in my brain. He thinks I turn into a caveman where Bailey is concerned, and he assumes it's because I have feelings for her. Maybe I just don't want my brother screwing my employee. Maybe that's a headache I'd rather avoid.

This is stupid.

I grab another drink from a passing waiter. It's crisp, bubbly champagne, and though I'd rather sling the glass against the wall to release some of this pent-up anger, I down it in one go then drop the flute back on the waiter's tray. His eyes are wide. I'm probably the first guest he's seen shotgun a glass of champagne tonight.

I finish my other drink and hand it off too.

"Uh, sir…can I get you something else?"

I shake my head and brush past him, unsure exactly where I'm headed until I spot Bailey across the room at the bar talking to my parents.

Hilarious. What in the world could they be discussing?

Cooper's nowhere in sight, but I'm sure he'll reappear near Bailey soon and do something else to raise my hackles, like kissing her cheek or wrapping an arm around her lower back. He held her hand during the ceremony. Fucking ridiculous. I don't like PDA, the touchy-feely bullshit. He did it to make me mad—he just admitted to that—and yet I don't forgive him. If anything, it makes me angrier. Does Bailey know she's just a pawn in his game?

It doesn't look like it. She got dressed up tonight. Her silky blonde hair is down and curly. Her makeup accentuates every one of her flawless features. She doesn't put this much effort into her appearance for work, and really, it's not necessary. The makeup and the outfit are nice, and sure, she's turning heads tonight, but I actually prefer her fresh-faced complexion. The cheekbones, the light blonde hair, the winning smile—she has a sort of girl-next-door charm that shines on its own.

Just for a moment, I indulge in the idea of considering her as I would any other woman. I ignore the complications of our relationship and think only of her fiery personality, her confidence and strength in the operating room. I drag my eyes down her tight blue dress and toned legs. A burning ache grips hold of me, but then it's doused with a healthy dose of guilt. Bailey isn't just a woman. She's my surgical assistant, and she doesn't want me checking her out.

"Matt!" my mom says as she sees me approach. "Bailey here was just explaining that you two work together. I had no idea!"

"I'm afraid we've been pestering her with questions," my dad adds, sending Bailey an appreciative smile. "Mostly about what you're like as a boss."

"I'm not technically Bailey's boss," I clarify with a hard tone. "I don't sign her paychecks."

My black cloud temporarily sours everyone's pleasant mood, but Bailey salvages it. "Just this week, we had an especially grueling surgery. Dr. Russell succeeded in doing a procedure only a handful of surgeons in the country could even attempt."

My parents' eyes are alight with wonder. I never talk about my job with them. "It wasn't that exciting," I clarify, slightly embarrassed by the attention.

My mom's hand bats my shoulder. "Oh stop. Now, Bailey, what do you do during surgery? I've never even heard of a surgical assistant."

"She's like my right hand. Closing, dressing the wound, passing me instruments. I wouldn't be able to operate without her."

I'm staring down at my drink when I say all this, but then the deafening silence is too much to ignore. I finally glance up and Bailey is staring at me with wide, shocked eyes. My mom's watching me with a curious little smile. My dad—thank God—is drinking his beer and keeping his lips zipped.

I sigh and rake a hand through my hair. "Bailey, can I speak with you for a second?"

Before she answers, I step forward, place a hand on her arm, just above her elbow, and lead her to an empty cocktail table across the room.

"Slow down," she insists. "You're nearly running and I can't move that fast in these shoes."

I sigh and slow my pace, aware of how tightly I'm gripping her arm—not painfully, but unyielding all the same.

Once we reach the table, I deposit her on one side and walk around until we're facing one another.

"Just to be clear," she says, pleasant tone gone. "I was just being polite in front of your parents."

Of course.

"What did Cooper say about this wedding when he invited you here tonight?" I ask, all business.

Her cheeks redden and she wrings her hands. "Um, I don't know…just that it was a small ceremony. No pressure, that sort of thing."

"He didn't mention me at all?"

"Obviously not." Her tone hardens. "Even though he definitely should have."

I nod. The next few minutes are going to be extremely painful, but I have to be honest with her about the situation or it's going to explode in my face. Cooper might want to play with people's emotions, but he doesn't have to face Bailey at work come Monday morning. I do.

"Do you have feelings for Cooper?" I ask, my head

tipped to the side, eyes narrowed.

Her brows shoot up. She glances away. "Feelings? Ah…"

She's all but grimacing with disdain and I want to grin, but I have enough sense to stifle the urge. "That's what I thought, and it's just as well, because Cooper only brought you here to make me jealous."

Nothing like having the truth shot right out of a cannon.

Her light brown eyes are focused on the cocktail table and there's untold emotion simmering there. Is she hurt by the revelation? Or just curious to hear the rest of the story?

I sigh and steel myself for her reaction as I continue. "It's too complicated and stupid to have to explain, but essentially, Cooper got it into his head that I didn't like you two dating. He's under the assumption that I have some burning desire to be with you, and he thought bringing you here tonight was the perfect way to test his theory."

Her brows scrunch together as she shakes her head. "That's the most ridiculous thing I've ever heard." At least we agree on something. "Burning desire? For *me*? Pfft."

Her gaze lifts to mine and a fist grabs hold of my chest.

Then, she does the absolute last thing I ever expected: she smiles.

"Honestly, I can't even be mad that he invited me here under false pretenses. I wasn't the one who agreed to this date."

What?

Now I'm the one leaning forward, waiting for answers.

"It was my little sister." She shrugs. "I really hate texting, so she started doing it on my behalf and got a little carried away. I didn't even know about this wedding until after she had agreed I'd go."

Relief floods my veins. "You're kidding."

She bites her bottom lip to stifle her smile and shakes her head. "No. She thinks I need to get out and date more. Cooper just happened to be the first guy to show any interest."

"That can't be true."

In a flash, her smile is gone. "Well it is. We're not all famous spine surgeons with thick hair and the brooding personality of Mr. Darcy."

I frown. "'Brooding personality of Mr. Darcy'…what in the world are you talking about?"

"Oh, c'mon." She waves her hand in my direction. "I don't have the energy to feed your ego. You're a doctor and you're attractive and if you bothered to go on a dating app, your thumbs would fall off from the amount of matches you'd get in 24 hours. They'd have to add a new server just to handle the overflow of traffic."

I shoot her a disbelieving smile. "How many drinks have you had?" She doesn't like my joke, rolling her eyes and moving to walk away, but I grab her wrist. "Wait."

There it is again: skin on skin. We've been doing it all night. Her fingers brushed mine when I handed her my wedding program. Our thighs pressed together during the ceremony. I held her elbow as I led her to this table. Now, I have her wrist, and it's so delicate it's like she'll bruise if I'm not careful.

"Usually we're wearing gloves," I say, suddenly sounding like I'm high out of my mind.

"What?"

I stare down at my hand. "In the operating room, when you hand me instruments, we're wearing gloves. That's why…"

This feels so intimate.

154

I swallow the words and release her hand.

"I think I should just go home. This night has been a total disaster."

I regret letting go of her as she starts to walk away.

I'm screwing this up, but there's no clear path forward. Do I let her go? Ask her to stay? We work together and she came with my brother and no part of this night makes any sense.

"What if my brother was right?" I say suddenly. "What if his experiment worked?"

She turns and her eyes collide with mine. I watch as the meaning of my questions sink in and *HOLY SHIT what have I done? Why did I say that?!*

"There you are!" Cooper's voice booms behind her. His timing is impeccable as he approaches us and drops his hands onto Bailey's shoulders. She flinches, but he doesn't notice. "C'mon, they want everyone to head into the ballroom. Dinner is starting!"

CHAPTER FIFTEEN
BAILEY

OH YES, JUST what I was hoping for: a five-course meal following the weirdest conversation of my life. I'm not hungry. My stomach has been replaced by a knot of tension, and yet here I sit at a banquet table with Cooper and his entire family. Short of feigning a sudden illness, there no way to escape sitting here for another hour or so. I keep trying to catch the waiter's attention so I can somehow signal for him to poison my food, or at the very least deliver me a drink with a heavy pour. Unfortunately, he just thinks I'm flirting—he passes me his number when he delivers the next course.

Dr. Russell is sitting across from me, brooding Mr. Darcy style and drawing the attention of every female in attendance who isn't related to him by blood. Even then, I think a few of his cousins would go there. Now, the waitress filling his water is focused so intently on his hair that she doesn't realize his cup runneth over. What is it about jet black, slightly rumpled, grip-it-while-he's-kissing-you-senseless hair that turns brains to goop?

She shakes herself out of her stupor just before the water starts to pool onto the table.

The banquet table is long, but not nearly wide enough. If I'm not careful, our knees will brush ever so slightly. It's happened twice now and the sensation of his smooth suit pants caressing my leg is nothing short of erotic. I find the only way to stifle a moan is by filling my mouth with bread. Consequently, the knot in my stomach has been replaced with a massive ciabatta loaf.

The other female guests aren't the only ones making googly eyes at Dr. Russell. Considering I'm sitting right across from him, I've had no choice but to peer at him from beneath my lashes and collect data like I'm a scientist and he's some newfound species of hunk. Here are my thoughts:

1) His eyes are the clearest blue, like that White Walker general in *Game of Thrones*. Fitting comparison considering they also share a similar personality.

2) The fact that he's taken off his jacket and hung it on the chair behind him is fine, but did he really need to roll the sleeves of his shirt up as well? We don't all need to be subjected to that level of forearm porn while eating dinner, tyvm.

3) He's a really terrible dinner companion. I think he's said three words to the people around him. I know this because I have one ear trained directly on him. If he so much as swallows, I notice.

4) He will not meet my eye no matter how hard I try. I think he regrets what he told me earlier.

I can't decide if I want him to regret what he told me earlier.

That's a door I've never considered opening before tonight.

"So Bailey, how long have you been a surgical assistant?"

The question comes from Mrs. Russell, who happens to be seated to my left. Oh yes, I'm surrounded by Russells on all sides. This would be a nightmare if Mrs. Russell wasn't one of the kindest people I've ever met. To continue the *Game of Thrones* comparisons, she would be Samwell

Tarly: kind, helpful, and always down for a snack. She's helping me finish off the bread basket.

"A few years now. I really like it even though it's not what I initially thought I'd be doing."

"Oh, really? Was medicine not always the end goal?"

"No, it was. I just thought I'd end up in a different role. I started out taking pre-med courses in college, but life got in the way a bit." Her brows crinkle with pity and I quickly add, "I really like what I do now though."

"Cooper tells me you take care of your younger sister? Is that what forced you to reroute?"

Reroute—what a nice euphemism for the chaos of that time in my life.

"Yes, but truly, it's better this way. I love having Josie live with me."

I'm expecting her to ask why my parents aren't in the picture, and I dread having to tell the truth. The tale is bleak: slick ice on a dark road. My parents were driving home from a holiday party when my father lost control of the vehicle. I flinch at the memory of their mangled car.

Fortunately, Mrs. Russell steers the conversation in a different direction.

"How old were you when you became your sister's guardian?"

"20."

"Goodness." She shakes her head in pity. "You've had to grow up so fast."

I shrug. "Maybe, but it taught me a lot. I don't resent having to take care of her."

Her hand hits my forearm and her eyes meet mine, and I'm embarrassed that I'm suddenly getting choked up. It's that kindness in her eyes making me feel like she's found the chink in my armor, the ooey-gooey center of my

Tootsie Roll Pop I try so hard to hide.

"I didn't know you take care of your sister," Dr. Russell says from across the table, his deep voice cutting through the chatter around us.

I still, keeping my gaze pinned on Mrs. Russell. I didn't know he was listening. With all the conversations taking place around us, it would have been hard for him to hear me clearly.

Unfortunately, when I finally work up the courage to glance over, those White Walker-blue eyes are studying me intently. There's no doubt he's heard every word. Dread fills my stomach. I want to go back to a few minutes ago when he was ignoring me, because the way he's looking at me now, it's like he's also seeing my vulnerable spot. What a dangerous development. He already wields so much power, and I've just hand-delivered him even more.

Cooper laughs loudly on my right and the sound jars me out of the moment. I'm thankful at least he is carrying on like he's at a wedding while the rest of us go deep into a therapy session. I don't need any more of an audience listening to my familial woes.

"I wish you had told me," Dr. Russell says, his dark brows crinkled in concern.

I clear my throat, trying to ease the tension there. "You've never asked about my life outside of the hospital."

He looks stricken by my comment, and I instantly regret the way it sounded. His mother is still listening, after all. I don't really think it's appropriate to chastise him in front of her.

"And," I clarify, "it's not something I talk about all that often."

After that, dinner lasts for another unbearable hour. I sit in silence, Dr. Russell nurses a few drinks, and Mrs.

Russell carries the conversation for all of us. I practically leap out of my chair when they clear away the last plate, bumping into the waiter who gave me his number.

"Hey, uh...I'm not sure if you came with anyone tonight..."

Oh dear GOD.

I sidestep around him and run for the bathroom, and even though I want to cut in front of the bride's grandma and a tiny flower girl hopping back and forth from leg to leg, I don't. I lean against the wall and wait my turn so I can lock myself in a stall and linger for as long as I damn well please.

Sitting on a crinkly piece of tissue paper covering the toilet, I check Uber and lament the ridiculous fee that pops up. It took us a while to get here. I knew the cost to get home would be expensive, but that's like can-I-pay-with-sexual-favors expensive. Walking isn't an option either because it's -139 degrees outside and my limbs would freeze and break off within the first mile.

"Hey! C'mon! There are only three stalls!" someone shouts before banging hard on my door.

"Oh! Sorry! I'm having diarrhea."

And then I pull up a YouTube video of Niagara Falls so I can finish researching my exit in peace.

Unfortunately, after a good deal of desperate searching, I'm left with no other option but to grin and bear it for a little longer until I can convince Cooper to take me home.

When I vacate my sanctuary (stall) and reenter the festivities, I expect him to be worried about my prolonged absence. No doubt word of my condition has spread through the ballroom, but I'm annoyed to find that I happen to be on a date with the Russell brother who loves attention. At this very moment he's in the middle of the dance floor smoothly transitioning back and forth between twirling the flower girl like a ballerina and shimmying beside the mother of the bride. There's a circle of people clapping around him and oh my god, he's doing the worm. Three bridesmaids hover nearby, licking their chops.

I turn in the exact opposite direction. Some people were made to dance, and some people were made to be wallflowers. I fall solidly into the second category.

I round the edge of the room, happy to finally have a moment to myself, but then I spot Dr. Russell sitting outside in the cold. He couldn't be farther away from the festivities unless he physically removed himself from the premises.

I watch as he brings a drink to his lips and takes a long drag. Then he lays his head on the back of the chair and stares up at the night sky. I press my hand to the glass and confirm it's just as cold as I thought it would be.

Stupid man.

He's going to get frostbite. I should let him.

What do I care?

And yet, I turn and walk back to the dining table to get our coats. His is thick wool and undoubtedly expensive and I want to wrap it around myself so badly, but I stuff my arms into my own puffy pink sleeves and resist the temptation.

At the door to the patio, I take a deep breath, appreciating one last second of warmth before I step outside and arctic air blasts my face. My extremities turn to ice. I lose feeling in my bare legs.

"Jesus, are you insane?!" I shout, scurrying over to him quickly. "What are you doing out here?"

He doesn't turn around, just holds up his tumbler as if in explanation.

"Yes, I get it: you're trying to drink yourself to death. You've been doing it all night—surely you're close by now."

He chuckles. "One more ought to do it."

His reply is lazier than usual. He's definitely drunk, and I'm definitely about to die when another blast of wind hits me.

I round his chair, fling his jacket onto his lap, and run back inside as fast as my legs can take me. I feel no pity for him anymore. He has his jacket. I'm going to walk right over to that nice roaring fire, plop down in the cozy sitting area, and pull up the Kindle app on my phone.

When I get closer, I realize I'm not the only one with this idea. A young girl is reading a worn paperback and she's so focused on it, she doesn't even notice me.

"Is this seat available?" I ask, pointing to the chair across from her. She nods without looking up and wow, this girl is my kind of people.

I sit there, warming up and reading on my phone, glad no one cares to bother me, right up until a pair of keys appear in my line of sight. I follow them up to a large hand, and then an arm covered in thick wool. Up even farther, my gaze clashes with Dr. Russell's.

"Drive me home?"

I scrunch my nose in distaste. "Can't you drive yourself?"

"That possibility flew out the window about four drinks back. Lily, mind if I steal your friend?"

The little girl shrugs and turns a page. Such betrayal. Here I was thinking we were forming a little book club. Where's her loyalty?

"Can't you ask someone else?" *Anyone else?*

Maybe Lily has a motorized scooter she could tie him

to.

He drops his keys and they plop onto my lap. "No. I know you want to leave too. This is called killing two birds with one stone. Now c'mon. I already told everyone we're leaving so you don't have to bother with saying goodbye."

Fine. It's just as well. My phone is about to die anyway.

Though he says I don't have to, I want to say goodbye to everyone because I'm not a complete jerk. There's no way Cooper will let me go this easily. No doubt he'll turn into a raging scorned lover when he finds out I'm leaving with his brother.

"Okay, cool. Drive safe!" he calls from the center of the dance floor, sandwiched between two bridesmaids.

Oh, right. Well...he must be very good at hiding his territorial side.

At least Mrs. Russell is sad to see me go.

"I hope we get to see you again soon, Bailey," she says, sounding as if she actually means it. Unfortunately for her, the chances of that ever happening are slim to none. One of her sons is doing the robot and has forgotten I exist, and the other is hovering near the door, anxious to get away from here and me.

Out in the parking lot, he walks a few paces behind me, drunk as a skunk.

I've never seen him like this. He's always so buttoned-up and high-strung. I bet he watches TV in his suit in the evenings. When he's watched exactly one episode of a documentary or snooze-worthy educational programming, he brushes each of his teeth for exactly 15 seconds and then he tucks himself into bed wearing a full pajama set, dressing robe, slippers, and little night cap.

I laugh at the image before realizing the real-life Dr. Russell is no longer following me. For no good reason, he's changed course and is toddling toward the dumpsters at the far end of the parking lot.

"Where are you going?!" I cry, running after him.

He laughs. "I can't remember the color of my car."

"Obviously."

Though I have the sober advantage, his legs are easily twice as long as mine. When I finally reach him, I'm breathing hard. Like a zookeeper trying to wrangle a wild bear, I'm careful not to get too close in case he decides to pass out and smother me in the process. Instead, I hover behind him, hands on his biceps as I half-shove, half-prod him in the right direction. It's not easy. With him resisting, it's like I'm trying to move a boulder.

We make it a few feet before he sees something on the ground that catches his interest and leans forward to grab it. It's a flower growing in the concrete. He picks it and offers it to me. "Here, please, a token of my gratitude."

I yank the tiny white thing out of his hand, shove it in my pocket, and roll my eyes. "All right, fine. Thank you. Now c'mon, we're almost there."

His Prius is just a few yards away, but he turns back to look over his shoulder and his bottom lip juts out like he's disappointed. I should despise him for what he's putting me through, but even inebriated, he's ridiculously hot. His dark hair is a slightly tousled, his tie tugged loose.

"You don't like it, do you? I'll buy you roses instead. Stop at a florist on the way home."

Oh Jesus. How did I get here?

I unlock his Prius and have a hell of a time getting him inside. It's like he's forgotten how his limbs work. His hand flies toward me and I have to duck.

"Do you have to be so big?"

I accidentally bonk his head as I force him down and he

groans, but eventually I have him stuffed in there and buckled up. I have to shift the driver's seat forward about twenty feet before I can reach the gas pedal, but a few minutes later, I'm on the highway with his address in the map app on my phone.

I'm so close to freedom I can taste it.

"Bailey, Bailey, Bailey," he says, head rolling back and forth on his headrest. "Why do you hate me?"

Okay, maybe not that close.

I glance over and his boyish charm hits me in full force. His head is turned toward me. His eyes plead with me to give in, though I have no idea what I would be surrendering to. His mouth is turned down in a sad frown. His hand is outstretched, palm up, resting on the console as if he's waiting for me to clasp it. I clutch the steering wheel extra hard.

"I don't hate you, Dr. Russell."

He groans like he's in pain as he redirects his gaze out the windshield. "My name is Matt. I don't know why you insist on—"

"Okay, *okay*." I'm quick to appease him. "*Matt*."

He sighs. "Say it again, slower."

Instead, I turn on the radio, set it to a country station, and blast the volume as loud as I can without permanently damaging our hearing. There's no more possibility of conversation for the remainder of the drive because a cowboy is singing about his achy breaky heart at max decibels.

His house is in a fancy neighborhood, but it's not an obnoxious stucco mansion with 45 bathrooms. It's a modern one-story farmhouse with white brick, large windows, and a glossy black front door. I lead him straight to it, much the same way I led him through the parking lot at the chapel (protecting my face), and when we reach the welcome mat, I wipe my hands clean and step back.

"All right. Well, good luck. See ya!"

He drops his head to the front door and makes no move to enter.

"Okay fine, let me just unlock this door and…there, now go inside."

I poke him in the back with my finger, but it's clear he has no intention of moving from his stoop. I could leave him there, but it's getting colder by the minute and I don't necessarily want his death on my conscience.

So that's how I find myself in Dr. Russell's—I mean, Matt's (!)—house, helping him down the hallway to his bedroom.

His arm hangs across my shoulders and I drag him forward like he's a wounded soldier. My legs are shaking from the weight. Every room we pass, I try to stop.

"No, no." He shakes his head. "That's my office. Keep going. That's a bathroom. I can't sleep in there."

"You're about to sleep right here if you don't help me out a little. I swear you're dragging your feet on purpose."

Finally, we make it to the end of the hall and I kick open the door to his bedroom. I'm expecting it to be in complete disarray just like his office, but instead, it's artfully decorated. Neat and tidy. His king-sized bed has white sheets and a fluffy gray comforter. Four oversized black and white framed maps hang on one wall. There's a plant in the corner that looks as if he waters it regularly. I half-expected him to sleep standing up, next to the power station he plugs himself into every night. The fact that he has such a warm, welcoming bedroom does weird things to my heart.

I need to get out of here.

"Do you think you can handle it from here?"

His hand drags along my shoulders and the nape of my neck as he steps away from me. He turns and meets my gaze. "Wait. You've been running from me all evening. Just stay for a second."

We're standing a few feet apart in his bedroom, staring at one another.

I'm aware of every breath I take.

"I need to go home."

He shakes his head. "Don't. Stay here. I won't try anything, I swear."

His brows pinch together in earnest, like he really means what he's promising.

I laugh like he's just suggested something absolutely preposterous. "You're very drunk and you have no idea what you're saying right now."

Truly, he won't remember any of this in the morning. I doubt he even realizes who I am at the moment.

He grunts bitterly and turns toward the bed. He plops down to sit on the edge and drops his head into his hands.

"I know what you think I am—*evil*. A man who shouts at you in the OR for every little mistake. Maybe that's true. Maybe I'm not a good man." He glances back up at me, and the moonlight filtering through his window catches the sharp contours of his face, the parts of him that intimidate me the most. "I had a wife. Did you know that?"

My heart races, trying to keep up with his erratic subject changes. He's inviting me to stay the night one minute then opening up to me about his marriage the next. I should turn and bolt, but my feet stay rooted in place. There's no way I'll leave when he's willing to offer up information his sober mind keeps tucked away.

"You're divorced?"

He nods and looks away. "We got married young, right out of college. Victoria was with me through medical school and part of residency. She liked the idea of being a doctor's wife, but not the reality of it. I was busy working 80 hours a week. She felt neglected."

I stay perfectly silent, waiting for him to continue.

He shakes his head and drags his hands through his hair. "She left me and she was gone for eight days and the only thing I noticed was that there was more space in our closet. The next time I saw her, I asked her if she got rid of some of her shoes. I can still remember her wistful laugh."

It's strange. I can't imagine him with a wife, even now. Before tonight, he was two-dimensional to me. He existed as a surgeon and nothing else. Now, seeing him in this room, hearing him talk about his past, I'm suddenly confronted with the idea that there's a heart beating beneath that suit, that maybe he has wants and desires that extend past the operating room.

I sense that he's waiting for me to condemn him for his divorce, so I sigh and take a tiny step forward. "You aren't evil just because you have a failed marriage under your belt. You were in residency—it was probably a hard time for the both of you."

"Maybe, but she's remarried and pregnant now," he says, the words coming out twisted and pained. "She's going to have a family and in all the years since our divorce, I haven't even had a serious relationship."

"That's because you're married to your job."

His eyes sweep up to me and he doesn't hesitate before replying, "Yeah, well maybe that's not enough anymore."

And then he collapses back on his bed with a heavy thud.

CHAPTER SIXTEEN
BAILEY

I STAND IMMOBILE, waiting for him to snap back to consciousness, but no, he is good and dead to the world.

Oh good grief.

The lower half of his body is hanging off the bed, and he's still wearing his wool coat and suit. I'm worried he's going to throw up in his sleep and die. I should let him—it would serve him right for putting me in this predicament in the first place. I look around as if trying to decide what to do, but there's really only one thing to do, the only decent thing: leave now and shoot up a prayer that he makes it through the night.

Just kidding.

I heave a reluctant sigh then step forward to take off his shoes. As I unknot the laces, I talk out loud, telling him things I'd never have the courage to say if he were awake.

"I hate you for doing this to me. This was supposed to be a fun night. I could be back at that wedding right now, dancing with Cooper and having the time of my life. Sure, I absolutely hate dancing, and yes, I'm not really that into him, but who knows—weddings do funny things to people.

"Also, how dare you ask me to sleep here with you?! What if I didn't have enough sense to realize you weren't being serious? You could really get a girl's hopes up saying things like that!"

Once his shoes are on the floor, I heave his legs up onto the bed and assess the results. His body is bent at an awkward angle. He's probably not that comfortable in his suit, but there is no way I'm undressing him. Also, with his weight on top of them, I can't exactly draw the blankets down. His coat should keep him warm enough. I button it up, just to be sure.

After I'm sure he won't roll off the bed, I head to his kitchen and pilfer a mixing bowl and a glass from his cabinets. I fill the cup with water and set it beside the bowl on his nightstand. Then, I think better of it and find a bucket in his garage so I can plop it onto the floor beside his bed. If he gets sick, I am *not* cleaning it up.

"I don't think you're evil, necessarily, though you are married to your job, which is probably why your wife left you. I don't really blame her. She probably *was* neglected. Patricia tells me you sometimes sleep in your office at work. I bet in your residency days you slept at the hospital more often than not."

I shake my head and realize now that he's asleep in his bed with strategically placed water and a bowl *and* a bucket in case he's sick, my work is done. I need to leave, except when I get my phone out of my purse to call an Uber, I find it's dead. D-E-A-D. It was all that bathroom dawdling and reading by the fire.

NO. NOooO.

After some quick Nancy-Drew thinking, I retrieve Matt's phone from the pocket of his coat, but it's locked. I try to break into it using his thumbprint, but it's no use. I need the passcode. What fresh hell is this?!

His phone will allow me to place a call to 9-1-1, and I actually consider it.

"Hello, yes this is a very serious emergency."

Josie is probably worried sick about me, but there's nothing I can do. Matt doesn't have a house phone. I've searched high and low. I consider knocking on a neighbor's door to ask to use their phone, but it's late and even though this is a nice neighborhood, there are crazy people everywhere. I'm not trying to end up in anyone's basement tonight.

Then it hits me: DUH, I'll plug my phone into Matt's charger and wait for it to juice up. I'll be on my way home in no time.

His charging dock is on his nightstand, so I drop my phone onto it and then slide down to the floor so I can rest my back against his bed. I take off my jacket and use it as a blanket, then I stand and steal a pillow so I can actually get comfortable. It smells like him and I try hard not to let the scent wind its way around me, but it's no use. I'm in his bedroom, listening to his steady breathing and using his pillow to cradle my head. I am all up in his personal space and I have free rein. I could snoop anywhere I want. I could turn and open the drawer of his nightstand. I shiver at the thought of finding condoms or some other proof that he's a living, breathing man with needs—sexy, R-rated needs.

I put up caution tape and roadblocks around those thoughts and turn my attention to the window in front of me. The curtain blocks most of the light outside, but I can still see a sliver of the moon. I'm admiring it as a yawn breaks free. My eyelids feel oh so heavy. The two glasses of champagne I had during dinner have made me extra sleepy. Maybe that waiter did give me a heavy pour after all. I fight to keep my eyes open, knowing my phone will be charged soon, but it's no use. My eyes flutter closed and I tell myself to stay awake...to check to see if my phone is charged...to...

I **HAVE THE** most delicious dream. I'm a princess and there's a dragon holding me captive in a medieval tower. Fortunately, there's a brawny prince with the bluest eyes and the darkest hair. He's brave and chivalrous and really knows how to rock a suit of armor. All the other princesses in the land think he's hot, but he's my prince. He's come to slay my dragon and rescue me from the tower. After an intense duel in which he comes out the victor, he finally reaches my room way up at the tallest peak, and he lifts me into his arms. I think we're headed out of the tower, but instead he carries me over to a bed. It makes no sense—we need to go in the opposite direction, out of the room. I really need to go home. I tell the prince my sister is waiting for me, but he insists I stay on this soft, warm bed as he tucks me under the blankets.

He moves to walk away and I say, "Aren't you forgetting something?" Then I make exaggerated smoochy noises with my lips. *Because, hello! This dream is not G-rated.* I want a kiss, dammit, but the prince just chuckles and walks away.

Pfft. Just my luck, getting a prudish prince.

This is the last part of the dream I remember before I jolt awake in a room that smells like sandalwood and pine, lying on sheets that are way softer than anything I can afford. It takes me all of three seconds to realize I'm still in Matt's house, and worse, I'm in his bed! Oh god, that means he must have picked me up and put me up here himself. He was the prince—and I begged him to kiss me!

I bolt upright and look around the room. He's not in bed with me. THANK GOD. I scramble out from beneath the covers and leap to my feet. With a shaky, nervous breath, I glance down. *Oh, phew.* Fortunately, I'm still in my dress from last night, though it's a little askew. I grab my phone from the charging dock and turn it on. Josie called me 37 times.

I call her back right away.

"OH MY GOD. I THOUGHT YOU WERE DEAD!" is the first thing she says as the call connects.

I hold a hand over my mouth, scared to make too much noise. I don't know where Matt is. He could be coming back any minute.

"Listen, I'm alive. It's a long story, but I'll be home soon."

She groans. "Good, I'm glad, but it's 5:45 AM and I'm going back to sleep."

The call abruptly ends.

Okay, well, at least that's taken care of. I tiptoe around and gather my things. My jacket is on the floor. My shoes are sitting neatly beside the bed. Matt must have taken them off for me like I did for him, and I shiver thinking of him undoing the little strap around my ankle. For some reason that seems more thoughtful than when I yanked off his dress shoes, but maybe I'm reading too much into it.

Once I have everything I need, I tiptoe to the door of his bedroom. If I make it outside without being noticed, I can just order an Uber from down the street, or who knows, I could always hitchhike home with some grizzly trucker. Last night, I was worried about crazy people. Now, I'm so embarrassed by how I behaved that a good ol' kidnapping doesn't sound so bad anymore.

I hear a noise behind me and freeze, glancing slowly over my shoulder like I'm expecting Freddy Krueger to make an appearance. A second later, Matt steps out of his bathroom, toothbrush swishing back and forth across his teeth. He's wearing gray sleeping pants and no shirt and I blink an untold number of times as if my eyelashes will flap hard enough to carry me right out of this situation.

"Good," he says with a quick nod. "You're up."

Then he turns and steps back into the bathroom so he can spit out his toothpaste and rinse his mouth. My eyes flick to his window and I wonder if I can make it across the room and outside before he's done. But no, a second later, he's back in his bedroom, brushing past me to get into the hallway. Now he's sans toothbrush and still sans shirt. I feast on the sight that is his tan back and broad shoulders and muscly biceps, but when he glances back to look at me, I shoot my gaze to the ceiling so fast, I think I sprain a muscle in my eye.

"C'mon, I'll make breakfast."

I laugh. "For a second there, it sounded like you said the word 'breakfast', but that can't be right."

He scrunches his brows in confusion. "Aren't you hungry?"

I hold up my hand. Why are we talking about food, of all things? Aren't there more important details we need to work out? Like, oh, *I dunno*, when we took the major leap from enemies to shirtless breakfast companions? "Hold on—did I or did I not fall asleep on the floor of your bedroom last night?"

He frowns and turns around, leaning one shoulder against the wall and crossing his arms. His abs are insanely toned. "You did."

"And did you or did you not lift me up into your bed and tuck me under the covers?"

"I did, but then I slept out on the couch. Nothing happened."

My cheeks burn because there's still one more thing I need clarification on. I rush the words out on one breath. "Good, okay. Also, I dreamed that I asked for a kiss—that didn't happen, right?"

His face completely transforms as his mouth breaks into a devastating smile. "No, that definitely did happen. It was cute. You puckered up and everything."

Just as I thought. I cross my arms and put my head down and fast-walk right on by him. I head straight for the door and I think if I pick up enough momentum, I won't even have to stop to open it, I can just barrel straight through the wood.

His hand reaches out to catch my shoulder and he tugs me back. "Wait, I said it was cute. You don't have to be embarrassed."

"Embarrassed isn't the right word. Traumatized is more like it. I'll need therapy."

He offers me a little half-smile and my gaze pings back and forth between that and his swoon-worthy bedhead.

"Well it's nothing worse than what I did. Getting drunk, forcing you to put me to bed—I don't think I've been that wasted since my college days."

Somehow, I doubt he was that drunk even then.

"You told me about your ex-wife," I admit in an effort to get everything out on the table as soon as possible.

He looks less than enthused. "Ah."

"And you told me the hospital was going to give me a massive raise."

He laughs and shakes his head. "Strange. I don't remember that part."

Then, much the same way I led him to his car and into his house last night, he puts both of his hands on my shoulders and pushes me in the direction of his kitchen. I have no choice but to allow him to direct me to his table and deposit me in a chair. There's already a freshly brewed pot of coffee waiting on the counter, and he pours me a heaping mug.

"Cream?" he asks.

"Please, and don't scrimp."

"Sugar?"

I arch a brow. "You're not going to lecture me about how bad it is for my health?"

He smirks. "I'm off the clock."

"Then yes, please. Just a little."

Matt making that cup of coffee is arguably the sexiest thing I've ever seen a human do. It's like when you see a hot dude holding a puppy. Alone, both things are adorable. Together, they're unstoppable. I try to contain my enthusiasm though. There's no need to drool on his wooden farmhouse table. I don't have enough in my savings to replace it.

He brings me the mug and has me taste it.

"Good?" he asks, watching for my reaction.

His toned abs are less than a foot from my face. I shoot him a thumbs-up in lieu of speaking.

With a nod, he heads back to the fridge and starts plopping ingredients onto the counter: mushrooms, spinach, cheese, eggs.

This all seems so remarkably normal, which makes me feel even more uncomfortable. How is he carrying on as if this is any other Sunday morning? Suddenly, I've had enough. I can't do it.

"What exactly are we doing here?" I ask. "Right now?"

"You're drinking coffee and I'm making omelets." He bends down to open a drawer in his fridge and I stare at his butt for two seconds before I realize what I'm doing and look away. "Do you want ham in yours?"

"Yes, of course—but that's not the point. Could you please just stop moving for a second?" I shoot to my feet and fist my hands by my sides.

He finally gets the hint and turns to face me.

"You said things last night that you can't take back," I begin, trying to keep my voice as steady as possible. "You said your brother's experiment might have worked. What did that mean?"

He heaves a deep sigh, like the subject seems daunting to him. "I think we should have this conversation after we've eaten."

I resist the urge to stamp my foot. "No. I want to talk now. As I was putting you to bed, you said even more things! Maybe they were just drunken ramblings, but they seemed like more, like you were actually opening up to me."

There. The truth is spilled across his kitchen floor, and I'm waiting for him to pick it up and discard it as he pleases. All he has to say is that he was drunk. Then we can shove all these weird feelings under a rug and get back to having a working relationship that's tenuous at best.

He leans back against the counter and crosses his arms over his chest. "I remember everything I said."

His gaze is heavy and intense.

I want to look away, but my next question is too important. "And do you regret any of it?"

There's no hesitation, no backpedaling on his part. He just replies confidently, "No. In fact, I stand by all of it. What I admitted to you last night about how it made me jealous to see you arrive at the wedding with my brother that was true."

My eyes bug out of my head.

"Oh..."

I have no clue what to say in response. I had a laugh and a *No worries, bud* ready in my chamber. I was going to play it off right along with him. *Yes, yes, what a strange night. Could you put my omelet in a to-go box please? Thank you. Bye!*

He sighs and steps back up to the island, starting to crack eggs into a mixing bowl.

"Would you mind chopping the spinach?" he asks. "I need food before we continue."

Who cares about spinach at a time like this?!

But, I do as I'm told, standing across from him at his kitchen island and helping him prepare breakfast. I sip my coffee and try to forget I'm still wearing a fancy cocktail dress and yesterday's makeup. He doesn't seem to mind, at least I don't think he does. I catch him studying me as I top off my mug.

"What?" I swat aimlessly at my face.

He shakes his head with a secret little smile. "Nothing. C'mon, let's eat."

"Okay, but first…for the love of God, you have to put a shirt on."

CHAPTER SEVENTEEN
MATT

I CAN'T BELIEVE how badly I've screwed things up. I think I've really terrified her. Bailey's sitting on the very edge of her chair, taking small, quick bites of omelet. Her knees bounce under the table. Her mind is working overtime, which is understandable; a lot has happened in the last 24 hours.

I woke up yesterday and Bailey was still categorized as coworker in my mind.

By the end of the night she'd slipped into potential love interest.

I haven't really come to terms with what that means, but we could figure it out together if she'd ever work up the courage to meet my eyes.

When I admitted that it made me jealous to see her arrive at the wedding with my brother, she looked terrified. Her reply said it all.

"Oh..."

Her face paled. Her eyes widened. I wanted to shout quickly, *Oh, HA HA. Just kidding!* like a fool.

Now, she pushes her food around, not really eating.

"Do you not like it?"

"Oh, no. I do!"

I watch as she takes a big bite and forces it down.

I don't think it's a good idea to continue discussing my feelings at the moment. She's tired. There are bags under her eyes, and I feel bad that she's still in her dress from last night. I offer her clothes to change into and she acts as if

I've just proposed marriage.

"No! Oh my god. No. Thank you though…"

Right.

Then, let's just sit here in silence.

After a few more tense, awkward minutes, we finish eating and I load the dishes. When I'm done, I turn to find Bailey standing at the threshold of the kitchen holding her purse and jacket. She's ready to go.

"Would you mind taking me home? I can get an Uber, but I thought I'd ask just in case…"

I frown. "Of course. Yes. Let me just grab my shoes."

I hate that I seem to be fumbling this. She doesn't have to rush out, but it's not really appropriate for me to ask her to stay either. It's not that shocking that she's ready to bolt when I consider the timeline of events from last night. She showed up to my cousin's wedding as my brother's date. I told her it made me jealous. Then I got rip-roaring drunk and rambled on and on about my depressing divorce and loneliness. She didn't come to my house willingly. She had to attend to a drunken idiot. It's no surprise she's counting the minutes until she's out of my presence.

I lead her outside and open the passenger-side door of my car for her. She thanks me and hurries to get out of the cold. I move to the driver's side, but when I sit, my knees collide with the steering wheel. It's like my car shrunk three sizes overnight.

Bailey stifles a laugh. "Oh yeah, sorry. I had to shift your seat up so I could reach the pedals."

Her laughter eases the knot in my stomach and I'm reminded that this doesn't have to be so bad. Sure, a part of me wants to turn to her at the first stop sign and speak candidly: *Bailey, I find you attractive and I want to ask you out on a date.*

Simple as that. Unfortunately, I don't think she'd say yes.

I'm watching her out of the corner of my eye. She's drumming her hands on her legs, ready to leap from the car at any moment.

When we arrive outside her house, she turns and thanks me for the ride. "I truly appreciate it."

I drag a hand across my chin. "It's the least I could do after you took care of me last night."

"It wasn't as bad as you think. I'm the one who begged you to kiss me in my sleep, remember?"

Her cheeks redden at the recollection.

I have to fight back a grin. "Like I said, it was cute. I knew you were dreaming."

"Yeah."

Her gaze flicks down to my mouth. She should get out and walk up to her house. We have nothing else to say to one another, but she doesn't move. She turns to face me and I furrow my brows in question.

She's a tiny thing and yet her presence fills up my car. Her jacket is so ridiculously pink and puffy. Her cheeks are rosy from the chilly air. I inhale and catch a whiff of her perfume. Her eyes are drowning in emotions she's not giving voice to. I want to order her to speak, but she's nibbling on her bottom lip and I don't want her to stop doing that either.

She turns to her door and fingers the handle, like she's thinking about getting out. Then she glances back to me.

The next few milliseconds pass like small eternities. My heart beats painfully in my chest. My hands leave the steering wheel and she leans an inch toward me. It's barely anything, really. I think she might not even realize it, but that inch is a plea and I don't hesitate. I slide one hand into her hair and bring her toward me.

This is insane.

I need to release her and let her go.

I've done enough.

"*Matt.*"

My name is a spell and there's no hope now.

My voice is hoarse when I speak. "I'm going to…"

Kiss you.

And I do. Our lips meet ever so gently at first, and I brace for the inevitable shove to my chest, the jerk of her head as she turns and offers me her cheek, but then she sighs against my mouth and I am a man without self-control. I want this girl and at this moment, she's sitting in my car, fisting my shirt, and pulling me toward her. My head tilts to the side and our lips fit like they were made for each other. Her mouth opens just enough so I can test the waters. My tongue touches her lips and my stomach tightens in response.

One of her hands glides up and around my neck. She strings her fingers through my hair and moans like she's been wanting to do that for weeks.

An innocent kiss turns into more and I want to haul her up and over onto my lap, but this space is too tight for those kinds of extracurricular activities. Fuck the environment—next time, I'm buying a Hummer.

We're kissing and hungry for one another and she's trying to speak, but I'm not letting her.

I have a hand tangled in her silky hair. I drag the pad of my finger across the sensitive skin just at the nape of her neck and she shivers. My dick strains against my pants. I could push us a little further. I could unzip the top of her dress and slide it off her shoulders. This could be a morning we'd never forget and maybe she knows that because she's pulling back now, catching her breath.

Her lips are swollen and red.

Her dress sits slightly askew on her shoulder because I was tugging at it, wanting it gone, wanting to drag my hand down her smooth shoulder and collarbone, lower until I felt the small curve of her breast. Her chest is flushed with color and it matches her cheeks perfectly. The rest of her is still porcelain, and it's a fitting combination: strawberries and cream. I want to lick her from head to toe.

Her hand presses against her lips like she's checking to see if they're still there.

I tug her hand away so I can lean forward and kiss her again. It's meant to be suggestive. I take her bottom lip gently between my teeth and the move says, *We could do this all day, Bailey, if only you'd let me.*

Her eyes widen and she jerks back, out of reach. "Oh my god."

That's all she says, but the three words bring the real world crashing back down around us. We're in my car, sitting outside Bailey's house. She's going to get out soon, disappear inside, and presumably enjoy the rest of her Sunday. Tomorrow, she'll step back into New England Medical Center and she'll be my surgical assistant, standing across from me at the operating table, off limits in so many ways.

She drags her hand down her face, and that's when I notice she's staring out the window, past my head. I realize then that the "Oh my god" she uttered wasn't in reaction to our kiss. Fresh hope blooms in my chest.

"We have company," she announces, biting down a smile.

I turn and sure enough, I spot a teenage girl's face pressed against a large window in the front of Bailey's house.

"That's my sister." She groans in embarrassment. "She probably saw all of that."

I smirk and wave. The girl's eyes widen before she ducks down out of sight.

"She's gone now."

"Yeah, right." She grunts. "She's probably just finding a better vantage point. I'd better get inside before she finds a pair of binoculars or something."

So much for giving her a morning she'll never forget.

I walk her to her door under the guise of chivalry, but really, I'm greedy for a few more minutes with her. I can't take her hand or draw her back into a kiss; it doesn't seem appropriate now that we're outside. Whatever magic that was in my car is gone. I stuff my hands in my coat pockets in an attempt to keep them occupied, and then before I know it, we're at her door.

In seconds, she'll be gone and I'll have an entire Sunday to myself. I'll do what I always do: work out, go up to the office, prepare for tomorrow's case. I'll take work and inflate it to fill every crevice of my life so I don't have to focus on all that's lacking.

"Here we are. Home sweet home." Her tone is self-deprecating. She thinks I won't like where she lives. True, it's an older neighborhood and the houses are a little rundown, but it's certainly nothing to be ashamed of. In fact, it seems like a nice place to call home. There's a Christmas wreath hanging on her front door and a bright red welcome mat with *HO HO HO* printed across the center. I realize I haven't put up a single decoration, but then why would I? It's only mid-November.

"I like it—the house, I mean."

She can't look me in the eye, but she nods and rocks

186

back on her heels. "Well thank you for the ride. I'd invite you inside, but…yeah…" She fidgets with her keys. "I'll just see you tomorrow."

Then she turns to go inside.

"Bailey—"

She shakes her head hard, cutting me off. "Be careful what you say—Josie is probably hovering on the other side of the door."

"Oh, c'mon!" a voice says from inside. "Are you kidding me?"

The door swings open and I'm suddenly staring at a miniature version of Bailey. They have the same freckles, the same shock of pale blonde hair, though her sister's is piled in a bun on top of her head. She's scowling at us, but it's cute, like a baby tiger practicing its growl.

She's wearing mismatched pajamas and in her hand is an empty plastic cup. When she sees me staring at it, she jerks it behind her back.

"I was just getting some water," she explains, feigning innocence.

Bailey groans and brushes past her to step inside. "No, you weren't. You were trying to use that cup to hear us better."

Her sister acts like the very idea of her spying on us is outrageous. "I was NOT. I would never do something like that to my own flesh and blood."

"Uh huh, then why did I see your little face pressed against the window a second ago?" Bailey asks as she hangs her jacket on a hook by the door and tosses her purse on a nearby table.

"I thought I heard the ice cream truck coming."

Bailey bursts out laughing. "You are so full of it!"

"Am not. And *wait*! Why am I the one under

investigation? You two were just making out in broad daylight! I bet Ms. Murphy saw it too!"

They continue volleying back and forth, completely unaware that I'm still standing on the doormat. I'm enthralled by their conversation and the warmth of their house. There are Christmas decorations everywhere, tinsel and a string of paper snowflakes spanning from one side of the living room to the other. I can barely see a small pine tree, it's so covered with ornaments and candy canes.

I step to the side to get a better view and Josie's attention snaps back to me.

"Wait! You're not the guy who picked Bailey up last night."

I smile. "No. That was Cooper, my brother."

"But…" She shakes her head. "No, that can't be right, because I recognize you…" She tilts her head to the side, studying me intently before she gasps and her eyes widen with recognition. "You're Dr. Russell! The hot doctor!"

Bailey leaps forward and grabs the edge of the front door. "Ooookay then. Well, Dr. Russell has to go now. Josie, move your foot. I'm trying to close to door. No, no, he has to leave, stop bl"—she shoves her sister out of the way—"ocking it!"

With an *oomph*, Bailey regains control and pushes the door closed all but one last inch. One of her bright brown eyes stares up at me from inside. I can only see a sliver of her mouth—the mouth that was just pressed against mine minutes ago.

"Well, thanks again," she says, all fake smiles and pretend geniality. "I'll, um—"

"BAILEY YOU WERE MAKING OUT WITH THE HOT DOCTOR!" Josie shouts behind her.

Bailey's eye goes wide and her cheek burns bright red.

"Hookay then, ignore her. See you at work! Goodbye now!"

Then the door slams and Bailey yells at her sister to stop shouting and I'm left outside in the cold with a big-ass smile on my face.

My last thought before I force myself to turn back to the street is that I wish I could spend the rest of the day with them. It would be the most entertaining Sunday I've had in a while.

CHAPTER EIGHTEEN
BAILEY

TO SAY THIS weekend was a rollercoaster of emotion is like saying the sun is kind of hot. On Friday, I spilled instruments, delayed surgery, and cried at work. Matt drove me home and told me to grow up. I was 99% sure I was going to quit. On Saturday, I unknowingly attended a wedding with his brother but ended up going home with him and sleeping in his bed. On Sunday, I made out with him hardcore. I was slobbering all over him, making a real fool of myself. My hands were in his hair. My vocal cords were producing the most ridiculous, slutty moans. He probably thought I'd never been kissed before. Now it's Monday and I'm expected to just walk into the OR like *Hey everyone! Everything is hunky dory!*

EXCEPT EVERYTHING IS NOT HUNKY DORY.

Can't a girl have a minute to process these developments? My body has run through fight or flight so many times it's not quite sure what we're doing. Staying? Crying? Declaring our love? Fending off his advances? ARE WE IN LOVE OR WAR?

When I press my finger to my pulse, my brain comes back with an error message: *too fast to compute.*

Even though Matt isn't technically my boss (the board of NEMC is), he *is* my superior and a surgeon and slightly intimidating. Getting involved with him sounds like a recipe for disaster. I've watched enough *Grey's Anatomy* to know I have to handle this situation delicately. I won't let this turn me into a nervous wreck. There can be no whispers in the halls or steamy sex eyes over the operating table. I will not be gossiped about. If this gets out (and it will) then it's going to be on my terms.

Which is why I'm sitting outside the HR office on Monday morning. It's ungodly early. The office is dark, but that's okay; I'll be the first person Linda sees when she arrives. She's the sole human resources officer for the entire hospital. I rarely see her around the building, and when I do, she's usually flustered, walking at a brisk pace and murmuring angrily under her breath. There's often a stain on her shirt. I've only ever seen her hair look wild and unkempt. With the number of employees this place has, I think she has her hands full. They really ought to hire someone to assist her. I'll be sure to tell her that when I see her, just so I'm on her good side.

There's movement to my right and I glance up to see her making her way down the hall. Her head is down, focused on her phone as she approaches.

I jump to my feet and paste on a big, cheesy smile.

"Linda! Hi, good morning."

She jumps out of her skin then glares up at me. "What? What is it?"

Not exactly a warm welcome, but I don't let that deter me. "Oh, well, I know it's early, but I was hoping to get a few minutes of your time to talk about something?"

I've never seen someone's heart break before my eyes.

"You're serious? It's Monday. The sun's not even up."

Then she shakes her head and brushes past me to unlock her office door. She flips the light on and—wow. I thought Matt's office was messy, but hers takes the cake. There are files and papers everywhere. Her desk is barely visible.

She plops her purse and her coffee down onto a side table then continues over to a tall filing cabinet in the corner.

"Who does the offense pertain to?"

"Offense? No. Well, the *situation* is between Dr. Russell and myself."

"All right. What form do you need?" She tugs the top drawer open. "Sexual harassment? Hostile work environment?"

"Form?"

She pulls out a slew of them: orange, green, blue, red, purple—one for any and every offense under the sun. Oh god.

I leap forward and hold up my hands. "It's not like that."

She's skeptical.

"Did he force himself onto you or put you in a situation where you weren't comfortable?"

Well, that Prius console *was* digging into my ribs while we were making out yesterday.

"No. *NO.*" I shake my head vehemently. "Nothing like that. It was completely consensual—*enjoyable*, even."

She drops the forms onto her desk and arches a brow, clearly confused by my presence in her office.

I decide to explain what happened over the weekend, albeit giving an abridged version. Though I'd rather not, I even reluctantly mention the make-out session in his car, though I keep it PG.

When I'm done, her eyes narrow and I notice the heavy bags, the disheveled hair. Maybe I shouldn't have come.

"So...you're just here to let me know you two consensually kissed and it was 'enjoyable'?" She speaks slowly, as if talking to a toddler.

I sigh. Good. She gets it. "Exactly. Just in case it's against the company guidelines, or some kind of rule outlined in the employee handbook, that sort of thing."

"It's not."

Oh.

Huh.

She stuffs the forms back into the filing cabinet and slams it shut.

Oddly enough, I'm disappointed that she's not going to forbid the relationship. "Is there any way you could double-check for me?"

Her eyes cut to the mountain of paperwork on her desk. Her computer pings with three new incoming emails. A woman skids to a stop in her doorway, breathing heavily, and announces that two nurses are at each other's throats on floor three.

She groans and moves to round her desk so she can take care of the situation.

I try to block her from passing by me. "So there's nothing you can give me? No angry orange form? No warning on my employee chart?" I chuckle like, *Ha ha, help a sister out here.* But no. She leaves and I'm left to stand in that HR office contemplating the twisting feeling in my gut.

I'm only now realizing I wanted our relationship to be against the rules. I couldn't sleep last night because I kept reliving Matt's kiss, every excruciatingly perfect detail of it, and that's not okay. I liked my life before the kiss. I only had to worry about being good at my job and taking care of Josie. I don't like these feelings stirring inside of me, the queasy sensation, the fear of what could happen if we get too carried away. I don't have the luxury of a quick fling. My life is complicated enough as is.

Dammit.

I need one of those forms. Talk about a perfect buffer, a

clean break. I could have given Matt a beautifully eloquent speech about valuing my position here too much to break the rules, but this HR lady gave me nothing. Not even a stern talking to.

I decide I have to take matters into my own hands.

MATT IS IN his office when I go searching for him. We have a case in a few hours and he's probably about to round with his resident, but this shouldn't take too long.

He's sitting behind his desk looking like Dr. Matthew Russell, foremost spinal surgeon, Hotty McHotpants. I think he got a haircut yesterday. His dark locks are trimmed short on the sides, thicker and fashionably mussed on top. They want to curl so badly, but they're not long enough. He's wearing his white coat. Underneath, his shirt is pale blue—a shade darker than his eyes. He shaved this morning, which means there's nothing between me and that perfectly smooth jaw.

His focus is on a file spread open on his desk. The side of his finger drags back and forth along his bottom lip as he reads.

I remind myself why I'm here and tell myself to get it together. Then, before his image can hypnotize me all over again, I knock loudly on his door and clear my throat as I step inside.

He glances up and his welcoming smile is like an arrow to my heart. I even stutter to a stop as if it were a physical blow.

He casually assesses me from head to toe before returning to the file.

"Morning Bailey."

His tone is warm and I wish his white coat were baggier. That stupid tailor of his really knows what he's doing. Would it kill him to let out the seams a little bit? Give a girl a break.

It occurs to me that I'm standing silent, talking to myself in my head, and he's waiting for some explanation as to why I'm in his office at this time of morning.

I clear my throat again and shake out the piece of paper in my hand.

"Yes, hello, Dr. Russell. I apologize for the interruption. I just needed to give this to you."

Good. My tone says I'm all business, and he catches the hint. Kind of.

His sly smirk says otherwise as he holds out his hand to accept the paper.

"You'll see that it's a contract," I explain.

His brows spike with interest and he stifles a grin. Dammit. Why does he look so amused by this? I'm serving him with papers!

"Just to sum it up for you, it's a legal document that states very plainly that we cannot date."

He nods. "I see that. 'Heretofore there shall be no touching or kissing of any kind.'"

Okay, yes—I Googled legalese on my phone.

He continues, "'Henceforth, Dr. Russell shall refrain from any suggestive smiles or flirting.'" He nods solemnly as if taking it very seriously. "Oh, I see. *Henceforth*. In that case..."

"Yes, and then it goes on to say—"

"'The plaintiff, Bailey Jennings, shall refrain from appearing or acting irresistible so as to not tempt Dr. Russell.'"

I'm not sure what plaintiff actually means, but I needed

a fancy word there.

"The document came straight from HR," I explain.

He wipes away his smirk. "Ah yes, it does sound like Linda."

I throw up my fists as if cursing the gods. "Ugh, if only there were some other way."

"Bailey." His voice takes on a serious tone and his eyes are earnest and sincere. Warning bells ring in my head. "You didn't have to do this. If you don't want to pursue anything with me then—"

"Good morning, Dr. Russell!" the resident sing-songs behind me. "I have your coffee right here, and don't worry, I didn't add any creamer to it this time."

Yes! What impeccable timing. I could kiss the man. Matt has to put a pin in whatever he was about to tell me. Good—I don't want to know. I want to pretend he's just a surgeon and I'm just his assistant, nothing more. In fact, I have work to do.

I make a move to slip out of the room. "See you in the OR!"

"Aren't you forgetting something?"

I glance back up and watch as Matt scribbles across the signature line of the contract then holds it out for me to take. I step forward and his gaze never wavers. When I try to pry it out of his hand, he doesn't let go. He indicates for me to lean closer so he can tell me something.

I have no choice. I have to lean down or risk him speaking loudly enough for the resident to hear.

"I don't regret Sunday and you shouldn't either."

HELLO! DOES HE KNOW HOW TO WHISPER?

I force out a hearty, fake laugh and shake my head. "Oh, Dr. Russell, you're so funny. I have no idea what you're talking about. Have fun on your rounds!"

197

Then I break out into a nice, brisk jog and I don't stop until I'm tucked safely inside the employee break room. As soon as I have time, that contract is getting laminated. Twice. If my heart is reacting like this from a few innocuous words, imagine how I'd feel if he tried to kiss me again?!

I get busy with preparing for our surgery, jumping into work with my full attention. It feels like it's been ages since I've been in an operating room, when really, it's only been two days. I make sure I prep everything to the best of my ability, and since I have a few minutes to kill before we get started, I review the case again so I absolutely know it by heart. There will be no crying, no spilled instruments, and no reason for Matt to shout at me today.

I half-expect him to continue the little charade from his office when he steps into the operating room later. In fact, I'm shaking with anticipation. I chance a quick peek up into the gallery and there have to be at least forty people shoved in there like sardines, excited to watch their version of Michael Jordan operate today. I hope he doesn't say anything to me that they might overhear. I take my job seriously and don't want my abilities in the operating room to be overshadowed by salacious gossip about whether he and I are getting it on—especially considering we aren't, in fact, getting it on.

At least not yet.

Oh my god STOP THINKING ABOUT GETTING IT ON.

When he pushes through the swinging door, I go perfectly still, though internally, my thoughts are more erratic than ever. *YOU HAD YOUR MOUTH ON THAT MAN. YOU MOANED, YOU TUGGED HIS HAIR, YOU—*

His eyes sweep across the room and crash straight into

me. I catch a hint of mischief behind his gaze, but it's gone before I really get a good look. He finishes checking in with his staff and I'm left holding up his gown and waiting for him to step toward me.

His mask and headlamp are in place. I can only see a sliver of his face and fortunately, it's the same for me. I like that I get to hide behind the mask on days like this when my emotions are brewing right at the surface.

"And how about you, Bailey? Is everything set?"

I nod. "Yes."

Then he addresses the room. "All right then. Our patient today is Hunter Larson. Ten years old. He was diagnosed with adolescent idiopathic scoliosis. He has a curve in his spine we're going to try to correct with a posterior fusion. I'll be placing rods and pedical screws from C5 to L4. Does everyone agree?"

His eyes lock with mine. I swallow and then speak up along with everyone else.

"Agreed."

He nods and steps up to the operating table. "Then let's get started."

When I say Dr. Russell is focused during the surgery, I mean it. We don't talk about a single thing that doesn't pertain to the patient, an instrument, or medicine. He executes a fusion that could make first-year residents fall to their knees and weep. His every move is meticulous and thoughtful. On top of that, there's no shouting, no snide comments on his end if I'm not as quick as he thinks I should be. He even stays to help me close so we scrub out at the same time. I swear to God, people stand and slow clap in the gallery as he exits the OR. *That's* how good he was.

I'm a little in awe of him, even now. We're alone,

scrubbing out side by side. I feel like I'm standing next to a celebrity. I tell myself to stop stealing glances at his forearms. They're nothing special. I repeat: NOTHING SPECIAL.

"You did well today," he says, breaking the silence. His voice has the same effect as a finger running down my spine.

I smile. "Careful, that almost sounded like a compliment."

I peer at him from beneath my lashes. He's smirking, but his attention is down on his hands as he rinses them under the faucet. "I'm trying something new: letting my assistants and nurses know I appreciate their hard work."

My eyes widen. "Color me shocked."

He finishes, grabs a towel, and rests his hip against the sink so he can assess me while he dries his hands. "Okay, now that we're done with that, I have a question."

Oh no.

I scrub extra hard, cheeks flooding with color. "What?"
Where's that blasted resident now?!

"Did that contract say anything about us being friends?"

My stomach flutters. "Oh, well…yes. That was in addendum two. I—I mean, *Linda* thinks that would be okay."

He laughs and shakes his head. I don't think he knows what to do with me.

"You're something else, Bailey."

I nibble on my bottom lip, trying to fight back a smile.

"Just for the record…" I finish washing my hands and he hands me a fresh towel. "I don't regret Sunday either. It's just…"

He holds up his hands as if he gets it. "Hey, no need to explain. The contract did a pretty good job of that." Then he holds out his hand. "Friends?"

I have to accept—any woman in her right mind would accept that outstretched hand—but the moment we touch, my gut clenches. It's like we're right back in his car, tearing at each other's clothes, lost in lust. It feels so intense just to have his palm against mine my knees nearly buckle. I forget he's waiting for me to speak until the dimple pops beside his mouth. He feels what I'm feeling. He knows there's no way we're just friends, which is exactly why he's proposing the idea in the first place. This is a game to him, just like the contract was a game to me.

His eyes say, *I know you want me to kiss you, but I'll bide my time and play along.*

I thought I was taking care of the situation by serving him with those papers. I thought it would give me the buffer I was so desperately seeking, but now I know it's too little too late.

Dr. Russell wants me, and there's a pretty good chance he's going to get me.

CHAPTER NINETEEN
MATT

I SHOULDN'T HAVE signed that damn contract. It was fake—obviously. Legally binding documents don't usually start with the phrase *To whom it may concern*. Nonetheless, it's still important. Bailey obviously freaked out after our kiss. I get it. It's not as if I've been flirting and courting her for weeks. There was a steep transition between us going from distant coworkers to lust-filled lunatics making out in my car, me tearing at her clothes like a bear. Just because I'm ready for more doesn't necessarily mean she is.

I want to make sure she doesn't feel pressured. I want to respect her wishes and give her the space she's clearly after. The trouble is, I'm not sure I can. Before we kissed, I might have written Bailey off as a passing fancy—a beautiful woman, yes, but not necessarily someone I should get involved with—but now, it's different. How am I supposed to forget what it felt like to have her kiss me like she was dying for it, like she couldn't get enough?

I catch her watching me in the operating room, the furtive glances she thinks I don't notice. When our eyes lock, her cheeks flood with color. When my hand accidentally brushes against hers as she passes me an instrument, she acts like I just whispered a sweet nothing in her ear.

She's a mess. After our surgery on Monday, she bolts as soon as possible. There's no chance to pull her aside or have a private moment.

On Wednesday, she comes to find me in the doctors'

lounge. She's standing in the doorway, wringing out her hands and catching the notice of a few of my colleagues, not necessarily for the right reasons. She's still in her navy scrubs and though she isn't trying to be, she's adorable. Blonde ponytail. High cheekbones. Dark lashes. When she catches sight of me, she smiles, and now she's not just adorable, she's drop-dead gorgeous.

I wish she had to wear my name embroidered on her scrubs in size 48 font.

"You can come in, you know," I say as I approach. "No one will shout at you."

She laughs but stays perfectly poised right where she is. I'm not sure she believes me. "Yeah, right. This place might as well have a red carpet leading up to it and a bouncer by the door." Her eyes widen over my shoulder. "Oh my god, is that a chocolate fountain in the corner?"

I turn and sure enough, it is. I'm slightly embarrassed.

"*Jesus*," she says under her breath. "Do you guys get your lunches catered every day?"

I shrug. "It's easier that way. None of us have time to brownbag it."

She snorts and shakes her head. "You know the vending machine in our lounge doesn't even accept dollar bills anymore? We have to go get change from the gas station down the street if we want a candy bar."

I smirk. "Did you come up here to campaign for a new vending machine?"

"No." She rolls her eyes then glances down at my plate. "Come *on*. Is that Boston cream pie?"

"It is. Want some?"

"No, I really shouldn't…okay, maybe just a bite."

I hand her the plate. "Here, take it. I'll get another slice. What did you want to talk to me about?"

She dips her pinky in the cream and brings it to her mouth to get a taste. It's innocuous, casual, and yet I'm staring at her lips as they pucker around her finger with such intensity it's a wonder they don't go up in flames.

"Matt?"

"What?"

"Did you hear what I just said?"

"Not at all."

She groans playfully. "I was asking if it would be okay if I knocked off a little early on Friday? I need to take Josie to a doctor's appointment."

I frown and shake away my errant thoughts. "Of course. I'll have someone fill in if my surgery runs long. What's wrong with Josie?"

"Oh, nothing. It's just a wellness visit."

"Good. Okay. Do you need a ride? You can use my car."

She seems taken aback by the offer. "No. Her doctor isn't far from our house, a ten-minute bus ride, tops."

"Let me know if you change your mind."

She's looking up at me as if I just offered to give her the shirt off my back.

"Why are you looking at me like that?"

She's smiling now, full-fledged, dimpled, I-know-something smile.

"Do you offer your car to all your employees?"

I wave away her insinuation. "Sure. It's nothing. Patricia drives it all the time."

She cracks up. We're still hovering in the doorway to the lounge and there are doctors trying to get past us, but they can fuck off because I haven't had an honest-to-God conversation with this woman in three days and I signed a stupid contract that forbids me from kissing her, but in this moment, that's all I want to do. I want to tug on that ponytail until her head tilts back and her chin tips up. She'd have to go up on her tiptoes a little, but I'd bend down and make it easy for her. It'd be better than the last one, I know it. I wouldn't have the constraints of a small car working against me.

Her knowing smile wipes clean. Her eyes widen. Her lips part. *Oh yes, Bailey.* I signed that stupid contract, but that doesn't erase these feelings. You're wetting your bottom lip because you're thinking the same thing I am. You're desperate for it and I wish you could see the shade of pink on your cheeks right now.

"Thank you for understanding, Dr. Russell."

I laugh and shake my head. I'm Dr. Russell again, like a name change will keep me at arm's length.

"Is that all?" I ask, brow arched.

She shakes her head no then nods yes, turns, looks back. "Yes. Okay. Thank you for the dessert. I'm going to go now."

She starts walking.

I tip forward, leaning out of the lounge. "The elevator is that way, Bailey."

She does an about-face. "Right. I knew that. I'm just going to…"

She doesn't finish her sentence before she promptly bolts. I laugh and turn back to finish my lunch.

She won't last another week.

WE FINISH UP the surgery on Friday on time so Bailey doesn't miss Josie's doctor's appointment. I offer her my car again, but she insists she doesn't need it. It's snowing outside, not a blizzard, but enough that I don't like the idea of her and her sister waiting at a bus stop.

I check the weather on my computer in my office, scowling when I see the little image of snowflakes falling from clouds every hour for the rest of the day.

I curse and it must be pretty loud because Patricia pokes her head into my office. "What is it?"

"Do we not pay Bailey enough? Why can't she get a damn car?"

"What are you talking about?"

She's confused, for obvious reasons.

I sigh and try to get back to my paperwork so I can get out of the office at a decent time. This is slightly hilarious on my part. I pretend like I want to hurry up and finish so I can leave and enjoy my life, but this *is* my life. In the last few years, I've spent more time in this office than I have at my house. I ignore that cold hard truth and forcefully open the file on my desk.

For the next hour, I work for fleeting moments between checking the weather, looking at my phone, glancing out the window, and then chiding myself for being distracted. At this rate, I won't finish my work until Monday.

The office clears out. Patricia scolds me for staying late on her way out, and yet here I sit, throwing my toy basketball up in the air and catching it over and over again. It's helping me think. Also, it's keeping my hands occupied. For some insane reason, I have the urge to pick up the phone and call Bailey. Her cell phone number is in her file, which is still housed in my desk drawer. I wrote it down on a sticky note and stuck it to the edge of my computer screen. It's taunting me.

I want to check in and see if she got home okay.

The phone call would be short, just a few seconds

really.

I reach for my phone and dial her number before I think better of it.

She answers after a few rings.

"Hello?"

Her voice sounds different.

"Bailey?"

"No. This is Josie. Bailey's in the shower. Who's this?"

I sit up and reposition a few papers on my desk, not sure how to proceed. I should hang up, but instead, I reply, "This is Dr. Russell."

"NO WAY. Hold on." Then she tilts her head away from the phone and shouts, "BAILEY HURRY UP— YOUR HOT DOCTOR IS ON THE PHONE!"

There's rustling on her end and muffled conversation.

"I don't believe you," Bailey says, clearly enough for me to hear. She must be out of the shower now. "You're not funny."

"Oh my god. She thinks I'm playing a prank on her," Josie says to me.

"Josie, you're not even that good at acting," Bailey continues. "I know no one is on the phone."

Josie laughs. "I swear he is! Here."

There's more rustling and I assume Josie is handing her the phone because a moment later, Bailey speaks, and it's much easier to hear her now. "Ha ha, very funny," she says, sounding confident she's caught Josie in a lie. "Hello Dr. Russell, I'm *so* happy you called because I was just daydreaming about you in the shower."

I chuckle and she screams.

"There *is* someone on the phone!" she shouts.

"I told you!" Josie responds.

Bailey clears her throat, attempting to compose herself. When she speaks again, it's calm and measured. "Um, hello?"

"Bailey? It's Matt."

"Oh hello, Dr. Russell. Please ignore everything I just said. I was just joking about the, err…daydreaming."

I smirk and decide to go easy on her. "I was just calling to see if you got home okay in the snow."

"Really?" She seems shocked.

"It looked like it was getting pretty bad out there," I say, suddenly self-conscious. I look out the window and there's not a hint of snow on the ground. It melted as quickly as it fell.

"Yup. Safe and sound," she says before speaking inaudibly to Josie. There's a heavy groan and then a slammed door. "Sorry, I was just kicking my little sister out of my room."

I lean back in my chair and stare up at the ceiling. "Does she answer your phone often?"

"She doesn't have a phone of her own, and she must have been browsing Instagram when you called. She's obsessed with the Hadid sisters."

"Who?"

"The models? Oh whatever. I won't keep you. We're back home. Thanks for checking in on me."

"Wait!" I don't want her to hang up. "How did Josie's appointment go?"

She's slow to respond, like she's not quite sure she wants to. "Fine. Though she likes to complain about my cooking, she's growing normally and all that. Did you honestly just call to talk about this stuff or is there something else?"

Oh, you want the truth? The truth is that I'm alone in

209

my office on a Friday night and maybe that used to be enough to satisfy me, but now suddenly, it's not. I want to know what pajamas you're going to put on now that you're out of the shower. I want to know what you'll make for dinner, if you'll watch a movie after or if you'll hang more candy canes on that stupid tree. I want to know what it feels like to kiss you again, but you won't let me so I'm calling you under the guise of checking in and maybe I'm more transparent than I think because I don't say any of this and I'm pretty sure you still hear it because your tone softens when you speak again.

"Is everything okay, Matt?"

I jerk forward and shake my head. "It's fine. I'll see you at work on Monday."

I slam the phone down onto the receiver.

CHAPTER TWENTY
BAILEY

AFTER MATT HANGS up on me, Josie and I dissect his call from every possible angle.

Maybe he just really wanted to make sure we got home okay.

Maybe he had something important to tell me but he chickened out.

Maybe it was just a friendly call, nothing more.

Friendly. Friends. Friend. I suddenly hate the word in all its forms.

I spend the rest of the weekend thinking of him when I shouldn't be. I consider how nice it was for him to offer up his car and to let me leave early on Friday. I think of how sexy he sounded on the phone. His voice was rich and deep, unforgettable. I make homemade Boston cream pie, savoring it for as long as possible only because it reminds me of him. It's stupid, I know. When Josie eats the last of it on Sunday night, I nearly weep.

I think I'm losing it.

I wonder if repressing sexual attraction can turn you into a crazy person.

Honestly, if I'd known he would respect my wishes in regards to that contract, I would have thought about it a little more before I forced him to sign it. I was overwhelmed. A lot had happened in a short amount of time and maybe I was a little scared. I wanted a chance to assess the situation with a clear head, but my head is anything but clear. If anything, it's foggier than ever, filled with thoughts of Matt and our kiss and annoyance over the fact that he's actually abiding by the terms of that phony contract.

It's Monday and we're in the middle of operating and I'm trying very hard to keep my focus on the procedure, but it's not easy. Today's case is more routine than most. I could assist him with my eyes closed, which means my mind is wandering in ways it shouldn't be. I want to know how Matt spent his weekend. He's a handsome guy. His scrubs do nothing to dull the rugged, masculine strength pluming off him like smoke. In this setting, he's a god. I wonder what women think of him out in the normal world. If he went to a bar, there's no way he'd go home alone. The thought makes my stomach turn. I wonder if he ever visits Smooth Tony's. It's right across the street. I bet he goes there to unwind after a long day. After all, that's where he was going to meet Cooper all those weeks ago.

If he sat alone at the bar, women would flock to him. He'd have to beat them off with a stick.

I feel queasy and suddenly I need answers.

"Did you have a good weekend, Dr. Russell?" I ask, adrenaline coursing through my veins.

He eyes flick up to mine. The surgical glasses do nothing to temper his piercing blue gaze. "It was fine. Productive."

Productive?! What does that mean? Did he sleep with *more* than one woman? I feel faint.

"Oh yeah?" I persist. "Did you get a lot of *work* done?"

"Yes." One word. I hate him. "Can you pass me that Bovie?"

I do as he asks, but I still continue my quest because now I'm a dog with a bone.

"Ah, well, that's good. I bet you had plenty of time to

unwind too…outside of the office."

His dark brow arches, but he continues to focus his attention on the patient. "It seems like you're dancing around a question, so just ask it."

I shake my head. "No, no. Just trying to get a better sense for how you spend your free time. Y'know, trying to make pleasant conversation."

He follows that with a disinterested hum and nothing more.

By the end of the surgery, I'm a ball of anxiety and repressed rage. If he spent his weekend with another woman, I want to know about it. *NO. I don't*, I tell myself. I'm going crazy. I made him sign a contract outlining all the ways he could not touch or flirt or kiss me, and now I'm the one outraged at the idea of him touching, flirting, or kissing another woman. I'm aware that I've done this to myself, but what does that matter because when I finish scrubbing out and walk into the hallway, I spot him chatting with a pretty nurse.

Oh god. I'm going to throw up.

I really am. She's put together in a way I'll never be for a standard work day—curled hair, loads of mascara. I self-consciously tighten my ponytail as I continue toward them. I wish I could turn in the opposite direction, but they're right by the elevators and the stairwell is creepy as hell, so I steel myself, square my shoulders, and continue walking.

She steps closer to him and drops her voice to say something, and my gaze flicks over in time to see Matt smile down at her. Considering how few smiles he's aimed at me in all our time together, I want to punch a hole in the wall.

I had no idea this hallway was so long. I can't speed up

because it'll look too obvious, but I swear I'm walking on a treadmill going nowhere. Maybe I could just sort of half-sprint, half-skip and no one would notice?

The nurse's hand touches his forearm and where is his white coat?! Usually he's in a suit or his surgical gown. Now, he's just wearing those navy scrubs and she could drag her hand up and down his tan arm if she wanted to. *Maybe she already has.* My face is a mask of horror at the thought.

I get within earshot and hear her say in a coy, flirty voice, "I was so surprised to see you there."

His response is inaudible.

My hands fist and I march right up to the elevators and press that button so hard my thumb aches. For good measure, I push it another dozen times.

"C'mon, c'mon," I murmur under my breath.

An imposing presence comes to stand beside me. Matt's scent makes my chest tighten. He's just a teensy bit closer than he should be. I stare straight ahead at the brushed steel reflecting our distorted images back at us. He stays perfectly still. There's nothing but silence. I wonder if he can sense how worked up I am. I have to force my fists to unclench. The numbers on the elevator blink in slow descension, and finally, the doors slide open.

I step inside and he follows. When the doors swoop closed, there's not an ounce of oxygen left in the small space.

We're the only two people in here. I press the button for the seventh floor and he presses nothing. I hole up in the corner, cross my arms, and stare straight ahead.

Matt turns as well so I'm only granted a view of his back. He's as cool as a cucumber. I wonder what he's thinking about—*her*, no doubt.

I'm shaking with jealous rage. I've never felt like this. I didn't know it was possible to be so worked up over something so little, and that only makes me angrier. I hate that I've turned into this person over a man who's clearly so uninterested he won't even turn around and address me.

I clench my teeth and snarky, antagonistic words fall out of me. "Honestly, if you're going to flirt with hospital staff, can you do it somewhere a little more private? Anyone could have seen you. It's just not really that professional."

He emits a little chuckle and shakes his head. His gaze stays pinned straight ahead.

Apparently, my remark isn't even worth a response.

"Where was she surprised to see you?" I ask, trying to engage him again.

The elevator dings, halts, and the doors slide open. A few people step in, and we're not at our floor yet, but our privacy is gone. My question lingers in the air between us, and now I have no hope of an answer. My heart is racing and there's no doubt everyone in the small space feels the tension simmering between us. I catch sight of a woman watching me, and I wonder if she can tell I'm currently in the throes of a jealous rage.

The elevator can't arrive on the seventh floor fast enough and when those doors slide open, I nearly tumble out, anxious for freedom. I gulp in a breath of air as if someone's been holding my head under water. A hand hits my elbow and I'm tugged painfully to the side of the hall, dragged inside what looks to be a supply closet. The door slams closed behind us. A mop gets wedged carefully beneath the door handle so no one can come in…and no one can get out.

Matt turns to me and I take a hesitant step back. With

215

only a little light filtering in from the hallway, his hard jaw and sharp features seem menacing and cruel. I'm standing in front of a ruthless surgeon—the man who makes grown men cry, the man who terrifies everyone who crosses his path.

"You made me sign that contract, Bailey," he says, stepping closer. "You insisted you wanted nothing from me, so why are you acting like this? Like you're jealous?"

My eyes widen. "I'm not!"

It's the most pathetic, transparent lie I've ever told. I'm a toddler with scissors and choppy bangs proclaiming she has no idea *who* cut her hair.

"You asked me what I did this weekend. Why do you want to know?"

I look away. "I already told you—I was making small talk."

"You're lying." I've never heard his voice quite so hard and challenging. "I ran into that nurse at the grocery store. She was shopping with her husband and daughter."

My cheeks burn and I desperately hope it's too dark in this tiny room for him to notice.

He takes another step forward and I hold up my hands as if to block him.

"I thought maybe you two were flirting," I admit, though it seems a bit too late for honesty.

"And if we were?" he asks, his tone as unyielding as it was a moment ago.

He has me wedged against a hard metal shelf. It digs into my back. Any moment now someone will need to get into this supply closet and notice that the door is jammed. The handle will shake and my heart will leap into my throat.

"Matt," I plead, suddenly genial and forgiving. "I'm

sorry. I shouldn't have let myself get so worked up over nothing. It was immature. I realize that. Now let me by and I promise I won't do it again."

The corner of his mouth lifts into a menacing smirk.

My insides liquify.

"Bailey," he says, reaching out to hook his finger underneath my chin. He tips my head up just a bit so my mouth is lifted to his.

I'm a shaking ball of anxiety at what he's about to do. He can't kiss me again. I'm still coming apart at the seams after the first one.

"I'd kiss you right now if I could." My chest is heaving as he continues speaking. No amount of air is enough air. "I'd bend down, just like this—"

His mouth hovers over mine. I feel the barest touch of his lips. Every hair on my body stands on end. My hands reach back and grip the metal shelf because without it, I feel like I'll float away.

"You want a kiss as badly as I do, and that's why you're wetting your bottom lip right now. That's why you're brushing your hips against mine." I immediately stop doing *both* of those things. "Your every desire is written across your face. *This face...*"

I stand perfectly still as he leans back and drags a finger around the edge of my forehead, down the curve of my cheek and chin, until he reaches the nape of my neck, and then lower...right to the V neckline of my scrub top. If he flattened his palm, my heart would corroborate his every word.

"You're flushed," he says as his smile turns condescending.

"And you're wrong," I insist, voice quivering. "You think I want you to kiss me? I'm *terrified* of you." His eyes spark as I continue, "You have all the power. If this doesn't work out, I'll be the one forced to find another job. When gossip spreads through the office, you'll look like a playboy and I'll look like the surgical assistant who couldn't keep her legs closed. I'm not going down this road until I'm absolutely certain it's what I want."

"And what about me? What if it's what *I* want?"

His hand curves around my throat and his thumb presses against my pulse. The action could seem threatening, but instead it's gentle and intentional. I think he wants to shake sense into me, but he doesn't. His eyes are locked with mine and there are a thousand emotions passing between us: longing, need, desire, want, jealousy, rage, and finally…impatience. I freeze as he tips his head down toward me again.

My heart soars and my breath catches as I brace myself for a soul-stealing kiss, but at the last moment—just before his mouth meets mine—he shifts and lets his forehead fall against the shelf beside me. His eyes pinch closed and he whispers my name like he's in pain then he slams his hand against the shelf and turns for the door. The mop is thrown aside and the sound of it clattering against the concrete reverberates around the closet as he storms out.

I'm shaking with residual panic.

It feels as if a bullet just whizzed past my ear.

I should be relieved more than anything, but the only emotion flooding my body at the moment is crushing disappointment.

CHAPTER TWENTY-ONE
BAILEY

I'M RESISTING MATT under the guise of being sensible and responsible. I tell myself I can't indulge my fantasies just because I might want to. I have to think about my future. I have to do what's best for Josie. I don't have the luxury of living solely for myself. It wasn't so long ago that I was worried about being out of a job. When Dr. Lopez retired, I was terrified of what would happen if I didn't find another position quickly. I remember what that uncertainty felt like, and I won't let burning-hot desire cloud my better judgment.

To curb temptation, I ban *Grey's Anatomy* from the house. Josie, of course, puts up a protest, but I don't listen.

"I can't watch it! I hate it! All those stupid doctors making out in storage closets. Guess what?! In real life, it's not so glamorous. Those metal shelves really hurt."

She stares at me with wide eyes and I hurry to amend my statement.

"At least, I assume they do…"

The following week is torture on par with waterboarding. I swear Matt wears scrubs that purposely accentuate his ass. He's tan and healthy while the rest of us are winter white. When he speaks, his voice has never sounded so deep and compelling. AND OKAY THE BEDROOM EYES HAVE GOT TO STOP. I'm boiling up inside.

I don't think Matt's faring any better than I am. Though he keeps his promise about treating his staff better, underneath his forced civility, I can tell he's a brooding mess. He might not be shouting orders at any of us, but he's still stomping around like he's angry at the world.

I give him a wide berth outside the OR so there's no chance of another steamy session in the storage closet, but it's hard work avoiding someone all day. When I get home from the practice, I have PTSD from looking over my shoulder and listening for his voice. I'm ready to collapse from exhaustion, but Josie only makes things worse by asking me about him incessantly. Now that I've banned *Grey's*, she's been checking out too many young adult romance novels from the library, and she's cast Matt and me as the main characters. Her questions might seem innocuous to someone else, but I know her tricks.

"Did surgery go well today?"

Yes.

"Was Dr. Russell there?"

Of course.

"Did he look handsome in his scrubs?"

Sure.

Every question is a little test to see how I'll respond. If I say he looked so hot I nearly wept, she'll accuse me of having a crush. If I say I barely noticed him, she'll accuse me of lying. So, I toe the line and attempt to seem unruffled whenever he's brought up, but of course, she sees right through it.

"You're so blind to matters of the heart, it's not even funny," she says to me one night over dinner before she walks away to continue reading, leaving me with the fallout of that emotional grenade.

The only respite I have is at the end of the day when I'm tucked in bed. I indulge myself by unpacking every moment I had with him that day, even if he was acting like an angry monster. It's better than nothing. I hoard every word and glance (okay, fine, every *glare*) he aims in my direction, and I dream about how it would be if things were different, if there were less on the line for me.

A few weeks after the supply closet incident, I overhear him speaking excitedly to Patricia in the hallway. I have my lunch in hand, en route to the staff lounge when I catch sight of him holding out a piece of paper for her to read. He's beaming from ear to ear. I haven't seen him look so happy since…well, ever. I freeze and stare, enamored by that smile and how it transforms his face. *Hello, Heart? Yes, it's me, Brain. Please control yourself.*

"It's an email from the grant committee," Matt explains proudly. "They're down to two proposals—mine and another one from an orthopedist in California."

Patricia beams. "That's awesome. When will they have the final decision?"

"Right after Christmas."

Of course, his grant—the thing I've heard so little about and the thing that must be weighing heavily on his mind. I know it's a big deal for him to be one of the final two nominees. I'm tempted to walk over and ask to read the email, but then he glances up and his gaze clashes with mine. Blue eyes pin me to my spot. In an instant, his smile fades. His eyes harden and any hope of congratulating him shrivels up and dies. I turn in the opposite direction and head for the stairwell. Creepy vibe or not, it's better than walking past him.

I'M LOOKING FORWARD to Christmas with equal amounts of excitement and trepidation. At the end of this week, the surgical department will close up shop for ten whole days so we can celebrate the holidays, but before everyone scatters across the country, the department will throw its annual Christmas party. It's always at a fancy location—a trendy restaurant or swanky hotel—and the food is worth stuffing myself into an uncomfortable dress. I always attend (re: food). Historically, Matt doesn't, and chances are he won't be there this year either.

I'm not sure how I feel about that.

I'm also not sure how I feel about not seeing him for those ten days. Sure, it won't be so different than how it is now. We aren't currently talking outside of the OR. For weeks, he's treated me how he would treat any other employee. When he speaks to me—and it's only ever about work—his tone is detached and aloof. He's not being rude, per se, but compared to the warmth I got from him when we were on friendly terms, it's torture.

I'm sitting with a few other surgical assistants in the staff lounge over lunch, picking at my sandwich and trying not to visibly mope, when Erika elbows me in the side.

"You have a visitor."

I glance up, follow her gaze to the door, and freeze when I see Matt's imposing figure standing at the threshold. He's wearing his suit and white coat. There are files tucked under his arm. His piercing gaze is aimed right at me and my stomach fills with dread. I lurch to my feet and hurry over.

"Is something wrong with Hannah?"

She's the patient we operated on this morning and I'm worried if he's here, it's because something is going wrong with her recovery.

His brows furrow and he shakes his head. "No. She's doing well. A new case just came in and I need to speak

222

with you about it."

I let out the breath I was holding and nod quickly. "Oh, okay. Of course. Let me just go toss the rest of my lunch."

He holds up a to-go box. "It's fine, you can finish it—we'll eat while we talk."

Then he takes a step into the lounge and I swear every person's breath catches from shock. Doctor's don't eat in here. They have chocolate fountains and catering. We have plastic utensils and Cup of Noodles.

If he's aware of everyone's attention on him, he doesn't seem to care. He claims an empty table in the corner, drops the files that were clutched under his arm, and makes himself at home. The silence in the lounge continues as I walk to gather my meager lunch and head over to join him. All eyes are on me. I'm sure everyone's wondering what's going on, why he would deign to grace us with his presence.

I shake off their attention and try to focus on Matt. If he's here, willing to talk to me, the case must be pretty important.

I sit down across the table and see he's already laid out a few pieces of paper for me to read, his lunch forgotten, so I follow his lead and forget about mine too.

"A colleague of mine in Chicago emailed me this morning about an emergent case," he says, launching straight into work. "A nineteen-year-old female presenting with extreme kyphosis and compression of her spine. She should have had surgery years ago, but her doctors and her parents chose to prioritize her other health concerns."

I frown and lean forward to read her file. "What other health concerns?"

"Leukemia." My breath hitches and I glance back up at him. His frown is deep as he continues, "They haven't

223

completely ignored her spine issues. She's been wearing a brace for the last year and a half, but it's no use—"

"She's too old," I conclude.

He nods with a grim frown. "Had they used a brace when she was younger, she might have stood a chance at foregoing surgery, but now it's a necessity."

"Why now? Why is this emergent?"

He pushes a document toward me, but the mass of words means nothing to me. I don't even know what I'm looking at. Then one word at the very top of the page jumps out at me: paraplegia.

"Because as of last week, June can't walk." My hand flies to my mouth before I can stop it. "The curvature of her spine is extremely severe. She's complained of numbness and paresthesia in her legs for the last few months. Last Monday, her symptoms intensified to the point of paraplegia. She's lost all motor function in both of her legs."

All I can think is, *Poor June.* To have endured leukemia only to now deal with this.

"What can be done?"

He gathers the papers in a neat pile and I watch as sheer determination sparks in his gaze.

"The paraplegia is a symptom, not a life sentence. Her spine needs to be decompressed to alleviate the pressure on those nerves. Hopefully, after the inflammation goes down, she'll regain motor function."

"Is your colleague in Chicago going to take the case?"

He shakes his head. "It's not his specialty. Even if it was, June's body has been through hell with chemo and radiation. There are additional risks. Most surgeons wouldn't take this on."

But Matt will. He has to.

His gaze meets mine and he must sense what I'm thinking because a moment later, he nods. "Her parents are bringing her here on the next flight out of Chicago. If we're going to do this, I'll need your help."

There's no hesitation.

I nod emphatically. "Yes. Of course."

I HAD NO idea what I was agreeing to. The moment I nod, he stands, tells me to gather my stuff, and we head back to his office. Patricia is standing at her desk as we approach, hurriedly writing on a notepad with her office phone pressed to her ear.

When she spots us, she tells the person on the line to hold on, presses the phone to her chest, and then launches into an update for Matt. "Dr. Buchanan is on line one. Dr. Mills says he'll call you back when he gets out of surgery. Dr. Goddard is still out for lunch, but I'll try to catch him when he gets back. Mr. and Mrs. Olsen will be on a flight with June from Chicago at 6:45 PM. I tried to get them a room at the hotel across the street, but it's booked with holiday travelers. I'm talking to another hotel now."

Matt listens and nods as he proceeds into his office. "Have Bailey take over the hotels. I need you to finish clearing my schedule. Push everyone you can into the new year. They'll protest—I'm sure they've all met their deductibles, but assure them we'll work with their insurance companies and figure something out." He continues inside, raising his voice so we can hear him. "They won't have to pay anything additional. I'll see to it." He turns back to address me. "Bailey, when you're done booking the hotel, can you help Patricia with rescheduling my patients?"

I nod and scurry to take the phone from her.

I have no idea what I'm doing. I need to book a hotel for the patient's family? Do we normally do that sort of thing?

"How many nights will they be in town?" I ask, gaze flicking back and forth between them.

"Start with four," Matt answers, tone hard and authoritative, before he picks up his phone.

The afternoon and evening pass in a blur. I barely have time to let Josie know I won't be home in time for dinner. It's nearly impossible to find lodging for the Olsens. Hotels are booked, everyone is here to spend time with their family and enjoy the holidays. Matt goes so far as to shout through his door that they can just "damn well stay with him", but I eventually sweet-talk my way into getting the family a room only a few blocks from the hospital. The price makes my stomach turn, but Patricia assures me it's fine. I book it with Matt's credit card then jump on the phone to start rescheduling patients.

Matt has a hell of a time with his task as well. Between our calls, Patricia explains to me in whispered tones that he won't be able to do the surgery alone. He's looking for a neurosurgeon to assist. With what June's body has already endured, he wants to take every precaution.

He's on the phone trying to call in favors, but like everything else, the holidays are impeding things. Most surgeons have their own cases to finish up before the end of the year. They can't rearrange their entire schedules, drop everything, and fly across the country to help Matt.

I'm sitting at Patricia's desk, crossing through patients' names as I call and reschedule their consultations and pre-op appointments when Matt shouts for me to come into his office.

I jump out of my skin, drop my pen, and hurry inside. He's pacing by the window, his white coat long forgotten, his shirt sleeves rolled to his elbows. His tie is hanging on the back of his chair and his shirt is unbuttoned just enough for me to catch a sliver of his tan chest.

He rubs his forehead like he's trying to ease a tension headache and then turns to face me. I've never seen him so stressed. His brows are knit together. His jaw is locked tight. "I need you to go see if Dr. Perry is still in his office. He's down on level three. If so, tell him I need to speak with him immediately."

I nod and hurry out of the room, fully prepared to mow down anyone who happens to get in my way, but the hallway is deserted. Dr. Perry's office is dark and empty, which seems strange until I glance down at my watch and realize it's half past eight. We've been going so nonstop I didn't even realize it was so late.

I drag my feet walking back to Matt's office. I don't want to be the one to tell him his colleague already went home. I have a feeling he might accidentally (on purpose) shoot the messenger.

"Dammit," he says after I tell him, and then he turns to face the window. He props a hand against the glass and stares out at the city covered in a blanket of snow. I'm torn on what to do. Give him privacy? Offer words of encouragement? I want to help, but I have no clue what he needs. He's been going full speed ahead all evening. It's a wonder he still has a voice after all the phone calls he's placed.

I stand immobile on the other side of his desk, giving him the chance to calm down while I desperately try to think of the right thing to say. I don't want to toss out some hollow phrase like *Have no fear! Everything will work out!* Because truthfully, I'm a little in over my head here. There's a pretty good chance this *won't* work out.

"Dr. Russell," Patricia says from the doorway, removing her glasses and rubbing her tired eyes. "I need to get home before the roads get any worse. I'll pick this back up first thing in the morning."

He doesn't turn from the window. "Of course. Yes. Go home and we'll finish tomorrow."

She frowns and heaves a resigned sigh before turning back to her desk to collect her things.

Matt and I stand there in silence for a long time, long enough for Patricia to leave, long enough for the quiet office to close in around us. I have the ludicrous urge to round his desk and wrap my arms around his middle and force him into a hug, but I stay right where I am, waiting for him.

He eventually speaks, turning to glance at me briefly before returning to his work. "You should go too. It's late."

He sounds so desolate and hopeless, my heart aches.

"And what will you do?"

He waves to the papers on his desk. "Stay here."

Of course. It might be late, but Matt still has plenty of work to do. I steel my spine and lift my chin, anticipating his response when I reply, "Then I'm staying too."

"No, it's late. You should go be with Josie."

Just as I expected. His rejection doesn't hurt because I was prepared for it. I step forward and take a seat in one of the chairs in front of his desk. He doesn't look up at me and he doesn't get back to work. His attention is pinned to a spot on his desk as he tries to work through a problem. I can practically see the weight of the world on his shoulders.

I take the hint and sit quietly, focused on the glowing

lights of the city behind him.

"Maybe I was crazy to think I could pull this off," he says finally, his voice nearly inaudible. "I told the Olsens I could do it and I've cleared my schedule, and yet—" He shakes his head and looks up at me, worry etched in his gaze. "Once I get in there and see what I'm working with, I might not be able to help her."

"I'm sure you've done similar cases," I venture.

He drags his hand through his hair, tugging on the roots, stressed and angry.

I won't let him give up on himself. If anyone can pull this off, Matt can. I lean forward and ask determinedly, "How can I help?"

"You can look through every one of those case files I pulled and find ones with CTs and MRIs that are comparable to our patient's." He's being sarcastic. He doesn't think I'm crazy enough to take on the task, but I push to my feet and turn to the stacks of files on the ground by his couch. They nearly reach my hip. "Bailey, I was kidding. Go home. I'll do that later."

It's too late. I'm kicking off my shoes and getting comfortable. I'm still wearing my scrubs from earlier. They're a little loose around my waist and pretty soft; I can totally trick myself into thinking they're pajamas. "So just look at the CTs and MRIs?"

"Bailey," he warns. "You don't have to do this."

I don't reply. I carve out a nice little spot on his couch, pick up a short stack of case files, and get to work.

He eventually leaves me to it, though he does think ahead and order some pizza. I insist he add on some warm chocolate chip cookies. Y'know, for morale.

I'm not a surgeon and I don't have the expertise Matt truly needs for this case, but he shows me exactly what to look for and it's not so difficult. He stays at his desk, working quietly. I'm too scared to ask him what he's doing, and besides, I'm here to help, not be a distraction. We eat our pizza while we work and I fight back a yawn. Josie texts me that she's too tired to wait up. I remind her to lock the doors before she goes to sleep. When I put my phone back down, I peer up at Matt from beneath my lashes. He's rubbing his finger back and forth along his bottom lip, eyes narrowed down at a file. He's lost in thought then he sighs and shakes his head, metaphorically balling up a piece of paper and tossing it in the trash. He flips a page and keeps reading. I should get back to work, but my eyes are tired from scanning image after image and they need a break.

He's my break.

He suddenly shifts in his seat, looks over, and I jerk my attention back to the file in my lap.

"What is it?" he asks.

My cheeks burn and I scramble for some excuse as to why I was staring at him. "Oh, I was just wondering if you had a blanket, by chance?"

It's a good deflection, and not totally out of thin air. I've been cold for the last thirty minutes.

He stands and grabs one from a small cabinet near his bathroom. I thank him with a smile and watch as he turns to grab his laptop from his desk before he comes back and claims the other half of the leather couch.

"My back was getting sore," he explains.

I nod and stay quiet. It feels like it could be intimate with us sitting so close, but the couch is big enough that we aren't in danger of touching.

I start to tuck the blanket around myself, only becoming aware of his gaze on me after I'm halfway done fully cocooning myself.

I blush. "Oh, do you want some blanket too?" I ask, holding up one corner for him. It isn't that big, and with me hogging most of it, he'd only be able to cover a few of his toes, maybe his ankle if he really tugged hard. He must appreciate my meager offer though because he smiles in amusement before shaking his head.

"I'm good. You take it."

He doesn't have to tell me twice. I wrap that soft blanket around myself and revel in the fact that it smells just like him. I reach for a case file and attempt to get back to work. It's hard now that my stomach is full of pizza and cookies and I'm extra cozy on his couch, with his blanket.

I haven't checked my watch in a while because I'm scared to look at the time, but I know it's late. Sleep is calling my name, and I do my best to stave it off, even jerking back awake after my eyes flutter closed of their own accord. It's no use, though. I tell myself I'll only rest my eyes for a few minutes, nothing more.

CHAPTER TWENTY-TWO
MATT

IT'S LATE. MY brain is fried. Bailey's slumped against the couch, asleep, and I'm tempted to join her. I need to get some rest before tomorrow, but with her huddled up, she's hogging most of the couch. For a small person, she really knows how to spread out. I kick off my shoes and set my laptop on the ground. She stirs and snuggles farther under the blanket. Any hope of wrestling some of it away from her flies out the window.

I could sleep on the floor, but I know my body will hate me for it in the morning. The couch is big enough. I shift her so she's a few inches closer to the edge and then I fill in the space behind her. Now her feet are near my head and vice versa. It's the only arrangement that will work. I keep expecting her to wake up, but apparently, she's a heavy sleeper.

I'm scared she's going to roll off, so I wrap my arm around her knees and prop my other arm up under my head like a pillow. It's not that comfortable, but it's...nice. It's the first time I've felt some semblance of calm since I agreed to take on this case.

I have a meeting with the hospital's legal team in the morning. Apparently, they caught wind of the situation and have a few issues they'd like to discuss before things go any further. There's a pretty good chance I won't like what they'll have to say, but I'll worry about that in the morning.

Bailey stirs and sits up, wiping her eyes.

"Matt?" she asks sleepily.

I hum.

"Are you comfortable? Here." She takes the blanket and splays it out over me. "This isn't big enough for us both. I should go home—"

She starts to move off the couch but I keep my hold on her legs. "Don't." She pauses and my attention drags up from her mouth to her questioning gaze.

It's late. I have no business thinking about kissing her, but I am. I'm imagining what it would feel like if she put her lips on mine, how easy it would be to untie those scrub pants and tug them down her legs.

"I won't stay if you keep looking at me like that." I quirk a brow and she shakes her head. "Fine, okay, but I'm going to flip around so we're both lying that direction. My feet probably smell."

I smile, but I don't protest. I lift the blanket and help her shift around so her head is only a few inches below mine. She plays at keeping a little distance between us, but the couch isn't big enough for that. I reach out and tug her close. Now she's nestled against my chest. Our legs are tangled. Our bodies are molded together and whatever need for sleep I felt moments ago is gone. Her soft curves and the feel of her hand pressed against my heart sends a shot of adrenaline through me. My palm rests against the small of her back under the guise of keeping her on the couch, but it brings her hips against mine and now she can feel how she affects me. We've done nothing but touch and I'm starved for her.

Her nervous gaze shifts up to mine and there's apprehension there.

If this were any other time, if she weren't half-drugged with sleep, she'd pull away and insist on putting space between us. I almost feel like I'm taking advantage of her, but she's here, isn't she? She's the one who insisted on staying and helping. Even though the temptation is killing me, I won't seduce her. My hands will stay exactly where they are and I'll only drop one chaste kiss against her forehead before telling her to go to sleep.

"Good night Matt," she says, her voice soft and sweet.

I stay awake a long time after her eyes flutter closed, studying her features and letting the rhythm of her heart steady my own. It's enough to have her in my arms. It's the peace I've been craving, the quiet calm that's been missing from my life since those early years with Victoria, and maybe not even then. I wasn't in need of a partner when I was younger like I am now. I was so focused on proving myself as a student and a resident, and then as a fellow. I regret the way I handled things with my ex-wife, but I don't regret that we went our separate ways. I can't recall ever lying awake and appreciating Victoria's presence like this, feeling grateful just to be near her.

Bailey's ponytail is loose and most of her blonde hair spills out around her. I can smell her shampoo. It's feminine and sweet and makes my stomach ache with need. I hate that tomorrow is an important work day. I want to jostle her awake and ask her about her life, about the hardships of the last few years and the fear she must have felt when she took on the role of Josie's guardian.

In sleep, she looks so innocent and young, her freckles dotted across her cheeks. I have the sudden need to care for her like she's cared for her sister.

Who takes care of you, Bailey?

Who's your guardian?

BAILEY'S AWAKE BEFORE me the next morning and when I blink my eyes open, she's hurriedly trying to fix her appearance in front of my office's large windows. I chuckle and close my eyes again, craving a few more minutes of sleep.

"You can use my shower," I offer.

I don't have to look to know her head jerks in my direction. "You're awake!"

I hum and burrow deeper under the blanket. "Not willingly."

"Wait…you have a shower in here?" She scoffs. "You surgeons are seriously spoiled."

I groan and force myself to finally sit up. "Hurry if you're going to use it. I need to rinse off before my meeting with legal."

"What about your clothes? They're all rumpled from sleep. I think someone—er…not *me*, but *someone* definitely drooled on your shirt a bit."

I smile despite myself. "I keep a spare suit in the closet. This isn't the first time I've slept here."

I sweep my feet off the couch, prop my elbows on my knees, and rub the heels of my hands against my tired eyes.

"Oh." I look up to see her looking down at herself. "Any chance you keep a spare pair of women's underwear in there too?"

Laughter spills out of me before I can help it.

She throws up her hands in defeat. "Oh well, I'll deal with that after I shower. Would you mind running down to grab me a new set of scrubs? I don't want anyone to see me like this."

She looks adorable, but I don't think that's what she wants to hear at the moment.

"Sure. Child-sized, right?"

"Ha ha ha," she mocks, making her way to the bathroom. "For that, I expect you to bring me back some coffee too."

I get her a new set of scrubs and grab two cups of coffee from the doctors' lounge. When I get back, Bailey's still in the shower.

I knock on the door. "Hey, I got your scrubs. I'll set them right out here."

"Thank you!" she shouts back. "Oh and I hope you don't mind—I'm using your soap! I'm going to smell like a rugged mountain man too!"

In an instant, desire burns up any last vestiges of sleep. Bailey's in my shower, rubbing my soap all over her naked body. In another life, I'd open the door and join her. She'd turn to face me and her pale brown eyes would widen in shock. She'd blush from head to toe as I stalked toward her and pressed her back against the cold tile. She'd be shy, but we've kissed before and I know she'd come alive for me with a little coaxing. She'd meet me in the middle, grind against me, wrap a leg around my hip, hot and needy for more. I'd kiss her endlessly, tease and worship her until a single touch could push her over the edge.

My dick stirs to life just from thinking about it. I'm going mad for a woman who's made it clear she wants to keep things platonic and professional. I've respected those wishes up until last night. Sleeping on that couch together wasn't professional in the least, and I wonder if she regrets it now.

The shower cuts off and a few moments later, the door opens an inch and one of her hands juts out, searchingly wildly for her scrubs. Considering she isn't brave enough to crack the door open a smidge more and actually look for them, she doesn't have an easy time finding them. Her fingers catch nothing but dead space and I hear her groan.

"A little to the left," I say, amused.

Her hand finally lands on them.

"Got 'em!" she shouts triumphantly.

While she gets dressed, I move to my desk to drink my coffee so I don't look like I'm lurking around like a weirdo. I'm doing a very good job of pretending to be occupied when she steps out of the bathroom fully dressed with damp hair and a fresh face. She runs the towel through her hair and shakes it out. I sit with my coffee midway to my mouth long enough for her to scrunch her nose in confusion.

"What?" she asks.

My gaze drags down her body and catches on her bare feet. Her toenails are bright pink and she wiggles them when she notices me staring.

"Do you need socks? I have a spare pair."

Socks. Nothing sexual about socks. At least that's what I try to tell myself.

She eagerly accepts the offer and once I hand them off, careful to give us about three feet of breathing room, I disappear into the bathroom for a shower of my own. I turn the valve so cold the pipes are liable to freeze. The water shocks my system and douses my desire. I tell myself to think of ice-cold water and not Bailey's hot mouth. *Fuck.* I lather myself and rinse off quickly, in a hurry to get to work. I have more than enough to keep myself occupied today.

Of course, I'm the idiot who forgot to bring his clothes into the bathroom. Usually, I'm the only one in my office so I don't have to worry about it.

I move to the door and open it, about to warn her when I catch a hint of conversation. She's on the phone.

"Yes, I slept here…We had a lot of work to do…No, I didn't sleep with him! We ordered pizza and worked. It was nothing…Yes. I know you're on winter break, but try to do something productive today. What'd you have for breakfast?" She groans. "Eat some kind of vegetable with your lunch, will you?"

I decide it's as good a time as any to retrieve my suit. Her back is to me and she's distracted by her conversation with her sister. I step out and move to the wardrobe.

"I promise I'll be home in time—"

Her voice suddenly cuts off and I glance over my shoulder to find her staring at me with wide eyes and a gaping mouth. I look down to check and yes, my towel is still slung around my hips. I'm not flashing her, though she's looking at me like I am.

Her sister's voice carries through the quiet room. "In time for what? Hey! Are you still there?"

Bailey can't close her mouth. Shocking her wasn't my intention when I came out of the bathroom in only a towel, but it's a convenient side effect. Yes. *Good.* I shouldn't be the only one going crazy here.

Her gaze sears my skin, jumping from my biceps to my abs to my chest. Her tongue is in danger of rolling out of her mouth. My workouts are intended to keep me capable in the operating room, but I appreciate them even more now that Bailey can't take her eyes off me.

I offer her a little wave, and it's enough to shake her out of the spell my partial nudity put her under. She whips back around to face the wall and I finish grabbing my clothes.

"HELLO ARE YOU DEAD?" Josie shouts through the phone.

Bailey clears her throat. "No! I'm not dead. Sorry. I

was…busy there for a second." She sounds flustered. "What was I saying? Oh right, I'll be home in time to make dinner. I have to go now, bye."

She hangs up as I head back into the bathroom. Though it'd be fun, I think changing out here would push her over the edge. I'm not trying to cause permanent damage.

"Everything okay?" I ask when I'm finished.

She doesn't turn to face me. She tosses a thumbs-up over her shoulder and adds a, "You betcha."

"You seem flustered."

"Just maybe warn a girl next time you're going to prance around in nothing but a towel," she says, her tone high-pitched and strained.

"You were on the phone. I didn't want to interrupt."

"Okay, well," she says, continuing to address the wall instead of me. "If I can't meet your eyes the rest of the day, don't take it personally."

WHAT STARTED OUT as a pretty great morning takes a sharp turn for the worst when I arrive for my meeting with our in-house legal team. Four sour-faced old men with thick glasses, starched shirts, and deep-set wrinkles line one side of a conference table while I sit across from them. I haven't had much exposure to them over the years. They're employed to protect the surgeons and staff at the hospital, but right now, they're standing between me and my patient. Their counsel has droned on and on:

"This case is a legal nightmare."

"The liability isn't worth the potential benefits to your patient."

"We can't ensure that the hospital's malpractice

insurance would cover this lawsuit in the event of a negative outcome. Your other colleagues have voted against the surgery."

Ah, yes—the three other assholes who are supposed to have my back. Dr. Goddard, Dr. Richards, and Dr. Smoot want to leave my patient permanently paraplegic on the advice of a few scrooges in bad suits.

They're in the room too, sitting to the left of the lawyers in their white coats, though at present they don't exactly deserve to wear them. They're unable to meet my eyes when I glance over at them. If I could, I'd wring their fucking necks.

"I wasn't aware my colleagues had reviewed the case as thoroughly as I have," I bite out. "Not to mention, a case like this isn't exactly their specialty. I could get a dozen reputable surgeons who specialize in scoliosis fusions on the phone who would back me on this."

"Dr. Russell, you aren't thinking clearly."

The accusation comes from Dr. Richards. He's finally worked up enough courage to speak for himself, but the glare I shoot in his direction makes him turn his gaze right back to the conference table. He doesn't say another word.

"C'mon, Dr. Russell," Dr. Goddard says, sounding exasperated as he takes up the charge for his friend. "There's what, a 10% chance you'll be successful in this case? What about the other 90%? What if you injure her further, or *worse*?

"Think of how that would look for the practice. We don't need publicity like that. The local news has already picked up this story. They're touting you as the hotshot surgeon, a hero, but when you fail, what will they call you then? Huh?" He shakes his head and looks to the doctors on either side of him for backup. "You think we're telling you no because we're heartless, but you've lost sight of your own limitations. You're foolish if you think you're going to help that girl."

"Not to mention the cost of the surgery itself," Dr. Smoot chimes in. "You're talking about a figure well over a hundred thousand dollars. Our department has a certain amount set aside for pro bono cases, and you've maxed that out, Dr. Russell. How exactly do you plan on covering this case?"

I'm seething. I knew there might be some resistance from my colleagues, but I didn't think they'd take it this far.

I stand up and offer a tight-lipped smile to the room. "Thank you for the information, gentlemen, but my patient and her parents are due to arrive any minute. If you'll excuse me, I don't want to keep them waiting."

"Dr. Russell!" Dr. Goddard shouts, but I don't pay him any attention.

I'm still shaking with rage when I finish climbing the stairs back to the sixth floor. I slam open the door to the stairwell and storm into the hallway. Bailey's pacing a few yards away and when she catches sight of me, she beams.

"They're here! They just arrived! Patricia has them set up in the conference room."

As I step closer, the hope twinkling in her eyes only makes me angrier.

"Good," I reply dryly. "They've arrived just in time for me to inform them there won't be a surgery."

"What?!" she cries. "What are you talking about?"

CHAPTER TWENTY-THREE
BAILEY

I DIDN'T THINK we'd get here: standing in the operating room, seconds away from starting June's surgery. The room is quiet, tense. The low hum and periodic beeping of machines are the only break in the silence. I'm looking to Matt, waiting for his cue.

It's not just him and me at the operating table today. There's a second surgeon with us, a friend Matt completed his fellowship with—Dr. Mitchell. He took a red-eye to be here in time, and he's working for free. In fact, we all are; it was part of the negotiation Dr. Russell made with the hospital.

The other spinal surgeons are up in the viewing gallery now, watching us like hawks. Their stuffy lawyers sit behind them as cheerful as the four horsemen of the apocalypse, but other than that, the gallery is empty. It's strange considering this is a hallmark case in Matt's career. Residents should be clambering over one another to get a front-row seat.

Matt follows my gaze and shakes his head, correctly guessing my thoughts.

"They don't want an audience in the event that I fail." He laughs sardonically. "In their opinion, the fewer witnesses the better."

"Dr. Russell?" The anesthesiologist dips his head around the drape. "Is there a reason for the delay?"

We've already completed the time-out. There's no reason for us to be standing here motionless, but then, I'm not Matt. I haven't put my career on the line to take this case. I might have fought tooth and nail to be standing here with him, but if things go south, it's not my name on that surgical board. It's not me those parents will turn to, looking for good news about their daughter.

Matt clears his throat and glances up at the clock. "Right. If everyone is good to go, we'll begin." He reaches his hand out, palm up toward me. "Bailey, ten blade."

I WAS THE first one to meet June when her parents brought her into the hospital. Patricia needed to get back to the phones, and I was as good a point person as any. I was surprised by how happy she looked sitting in a wheelchair beside her parents. Happy and thin, her fragile frame seemed in danger of toppling over in a heavy wind, but there was a fierceness in her eyes that I could relate to.

I stood in that room while Matt explained to them the challenges he faced in performing the surgery. Not only did it come with a whole slew of risks, but on top of that, it would be extremely expensive.

After years of paying for cancer treatments by remortgaging their home, taking out loans, and maxing out credit cards, June's parents weren't in a position to offer much, but Matt was determined not to let that stop him.

On top of all that, we still had the hospital to contend with. Back in his office, Matt, Patricia, and I worked tirelessly, trying to come up with a solution that wouldn't involve Matt being slapped with a lawsuit from the hospital. I could tell he was at his wit's end, so I spoke up, throwing out a simple, ruthless suggestion.

"Why don't the other doctors and the legal team meet

her? They're the ones who don't want to do the surgery. Why should you have to be the one to tell her no? Make them do it."

It took some convincing, but between Patricia and me, we wrangled the three surgeons into the conference room. Dr. Goddard was the easiest to sway, though technically I did promise him it would just be him and me in there and maybe there were some suggestive hand gestures I'm not proud of.

Matt gathered everyone else, including the head of the surgical department, the person who really could make or break it for us.

I'd warned June what it might be like, that even after pleading her case, the hospital might still say no, but I soon realized I'd underestimated her sheer will to overcome the obstacles life had thrown at her.

Matt and I stood outside the conference room with her parents. June had requested to speak to the other doctors in private, a feat I'm not sure I'd have had the courage to do if I were her.

I watched as those eight men sat silently, listening as one brave girl fought for her right to have this surgery. I watched as tears gathered in her eyes, but they never fell. She spoke bravely, keeping it together just long enough to win her case.

When all three of the surgeons walked out of that room, I knew she'd convinced them to change their minds. I knew it even before Dr. Richards sighed and before Dr. Goddard lifted his head and offered Matt a resigned glare.

The head of the surgical department was the last person to leave, and he said simply, "I won't let the hospital eat the cost of this surgery."

"I never said it would," Matt said calmly, aware of how

close he was to winning. "I already have a team in place, willing to work for free. I'll cover the cost of supplies and any devices used during the procedure."

He shook his head and brushed past us, defeated.

I wanted to punch the air. Instead, I turned to Matt at the exact moment he turned to me, both our eyes saying, *HOLY SHIT! WE DID IT!* and in that moment, I could have flung my arms around his neck and kissed him senseless.

JUNE'S SURGERY IS long and meticulous. I've endured difficult surgeries with Matt before, but this is different. I've never seen him so tense. His attention to detail is only surpassed by his inability to trust himself. I can see it in the way he rolls his shoulders and when he tilts his head from side to side, as if trying to loosen himself up. He's let everyone's doubt seep into his head. He's worried about making a mistake. I want to shake him and remind him who he is: Dr. Matthew C. Russell, a freaking superhero if I've ever seen one!

Instead, I stay quiet and focused. If something goes wrong, it won't be because of me.

Six hours in, he insists I take a break and eat something. I want to protest, but I don't want to waste any of his time or energy arguing, so I do as I'm told and let another surgical assistant take over for me. Matt doesn't get a break though. Even if he could, I don't think he would take one. This is what he was made to do, what he's trained his body to endure. He won't leave that operating room until June does.

After I run to the bathroom and scarf down a protein bar, I pass June's parents in the waiting room. I can't speak with them, though I wish I could. June's mom catches sight of me and I offer her a small smile. I don't linger long, but it's still enough time for things to go sideways in the operating room. As I step back out of the elevator, I hear curses and shouts and then I realize it's Matt yelling from down the hall.

I break out into a sprint, grab a mask, and slam my hand against the swinging door in time for him to bellow out, "Page a vascular surgeon and get someone up here. NOW!"

Shit. That means he's nicked an artery. June's losing blood and every machine in that operating room is blaring at us to do something. I scrub in as quickly as I can then step into a new surgical gown. I shout at someone to tie the back for me and my hands are pushed into sterile gloves. In a few moments, I'm already back at the operating table, grabbing the suction handle from Dr. Mitchell so he can better assist Matt.

"Her anatomy isn't textbook," Matt explains to me, to himself, to everyone. "There shouldn't have been a fucking artery there."

It's a tense few minutes while we wait for the vascular surgeon to arrive. I suction as best I can, but then Matt takes over for me, worried I'm not doing enough. They add another unit of blood. People are scrambling, and then finally, the vascular surgeon arrives.

"I'm occluding the ruptured vessel, Dr. Brown," Matt shouts impatiently as she walks in. "Get over here."

She's calm compared to the rest of us, but then I suppose you have to be to go into such an intense specialty.

After a few minutes of working in silence, she assures us confidently, "The vessel is clamped." Then she twists her head a little to the left so her headlamp better illuminates the surgical site. "You," she says, speaking to me. "Suction right here until I tell you to stop. Quickly—I need this area clear if I'm going to suture."

I do exactly what she tells me to and I'm rewarded with a nod.

"I'm surprised you didn't tackle this yourself, Dr. Russell," Dr. Brown says as she sutures the tear in the artery. I watch her steady hand, amazed at how meticulous her movements are. "You could have done it."

"I didn't want to take any chances with this patient."

I glance up, trying to meet his eye, but his focus is on June. I understand. We're still in the middle of battle and there's a chance—now more than ever—that this won't work out the way we want it to. This was a toss-up even in the best of circumstances, and now, with this... I don't let myself finish the thought. I have to stay optimistic.

I think of that girl fighting in the conference room and I try to stay calm for her, try to endure this as bravely as she endured that.

I HAVE A realization during that surgery with Matt, a sort of are-you-a-freaking-idiot slash come-to-Jesus moment. I have this epiphany mostly because there's a lot of time to think during an eight-plus-hour surgery, a lot of time to take stock of your life and decide whether you like the direction you're headed in or if you need to change course.

It's obvious to me now more than ever that the feelings I have for Matt aren't going to go away just because I'd like them to.

Working with him complicates things because it's hard to be around a man like Matt and not engage in at least slight hero worship of him. In the operating room, he's a force to be reckoned with. A little bit of me has a crush on his surgical abilities alone, but the real problem is that outside of the OR, he's even better. It's hard to see the good side of Matt because he's made of tough stuff, grit and ego and *many* layers of muscle (as evidenced by that towel situation a few days ago), but there's a lot to love underneath all that. He's a man who fights for children who can't fight for themselves, a man who donates his time and money not because he wants notoriety or appreciation but because something inside of him needs to do it. I'm not sure I've ever met a more selfless human.

It's funny because I think if I asked him if he thought he was a nice guy, he'd say no, which is exactly the point. He doesn't see what I see, and maybe not many people do, but now I can't *un*-see it: the real Matt, the soft version of him that cuddled with me on that couch.

Suddenly, I want to be the woman who gets him, in and out of the OR.

I've pushed him away from the beginning because by anybody's standards, it was the safer, better option. A passing crush isn't worth jeopardizing my career over, but now I'm confident this isn't just a crush. Now I think I might be stupid if I *don't* jeopardize my career for him.

There are other surgical assistant jobs.

There is only one Matt Russell, M.D.

CHAPTER TWENTY-FOUR
MATT

I FEEL EXHAUSTION deep in my bones. I could fall asleep in an instant and stay asleep for a week. I've experienced difficult surgeries, but none of them have come close to June's. I want a celebratory milkshake and a celebratory nap. I'm scrubbing out by myself, collecting my thoughts and trying to convince my body it can calm down. I force another deep breath. The fight is over. June is getting wheeled to a recovery room and in a few minutes, I'll go to the waiting area and have the privilege of letting her parents know their daughter's surgery was a success. I'll skip over the parts where my heart was pounding and serious doubt crept in, when I nicked her artery and clamped my fingers on her vessel to curb blood loss, when I waited with baited breath as we took the final x-ray and measured the curvature of her spine.

Her spine is as it should be, but that doesn't necessarily mean she'll regain full function of her lower extremities once the inflammation subsides. The human body is a finicky bitch.

We just have to hope for the best.

I finish rinsing the suds off my hands and reach for a towel. Bailey's still inside the OR, helping clean up. I know she's just as tired as I am. The last few days haven't been any easier for her, and yet she's in there laughing with one of the nurses, doing her part to turn the room over for the cases that will come after the holidays. She doesn't have to stay in there. I told her to scrub out and go home, but she insisted on helping. It's been three days since she slept with me on that couch and ever since then, she's been in the trenches right alongside me, doing everything from prepping the OR to checking in on June's parents.

On top of that, I know she's been going home to take care of Josie. She mentioned that she went to the grocery store after work yesterday, which means she took the bus from here, to the store, and then home, and probably didn't get there until after nine. When I asked her why, she shrugged and explained, "Josie requested spaghetti with meatballs. It's her favorite." Simple as that. As if anyone would do what she does on a daily basis.

This morning, she was in the office extra early, coffee in hand, hopeful spark in her eyes. She was excited for this case. She rocked back and forth on her heels in my doorway, anxious to be put to work, and in that moment I realized she loves this world as much as I do.

She was vital in this case. In fact, she's the only reason I made it through today.

I watch as she waves bye to the nurses and techs and pushes past the swinging door to join me. Her raised brows let me know she's surprised. I should be finished by now, but I was taking my time, thinking.

"How do you feel?" I ask hesitantly, throwing my towel in the hamper by the door.

Her short laugh is mixed with a heavy sigh. It says it all.

"This might have been the craziest day of my life. I could collapse on this spot and never get back up."

I chuckle and lean back against the doorjamb, fighting back an audible sigh. It's no bed, but it's pretty nice. "It's definitely one I won't forget."

She turns and presses her cheek against her shoulder so she can look back at me. Her mouth is curved into a thoughtful smile, but I can only see the very tip of it. "I can't believe you pulled it off."

I return her smile, fighting the urge to step closer. "It wasn't all me."

She laughs and shakes her head, turning back to wash her hands.

Anything outside of food and sleep shouldn't be on my mind, but I still want her. I always want her.

"Matt, you're amazing. What you do for people…it's—" She shakes her head and stares down at her hands. "I'm just happy to even be in the same room with you. I'm really glad I took this job."

My heart swells and I have the sudden urge to tell her about the grant and everything that could happen if they award it to me, but there's not enough time. I need to go talk to June's parents. They've waited all day to hear about their daughter and I won't keep them waiting any longer.

I tell Bailey that then nod to the door. "Come with me?"

She's taken aback by the suggestion. "Seriously? OKAY! I've never done that before."

I NOTICE I have a few missed calls from my mom waiting for me when I finally get home. She asks me about Christmas and demands I let her know my plans. I've completely forgotten we're only a few days away from the holiday. Red and green decorations crowd every available space at the hospital. The doctors' lounge is filled with tins of gingerbread cookies, bags of fudge, and cartons of fruitcake my colleagues insist they have to get out of their houses while patting their growing midsections.

My mom has been pestering me about whether or not

I'll be at Christmas dinner for weeks now. I haven't decided. I could use the time to catch up on work. It sounds infinitely more tempting than enduring a meal in which my mom asks me if I'm seeing anyone and then follows up her line of questioning with not-so-subtle hints about how my ex-wife has moved on and is due to deliver her first child any day now.

I wonder how Bailey will spend the holiday. Her house was already decorated weeks ago, so clearly, she celebrates. Maybe she has a big family with lots of cousins, but somehow, I doubt it. From the little I've heard, it seems like it might just be her and Josie.

EVEN WITH THE day I've had, I have a hard time getting to sleep that night. I thought I'd hit my mattress and instantly be dead to the world, but I'm staring up at the ceiling, one hand on my chest, the other behind my head, still thinking about Bailey.

I can't remember the last time I had feelings for someone like this. It's like I'm back in high school, like Bailey is the unattainable girl next door and I'm the nerd who can't get her to agree to a date. I should just accept defeat.

Apparently, she hears my thoughts all the way at her house because my phone lights up on my nightstand and it's her.

I answer on the second ring, a smile on my face and in my voice.

"Bailey."

"Hey," she says, sounding uneasy. "I know it's late, but I was wondering if you had an update about June?"

"She was recovering well before I left. I'll head back over first thing in the morning."

"Oh," she says with an interested lilt to her voice. "That's awesome. Any signs of movement in her legs?"

"Not yet."

There's a break in conversation, the transition between the reason she called and the reason we're both still lingering on the phone.

"Y'know, today was the last surgery we have before the holiday break," she offers, and just like that, she's saying, *I don't want to hang up just yet. Talk to me.* "Ten days with no surgeries—how will you occupy yourself?"

I hum. "I'll still be up at the hospital most of the time."

She laughs. "Seriously? You need a break more than anyone. I sort of assumed you'd be taking a beach vacation or something."

I smile ruefully. "I'm not really the beach vacation kind of guy. I hate sand."

She finds that incredibly funny. "Actually, that doesn't surprise me in the least. Now that you mention it, I can't really imagine you taking any sort of vacation—*ever.*"

"I have," I protest. "Just not in the last decade."

"Well, you'll at least make it to the Christmas party tomorrow night, won't you?"

"I hadn't thought about it."

I don't usually go. Forced small talk with my colleagues and their spouses isn't really my thing.

"Well, you should. I have a present for you," she says, her voice taking on a slightly seductive edge, though it could just be wishful thinking on my part.

"Can't you just bring it to the hospital?"

"Maybe I'm trying to bribe you into showing up to the party," she quips.

Suddenly, I've had enough of this dancing around one another, this will-we, won't-we bullshit game Bailey insists we play.

"What does it matter if I'm there or not?" I push, desperate for honesty.

"It won't be the same without you."

I tug my hand through my hair and resist a groan. It feels like she's being a tease, pushing me away at the same time she's reeling me in, but Bailey isn't like that. She's genuinely being nice, inviting me to the party because she wants me there. Simple as that.

"I'll think about it," I promise, swallowing my anger. "Are you bringing a date?"

"No," she answers quickly. "Wait, *are you*?"

I laugh and decide on a whim that I'm tired of pretending. She asked the question, she's going to get the truth. "No, I'm not bringing a date. The only woman I want to ask had me sign a Word doc instructing me to stay away from her."

I know I should keep pretending I don't want her, that arm's length is my preferred proximity, but I can't. Every day I'm forced to work alongside her and every day she digs a little more under my skin, carving into me so deep I couldn't get rid of her if I tried.

"Are you referring to our legally binding *contract*?" she teases.

I don't laugh. In fact, I nearly growl. "I'm done, Bailey. I'm not abiding by that stupid list of demands anymore. Do you hear that? It's the sound of me tearing that 'contract' in two."

She stays silent, no doubt contemplating the weight of my words.

I smirk as I continue, "I'll come to that party tomorrow

night. In fact, I'm looking forward to it now. Don't forget
my gift."

CHAPTER TWENTY-FIVE
BAILEY

IT'S SNOWING OUTSIDE. Big, fat flakes drop from the sky and accumulate on the ground, turning the parking lot into a winter wonderland. It's fitting considering the interior of the restaurant NEMC rented out has been transformed to match. The party planners spared no expense. There are little Christmas vignettes in every corner of the room, fake deer and Christmas trees and those big, wrapped presents with nothing inside of them. There's enough food and drink to fill us all ten times over. The heads of the hospital might have protested about spending money on June's surgery, but they apparently have no qualms about dishing out big bucks for an event like this.

I shake away the thought and try to get into a more festive mood. There are only a few more days until Christmas! I have paid time off for the next ten days! SANTA IS COMING!

It's no use though. There's no room for cheer when I'm on high alert, scanning the room every few minutes on the off chance Matt arrived while I wasn't looking. The event is even more crowded than Dr. Lopez's retirement party. Every surgeon in the entire hospital is here with his or her family. Kids run around, high on sugar and the fact that they don't have school in the morning. I'm standing in a group with Megan and Erika and their dates. I don't have a date. Well, I have Josie. I glance over and find her exactly where I left her: sitting at a table by herself, reading a book and double-fisting bacon-wrapped shrimp. I watch as a cute boy her age—Dr. Richard's son, if I'm not mistaken—walks over to try to engage her in conversation and she waves him away, not bothering to look up from her book. For my sake, I'm glad she's currently choosing Harry Potter over boys. I'm not quite ready to play the role of angry, shotgun-toting father.

"No date tonight, Bailey?" Erika asks.

How dare she call me out in front of the whole group?!

For all she knows, I'm actually a loveless loser and not just pining after my angry, hot boss.

"Nope," I reply, affecting a casual tone. "Just my sister."

They glance over in time to see her steal yet another bacon-wrapped shrimp off a passing tray. *Boy are we related or what?*

"What about that blond guy from Smooth Tony's?" Megan asks, tilting her head. "He was cute and he seemed into you. Did anything happen with that?"

Ha. *Cooper.* Boy are they behind. I'd need a million years to catch them up so I just shake my head and pretend I'm disappointed when I reply, "Nah, didn't really pan out. He wasn't ready for a relationship."

It's as good a lie as any and as they throw me sympathetic frowns, I chance another glance at the door, my heart leaping when I catch movement. Unfortunately, it's only Dr. Goddard and his wife, followed by three blond children walking in perfect unison. Though adorable, they're stuffed into uncomfortable-looking Christmas outfits that coordinate perfectly with Dr. Goddard's suit and his wife's dress. The whole effect is a little ridiculous.

"So how has it been working with Dr. Russell?" Megan asks, aiming a conspiratorial smile at Erika before continuing, "I'll be honest, we didn't think you'd last this long."

Surely there's something better to talk about. Maybe I should have launched into that discussion about Cooper after all. It's better than having to look them in the eye and make up some phony reply about how, *Actually, it's not so bad guys. Ha ha. Yup, I just had to tough it out for the first few weeks and now we've really hit our stride.*

Truthfully, that no-good jerk of a surgeon has stolen my heart and he's about to walk through the door of this restaurant any minute and I'm not ready to face him. That phone call last night left my nerves frayed.

"Do you hear that? It's the sound of me tearing that 'contract' in two."

Ha! Well too bad, buddy, because I made copies!

I can still hear the determination in his voice. He really thinks I'm just going to throw caution to the wind and give in to this…this *lust* that's been building inside me for the last few weeks.

I'm considering all of this, of course, as he arrives. One minute, the doorway is empty, and the next, Matt is striding through with all the confidence of a king. My entire body stiffens as I take him in from head to toe. He's impossible to miss in a tailored black suit. No tie. His tan complexion stands out against his crisp white shirt. His slightly curly hair is inky black and thick. Heads turn in his direction, conversation halts around him. It's as if God himself is making a debut at the party.

Before June's surgery, his reputation was already larger than life. Now, it's completely out of control. Surgeons from every floor of the hospital rush over to greet him and shake his hand. They clap him on the shoulder and act as if they're the best of friends.

He smiles slightly and makes a good show of greeting

everyone, but his eyes scan the room looking for…me.

HE'S LOOKING FOR *ME*.

I panic and turn back to the group, suddenly 100% positive I need to get the hell out of here.

I shouldn't have come tonight.

My nerves are shot.

He's a dream in that black suit, and Josie talked me into wearing this silky, short dress that seemed daring and sophisticated back at home but now just seems downright inappropriate. I look around for a jacket and home in on Erika's date. He's a big guy, wide around the middle—his jacket would cover me and then some.

"Hey, bud." I say bud because I was distracted while he was introducing himself. "Could I borrow that jacket?"

He crosses his arms protectively over his chest and then replies weakly, "I'm actually kind of chilly."

What kind of men are we raising in this country?!

I have half a mind to just rip it off him, but I don't want to cause a scene. In fact, I want to do the exact opposite. I want to slink out of this party without Matt noticing me and run all the way home.

On a whim, I grab a flute of champagne from a passing waiter, down it in one long sip, and then hand it back. The group stares at me as I wipe the back of my hand across my mouth.

The waiter is deeply impressed with my abilities. "Um, would you like another glass, ma'am?"

I want every flute on his tray, but that won't solve my problem. I shake my head and thank him before addressing the group.

"Listen, guys, I'm not feeling well all of a sudden—"

"Probably because you just shot-gunned champagne like you were at a frat party," Erika cuts in, deeply suspicious of my weird behavior.

I wave away her insane suggestion. "No. I was feeling bad before that."

"What hurts?" Megan asks, concern oozing from her pores. She's way more gullible than Erika, clearly.

"My head." That's not enough to convince Erika, so I add, "And my…" I suddenly can't think of a single part of the human body. "Aaarm? Yes, my arm." I cradle it against my chest. "I'm going to head home. Merry Christmas, everyone!"

I turn and scan the party for the best route. There's only one entrance and Matt's blocking it, but I'm hoping by the time I reach Josie, one of his many admirers will have drawn him farther into the room and I'll sneak out without him even knowing I was here. It's the only option I have. I move quickly, like I'm on a stealth mission. I push my hair over my left shoulder and use it like a curtain to shield my face on the off chance Matt looks in my direction.

It takes me forever to reach Josie because I'm forced to duck behind Christmas trees or bend down to adjust my heels just to throw him off my scent. I nearly do a barrel roll before I think better of it.

"Josie!" I hiss as I rush forward and slam her book closed. "Hurry. We have to go."

She groans. "Are you kidding?! You just bent my page! And I didn't have a bookmark in there. It'll take me forever to find my place."

"I'm sorry. I really am." I round the table and hook my hands under her arms to haul her to her feet. "C'mon, I'll buy you another book—*ten* books. Just—"

A hand wraps around my bicep and I jump out of my skin.

"Bailey," Matt says right beside my ear, cool and

263

unaffected. "Not running off already, I hope?"

Josie jerks away from me to reclaim her seat and Matt uses his grip on my arm to spin me around slowly. I keep my gaze carefully pinned on his chest. My cheeks burn. The amusement in his tone makes it clear he saw every bit of that little charade. I'm more glad than ever I didn't attempt that barrel roll.

I gulp and nod. "I am. You see, my arm is—" I look down at my useless, perfectly functioning arm. "Injured."

It sounds pitiful even to my own ears.

He laughs acerbically then bends down to address my sister. "Josie, if you'll excuse us, I need to have a word with your sister."

"No she will not ex—"

Josie yanks her book back to her side of the table and starts to flip through it to find her page, unbothered by Matt's grip on my arm. "You're excused."

Choosing Harry Potter over her own flesh and blood?! I would do the same, but how dare she?

Matt keeps his hand on my arm as he leads me away from the table and over to a corner of the room partially concealed by one of the more over-the-top holiday scenes. Massive deer leap through the air, frolicking around white-flocked Christmas trees. I ask Matt if he likes the decorations and his eyes narrow on me.

Oh, I see. The pleasantries are gone now that we're all alone.

"Did you or did you not ask me to come tonight?" he asks, tone deceptively calm.

I swallow and look away. "I did."

"So then why were you about to leave?"

I'm not ready to admit the truth—or rather, I'm too embarrassed.

When I don't speak, his grip on my arm loosens and then he releases me. Disappointment hits me square in the chest.

"I won't do this, Bailey. I won't chase you. I told you last night I'm done with the contract. If that scares you, I'm going to listen and respect that. Do you understand? I won't force my way into your heart."

"'Force your way into my heart?'" I echo back at him, sounding incredulous. My gaze clashes with his in outrage. "You think you still need to force your way in? You're there, Matt! In every damn nook and cranny. That's why I'm running! That's why I drew up that silly contract!"

He reaches for my hand and I don't realize I'm trembling until I feel how steady his grip is on me.

"What are you saying?"

"I can't be any clearer."

He laughs, his face betraying every ounce of his elation. I've never seen him so breathtakingly handsome. "Well you'll have to be because I don't want any more misunderstandings."

My eyebrows pinch together. "Do you honestly expect me to declare my feelings for you here of all places? That deer is following me with its eyes. Everyone in this room is looking at us right now. They saw you drag me over here like a caveman, and I'm sure they're waiting for something to happen, a kiss—or a slap, more like."

"Out of the two, I know which one I'd prefer," he replies coolly, unbothered by the idea of everyone watching us. I suppose in some ways, he's used to it.

I, however, am not.

Matt steps forward and threads his fingers through mine. The gesture is intimate. I can hear my heart pounding in my ears. My stomach quivers as his gaze falls heavy on my mouth. He's going to kiss me right here in front of everyone! He'll do it! And that's the only reason I force him to follow me down the hallway just to our right and drag him through the first door I see.

It's a bathroom. Good! I lock the door and whirl around to face him, finger poking his big, manly chest. Admittedly, it probably hurts me more than it hurts him, but he needs to know I'm serious.

"You were going to kiss me out there!" I say, outraged. "In front of everyone!"

His hand reaches out and he fists the front of my dress, using the silky material as a means to pull me toward him. I stumble over my heels and collide into him. He's a rock, unmoving even when my full weight knocks into him. His hands at my waist keep me steady. His muscular thighs press against mine. My hands are on his chest, palms flat so I feel every breath, every heavy thump of his racing heart. His fingers twist the fabric of my dress and the silk brushes against my thigh, hiking up a few more inches so my bare legs brush against his suit pants.

I force myself to glance up at the tall, daunting man poised to wreck my world. His dark brows are tugged together. His blue eyes hold back a storm of emotion as he stares searchingly into mine, trying to find the answer to some unspoken question.

I'm shaking as if he has me on the edge of a cliff. One single finger could push me over. I'd tumble down, and right now, there's no way to know what awaits me at the bottom. Pain, love, heartache, elation—each is as likely as the last and I can't willingly do this to myself. I can't give myself over to a man who has the power to upend my life so easily.

I make a small move to step away at the exact moment

he bends his head and captures my mouth in an endless, passionate kiss. His strong grip keeps me there, pressed against him. I feel drugged as he kisses me again and again, his hands shifting higher, stroking and teasing and caressing everywhere within his reach. His thumb curves around my ribs and brushes the very edge of my breasts through my dress. His mouth slants over mine and I shudder. It's seduction, pure and simple. I'm helpless and frozen, using all of my wits just to stay standing, let alone kiss him back. My hands haven't moved from his chest. I've forgotten how to execute the simple act of breathing.

He pulls back and his hand wraps around my chin so he can lift my face toward his. His beautiful features are masked by desperate need. It's nearly enough to break my heart when his lips press against my temple, my cheek, the delicate groove just below my ear. My eyes are pinched closed as tingles ricochet down my spine.

"Kiss me," he pleads, his hands sliding around me, hauling me up against him so there's no space left between us. "Bailey...*kiss me*."

The words are as effective as a puppeteer's strings. The longing in his tone breaks the final chains straining around my heart. His parted lips find mine again and this time, I'm not frozen. I'm a woman taking exactly what she wants. I moan with hot need, tangling one hand in the thick hair at the base of his neck at the same moment my mouth opens and my tongue teases his. I kiss him with a hurried fervor, suddenly too anxious for this. I kiss him with all the desire I've foolishly tried to repress, every bit of longing that's built up over the last few weeks.

His response is a deep, hungry groan and it lights a fire inside me. Now we kiss with no holds barred. His hand wraps around my thigh and my leg lifts of its own accord.

My dress slides up to my waist and his hand shifts higher, dragging across the heated skin of my upper thigh so he can keep my leg wrapped around his hip. My stomach tightens in anticipation. Sizzling desire floods my system.

We kiss until my lips are sore, until I have to break away and gasp for breath, until I feel lightheaded and dizzy with need. If I had a bottle of water within reach, I'd dump it on my head. Everywhere he touches, it feels like he's dragging a flame across my skin. It sears. It ignites. It turns me on to the point of clothes-tearing, nails-dragging, teeth-biting insanity.

My hands are on his suit pants and I'm fumbling with the button, like *gimme, gimme, gimme.*

I want him to push me up against this wall and end my three-year dry spell. I want to finally know what it feels like to have Matt drive into me and lose control, rock his hips against mine and…I'm saying all of this to him. Every word spills out and Matt is cursing under his breath and tugging on my panties, trying to drag them down my hips, and *Jesus.*

"Just tear the damn things!" I plead, near tears.

He does and stuffs them in his pocket. *Dammit*, those were my good panties, but who the hell cares, because Matt's fingers are between my legs and I've watched him operate with those hands, but this is what they were really meant to do. This is…this is…

DEAR GOD.

His hand glides back and forth and he likes how ready I am, how very, very, very wet I am. For him.

He presses his mouth to the shell of my ear and tells me how good I feel as his finger slides into me.

My mouth drops open and I'm not one hundred percent sure my jaw doesn't come unhinged because DR.

RUSSELL drags his finger out slowly and adds a second, and that gentle pumping turns *not* so gentle. I'm grinding against the heel of his palm as he shifts us to the left and pushes me against the wall. It's almost humiliating how easily I'm coming undone, how easily two little (*okay*, big) fingers can make me mewl like a kitten.

"I want you," I demand sharply, sounding nearly possessed with need, but he's the one thinking clearly, because he shakes his head and uses the pad of his thumb to swirl in the exact spot that makes my toes curl and my eyes pinch closed.

Those first few waves of pleasure start to crest, but he staves them off, working me up even more before his thumb returns, swirling just slowly enough to put me in a straitjacket.

"There's not time," he insists, his voice velvety and commanding before he quiets my protests with his mouth. His teeth bite my lip and he's a little rough, but then I knew he would be. That softness he hides from the world is lost in this moment too. The man doing wicked things to me in this bathroom is the same man who inspired that devil picture in the lounge. This is the hotshot surgeon with all the confidence in the world, the man who scares me as much as he excites me.

He pulls back and watches me with hooded eyes as his fingers continue killing me slowly. His faint smirk tells me he's pleased by every one of my moans and whimpers.

Except for one hip pressing me against the wall and his fingers pumping in and out, he doesn't touch me. He stays just like that, disengaged enough that he can watch what he's doing to me. It feels like I'm performing for him. Maybe later, I'll be embarrassed by my flushed skin and swollen lips, but right now, I like his eyes on me. I like letting him do this to me.

A heavy fist knocks on the bathroom door and I jump out of my skin.

Matt's fingers curl into me.

The door handle jostles as a deep voice asks, "Is someone in here?"

Matt's thumb swirls faster and I bite down on my bottom lip to keep from crying out.

His gaze finds mine and he shakes his head, pressing a finger to his mouth.

There's another knock as the person grows more impatient. I have half a mind to shout, *WE'RE ALL IMPATIENT, OKAY, BUDDY?!*

I've waited so long for this moment, and the idea that it could be taken away in an instant makes me more desperate than ever. My chest rises and falls in quick succession. My hand hits Matt's wrist and I grip it hard. The gesture says, *If you stop, I'll kill you.*

His smirk turns him into a devil and he gets the hint because there's no slow teasing anymore. There's only his thumb and his eyes on me and "I'm going to come," I whisper. His hand covers my mouth at the precise moment the peak of pleasure crashes into me. Ricochet after ricochet. Tingles rack me from head to toe. I cry out against his hand and he smothers the sound as best as he can, but it's still probably not enough. The pope, my first-grade teacher, and my grandmother could be standing outside that bathroom door and I wouldn't be able to stay quiet.

Matt's hand makes it hard to breath, but this orgasm is never ending, and I live in the clouds now. I refuse to float back down to earth. His mouth presses against my forehead in a chaste kiss and his hand eases a little bit.

"Bailey?" he asks, his tone tinged with amusement.

270

"I'm going to move my hand now."

I nod to let him know I'm not going to do anything crazy, like proclaim, DR. RUSSELL IS DOING DIRTY THINGS TO ME IN HERE, EVERYONE.

Though, just to be clear, a part of me does want to do that.

He steps back, slowly pulling his hips away from mine, and I take stock of my body: my limbs are somehow still intact, my breathing is slowly returning to normal, my cheeks are still flushed, and they'll probably stay that way as long as Matt is looking at me with that knowing gleam in his eyes. I adjust my dress, step toward the mirror, and cringe. My mouth says, *I've been naughty.* My hair is a riotous mess. I drag my fingers through it and try to get it to lie as flat as possible, but there's no way to get it back to normal.

I groan as reality sinks in.

We're at the company Christmas party.

I'm not wearing any panties.

There's still someone waiting outside the door.

"How the hell are we going to get out of here?" I ask, peering at his reflection over my shoulder.

Matt's apparently already thought of that.

When I'm good to go, I give him a thumbs-up, and he tugs open the door just enough to stick his head out.

"Dr. Richards." He winces gently. "I need help. I've been throwing up nonstop—food poisoning or something."

"What?!" Dr. Richards groans. "Are you okay? You didn't have the spinach dip, did you? Dammit, I knew I shouldn't have gone back for seconds."

"No, no. Just go get me some water, will you? And something to settle my stomach if you can find it."

Dr. Richards mutters something under his breath and

271

Matt watches carefully as he turns down the hallway to complete his errand. The moment he's out of sight and the coast is clear, Matt straightens, adjusts his coat jacket, and offers me his elbow.

"Let's get out of here."

I shake myself out of my impressed stupor.

"Honestly, you went into the wrong profession," I tease. "That performance was worthy of an Oscar."

CHAPTER TWENTY-SIX
MATT

LET'S BE PERFECTLY clear: everyone knows what just happened in that bathroom. Dr. Richards is the only one who still thinks I'm having stomach problems. As I take Bailey's hand and lead her back to her sister, he rushes over to me with water and some antacids he found in his wife's purse. Sweat drips down his forehead as he presses a hand to his stomach. "Now that you mention it, I don't feel so good either."

Bailey has to stifle her laugh with a poorly executed coughing fit, and I tug her along before she can blow our cover.

"Really?" I chastise, unable to wipe the satisfied smirk off my face.

She shakes her head and covers her smile. "I can't stop."

She's giddy from her post-orgasm high. At least that makes one of us. I'm still so hard, a soft brush of her hand across my crotch and I'd be a goner. It's pathetic. I need to get the hell out of here. My mission is done. I came, I saw, I conquered. Well, I did the second two.

"People are still staring at us," Bailey hisses under her breath.

"Huh." I sound bored. "Are they?"

"You know they are," she says, wrapping her free hand around my forearm, shielding half her body behind mine. A few minutes ago, she wanted away from me as fast as possible. Now, suddenly she can't get close enough. It's the best case of whiplash I've ever had.

"Just smile and look confident. They'll move on. Look, Dr. Goddard and his wife are over there making fools of themselves. No one even cares about us anymore."

It's true. Dr. Goddard is stamping his foot and insisting the children "stand in descending order by age, not height" for their photo with Santa while his wife shouts back angrily. Still, half of the room remains laser-focused on us. I should probably let go of Bailey's hand. It's not helping matters. Instead, I tighten my grip.

"Just to be clear," she says, leaning in and dropping her voice so only I can hear. "Holding hands right now is as good as getting on a loudspeaker and announcing to everyone that we're a couple. If you want to be discreet about this, I'd let go if I were you."

"I'm not letting go," I reply confidently.

Her mouth forms a perfect O.

I lift my chin. "Are you changing your mind?"

"About what just happened in that bathroom?" she quips, lazy smile back in place.

"About agreeing to give us a try."

She laughs. "Ooooh, I didn't realize that's what was happening back there." I shoot her a teasing glare and she wiggles her fingers against mine. "Fine. Okay! *Yes*! Let's give us a try, but if it doesn't work out, you have to tell everyone I'm really good in the sack and super smart and that *I* left *you*."

She's teasing but her words still sting.

She tries to catch my eye, but I tug her along. "C'mon, it looks like Josie finished her book and there's a group of boys trying to talk to her."

"Oh good! Scare them all off, will you? She's not allowed to date until she's 40."

I WAS WORRIED about how people would treat Bailey after our little show. I probably should have given her the choice about where and when she'd like to inform people about our relationship, but…well, things happen. Our plan was to leave soon after getting back to Josie, but there were too many people eager to hear news about June and her recovery. I hadn't even told Bailey the best of it: June tested positive for motor and sensory function this afternoon. She'll still need physical therapy, but I have no doubt she'll regain normal use of both legs. I watch Bailey's face as I tell this to the group of surgeons crowded around us. Her eyes well up and she forcibly swallows as if that might keep her emotions at bay. I want to wrap my arm around her and tug her close, tell her she has as much to do with June's recovery as I do, but my colleagues crowd in like a tidal wave, eager with questions.

I play at politeness for a little while, appreciating how sour Dr. Goddard's face is every time we make eye contact from across the room. Dr. Richards and Dr. Smoot are quick to amend their original stance on the subject. *"We didn't have the forethought you had, Dr. Russell."*

With the amount of press coverage from the case, New England Medical Center won't be hurting for surgical patients any time soon.

As the night continues, I give Bailey every opportunity to break free and save herself. She could go hang out with the other surgical assistants or find her sister, but instead, she stays by my side. My colleagues notice. They try to be sly about it, but they're definitely inspecting how close we're standing. They pay careful attention when I whisper something in her ear and Bailey smiles. A few of them even toss her a question or two about June's case, and to Bailey's credit, she doesn't cower. She lifts her chin and holds her own in a group of egotistical surgeons, every bit as confident as the day I met her.

No one asks about our relationship outright. I think they're minding their business because they know better than to pry.

Bailey thinks that's hilarious and informs me they're actually whispering nonstop behind our backs, but no one is brave enough to ask us directly if we're dating because they're terrified of me. I smile at the thought. There is one person who's brave enough to address the elephant in the room, though.

Patricia walks by at one point with a plate of desserts in hand. She pauses beside us, drops her chin, and stares pointedly over the brim of her glasses at our joined hands. Then she emits a half-interested hum and keeps walking. That's it.

"I swear she smiled a little," Bailey insists, watching her walk away over her shoulder.

"Patricia? I'm not sure she knows how to smile."

THE SNOW'S STILL coming down hard when we finally manage to escape the party and I insist on driving Bailey and Josie home. Bailey's conspicuously quiet in the passenger seat. Her hands are wrapped around her purse and I can see the edge of a present sticking out of the top— *my* present. Josie, meanwhile, sits in the middle of the back seat, doing her best to catch up on all the changes in the last few hours. For every question a colleague of mine suppressed at the party, Josie asks five.

"So you two are really dating now? Like it's Facebook official?"

"I don't use Facebook," Bailey replies quickly. "But sure, yes. Can't you go back to reading now?"

"I finished my book. Harry's back at Privet Drive for the summer. So, Matt, can I call you that? Or do I have to call you Doctor?"

I laugh. "Matt's fine."

"Right. Matt, have you had many serious girlfriends in your life?"

"A wife." I meet her gaze in the rearview mirror. "Does that count?"

"A WIFE?!" Josie acts outraged, and I have to stifle a laugh as Bailey drops her head in her hands and groans.

"Why don't you just let us out here?" Bailey suggests. "Yes, this is fine. We're only, what, four miles from our house?"

I ignore her and give Josie a CliffsNotes version of my relationship with Victoria.

"So it was ages ago?" Josie asks once I finish.

"Ages," I confirm.

She nods and leans forward so her head hovers between Bailey and me.

"Well, Bailey here hasn't had a serious boyfriend ever. Have you told him that, sis? Seems like something a guy would want to know before he commits."

Bailey reaches to unlock the car, presumably so she can leap to her death on the highway, but I'm too fast at re-engaging the lock.

"As a matter of fact, Josie"—I grin—"she hasn't."

Josie nods. "Yeah, I mean if I were her age and had only ever dated—how many guys is it, Bailey? Two?"

"THREE," she corrects, crossing her arms and staring out the window. "And I'm no longer participating in this conversation."

"Right, I mean three's not that many. Hell, I kissed three boys in kindergarten alone."

I have to fight down a surge of laughter.

It continues like that the whole way to their house. Josie's got the innocent act down pat, but I'm confident she knows exactly how to torment her sister. It reminds me a lot of how Cooper and I act when we're together.

After a few detours because of heavy snow, I eventually make it to their house and pull into the driveway.

"Want to come inside for some hot cocoa?" Josie asks excitedly.

I glance to Bailey, wondering what she wants me to do, and to my relief, she smiles and shrugs.

"I was going to suggest the same thing, but she beat me to the punch."

When we get out and walk up the path, Bailey takes my hand before I can take hers. We've done so much hand-holding tonight I should be sick of it, but I'm not. I can't remember the last time I just wanted to hold on to someone like this. It feels silly, and yet I can't stop doing it.

We kick off our shoes in the foyer and Bailey turns to her sister.

"Josie, why don't you go make the hot cocoa? I'm going to talk to Matt for a second."

"Okay! I'll pick a movie too!"

Bailey smiles weakly as her sister skips into the kitchen. "Sorry, you probably didn't think you'd be hanging out with a teenage girl tonight."

"I happen to think she's funny."

Bailey rolls her eyes. "Well, whatever you do, don't tell

her that. Now c'mon, I'll give you the grand tour."

If possible, their house has even more holiday decorations inside of it than it did the last time I was here. The Christmas tree we walk past is covered with so much tinsel it's in danger of tipping over. There are a few gifts under the tree—not nearly as many as I had growing up. I narrow my eyes, trying to see if any of them are addressed to Bailey, but she tugs me along before I can get a good look.

"The carpet is old and stained. Ignore it. It's from the 80s, and we only made it worse when we fostered a dog for like three weeks last year. It didn't take long for me to realize I couldn't handle raising Josie *and* a puppy who wasn't housetrained. I mean, Josie *barely* is," she quips with a smile.

If she thinks I'm looking at her carpet, she's insane.

"Now this," she says, patting the wall with a teasing glimmer in her eyes. "This here is *grade-A* wood paneling."

"Fancy," I say with a smile.

"You can't just get this type of high-end finish in any ol' house."

I laugh and step toward her so I can wrap my hands around her waist and match her step for step as she continues walking backward to her room. "What about the 70s-style wallpaper in the bathroom up ahead?" I ask, nudging my chin toward it.

She pats my chest teasingly. "The pinkest, most ugly thing you've ever seen."

We arrive at a door beside the bathroom and she reaches behind her to turn the handle, her eyes staring up at me while she does it. "Are you ready to see the main attraction?" she asks, wiggling her eyebrows.

I grin and push us forward until her door opens wide

and I'm standing on the threshold of Bailey's bedroom.

The first thing I notice is the twin bed. I have to stifle a groan. Really? A twin? I haven't had sex on a twin bed since my freshman year of college—not that we're about to have sex. Yet.

She follows my gaze and bites her lip. "Yeah, I've been meaning to upgrade. Also, not to further disappoint, but it's hard as a rock."

I nod and drop my hands as I move past her, anxious to uncover the secrets of Bailey Jennings.

In lieu of a nightstand, she's stacked pre-med textbooks beside her bed so she can rest a glass of water and what looks to be a half-finished copy of *When Breath Becomes Air*—a book I read the day it released—on top.

"You're judging," Bailey accuses, crossing her arms by the door.

I step farther inside and turn in a slow circle. "I'm not. Really." I glance at her with a smirk. "It's only fair. You got to snoop around my room when I was passed out drunk. Now I should get to do the same."

She chuckles and shakes her head. "Actually, I didn't. I was too scared of what I would find in your bedside table."

"There isn't anything too terribly shocking. A pack of condoms." I shrug nonchalantly. "Some ball gags."

She chokes out a laugh, and then her eyes widen and she jerks her head out into the hallway.

"Oops." I'm not used to having to watch what I say. "I don't think she heard. Also, for the record, I'm kidding."

Bailey lets me take my time looking around her room. I browse through her books (she has good taste), test out her bed (rock hard, as promised), and then stop short when I realize there's not much else. Her walls are bare. Her bed doesn't even have a headboard. Her box spring is sitting on the floor.

Josie shouts from the kitchen that the hot cocoa is ready and *Elf* is cued up on the TV.

"Not one for interior decorating?" I ask as we step back out into the hallway.

Bailey deflects. "Haven't really had the time."

I don't quite buy her answer, especially when we pass Josie's room and I see it's stuffed to the brim. She has two bookshelves fully stocked with what looks to be the entire contents of the teen section at Barnes & Noble. Posters of One Direction and some guy named Ansel Elgort cover the wall above her bed. She has a little writing desk, and a bean bag, and a blue and white striped rug.

It confirms everything I already know about Bailey.

When we arrive in the living room, Josie has confidently claimed the middle of the couch. She has a blanket over her legs, a bowl of popcorn on her lap, and her mug of hot cocoa cooling in one hand. The remote is poised in the other, aimed for the TV.

"*C'mon*, you two," she says impatiently.

"Josie, why don't you scoot over," Bailey suggests, waving to the left side of the couch.

Josie's nose scrunches in protest. "What? But you know I like sitting in the middle. The cushion has a nice little indention from my butt."

"*Josie*," Bailey hisses, obviously trying to convey something to her sister, which the fourteen-year-old completely misses.

Her bottom lip juts out. "But I like being in the middle."

So that's that. Bailey and I are forced to sit on either side of her. I fight back a laugh as we lock eyes behind her head.

"Sorry," Bailey mouths, shooting me a defeated half-smile.

I reach my arm along the back of the couch and brush my thumb back and forth across her shoulder.

"Quiet!" Josie insists. "The movie is starting!"

The irony is that Josie herself talks through the whole movie, pointing out her favorite characters and explaining to me why certain jokes are funny then looking over to see if I'm laughing too.

I chuckle because there's nothing else to do. This night is nothing like I thought it would be.

I catch Bailey glancing over at me every now and then. There's tension between us, and during slower parts of the movie, I can't help reliving moments from the party, specifically every second we spent in that bathroom together. I fidget in my seat and lean forward to take off my coat.

Then I stand to get water and Bailey shoots to her feet to join me, explaining to Josie that she needs to show me where the cups are.

"Okay! I'll pause it."

Bailey laughs. "Oh good."

Their kitchen is right off the living room, small and just as dated as the rest of the house. Bailey walks over to a cabinet and reaches up for a cup and I come up behind her, hands on her hips, turning her slowly toward me.

Her eyes widen in shock then her gaze darts toward the living room. "What are you doing?" she whispers.

In response, I tip my head down and kiss her slowly. My mouth claims hers and my hands curve around her ass, tugging her toward me until our hips meet. *Fuck.* I *need* her.

Our kiss turns hotter as I try to convey every ounce of torment I feel, but then Josie's voice carries into the kitchen and we leap apart.

"Hey!" she shouts. "Could you bring me some water too, please?"

Bailey whirls around to the cabinet and grabs another glass. "Yes! Got it!"

Obviously, I don't pay attention to the rest of the movie. My focus is on Bailey. Every little move she makes, every time she smiles or laughs. I'm hypnotized, worked up, and slightly annoyed Josie's bedtime isn't 8:00 PM.

I suspected the snow was piling up outside, but I'd put it out of my mind. Once the movie is over and the mugs of hot cocoa are sucked dry, I face the fact that I probably can't drive home. The three of us stand at the door, staring out at the driveway. A thick layer of snow covers my car.

"You shouldn't drive," Bailey says, tapping on the glass. "Look at how icy the walkway is."

"Yeah, I bet the roads are just as bad. You'll just have to stay here." Josie nods before turning to look over at us. "But, wait, where will he sleep?"

"THE COUCH!" I shout, a little too forcefully. "He'll take the couch, of course."

Matt smiles at how flustered I am, but I refuse to meet his eyes. This entire charade has gone on long enough. The last few hours have been absolutely unbearable. *Oh yes, please, let's all sit and watch a movie together while visions of Matt in that bathroom dance in my head. What a wise idea!*

I'm burning up on the inside and I'm worried Josie can tell something's up. I swear I'm flushed from head to toe, a human-sized cherry. I think I wrung out my hands through the entire last half of the movie. My heart hasn't slowed its rapid pace. I'm a jittery, turned-on mess.

I curse the weather as I march to the linen closet down the hall, relieved that I happen to have clean sheets and a blanket for Matt. There are no spare pillows, so I grab him one from my bed and then hurry to make up the couch for him.

"I can help," he says, reaching for the sheets.

I shake my head adamantly. "No. I've got this. Why don't you just…stand over there, will you?"

I place him beside the Christmas tree and I swear his eyes are filled with amusement.

The space is necessary. If it weren't so cold, I'd make him stand outside. If he comes near me again, if he tries to kiss me like he did in the kitchen, I'm going to give Josie a show that will scar her for life. My little sister doesn't need to see that. She's still so young and naive. She even asks Matt if he wants something to read.

He must look confused because she continues, "I read before bed every night and it helps me get to sleep. Here, I'll go get you something."

I nearly shout at her to stay put, but she's already disappeared down the hallway. Matt steps toward me and I start working double time. That sheet and blanket are laid out so quickly I should probably contact the nearest Best Western about working in housekeeping.

"Thanks for letting me stay," he says from behind me, his voice smooth velvet.

I turn and give him a quick nod and a bow. A BOW, because that's how awkward this evening has become.

If Josie weren't here, we'd have had sex four times over.

I know it. He knows it.

God, this is terrible.

"Here you go!" Josie says, walking back into the room with a stack of books. "Have you read *The Hunger Games*? The series is kind of old now, but I think it's held up nicely. This is the first book."

Matt smiles and accepts it, promising to read a few pages before he goes to sleep.

I busy myself with clearing the dishes and unplugging the Christmas tree and brushing my teeth. I change into a button-up flannel nightgown and a pair of fuzzy socks. It only occurs to me afterward that I could have chosen a sexier outfit to sleep in, but that would be complicated seeing as I don't own any sexy pajamas. It was either this or a holey oversized t-shirt.

Once I'm finished, I venture back into the living room.

Matt's sitting on the couch, on top of the blankets,

checking his phone. His shirt is untucked, but other than that, he hasn't changed. He glances up and his gaze catches on my nightgown. I look down to ensure I didn't miss a button or anything, but nope, everything is in place. I could easily pass for a ten-year-old at a slumber party.

"Cute," he says with a wry smile.

I nibble on my bottom lip and finally think to ask, "Do you want some clothes?" I squint one eye as if sizing him up. "I might have a big t-shirt that would fit you, or maybe I could fashion you a toga out of a sheet?"

He smirks. "I'm fine. I'll take my shirt off once everyone's asleep."

Josie finishes up in the bathroom and then comes to stand beside me.

"Night Matt! Hope you like the book." He tells her good night as well and she turns to go to her room, but then she pauses at the doorway and looks back at me. "Bailey, aren't you going to bed too? You guys aren't going to stay up late without me, are you?"

She's concerned she's going to miss out on the fun, like we're going to bring out cupcakes and a disco ball once she's tucked in bed.

I stare at Matt, trying to work up some reason for why I need to speak with him alone, but nothing comes to mind.

"I—" All I see is his perfectly handsome face grinning up at me. He thinks this is funny. He loves how much I'm squirming. I sigh, finally coming to terms with the fact that tonight's not the night for Matt and me. "No, we aren't staying up late. I'm going to bed too. Night Matt."

Josie hooks her arm around mine as if escorting me down the hall. It's all innocent. I truly don't think she realizes what she's doing, but it's funny all the same. I deposit her in her room with strict orders not to stay up too late reading. She shoots me two thumbs up and then leaps onto her bed.

I walk into my dark, lonely room and stand just inside the doorway, at a loss for what to do. I can't go to sleep. I can't sneak back out there while Josie's awake. With a sigh, I walk to my bed and prop my pillows up so I can lean against them and read. Well, I pretend to read. My book is a useless prop. I don't even bother turning pages. I sit there, chewing on my bottom lip and contemplating what Matt could possibly be doing. Surely he's not reading *The Hunger Games* like it's any old night. I wonder if he's taken his shirt off now that Josie and I are tucked in our rooms.

Good GOD, if that man is out there shirtless, on my couch, I will…I don't know…I can't finish the thought. I have to fan my face.

I've had enough.

I slap my book closed, push off the bed, and creep out into the hall. Josie's lamp is still on in her room. I see the faint light peeking out from underneath her door, so I turn and go into the bathroom. I close the door and stare at my reflection. It wasn't a good idea to come in here. Being in this bathroom reminds me of being in *that* bathroom with Matt.

I splash water on my face, pat it dry, and then yank the door open.

A pale light glows in the living room and I take a hesitant step toward it before fear douses my courage. *No! This is stupid!* I should just accept the fact that nothing more is going to happen tonight, lie down in my bed, and go to sleep.

I should do that…I'm going to do that…I have every intention of doing that, except I don't.

I tiptoe to the very end of the hallway, careful to be extra quiet as I pass Josie's room, then I press myself flat against the wall and peek my head around the corner.

Matt's sitting on the edge of the couch, head in his hands. *The Hunger Games* is forgotten on the coffee table in front of him.

His shirt is off, but his pillow and blankets are still right where I put them, untouched. He's been sitting there, dragging his hands through his hair like he's doing now. He looks agitated, and I'm not surprised. He's probably annoyed that our night got derailed by hot cocoa and *Elf*. Not exactly a sexy night in…

I study the contours of his smooth, tan skin, the bunched muscles of his shoulders and biceps. He's too big for that couch—for this house, really.

He shakes his head as if deciding something and then looks up. I freeze as his gaze clashes with mine.

I've been caught.

Snooping.

I press my lips together to keep from speaking. Neither of us says a word. Josie will hear us if we do.

He's still leaning forward with his elbows propped on his knees. He doesn't move as he stares up at me. I want him to give me some signal that he's glad to see me standing here, but the only guidance I have to go on is the storm brewing in his eyes. Those are not the eyes of a man who wants to lie down and go to sleep.

I take a hesitant step out from behind the wall and he sits up straight.

I hug my middle and take another step toward him. Then another.

He doesn't move and he doesn't meet me halfway.

I start to shake a little as I keep walking, nerves racking

through me. I could be reading the situation wrong, but it's too late to turn back now. I'm already too close and the moment I step within reach, Matt's hand shoots out and tugs me forcefully between his legs. His warm palms grip the backs of my knees, and I'm so out of my league it's not even funny. His face is level with my chest. My fingers weave through his thick hair, disappearing into the dark strands. I bend down an inch and he tilts his head back. Our lips brush together and it's gentle at first, a teasing, could-be-more-if-we-want-it-to-be kiss. His hands skim up the backs of my thighs and then his fingers knead into my soft flesh. It's the first sign of his impatience, followed swiftly by a low groan. He tilts his head and deepens our kiss; his tongue touches mine, and I'd press my thighs together if he weren't currently prying them apart. He leans back so I can climb on top of his lap, and I do just as he wants me to. My nightgown bunches at my waist and I hook my knees on either side of his hips. His suit pants brush against my panties and I can't help but roll my hips reflexively. The way his hands squeeze my hips lets me know he likes it. He rocks me back and forth against his length as his mouth teases mine. We're grinding together and finding a rhythm.

I'm losing my mind.

He's impossibly hard.

His hands are everywhere: in my hair, on my hips, cradling my head so he can tilt my chin up and sweep kisses down my neck. It's so heady when his fingers tease the top button on my nightgown. *YES*, I think. I'm more than ready to feel his hands on my bare skin, to have him touch me in places I've only imagined, but thankfully my brain catches up before we get too carried away.

My little sister is still awake, like ten feet away from where we're currently mauling each other. If we're going to do anything in this house, it has to be in my room, with the door locked and (preferably) a loud marching band performing out in the hallway.

I jerk back and break our kiss.

Matt's gaze meets mine, his brows tugged together in confusion.

He thinks I'm pumping the brakes.

No, you fool.

I'm changing locations.

I scramble up off the couch, reach down for his hand, and tug him after me. We cross that living room in half a second. We're down the hall, pressing fingers to our mouths and stifling laughter before I shove him into my bedroom, close the door, and freeze.

I listen for any sound of Josie stirring in her room or the subtle pad of footsteps on the carpet.

Blissful silence greets me.

I grin and turn to Matt.

We just might be able to get away with this.

I stand in front of him, half a room away as my hands find the buttons of my nightgown.

Am I really going to do this? I ask myself even as my fingers start to move of their own volition. My stomach quivers as the first button is undone. Then the next. Cool air hits my chest and a shiver racks my spine as I work the third button free. His eyes slash down to where my hands are working and the cool air is replaced with searing heat. My hands start to shake and that fourth button proves especially tricky.

He stays right where he is, watching me as I undress for him. He's still wearing his suit pants, but his feet are bare. His hair is in disarray, but his features are as sharp and calculating as ever. Without his shirt, he's a wall of tan skin and hard muscle. My mouth waters and I swallow, in awe of the effect he has on me. No words, no touching—just him, standing in my room, shadowed by the moonlight.

"Keep going," he urges, his voice husky and low, and I realize then that I've paused, too preoccupied with staring at him.

I force my attention down to my nightgown and find the fifth button. The two sides of the dress sag open just enough to reveal a hint of cleavage. My skin glows like porcelain in the dark room and when I work the sixth button free, Matt growls and steps toward me.

He reaches me in two long strides, gripping my waist with one hand and using the other to push the flannel fabric off my right shoulder. The thick material scrapes across my sensitive skin as his mouth finds the base of my neck, my collarbone, and then the very center of my chest. He bends before me and strings kisses along my skin until he reaches the curve of my breast exposed by my nightgown. His fingers push the flannel aside reverently, baring me. *Finally*. My chest heaves as he stares down, almost in awe. His finger traces along my breast and then he hauls me against him at the same moment he takes the very tip into his mouth, sucking and kissing with a fervor I've never felt. My knees give out but he holds me up, dragging his tongue across me.

Heat spreads through my body as he takes his time worshiping me. It nearly feels like I'm the one doing the seducing, which couldn't be further from the truth.

He's the one in control, loosening another button on my nightgown so it's easy to push off my other shoulder. The fabric pools at my feet and I'm standing before him in nothing but a silky pair of underwear and red fuzzy socks.

Standing before him like this, it feels like there's so

much more of him than there is of me. His hands are bigger than mine. He's stronger, older, more confident. He bends to kiss my other breast and my hands roam across his back, trying to feel every contour of muscle, every inch of heated skin.

He wraps his hands around my hips and pushes me toward my small bed. There's no use trying to keep up with his deft movements. We're backing up at the same time his hands slide into my panties and cup my ass. He uses his grip to bring me against him and his hard length grinds into me. I can feel him through his pants. I know how patiently he's waited. For hours—*weeks*.

He whispers against the shell of my ear, telling me how badly he wants to feel me wrapped around him.

His hips roll and my eyes pinch closed. There are still layers of clothes between us, but the sparks are there, warning me. I don't want to come like this, just from his hips grinding against mine.

But I will if he continues.

I beg him to slow down because I'm coming undone too easily, but he doesn't care. My silk panties brush against overly sensitive skin as he continues his seduction. His hand skims down and he brushes his fingers across me, on top of the fabric. He's relentless and I'm angry with him, mad that he's doing this to me when we're so close to feeling skin on skin, so close to the real thing.

He kisses me relentlessly and continues teasing me right up until my toes start to curl, until I've completely surrendered to the beginnings of an orgasm. I don't care about anything now that I'm so close. I can feel the tingles start to trickle up my spine and then suddenly he pulls back and deposits me on the bed. The shock of cold air jerks me sharply away from the edge.

If I was angry before, now I'm on fire. I scramble up and over to him, yanking on his pants at the same time he unzips them and pushes them down. They're on the floor and his briefs are next. I lose my breath as I finally catch sight of his length. My reaction must be funny because he chuckles and pushes me back onto the bed.

"Not so angry now?" he teases right before his mouth meets mine.

A kiss.

God, it feels like ages since his mouth has been on mine, but it's only been a few seconds. I'm reminded why we're here, why I'm spreading my thighs and begging him to continue, to finally let this happen. My anger burns away and there's nothing but all-consuming need left behind.

"We need to be quiet," he warns as his hand drags down my body. His fingers hit the edge of my panties and I dig my nails into his shoulders. He pushes past the top of the fabric and then his palm covers me. We've been here before, his fingers sinking into me, but this time it's infinitely better because his weight is on top of me, his naked heated skin covering mine.

I offer some inaudible plea and he shakes his head, bending down to kiss me.

His finger sinks inside me again, burrowing deeper.

"You nearly got us caught earlier," he reminds me. "Maybe we shouldn't do this."

Even as he threatens me, his fingers drag back out and then in, stretching me, teasing me.

My orgasm—the one he stole from me a second ago—comes roaring back to life, and if he'd only just keep…doing…*that*.

"I won't make a peep," I promise as my gaze finds his. My fingers wrap around the sides of his biceps and I use all of my strength to keep him there on top of me. His eyes are hooded as he stares down at me. I arch my back and my breasts brush against his chest. "*Please*," I whisper desperately, and finally, a quiet groan tears through him and he claims my mouth.

My panties are tugged off and thank God he's quick with the condom he pulls out of his wallet because I'm dying a slow death as he settles himself back between my thighs and thrusts into me...slowly...slowly...and then all at once. A moan rips through me as I *finally* orgasm just from that one, hard thrust. Fireworks dance behind my closed eyes and Matt's mouth crashes against mine. His kiss is painful and biting and he's angry at me for breaking my promise to stay quiet. He punishes me when he thrusts harder again and again. I wish I could tell him I'm not in control. My body is his, these limbs and mouth and that delicious spot in the center of my thighs are his to do with as he pleases. I wish I could tell him this is no punishment. This is a gift.

He hoists himself up onto his hands and uses the leverage to his advantage. With a confident grip, he hikes my bent knee up so my thighs are spread wider for him. One of his hands presses my leg into the mattress and he rolls his hips, grinding into me at an angle I've never experienced before.

My breathing is labored because I have one hand over my mouth. I'm scared I'll unintentionally cry out again. My other hand is everywhere, fisting his thick hair, dragging down his back. I feel his muscles shift and I indulge myself and grip his hard ass as he thrusts into me again and again.

His mouth is at my ear and he's apologizing that he can't last much longer, that tonight has been too tortuous and drawn out. Then he pulls back up and bites his lip and concentrates on where our bodies are meeting. Sweat collects on his brow and I'm taking snapshots to remember later: the bunched muscles of his abs as he rolls his hips, the tension in his jaw as he tries to stave off his orgasm, the softness in his eyes as his gaze meets mine.

He brushes my hair off my face and I tilt my chin up in invitation.

He bends and kisses me languidly, teasingly. My tongue rolls with his and he moves his hand between my thighs. I wish I could say I put in a good effort fighting off that second orgasm, but the truth is that after only a few hours, Matt knows my body too well. His thumb swirls in time with his thrusts and I'm shattered. I can't take another. "I'll die," I tell him.

He laughs huskily and drops his mouth to my breast, taking the tip into his mouth. It's his answer, and it's every bit as confident as him blatantly replying, *Oh yes you will. Now come.*

I do, and this time, I manage to stay as quiet as a church mouse, mostly because I'm so preoccupied with watching Matt lose himself. He can't hold off any longer and I kiss his cheek, begging for him to let go as well. His shoulders bunch and his face falls into the crook of my neck. His hips jerk and it's nearly painful how deep he is inside me. His fingers intertwine with mine over my head as the waves of pleasure shoot through his body. I'm lost to the sensation of it, the sheer bliss of making a man like Matt come apart at the seams.

He stays on top of me just like that as our breaths start to even out and the details of real life start to filter back to us. For the first time since we began, I'm made aware of just how tiny my twin bed is. Matt's nearly falling off. My body is wedged painfully between the wall and him.

I drag a hand down his spine and he moans but doesn't move.

"You're going to fall," I warn him with a little laugh.

He shifts to the left and covers me even more.

"*Matt.*"

"Shh, I'm sleeping," he teases, hand dragging up and finding my breast.

"Oh, okay. That doesn't feel like sleeping to me, sir."

He lifts his head and his eyes blink open. He stares down at me for a few seconds and my realizations go as follows: Matt and I just had sex, write-home-about-it sex, and honestly, it felt a lot like we were making love. Yes, that four-letter word creeps into my mind like an uninvited party guest. *Ohhh, you just wanted a casual fling? 'Cause I thought it'd be more fun if we tumbled head over heels.*

His brows tug together in thought and he lifts his hand to wipe my cheek with his thumb. Oh dear god. Those are tears he's wiping.

When was I crying?!

"Did I hurt you?" he asks, deeply concerned.

I shake my head back and forth on my pillow as his finger curves below my chin so he can tilt my face toward him.

"Are you positive?"

I nod.

His mouth curls into a panty-melting smirk. "Was I so good you've lost the ability to speak?"

I try to hide my face behind my hands, but he doesn't let me.

"Do you want me to change the subject?"

"Desperately."

"Okay, but if it helps, you look adorable right now."

I bark out a laugh and his gaze shoots to my bedroom

door. Oh god, I completely forgot I need to be quiet. I'm really bad at this. I press a finger to my lips to let him know I won't mess up again. He rolls off me and stands, and *presto chango*, I'm now treated to a magnificent view of his backside as he walks toward my bedroom door. Wide shoulders, tapered waist, very nice rear end. All in all, I'd give him a 10/10, and I tell him so.

"Stop staring at my butt and c'mon. I need you to go out first and confirm the coast is clear," he says quietly, glancing back at me over his shoulder. Something gives him pause and I swipe at my cheeks to make sure I don't have any residual tears, but I don't think it's that. His gaze drags languidly down my body and *oooh, right. I'm naked.* Men are such simple creatures. When his gaze finally meets mine again, I try to ignore the mischievous glint I see there and instead return to the task at hand.

I sit up and whisper, "What happens after I check if the coast is clear?"

"Then we sneak into the bathroom and rinse off," he says, as if it's obvious.

"I meant *after* that."

He chuckles and shakes his head. "Then we're going to see how easily you can fit two adults onto a bed made for ants." I must look worried because he adds, "Bailey, I'm not going to sleep on the couch. I'll set an alarm on my phone and move back out there before your sister wakes up. She'll never know."

He says all this while he strides confidently back toward me. I make a move to get off the bed, but he's quicker. He bends down and grabs my knees, tugging me so my butt is right on the edge. I think he's going to help me up, but instead, he pushes me back down with one hand on my chest.

My heart leaps into my throat. "I thought we were going to the bathroom," I say, voice faint.

He's staring down between my legs, a drugged look in his eyes. "We are...just as soon as I've finished."

"*Matt*," I warn, but it's no use.

He smiles and gets down onto his knees. "Maybe try not to wake the entire neighborhood this time."

I toss my hands up over my head in defeat. I highly doubt we'll be getting any sleep tonight.

CHAPTER TWENTY-EIGHT
MATT

THE NEXT MORNING, Christmas music blares at full volume, a fresh layer of snow coats the ground outside, a steaming pot of coffee waits to be poured, and I'm trying to wrestle a wooden spatula out of Bailey's hand.

"Hand it over, Matthew, or so help me."

That's her taunt and I can't help but laugh. She's diminutive. I could pluck her up with two fingers and deposit her elsewhere.

My brow arches, and with one tug I yank the spatula out of her hand and hold it up over my head. She jumps to get it and I move it just a little farther out of her reach. Suddenly, I'm a middle school bully. I'll stuff her in a locker next.

"Can't you just go enjoy your coffee in the living room?" I press a hand to her chest. "Go cocoon yourself and watch the snow falling. Doesn't that sound nice?"

This is hard for her, me making breakfast. Instead of listening to me, she lingers in the kitchen, asking if I need help with anything. I scramble eggs and fry up some bacon, both of which I had to run down the road to purchase before she and Josie woke up. Her fridge had only four items in it when I checked this morning, and none of them looked fit for human consumption.

I drop some bread into the toaster and she rushes over, explaining to me how it works.

"Ohhhh, I see," I reply, as if enlightened to the art of toast for first time in my life. "You put the bread in the two little slits and push down right *here*. Got it. I always thought there was more to it."

My sarcasm is lost on her. She flies over to the fridge. "Why don't I make us some fresh-squeezed orange juice?"

She bends down and roots through the empty drawers, no doubt trying to find the orange I saw earlier. It was growing a Petri dish's worth of mold. It's now in the trash.

"Bailey," I chide, dropping my hands on her shoulders and directing her into the living room. She attempts to dig her heels in, but my size makes it a futile fight. "When was the last time someone cooked for you?"

She frowns up at me, having to think hard. "Josie tried to make me pancakes a few months ago, but she set off the smoke alarm and then like a dozen firemen showed up." She waves her hand. "It was a whole thing."

Josie, who's sitting on the couch eating cereal (which I also bought), smiles proudly. "It was actually pretty cool. One of them let me try on his uniform."

I chuckle and turn back to Bailey. Her eyes say, *Please let me help.* I shake my head, tip her chin toward me, and am about to give her a chaste kiss when I realize her sister is watching us. Instead, I straighten and gently shove her down onto the couch. "Sit." She tries to stand. "*No.* I said sit." I step back and hold up my hands, retreating hesitantly. "Stay."

"You're talking to me as if I'm a dog," she says pointedly.

"If only you were—maybe then you'd actually listen."

She narrows her eyes before I return to the kitchen. To Bailey's credit, she stays put for the entire ten minutes it takes me to finish up the bacon and eggs. I fix our plates, top off our coffee mugs, and then set the table.

Bailey is inexplicably touched by the gesture. "You

didn't have to do all this," she says, waving to her food and the bouquet of flowers I picked up at the checkout counter on a whim. I felt foolish carrying them in earlier, like maybe it was a little too much, but then Bailey walked out of her bedroom, wiping sleep from her eyes and dragging her feet. She paused, face frozen, mouth agape, and then she asked very slowly, "Are those for me?"

A million responses leapt to my mind, none of which seemed appropriate at that moment, so I settled for a simple, "Merry Christmas."

I've never seen someone fuss so much over a few damn roses. She trimmed them carefully and arranged them in a vase. They sit on the table between us now, and she's staring at them as she takes a big bite of scrambled eggs.

Josie opts to finish her cereal in the living room. Apparently, there's some kind of holiday movie marathon on TV that she doesn't want to miss.

"Matt, this is amazing." Bailey grins.

"It's nothing. I make myself breakfast every morning."

She levels her gaze on me. "You know what I mean. I really appreciate it."

"How will you ever thank me?" I ask, hoping Josie is too enamored by her cheesy movie to catch my innuendo.

Bailey's eyes light up. "I can give you your presents!"

"Presents, as in more than one?"

She leaps to her feet and hurries out of the room. A second later, a wrapped box is dropped onto my lap. There's a pink bow right on top.

"Open it, open it!" she insists.

I have a weird urge to protest. *If I open this now, what will I have to open on Christmas morning?* But then I remember I'm an adult, not a ten-year-old boy. Not to mention, I don't want to kill Bailey's excitement. I start to unwrap it and I'm so careful with the bow and wrapping paper it's like I'm going to go home and put it all in a scrapbook. Bailey notices.

"God, are you meticulous about *everything*? I should have known a surgeon wouldn't just tear into a gift with full abandon."

"Ha ha," I mock, flattening the wrapping paper on the table just to mess with her. Then I fold it in two, and again, hotdog style.

She's nearly convulsing with impatience.

There's tape across the top of the box. I reach my hand toward her and demand, "Scalpel."

She feigns pulling out her hair, clearly over my jokes, so I open it quickly, blinking with confusion at what stares up at me.

Her smile is self-conscious. "It's a little scoreboard—y'know, for the basketball hoop in your office."

I laugh. "Awesome."

I pick it up to see how it works and my gaze catches on the second thing Bailey put in the box.

A picture of me.

A picture of me with devil horns and a little red tail.

She rolls her lips together before clarifying, "That is, well…you might have heard, but it's a picture that was hanging in the staff lounge."

"What a thoughtful gift," I reply dryly.

"It's not really a gift." She tilts her head in thought. "I guess me taking it down is sort of a gift, but I think the fact that I, er…was the one to put it up in the first place kind of negates that. Don't you think?" My eyes catch hers and she offers a helpless smile. "It was before I worked for you. Kirt was crying, really making a scene, so I did it to make him laugh."

"You drew the devil horns?"

She grimaces. "Guilty. Please don't hate me."

If I'm honest, it's actually extremely funny that Bailey was the culprit behind the photo. I mean, talk about a twist of fate.

"You can draw an embarrassing photo of me and hang it in the doctors' lounge if you want!" she adds hurriedly. "Just to even the score."

My gaze levels with hers and I reply as seriously as possible. "All right. You can pose for me after breakfast."

Her eyes widen as she catches my meaning and she flushes from head to toe.

"Matt."

I smirk and drop the picture back into the box. "Consider us even."

"You're not mad?"

"Not at all. In fact, I love *both* of my gifts. Now finish your breakfast. I need to head over to check on June while the roads are still clear, and you can come with me if you want."

She scrambles for her fork. "Yes!"

THE DAYS LEADING up to Christmas pass quickly. I'd planned on taking full advantage of an empty office to catch up on work, but somehow it never happens. It's easy to see where I go wrong, and it's largely in my inability to say no to Bailey. On that first day, after we check on June, we drive by an outdoor holiday market with vendors selling last-minute Christmas gifts. There are carolers and food trucks and even a little skating rink.

"We have to take Josie!" Bailey exclaims, her face and

hands pressed to my passenger window. "She'll love it!"

So, of course, we do. But first, we stop off at my house so I can shower and change into some clean clothes. After I rinse off, I step back into my room with a towel wrapped around my waist and find Bailey packing some of my clothes into one of my duffle bags.

"What are you doing?" I ask, glancing down to see what she's packed. There are like 45 pairs of socks, but not much else.

"I figured it'd just be easier for you to have some clothes at my house."

"Oh?"

She turns toward me in a panic, face suddenly pale. "Unless I'm reading this situation wrong? Oh crap—was this just a one-night-stand sort of thing?"

Before I can reply, she proceeds to turn the duffle bag over and spill the contents of it out onto my bed. Just as I suspected, it's all socks. At least there's an assorted variety.

I laugh. "No, Bailey. I was actually going to pack some clothes, but you were off to a good start."

She watches me as I walk into my closet to grab a pair of jeans and a flannel shirt.

"Wait, umm…before you get dressed…"

Her voice drifts off as she rubs her arm, clears her throat, and stares up at the ceiling. I carry my clothes back into my bedroom and lay them across the bench in front of my bed. I know she's suggesting we have sex, and the idea that she thinks I was planning on leaving my house without doing that first is adorable.

I smile tauntingly. "Finish your sentence."

She turns away and scrunches her nose then squints her eyes at my headboard like she's deep in thought. "I was just going to say…because you have a king bed and we only had my twin bed last night…" I step toward her and start to tug her shirt up over her stomach and chest. She holds up her arms dutifully and her shirt gets tossed to the floor. "Not to mention, you have an empty house and Josie thinks we're still checking in on June…" I unbutton her jeans and start to slide them down her legs. "It really just makes sense for us to have sex right now!" she finally finishes on a heavy exhale.

I smirk and bend down to kiss her.

"Funny, I was just going to suggest the same thing."

The morning after the holiday market, I force myself to spend a couple hours up at the hospital. I need to check in on a few patients and catch up on work, but it doesn't last.

> **Bailey**: Are you done yet?
>
> **Matt**: I've only been up here for a couple of hours. I just finished with my patients.
>
> **Bailey**: Well, our Christmas tree is officially dead. Apparently, there's a finite number of decorations one tiny tree can withstand. I think we'll have to go get a new one. Poor guy sort of split in two.

Then she sends a picture of Josie leaning over the tree, frowning, and doing a thumbs-down.

I wonder if Bailey ever just has a normal, boring day. Somehow, I doubt it.

That evening, we drive to a tree farm and luck out when we see that all the trees are on sale.

"Duh!" Josie says from the back seat. "It's Christmas Eve tomorrow!"

I hadn't even realized. Crap. I should have called my mom back days ago, but it completely slipped my mind. She's probably given up my spot at the Christmas dinner table, or if not, she'll have ordered a cutout version of me to place there. It'd probably be as jovial as I tend to be during the holidays.

I leave Bailey and Josie to browse through the trees and tell them to find a good one, and then I head back toward my car to dial my mom.

"Well, if it isn't a Christmas miracle," she teases as soon as she picks up.

I smile. "Hey. Sorry, it's been a crazy few days."

"Aren't they always? Let me guess, you're up at the office now, working even though you should be enjoying the holidays?"

I rub the scruff of my neck and turn in time to see Josie point to the back of the lot, where they keep the behemoths, and then I hear her tell the attendant, "We're looking for something bigger!"

Oh lord.

"Actually, I'm at a tree farm with Bailey and her sister."

"*Bailey*…" She says the name like she's trying to jog her memory.

"The woman I'm seeing," I clarify at the same moment she exclaims, "Your surgical assistant?! The woman Cooper brought as his date to Molly's wedding?"

I watch as Josie points to what I swear is the biggest, widest tree in the whole damn lot and then asks the attendant to wrap it up. Bailey turns back to me and holds up her hands like, *What are we going to do?*

I laugh and shake my head. There is a 110% chance I'll be driving home with that tree attached to the roof of my Prius.

My mom makes a funny, well-isn't-that-interesting noise. "So she got you out of the office, huh?"

I sigh. "Seems so."

"I'll be damned. Are you going to spend Christmas Day

with her as well?"

Bailey made it clear I was welcome to. Well, technically, Josie was the first to insist upon it. *"You have to! Bailey makes the best cinnamon rolls in the world! It's a Christmas tradition!"*

"I might."

"Well, you're welcome to bring them over to the house. It'll just be a few of us. Your Uncle Pat and his wife are coming, and Molly and Thomas are back from their honeymoon so they'll be there too. Cooper's staying up in Cincinnati."

"Okay, let me run it by Bailey and I'll let you know."

I expect Bailey to flinch at the idea of spending Christmas with my family, and I don't even work up the courage to suggest it until we're halfway home from the tree farm. It's taking longer than usual because with the tree on my roof, I can barely see out the windshield.

"Really?! I'd love to go to your parents' house on Christmas!" she says, smiling. "Honestly, the holidays can get a little lonely with just Josie and me, and it's a hassle making all that food for only two people. We usually just skip right to dessert." She turns toward the back seat. "What do you think, Jos? Do you want to go?"

Josie leans forward and props her hand on my headrest. "What kind of food are we talking? Your standard turkey and stuffing?"

"And ham too, probably."

Her eyes narrow in serious contemplation. "Will there be sweet potato casserole?"

"Always."

"Green bean casserole?"

My grin widens. "Definitely."

"How many dessert options, give or take?"

"Josie," Bailey cuts in, eyes wide in warning.

"At least half a dozen," I brag.

"Fresh-baked rolls?"

I smirk, knowing full well I've got her. "My mom uses an old family recipe. Word is she uses half a stick of butter for each one."

She grins and taps my headrest twice. "All right then. I'll wear my stretchiest pants."

CHAPTER TWENTY-NINE
BAILEY

I'M SO JOLLY on Christmas morning I might as well be Mrs. Claus. I wake up before the sun and am careful not to wake Matt as I sneak out of bed. For the record, he's a cuddler, and I have to simultaneously pull my body out from beneath his arm and slide a big fluffy pillow into its place. It works like a charm.

I'm a little elf doing Santa's bidding as I tiptoe around the living room. I lay stockings out on the coffee table for Matt and Josie. Matt's is homemade (Josie had some fun yesterday with felt letters and a hot glue gun), and sure, it's a little wonky—she made M-A-T so big she had to put the last T on the back—but it's the thought that counts. I fill both stockings with candy: cherry cordials for Josie and the darkest dark chocolate I could find for Matt. Josie and I both groaned in protest when he told us that was his favorite treat.

Once that's done, I light the tree and put out Josie's "gift from Santa". It's tradition. I always wrap a few things for her, but the real present—the big kahuna, if you will—always sits unwrapped in front of the tree, waiting for her to run out and see it and squeal with delight. Last year, it was a Kindle. This year, I scrimped and saved and got her tickets to see *Harry Potter and the Cursed Child* on Broadway. We'll take a train into the city and make a whole day of it. I'm giddy just thinking about it. She's definitely going to scream, maybe even cry. I should set up my phone to record the whole thing.

After everything is arranged in the living room, I head into the kitchen, AKA where the real magic happens on Christmas morning.

I flip the light on and the quiet, empty room sends a pang straight to my heart. I'm careful around the holidays. After so many years without my parents, I've learned it's a slippery slope to dwell on their absence too much this time of year. The first years without them, Josie was so young, to her it didn't matter so much that our parents weren't with us as long as there were presents waiting for her under the tree. Dollar store trinkets lit up her eyes and a frozen turkey dinner was as good as any. Meanwhile, all I wanted to do was curl up into a ball and cease to exist, but with Josie relying on me, I pulled myself together and cranked up the holiday spirit.

In the years since, we've slowly started to incorporate my parents into the festivities more and more. It doesn't scare me as much as it used to. Now we hang my mom's vintage ornaments on the tree, and every time *Feliz Navidad* comes on the radio, we sing along at the top of our lungs just like my dad used to do. My favorite tradition is baking on Christmas morning. It's something my mom and I used to do together. She and I would wake up first and take care to be extra quiet as we padded into the kitchen so we wouldn't wake up my dad and Josie.

Her maple-glazed cinnamon rolls were out of this world. To this day, Josie talks about them every day of December, discussing ad nauseum every little detail that makes them so dang delicious. The thought makes me smile as I pull the recipe card out of a tin box and run my finger pad across it. I know I shouldn't. My mother's instructions are written in pencil and they're already fading, but I just can't help myself. Being in here now makes me feel closer to her, as if she and I are still doing this together.

God, I miss her.

"Ugh, I could have sworn I already smelled cinnamon rolls, but I must have been dreaming."

I jump out of my skin and whip around to see Josie standing at the kitchen door, rubbing sleep from her eyes. Her blonde hair is sticking up in every direction and there's a little drool dried on her chin. Her sleeping shirt says, *All I want for Christmas is you food*.

"Oh no. I didn't wake you, did I?"

She wraps her arms around herself to keep warm and shakes her head. "No. I was just too excited to sleep."

I quirk a brow. "You didn't go into the living room yet, did you?"

Her eyes light up with the realization that there are presents with her name on them waiting just in the other room. She turns as if preparing to sprint.

"Wait!" I plead. "Help me bake first. *Please*? We'll go look at your gifts in a minute."

She groans and I can tell she really wants to go see her presents, but something in my tone must tip her off to the things I'm not saying, to the memories we tiptoe around so carefully, because she relents and walks over to me. Her arms wrap around my waist and she rests her head against my shoulder.

"Merry Christmas, Bailey," she says wistfully.

I lean down and kiss her forehead. "Merry Christmas, Josie."

I'M EXCITED TO go to Matt's parents' house for Christmas, but I wish he'd sprung it on me a little earlier, like maybe *before* all the stores closed. I would have liked to bring his mom something: a candle, a tea towel—I don't know. I've never had a boyfriend, therefore I've never had to impress a boyfriend's mom, so I'm just going off of what I think Reese Witherspoon or Joanna Gaines would do, and they'd sure as shit bring a gift for Mrs. Russell.

Matt assures me it doesn't matter, but when I persist, he caves and we swing by his place for some wine on our way to their house. I feel a lot better cradling that bottle on my lap. Josie also helped me bake snowball cookies after breakfast, so between the two gifts, Mrs. Russell will have to like me. Right?

At least I look the part. I'm wearing a red cashmere sweater. I've never owned anything cashmere before and holy heck, how is this material so soft? The sweater was a gift from Josie. When I opened it this morning my first thought was, *OMG I LOVE IT*. My second thought was, *Oh god, how did Josie afford this?* I might have accused her of petty theft before she clued me in to the fact that she's been shoveling the snow off Ms. Murphy's sidewalk and taking out her trash for the last two months so she could afford to buy me something. It was such a sweet gesture that I cried. Josie told me to get it together, but the tears just kept coming. This morning has been one emotional gut punch after another. Like for instance, Matt somehow managed to sneak away long enough in the last few days to get both Josie and me a gift. I wasn't expecting anything, but when he produced a present for each of us, the tears were back.

Josie groaned. "Honestly, do you need a minute to compose yourself?"

"No! I'm fine. I swear!" I protested, snot running down my face. "Here, let me use your pajamas to wipe my nose."

Josie opened her gift first.

"It's a journal," Matt said, somewhat nervously. "I thought since you enjoy reading so much, you might enjoy writing as well."

What's that painful feeling? Oh yes, it's my heart swelling to ten times its normal size and encroaching on all my other organs.

He brushed the back of his neck self-consciously. "Also, there's a Barnes & Noble gift card in the bottom of the bag, just in case you hate that."

Josie—the girl who has never once had a difficult time finding words—was speechless. She stared down at the journal and nodded. Matt cleared his throat and picked up his empty coffee cup, inspected the contents, and then set it back down.

"Also, I have the receipt in my wallet if—"

She shook her head quickly. "No! It's perfect."

Then she cradled it against her chest like it was a baby bird as Matt leaned forward to grab a tiny red gift bag off the coffee table for me. I took it from him with a smile and started tugging out tissue paper carefully. At the very bottom there was a small black velvet box.

A ring box.

OH MY GOD. WHOA. TOO SOON. BUT YES OKAY!

I yanked that sucker out of there and whipped it open, a *YES* locked and loaded on my tongue right up until my eyes registered that there were not one but two twinkling diamonds nestled in the box, and they were attached to studs, not a band.

"Earrings," I said slowly, instantly regretting not showing more enthusiasm.

THEY'RE DIAMOND-FREAKING-EARRINGS, BAILEY! Get it together!

"I know jewelry is sort of cliché, but since you always wear your hair up at work—"

Josie put up her hand to stop him from continuing. "Every girl wants diamonds. You did good."

"Bailey?" he asked.

My mouth opened and words were supposed to be spilling out, but my brain couldn't quite handle the shock of the last few minutes. I literally thought Matt was proposing to me after like a week of dating. I've gone mad.

"They're beautiful," I whispered, hoping he wouldn't scrutinize my reaction too much.

I'm wearing the earrings now and I've already flipped open the mirror on the visor in Matt's car twice to inspect how they look in my ears. I curled my hair and pulled it up into a ponytail so I could show them off. Combined with the red sweater, I can't remember a time in my life when I felt more beautiful.

"You like them?" Matt asks from the driver's seat, glancing over to me.

"They're perfect," I reply, reaching over to take his hand and cradle it in my lap.

"All right, enough with the lovey-dovey stuff," Josie groans in the back seat. "Can someone turn Christmas music on? I'm ready to sing!"

CHAPTER THIRTY
BAILEY

NORMALLY, I'D FEEL a little sad to see the holidays go, but this year is different. I'm ready to start working again. I'm anxious to get back into the OR with Matt. His schedule will be jam-packed because of the cases we had to delay for June's surgery, but I've already told him I'm willing to work as much as he needs me to. We'll tackle it together.

Even though I'm ready to get back to the hospital, I can't believe how fast the holiday break flew by. Matt and I spent nearly every moment of it together. We were with his family on Christmas Day. After dominating a round of charades, his aunts and uncles enthusiastically embraced Josie and me as if we were one of them. His mom made me sit right by her during dinner, and she even stealthily showed me embarrassing photos of Matt and Cooper when they were babies. That night, Matt and I happily crammed ourselves onto my twin bed.

In the days that followed, we (I) baked cookies and ate them straight out of the oven. We spoiled Josie and took her to spend most of her Barnes & Noble gift card. She has enough books to last her a lifetime, though I fear she'll finish them all within a week.

Things are moving fast between Matt and me. This isn't just a casual fling and though I'm ready to go all in, I worry it might be too much for Matt because I start to notice a subtle shift in his demeanor the weekend before we're due back at the hospital. It starts when we're driving home from dinner on Friday and I ask him something, nothing important, really, but he doesn't reply. I glance over to see he wasn't even listening. When we get home, I work up the courage to ask him if everything is okay, and he brushes off my concern as if it's nothing and tugs me in for a kiss, worries be damned.

Saturday, we take Josie to go see a movie and he doesn't watch a single minute of it. Sure, he's sitting there, looking up at the screen, but his mind is somewhere else. I know because we talk about it on the way home and Matt can't even name the main character. Josie teases him about it, but I keep quiet, wondering if I've done something to give him second thoughts about us.

At dinner, I catch him checking his email incessantly and then that night, I wake up to see him sitting on the edge of my bed, his head in hands.

At first, I think he's sick.

It's 2:30 AM. *Why is he awake?*

"Matt? Are you okay?"

He jerks up straight and glances at me over his shoulder. "Yeah, I'm fine. I just couldn't sleep."

He reaches back and finds the hand I extend out for him. Something doesn't feel right. I've never suspected him of lying to me, but I swear he's not being honest now.

"Are you sure? Do you want me to get you some water or something?"

"No, I don't need anything." He shifts and crawls back under the blankets to get to me.

I'm greedy for his warmth and I tuck myself right beside him. It's my favorite spot.

"It seems like you've had a lot on your mind the last few days," I venture, brushing my finger back and forth against his chest.

He sighs. "I'm supposed to hear back about that grant any day now. That's what's been on my mind."

Of course! I should have realized. I heard him talking about it with his parents on Christmas Day, but I was too far away to catch much of the conversation.

Relief rushes through me. I was really worried he was having reservations about us.

"That's exciting, Matt. Will you tell me about it?"

His arm wraps around me and he draws me even closer. "Sure. In the morning. We should get to sleep."

That conversation never happens though. The next day Matt has to head up to the hospital early, and by the time he gets back to my house, I've finished making lasagna and Josie ushers him straight to the table she's set. Then, she proceeds to dominate most of the dinner conversation, and I don't mind because I'm busy watching them. They have an easygoing relationship. He seems so relaxed around her, as if he can't help but smile at her ridiculous take on life. After we finish eating, Matt offers to do the dishes—and by offers, I mean he forcibly removes me from the kitchen.

One day rolls into the next and the grant is the last thing on my mind.

We settle into a happy pattern, one I could easily get used to. Matt and I operate together three days a week and he stays over at my house most nights. We share my tiny twin bed and his cuddle habits grow more out of control. Soon, I'll have to build a pillow fort between us just to get some sleep. I secretly love it.

I cook him and Josie dinner most nights, or when we have a late surgery, we opt for takeout. Matt insists on paying for groceries since he's the one eating most of the food. Tuna is a thing of the past, and I couldn't be more grateful. We watch movies with Josie on the weekends and sneak out for a date night here and there, usually just hightailing it over to his house so we can have sex without fear that Josie will walk in on us. Also, I take full advantage of his washer and dryer. While our clothes tumble dry, we tumble right back into bed.

It's the best month I can remember, weeks so jam-packed with happiness I completely forget about the grant until I arrive at work one Monday and find half the hospital standing outside Matt's office, clambering to get inside.

There are balloons tied to the door handle and laughter spilling out into the hall. I can't get within ten feet. I can't even *see* inside to try to decipher what could possibly be going on.

At first, I assume this is all excitement about June because she took a few steps on her own in physical therapy the other day, though that doesn't make sense because this is way too over the top.

Someone nudges their way through the crowd with a cake that says, *Congratulations!* Another person shouts, "Dr. Russell, you're the *man!*"

I spot Erika hovering at the back of the crowd, pressing up on her toes to try to see into his office. I head in her direction and ask what's going on.

She turns and her eyes widen. Her hands grip my shoulders and she shakes me back and forth. My brain rattles in my head. "Oh my god! I can't believe he got it!"

"Got what?" I ask, dumbfounded.

"The MacArthur Grant!"

OH MY GOD!

My hand covers my mouth in excitement. I can't believe it! He's probably freaking out! Look at all these people here to celebrate with him. I've never even heard of the MacArthur Grant but it sounds fancy as hell.

"That's amazing!"

"I know! Apparently, he was awarded full funding for his spine clinic in Costa Rica! Isn't that insane?! Wait." She shakes her head and laughs. "Why am I telling *you* this?"

Wait. *WHAT?!*

Spine clinic?

Costa Rica?!

I blink and try to make sense of what she could possibly mean. Costa Rica—is that a fancy suburb of Boston or something? Surely she isn't referring to the country a million miles away from where I currently stand.

"It's so crazy! I can't believe you kept the secret too," she continues. "None of us even knew he was in the running for it until this morning when we found out he won. I bet he's been a nervous wreck."

I laugh half-heartedly. "Oh, yeah. Super nervous."

Her brows furrow and she tilts her head, studying me. "Did he not tell you he won?"

I shake my head infinitesimally and then admit the sad truth. "No. I mean, we haven't talked this morning…"

He didn't tell me he won. He didn't tell me anything about the grant or the spine clinic or what that could possibly mean for us. I mean, I knew he was waiting to hear back about *a* grant, but I thought it would just be money that could go toward more pro bono work here, or, I don't know, more chocolate fountains in the doctors' lounge. I had no idea he was trying to open a clinic in another country.

I feel like the floor is falling out from underneath me. Am I dreaming? Did I eat too much leftover Christmas candy last night and now this is some weird sugar-induced nightmare? I press a hand against my stomach and try to steady myself, and now Erika is actually concerned by how I'm taking the news. "I'm confused—aren't you two dating? Everyone just assumed with how you acted at the Christmas party, and you've been inseparable around the hospital ever since…"

I give her a sort of half-nod, half-shake of my head. Yes, sure, I thought we were dating. All signs point to the two of us being a couple. I'm wearing diamond studs he gave me. He's practically living with me. He kissed my cheek in the wee hours of the morning before he left for work today. Until this moment, I thought we had a future, but this is throwing me for a loop, and why the heck are there so many people out here right now? I couldn't get into his office if I tried. It'd be like attempting to push my way to the front row at Coachella. No thank you. It's a little too early in the morning to get elbowed in the head.

"I didn't mean to upset you," Erika says, dropping a hand onto my shoulder in solidarity.

Oh Erika, you kind soul. You aren't to blame in this.

Matt is.

Matt with his stupid secrets and his big plans.

I shake my head. "It's nothing. Really. I'm just a little flustered because of this surgery I have in a little bit. Actually, I better get down there."

It's such a good excuse she doesn't even try to stop me. I walk numbly down the hall and away from the chaos. The elevator opens and a deliveryman steps out with an extra-large Edible Arrangements bouquet and an armload of balloons. There are so many, I sort of get tangled up in them as I try to step into the elevator.

"Oh, oops!" The deliveryman laughs. "Here, let me just—"

I flail my arms and kick my legs and let out a guttural

322

groan before I finally break free onto the other side.

"Sorry about that! Death by balloons, ha ha."

I barely contain my snarl as I repeatedly press the *Close Door* button in the elevator. The surgical floor is blessedly empty when I arrive. It shouldn't be a surprise considering every human in the building is up in Matt's office bowing down and kissing his ass.

I head straight for the surgical board, confirm our assigned room, and get to work.

I keep my head down, stay focused, and let the rhythm of my job take over.

This is what I know.

This is what I love.

It's simple and methodical and before Matt swelled my heart to ten times its normal size, it was enough to keep me happy.

My coworkers start trickling in as I finish my prep. I nod to each of them and feign a smile as they mention Matt or the grant or all the children in Costa Rica who will be affected by the clinic he's going to open. There's an undercurrent of excitement in the air. Everyone's glad to be working with Matt today—everyone except me.

It makes me mad that everyone seems to know more than I do, and even more mad that I shouldn't be mad. He's going to help children! He's going to be a hero! I can't hate him for that, and yet deep down…I'm angry. Blisteringly so.

I'm scrubbed in and standing at the operating table by the time he walks in.

His gaze is aimed straight at me as he makes a beeline for my side.

The anesthesiologist tries to catch his attention, to congratulate him, and Matt barely throws a glance in his direction.

"Bailey, I've been trying to call you all morning."

"Not all morning."

"What?" he asks, brows furrowed.

I clear my throat, aware that every person in that OR has stopped what they're doing to listen to us.

"I checked my phone when I was on my way to work and I didn't have any missed calls," I clarify, turning to the patient. "Everything is ready to go. Let me grab your gown and I'll help tie it."

That's my way of trying to tell him, *Not now. Not in front of everyone. Please don't tell me you're moving to Costa Rica now because I will definitely sob and I'd like to maintain some dignity in front of my coworkers, thank you very much.*

His eyes lock with mine and they're imploring me to do…something. *What? Do what, Matt?!*

I turn to retrieve his gown and as I tie it onto him, we don't say a word. As we go around the room for the time-out, confirming we're all ready to get started, I stare up at the gallery, at all the eager faces staring right back down at me. They're watching, waiting. My fledgling relationship with Matt is probably just as interesting to them as the surgery they came here to watch.

"Bailey, you're up," Matt says, his voice distant and cold. It's the surgeon talking—that's what I tell myself so I don't have to feel hurt when I turn and see he's staring at me like he doesn't even recognize me.

I'm the same person I was yesterday, Matt.

You're the one who's changed.

HE FINDS ME after I finish scrubbing out. I'm walking down the hall when he steps out of a post-op recovery room and heads in the opposite direction. His presence might as well take up the whole damn hallway. He's half a foot taller than everyone he passes. His hair is ten shades darker. He turns heads without even trying.

I don't consciously decide to walk right by him. I have work I need to catch up on, but he blocks my path and narrows his gaze down at me. He looks like a giant who wants to crush me under his shoe.

"Can I speak with you for a moment?"

I'm sure he's expecting a fight, but I won't be immature about this. I nod and offer a tight-lipped smile.

"Of course. Where would you like to speak?"

He grips my elbow and tugs me hard into a nearby on-call room.

Metal bunk beds are stacked against one wall. A wooden desk fills what's left of the small space. The lights are dim as I turn to face him and decide to speak first.

"Congratulations on the grant, Matt. I'm really happy for you."

Shockingly, it's the truth. Separate from being hurt, I *am* happy for him. I can't think of another doctor who deserves this as much as he does.

"I was going to tell you about it," he says quickly, coming toward me. I hold my ground and it only takes him two strides to reach me. His hands wrap around my biceps and he speaks quickly, words rushing out one after the other. "I just didn't want to make a fuss about it until I knew for sure whether or not the committee would pick me. There was every chance the other surgeon would win." I nod, trying hard to give him the benefit of the doubt. "And I wasn't sure how to say, *Oh, by the way, I could be moving to Costa Rica soon.*"

"So instead you opted to keep me in the dark," I clarify with a rueful smirk.

He rears back like my words sting him. "No, Bailey. *No*. I wanted to preserve what we had before complicating it with *this*."

I sigh and nod, sad for us both. "Sorry, I didn't mean that. I just really wish you had told me."

"I'm sorry, I am. It was selfish of me."

He's saying all the right things and I'm somehow not making a complete ass of myself. This should go down as the most mature fight any couple has ever had, but I can't seem to care. Just because he's clarifying things for me now doesn't change the fact that he's leaving.

"When will you go?" I ask, my voice emotionless.

He frowns. "Summer at the latest."

Well there's our timeline: a few months. Maybe we can really make them count. Maybe I can cram in a lifetime's worth of memories with Matt before he leaves.

"Please don't be angry, Bailey. This doesn't have to be sad. In fact, I've been thinking…" He bends to my eye level. "You could come with me."

"Come with you?" I repeat in disbelief.

The suggestion lights a fire under him. He releases me and starts to pace quickly, hand brushing the nape of his neck.

"Yes. Come with me! Honestly, I've been considering it for weeks. This clinic is going to be impossible to run without you. I need you by my side."

I'm shaking my head, trying hard to keep up. When I speak, I sound as if he's proposing the most ludicrous idea I've ever heard. "What are you *talking* about? My life is here, Matt. My sister is here. I can't just pick up and leave."

His brows furrow. "Josie will come too, of course. I want her to! This is perfect. You and I will build the clinic together. You'll be by my side. There are tutors I can hire for Josie or we could enroll her in an American school there. I've already been calling around. This weekend, I emailed a colleague—"

He's talking a mile a minute, acting as if this is a real possibility. I suddenly feel the urge to throw up.

"STOP!" I'm seething. "Just stop! You've been calling around and making plans and yet it didn't occur to you to *include* me in these plans? Jesus, do you really think I'd move Josie to another country just like that?" I snap. "We've been dating for a few weeks, Matt. Put yourself in my shoes. Think about what you're asking of me!"

Just then, the door to the on-call room opens and a resident steps in, rubbing her eyes. When she glances up and sees us, she freezes. "Oh, crap. Sorry." Then she jerks around and scurries out of the room.

I want to follow her, but instead, I take a steadying breath and choose my next words very carefully. It's easier to think when I keep my attention on the door and away from him.

"I'm very, very happy that you won the grant. No one deserves it more than you. I wish you had told me about it, but I understand why you didn't. Things are new between us and you didn't want to rock the boat. I get that. I forgive you for that. I just…need a little while to wrap my head around this. That's all."

He nods and tugs me toward him by the front of my scrub top so he can wrap his arms around me. We hug, and at first, it's the last thing I want. It feels awkward and tense. I don't give in. I keep my arms hanging limp at my sides in silent protest. My gaze is focused on the wall behind his head. A part of me wants to step away and deny him this hug, but then his arms tighten around me and I let my forehead fall against his chest, against my better judgment. My breathing slows and my anger is fleeting, replaced by an overwhelming urge to accept this small comfort.

He dips down so his head rests against my shoulder, and my heart breaks a little at the idea that this could be one of the last times we're this close to one another. By the time the snow melts and the flowers bloom again, he'll be gone.

"This doesn't have to be the end," he says, hopeful. "This grant could be the start of something for both of us. *Please* think about it."

CHAPTER THIRTY-ONE
MATT

WHEN I MAKE it back to my office, it's back to normal—messy, but at least it's *my* mess. Patricia worked her magic in clearing everyone and everything out. The balloons and bouquets were sent down to my patients. The congratulatory cookies and cupcakes and fruit baskets were dispersed to different lounges around the hospital. I'll be everyone's favorite doctor by the end of the day. I sneer at the thought. With my office back in order, it's almost as if this morning never happened, but unfortunately, that's not the case.

"The phones have been ringing off the hook," Patricia says, leaning her head past the door and holding out a thick stack of messages for me. "I think everyone on Earth is trying to get in contact with you, but I've told most of them you're too busy to talk. Dr. Lopez is holding on line one though. He didn't buy my excuse."

I drag my feet walking to my phone. As the closest thing to a father figure Bailey has, Dr. Lopez isn't exactly someone I want to speak with at the moment, but I can't just ignore him. He's so polite, he'd probably wait on the line all afternoon.

I stay standing as I connect to line one, greeting him with a knot of apprehension in my stomach.

"Dr. Russell!" he says, his tone full of excitement. "If it isn't the man of the hour!"

I grow uncomfortably hot.

"Hey Dr. Lopez, good to hear from you. How's

retirement treating you?"

"Oh, it's fine. A little boring, but Laurie says I'm still adjusting to a slower pace. Truth be told, I've picked up about ten hobbies—grilling, gardening, woodworking—none of which I actually like yet."

I muster up a shallow chuckle.

"Listen," he continues. "I heard about the grant. What an accomplishment. You must be beside yourself."

Beside myself? Try depressed as hell.

"It's great."

Dr. Lopez hums skeptically. Maybe I should feign a little more enthusiasm. "I've been getting calls about it all morning. I'm really proud of you."

"Thank you for calling. It means a lot."

"While I have you here, I was also going to ask, how's Bailey doing?" There it is, the question that makes my heart drop. I must hesitate for a moment too long because he laughs. "Don't tell me you've already run her off? It's only been a few months."

"No." I scramble quickly. "I haven't. She still works for me."

I can hear the smile in his voice as he continues, "Good. I'm glad to hear it. I hope you'll try to find a position for her at the hospital before you leave for Costa Rica. Last I heard, the board is looking to bring on another surgeon now that you're leaving, but if that isn't a good fit for Bailey, tell her to give me a call. I can check around with a few of my old colleagues. I worry about her." He sighs. "You aren't stressing her out too much, are you?"

Stressing her out? Well, I just proposed she move to another country with me—how's that for stress?

"No. I'm going easy on her," I lie.

"Somehow I doubt that." He chuckles. "Well, all right, I

330

can tell you don't really want to be talking right now. You're probably as busy as ever so I won't keep you, but please pass on that message to Bailey and let her know Laurie and I are thinking about her. And congratulations, again. The work you're going to do in Costa Rica will impact a lot of lives. You should be proud."

His words magnify my guilt tenfold.

After we hang up, I sit at my desk, staring out the window, wondering how I could have possibly screwed up so badly. Just this morning, I woke up in bed with Bailey. Now, I'd be lucky if she even took my phone call. When Patricia speaks to me through the intercom and reminds me I'm running a few minutes late for a consult, I sigh and push to stand so I can head toward the conference room.

I should have told Dr. Lopez the truth about my situation with Bailey and asked for his advice. He knows her well. Maybe he could have told me how to proceed. Then the thought makes me smile. Yeah right. More than likely he would have chewed my ass out for hurting her feelings in the first place.

Admittedly, I'm not good at relationships. I've perfected every spinal procedure in the book, but when it comes to matters of the heart, I'm a complete idiot. *Good thing I didn't go into cardio.*

I push through the rest of my day, try to stay focused, and do a piss-poor job of it. After I mix up two patient files and nearly perform a pre-op exam on the wrong person, I decide to ask Patricia to postpone everything else on my schedule and knock off early. It might be the first time I've ever taken a personal day.

Patricia is so confused by the request, she asks me if I need to be admitted to the hospital. *"Are you dying?"*

I'm at a complete loss for what to do with myself when

I get home. For the last few weeks, I've been at Bailey's house in my free time. My cold, quiet home matches my mood a little too well. I turn on the TV in the living room just for some background noise. I check my phone to see if she's called, and when she hasn't, I check my email. It's jam-packed with messages of congratulations. I keep scrolling, come to an email from Victoria, and opt to ignore it. I have enough on my plate at the moment. Whatever she wants to talk to me about can wait. *By the way, I'm not just having one baby. It's twins!*

I think about reaching out to Bailey, but I don't think it'd be a good idea.

She asked for space earlier. She needs time to process everything I threw at her, and maybe that isn't such a bad idea. I'll respect her wishes, but I'll use my time wisely.

I have a lot to do.

This grant is important to me because in the past, my work abroad has been limited to week-long medical mission trips. I'd assemble a volunteer team and we'd travel to the National Children's Hospital in San Jose, Costa Rica. There, we'd have to race through a waiting list filled with hundreds of children in need of surgery. Every one of them was as deserving as the last, but with limited funds and time, we were only ever able to operate on a handful of them.

It wasn't enough.

I want to do more, and now, with this grant, I can.

I'm not moving to Costa Rica forever. My goal is to be there for a year or two. I'll use the aid to establish a clinic and train surgeons and staff at the hospital there.

I can't do it on my own, though. I need a team around me. The nonprofit I'm partnering with will send a few people, and the hospital will have host surgeons and residents, but I'd like to have my own surgical crew as well, people who already know my methods, people I can trust.

People like Bailey.

With that thought, I grab a notepad, a pencil, and a cup of coffee, and I get to work in my home office. I don't plan on leaving this spot for the rest of the evening. I need to make a proposal so damn convincing, Bailey can't possibly turn it down. I need to explain everything clearly so there won't be any more surprises.

I research everything from education options for Josie to rental homes around the hospital. I call my contacts at the nonprofit and they pass along helpful information.

I'm on a call with a friend of a friend who runs the pediatric department down at National Children's Hospital, getting advice about schools, when I realize I haven't eaten since breakfast and it's already half past eight. I take my phone with me into the kitchen and continue talking as I make a peanut butter sandwich. After I scarf it down, I throw a handful of spinach into my mouth—*for health*—and then get right back to the grind.

I don't stress over the fact that Bailey hasn't reached out.

I don't worry that she might have already made up her mind not to come.

I don't consider that she might not forgive me for keeping this from her for so long.

Instead, I keep going. Keep Googling. Keep typing. Keep changing the fucking font on this Word document to something friendly and non-threatening. I'm looking for something that says, *This proposal is a good idea. Listen to your boyfriend.*

Move to Costa Rica.

CHAPTER THIRTY-TWO
BAILEY

I'M A WRECK. I keep wishing I could snap my fingers and go back to last week. I want to pick up the phone and beg Matt to come over so we can patch things up, but I don't have my head on straight yet. Having him come over, dragging him into my room and onto my bed would only confuse me more.

Although would it? Maybe a good romp in the hay would really clear up this whole debate for me. I'd better call him right this second—

No. Bad Bailey!

Change is inevitable. In a few months, Matt's going to move to Costa Rica and I have two options: go with him or stay here. The idea of going with him is still completely out of the question. Chances are, he wasn't even being that serious when he suggested it. He was probably trying to spare my feelings. Even if he was serious and he does want me to come, how would that even be possible? I can't just upend my life on a whim. *Pack your bags, Jos, we're going abroad!*

Unfortunately, option two—him moving without me— is too hard to even contemplate.

So, you see, I'm stuck in the middle, feeling like a fool for how torn up I am over this. We've only been together a few weeks, and yet the thought of him leaving drags me right back to the dark place I haven't visited since I lost my parents. I'm up at all hours of the night, tossing and turning. Food has lost its appeal. I walk around in a malaise, trying and failing to put on a good front for Josie. I force fake smiles she sees right through.

She knows something's up, but I haven't told her about the grant. I don't think I should until I know for certain what I'd like to do. She's as attached to Matt as I am at this point. She insists upon writing him a thank you letter for her Christmas gifts and asks why he hasn't come over for dinner this week. She even tucks *The Hunger Games* into my purse so I can drop it off for him at work. *"Just in case he wants to read it!"*

I was stupid to bring him into our lives as quickly as I did. I should have made sure this was a real, lasting relationship before I introduced her to him.

Now when he leaves, she'll be just as heartbroken as I am.

Over the next few days, I spend untold hours researching Costa Rica. I have a password-protected folder on my laptop codenamed "very boring work stuff" where I've saved everything I've found so far: information about the MacArthur grant, articles highlighting Matt and his proposal. I look into the hospital, and I even find pictures of Matt on past medical mission trips. One in particular guts me: he's leaning over a hospital bed, handing a teddy bear to a girl no older than ten. She's hooked up to a million machines, but that doesn't dull her megawatt smile. The caption below explains that she's just undergone a life-changing procedure thanks to Matt and his team. She'll get to live a fuller, more pain-free life because of him.

The picture proves what I already know: Matt has to go to Costa Rica.

On the Thursday after Matt and I had our fight in the on-call room, I'm sitting at dinner with Josie and I decide to broach the subject of moving.

"Do you like it here?" I ask, trying to sound vague.

She scrunches her nose, confused. "Like in this house? It's fine. I mean, ideally I'd have a bigger room and more storage space for my books but—"

"No, here as in this city, your school—that sort of thing."

She shrugs and takes a bite of spaghetti before she replies, "Yeah, it's cool."

Fourteen-year-olds are some tough nuts to crack.

I persist, trying to keep my questions general enough that she won't grow suspicious. "Have you ever thought about living somewhere else? Like as a foreign exchange student?"

Her gaze flips up to me and she looks concerned. "Are you thinking of shipping me off somewhere? Because I know I said I'd put away the clean dishes before you got home from work, but I was doing my homework and—okay fine! I was actually finishing up a reread of *Twilight*, but I swear I'll do it right now!"

Her chair screeches against the floor as she hops to her feet.

I shake my head, trying not to laugh. "No! No, nothing like that. I just remember when I was your age, I always thought it'd be cool to live abroad for a year or two. A lot of my friends traveled in college, but I didn't get the chance."

She nods and sits back down, finally understanding. "Of course. Duh. My friend Sarah went to live with her dad in France last summer and she came back with the coolest stories and a million cool pictures to post on Instagram—" She suddenly stops and glances up at me tentatively. "I mean, sure, it'd be fun, but all that stuff doesn't matter. I like living here with you."

She waves to our kitchen and I realize she's trying to spare my feelings. To her, this conversation is all hypothetical. We don't have the money for travel. The closest she'll likely get to going abroad is watching a documentary on the travel channel.

I spend the rest of the night hunched over my computer, researching.

THE NEXT DAY at work, I head straight to the operating room. It's been my M.O. for the last few days and it's proven successful so far. By hiding out in here, I limit the chances of having any awkward hallway encounters with Matt. We only see each other when we're scrubbed in, surrounded by a dozen people, ready to operate. I hide under my layers, glad for the mask and protective glasses. If we speak, it's about the case at hand, though there are still subtle hints that let me know this distance is killing him as much as it's killing me. I see it every time our eyes meet. A storm. A longing. The words that live and die on his tongue.

He doesn't linger after surgery. He doesn't try to corner me in the hall or ask me if I've thought any more about his offer, though now more than ever, I wish he would push a little. On Monday, I needed space. Tuesday and Wednesday and Thursday, I needed to get my head straight, but now—*now* it's been five days since I've felt Matt's mouth on mine, since his hands have been on my skin. I miss him in my bed. I miss having to make do with the tiny wedge of mattress between Matt's body and the wall. Without him, it feels like I might as well be sleeping on a bed made for Shaq with the amount of room I have to spread out. I hate it. I miss him.

I won't survive the weekend like this.

I don't care about Costa Rica or our future. Responsibility *shmonsibility*. I want to be impulsive and dumb. I want to put a pin in my decision-making process and feel like us again, even if just for a moment.

The door to the OR swings open and Matt steps in. My breath catches in my throat and an electric feeling buzzes through me. It's painful—being this close to him every day, keeping my thoughts carefully contained. He greets the team and checks in on the patient. Meanwhile, I stand at the operating table, unable to tear my eyes away from him. It takes him five and a half years to cross the OR and step into the gown I'm holding open for him. When our gazes meet, my stomach tightens. It's a sucker punch every time.

"Morning Bailey," he says with a nod. "Everything set?"

"Let's not fight and I think you should go to Costa Rica and I wish I could go, but I don't think it would work with Josie and we only just started dating and that navy scrub cap really brings out your eyes and I think I'm falling in love with you even though we haven't talked in days. And were you serious about me coming with you because I might just be insane enough to take you up on the offer."

Those are the things I leave unsaid as I clear my throat and look down at the trays I finished setting up a few moments ago.

"Everything is ready to go."

"All right then, let's get started."

"EXCUSE ME, ARE you the woman who was assisting

339

Dr. Russell in the OR earlier?"

I pause in between bites of my sandwich, annoyed that someone is interrupting my lunch. I've learned my lesson—I can't eat in the staff lounge. All anyone wants to talk about is Matt and his grant and how I feel about it and are we dating and are those new diamond earrings really from him? So today I planned ahead and went down to the hospital's lobby to eat my lunch. I'm tucked away in a massive leather chair in a corner near the front windows. I thought I was hidden pretty well, but apparently not.

I hold a hand next to my mouth and hold up a finger—the universal sign for, *Just one second, I'm chewing.*

"No worries." The woman laughs softly. "I'm the one interrupting your lunch break."

I gulp down my bite and then force a smile. "It's fine, really. Um, in answer to your question, yes, I was assisting him earlier."

She grins, pleased with my answer, and then she takes the seat opposite me.

Alrighty then. Help yourself.

I was sort of hoping this would be a two-second conversation—*yes, I was in the OR. Okay, bye now*—but apparently not. I longingly look down at the second half of my sandwich, and then I force my attention back to her. I notice then that she doesn't really fit in with NEMC's usual crowd. For one, she's a total hippie. She's beautiful, but not in an intimidating way, more in a salt-of-the-earth, ethereal-art-teacher way. The pattern on her long maxi skirt is made of abstract swirls of magenta and blue, and her cream turtleneck stretches adorably over a very round baby bump.

"I'm so relieved to have found you. I've been trying to get in contact with Dr. Russell for weeks and I can't seem to track him down." She reaches into her purse and pulls out a small chocolate bar. "Do you mind?" I nod, dumbly, and she tears into it. "Sorry, this baby really likes chocolate. I wasn't even really a fan of it before, but it's all I want to eat these days."

"Umm…"

I look around us, wondering if anyone else in the lobby can see this woman. Am I hallucinating? I know I haven't been eating much lately, but…

She must sense my confusion because she laughs and smacks her forehead. "Of course. Where are my manners? I'm Victoria, Dr. Russell's ex-wife."

My mouth drops and I say very bluntly, "No way."

Her shrugs. "Guilty as charged I'm afraid." Then she flinches. "Oh, don't tell him I said that. It was meant as a joke, but now it just seems mean. He's truly not such a bad guy. Not so good at returning phone calls—or emails, for that matter—but other that, he's decent." She laughs again. "I don't know why I'm telling you this. You work for him—*you* probably know him better than I do nowadays."

Maybe so considering I also sleep with him…at least I used to.

I swallow that thought, stay quiet, and nod.

This can't be right. In my head I'd pictured her as a caricature of an ex-wife: bitter and out for blood. This woman sitting across from me is neither of those things. She's a glowing pregnant lady nibbling on chocolate.

"We were married a *long* time ago," she emphasizes before pointing one finger down at her belly. "Obviously "

"Congratulations," I say, because what the heck else am I supposed to say? "About your pregnancy, not about it being a long time ago."

She grins. "Thank you. Want a piece?" Her chocolate bar is outstretched toward me and I've had a terrible morning, so of course I accept a few squares. We munch for a moment or two in silence and then she continues. "Matt—er, Dr. Russell hasn't been returning my messages and I really need to speak with him. We invested in this tiny condo when we were newlyweds, and I put it up on the market last year. It finally sold and—" Our gazes meet and she stops suddenly, realizing none of this is really my business. "Sorry, I'm an over-sharer. Don't ever sit by me on an airplane or I'll chat your ear off the whole flight."

"It's okay."

She flashes a remorseful frown. "You probably just want to get back to your lunch, but I was hoping you'd help me track him down. He wasn't in his office when I went up to speak with him after the surgery, and his assistant said she couldn't tell me when he'd be back. Also, she sort of yelled at me to leave him alone."

I resist a laugh. Matt probably needs peace and quiet after the week he's had. Patricia is likely scaring everyone away on his orders.

"Yeah, Patricia's fiercely loyal. She's been with him since he started here."

"What about you? Have you two been working together for long?"

I was wondering if our conversation would veer in this direction. In fact, I've sort of been dreading it. I could smile and tell her I just started working with him, or I could be honest and volunteer that he and I aren't just coworkers. I really want to choose the first option, but I've never been very good at deception.

Not to mention, this meeting could be used as an opportunity of sorts, one I might not ever get again. Perhaps I'd be silly to pass it up because Victoria knows more than anyone what it's like to be in a relationship with

Matt, and right now, I could definitely use some advice.

So, I take a deep breath, put down my sandwich, and lay out the truth. "Matt and I aren't just coworkers. We're dating."

Her brows arch and she blinks a few times in quick succession. I think I've really surprised her.

"I didn't know Matt was dating."

I blush. "It's new."

She waves her hands hurriedly. "That came out wrong. I just meant I wasn't *aware* he was even interested in dating, let alone dating someone seriously. What's your name?" she asks tentatively, and I'm surprised to find it's not speculation or annoyance in her eyes—it's curiosity, and maybe even a little relief.

"Bailey."

She smiles. "Can I be honest with you, Bailey?"

I nod, bracing myself for some salacious piece of gossip that will tear through my heart.

"You seem like you're too sweet for Matt."

Funny. Most days I think it might be the other way around. No one at New England Medical Center would believe me though. In this building, he walks around like a hulking beast with a short fuse and a ferocious growl. They have no idea of the man he truly he is.

"Matt's told me a little bit about your relationship," I venture, curious to see her reaction.

"Oh god," she groans. "I was a real bitch there at the end. I hope he didn't paint me too poorly."

I smile. "Not at all. He actually puts a lot of the blame on himself."

"That doesn't surprise me." She leans back in her chair and nibbles off a bite of chocolate. "We were both young. We wanted different things." Her gaze shifts and she studies me as if contemplating her next words very carefully. Then she continues solemnly, "Matt's not ever going to change. Work will always be his mistress and you'll always have to look the other way. When we were married, I tried to keep myself busy. I volunteered at the library and got a part-time job. I never wanted to be a nag when he didn't show up for dinner or missed my calls. I really toughed it out for a while, but in the end, I just couldn't see what the allure was for him. I couldn't understand why he couldn't prioritize me over his job." She shrugs. "But he worked himself ragged then. Maybe he's different now."

I think of the spare pillow and blankets in his office and laugh. "He's not."

Her mouth twitches in disappointment. "I'm not trying to warn you away from him, honestly. Matt just always seemed slightly out of my reach even when we were married, like I always loved him a little more than he loved me. It drove me crazy. I guess I just want to be sure you know what you've gotten yourself into."

I look down at my hands and let her words settle over me. She's not exactly telling me anything I didn't already know. I half-expected her to launch into a tirade about all his idiosyncrasies like ex-spouses do when they've been pushed well past their limit. *Here's another thing: he never put the toilet seat back down after he went to the bathroom! And is it that freaking hard to load your dish in the dishwasher instead of leaving it in the sink?*

This warning about a man who is devoted to his work is exactly the version of Matt that tugged on my heartstrings in the first place.

"It's funny, I hadn't really thought about it until now, but it makes perfect sense for him to fall for someone like you." I jerk my gaze back to her and find that she's been studying me intently. "You're beautiful, obviously, but it's more than that. You seemed so competent in that operating room earlier. I stood in the back of the gallery and watched the way you two worked together, almost as if you were one person instead of two." Then she laughs, thinking of something. "And God knows you won't have to worry about spending enough time together. That surgery lasted forever! I was tired just watching it."

I smile and just then, a deep voice calls her name near the entrance of the building. She turns and waves cheerfully. Meanwhile, my heart lurches in my chest. I lean forward so I can peek one eye around the wing of the leather chair and watch as Matt veers from his route toward the elevator bank and makes his way over to us. My eyes widen. My heart starts racing. Should I lean back and pretend I don't see him? Make a mad dash for it?

With the subtlety of a freight train plowing straight into me, Matt's attention swoops in my direction. The surprise on his face vanishes. His blue eyes cloud over and now I swear he's taking even faster, longer strides. The ball of tension I've been living with all week is back and bigger than ever.

He reaches us and comes to stand beside my chair, gripping the top edge. I peer up at him from beneath my lashes but don't say a word. From this angle, his jaw looks especially chiseled.

Victoria is actually the first one to speak, and her voice is light and amused when she explains, "I've just been chatting with your surgical assistant, Matt."

The look he aims down at me cuts me deep. Furrowed brows, sad eyes—it's like he thinks I introduced myself to her as his surgical assistant and nothing more.

"I also told her we're dating."

Well...we were.

Relief floods his gaze before he turns to Victoria.

She's beaming at us.

"You two make a striking pair in your matching scrubs," she says, waving her hand up and down us. "Though I have to be honest, I already told Bailey she's way too good for you."

He smiles tightly and shakes his head. "Well, let's hope she doesn't listen to you. I hear pregnancy brain is a real thing."

She tosses her head back and laughs, and I sit like a statue, suddenly uncomfortable to be sitting here with them. Maybe I should give them a moment of privacy. I shoot to my feet and my sandwich hits the ground with a dull smack.

Oh, right, my lunch. My stomach lurches in protest at the sight. I couldn't finish it now if I tried.

Matt's hand hits my shoulder and his grip is just the slightest bit too tight. The message is clear: he doesn't want me to leave, but I need to. I want to give them the chance to talk, and I want to absorb what Victoria just told me. I want to gather myself a bit before I have to speak to him in full, comprehensible sentences.

His gaze implores me to stay, but I shake my head and step out of his reach. "You two have things to discuss. I'll be up in your office." His brows rise in shock at my promise, and I offer a reassuring smile before turning to Victoria. "It was really nice to meet you."

She grins and hands me the last half of her chocolate bar. "Want it? For the road?"

Of course I do. I eat that chocolate bar on my way up to Matt's office and I half-expect Patricia to block my entrance, but I breeze right past her as she continues flipping through her magazines.

"Been wondering when I'd see you again," is all she says before I shut his door behind me.

I stand there at the threshold as my gaze sweeps from the couch to his desk to the open bathroom door. Memories fill every nook and cranny as Victoria's words replay in my mind.

Matt's not ever going to change.

Work will always be his mistress.

It makes perfect sense for him to fall for someone like you.

The way you two worked together, almost as if you were one person instead of two.

Yes, Matt's passionate about his career and he'll always be pulled in a million different directions. He won't answer every one of my calls or be able to make it home for dinner every night. I'll always have to share his attention. For some people, that might be a deal breaker. For me, it only solidifies what I already love about him.

I understand Matt in a way not many people do. I'd never ask him to pick me over his career. It'd be like trying to split a heart in two. Matt lives and breathes medicine, and I wouldn't have it any other way. In fact, it's enough for me just to be a part of it, to watch him save lives, to walk alongside him as he strives to make a difference in the world around him. I want to help carry some of the burden. We could build that clinic together. I could be his right hand in life just like I'm his right hand in the operating room.

We're a perfect fit, and maybe I'm the last one to realize that.

Maybe it's time I tell him exactly how I feel.

When he throws open the door to his office a few minutes later, his eyes rove wildly across the space, looking for me. I push up off the couch as he steps in, and he sighs with relief when he sees that I fulfilled my promise to wait for him here. He shuts the door, and the heavy wood shoves my good sense and restraint out into the hallway. All that's left is the wild beat of my heart, my feet carrying me toward him in quick strides. Without a moment's hesitation, I fling myself into his arms.

My face is buried in his scrubs. I inhale his cologne as his hand caresses my hair. His arm is clamped around my waist and we stay like that for so long, just breathing one another in. My feet are a few inches off the ground. His chest is broad and warm. I think he took the stairs to get up here—he's breathing heavy and his heart is racing and I'm floating and Matt's telling me he's sorry again for doing this to us, for keeping a secret, for our shit luck and bad timing.

I squeeze my eyes closed and wrap my arms around his neck and hang on, hang on, hang on to him and to this moment before real decisions get made. Life continues outside his office, but right now, it's just us, squashed together so tightly neither one of us can catch a full breath. He sets me down slowly and his hands cradle my face. He tilts my head up and I wet my bottom lip instinctively.

"Bailey."

He sounds hoarse, and there's a deep crease between his brows.

My hands fist the front of his shirt and I'm up on my toes, eyelids fluttering shut as his mouth descends on mine.

Our kiss is slow and gentle, a testing of waters. I'm the one to increase the tempo. "I need this," I beg breathily, and Matt delivers. My knees buckle as the kiss intensifies.

Our tongues touch and there's a flutter in my stomach. I have a need only Matt can satisfy with his big hands and his impatient growl. I'm lifted up off my feet again and carried to his couch.

God, we have so much to talk about, but even more than that, we have moments to make up for. Moments we lost this last week. Moments in which his mouth drags down my neck. Moments in which his hands dip under my scrub top and untie the little bow at my waist. My pants are loose enough that it's easy for him to slide his hand down, skimming across the seam of my panties and then confidently dipping his hand right past it.

We absolutely have to stop. We're in his office in the middle of a work day. The sun gleams bright through the window behind his desk and I can hear Patricia on the phone outside, yet my hands are tugging angrily at his scrubs. I want to shred the fabric into pieces.

I'm stripping him quickly, but he still beats me to the punch. Our clothes are kicked off and forgotten on the floor and *Hello, Matthew's firm ass. I've missed you.*

Cold leather hits my back as he lays me down. Our fingers entwine as his mouth finds mine and then he forcefully moves my hands up over my head and holds them against the cushions. His hard chest crushes me and our hungry kisses turn hot and teasing. I'm an animal as I bite his lip and grind my hips up against his.

More.

He lets go of my hands and I hook my arms around his neck, keeping him pressed against me as his knee spreads my thighs apart. He skims a hand down across my breasts, teasing each one before he moves down to my navel...and then lower. My eyes squeeze closed as his middle finger finds my wetness. Slow, torturous circles spin me right out of control. I arch my back and meet his hand, encouraging him to continue, and I think he's as impatient as I am because our foreplay lasts about thirty seconds and then he's finding his wallet. I yank it out of his hand and find the condom tucked inside. No, crap—he's better at this than I am and now I've delayed us even longer. He laughs as he takes it out of my hand and rolls it onto his hard length. My tongue lolls out of my mouth and my eyes are as wide as saucers, but he's too focused to notice my reaction. *Thank God.*

"Bailey?" he asks gently, glancing up at me from beneath his dark brows.

I wish I could frame a photo of him exactly as he appears in this moment. With his black hair tousled from my hands and his lips dark red from my kisses, he's my fantasy come to life.

I nod and bite my lip, more than ready when he slowly thrusts inside me.

It's there, in that slow roll of his hips, in the deep, real connection that I finally feel clarity sink into my bones. I grip his cheeks and force his gaze up, and then I say very simply, "I want to come with you."

He's shocked—obviously—because he stops mid-thrust and asks me to repeat myself.

I laugh and kiss him quickly. "I want to come to Costa Rica. It's wild, but not totally out of the realm of possibility. I've been looking into it all week."

His eyes betray how taken aback he is by my words. "Are you serious?"

I nod and run my fingers gently down his back. I can't believe we're having this conversation right now. *In this position.*

"I still have to talk to Josie. If she doesn't want to go, if she doesn't want to leave her friends, I won't make her."

"Of course. I know that. I would never ask you to."

"So I might have to stay…"

I think we're about to discuss whether or not we'd try out long distance but he completely blindsides me.

"If you stay, I'm staying too," he says calmly, confidently, as if his mind is already made up. "I'll turn down the grant."

"Matt," I say incredulously.

"Bailey," he replies, mimicking my tone.

"You have to go."

He starts to move again, slowly dragging himself out and thrusting back in. I arch my back and he smiles, happy about my reaction.

"There's no point in trying to talk me out of it," he continues. "There will be other grants and other opportunities like this. There is only one of you."

I shake my head but he picks up the pace, and my body isn't quite sure what it's supposed to be focused on. My heart breaks at the idea of him giving up on Costa Rica, and yet I can't quite think of a logical argument to use against him because it's impossible to stave off this orgasm for much longer and then he makes it that much harder when his hand moves to my breast. He rolls his palm across my nipple and every thought flies right out of my head.

No! I chide myself. *This is important!*

"This is still so new. We could still crash and burn so easily," I point out as his hand moves down between my legs.

The side of his mouth hitches up in amusement. "Maybe. I've heard I'm pretty hard to tolerate. You'll probably get sick of me soon enough."

"Ma…*Matt*!"

351

I mean his name to come out as a reprimand for not taking this conversation seriously enough, but midway through it changes into a moan because his finger finds the exact right spot between my thighs, just above where he's sliding in and out of me.

"What?" he taunts, brow quirked.

He's daring me to continue this, to try to come up with sentences that have nouns and verbs and all I can do is pinch my eyes closed and grip his muscled shoulders as his finger speeds up and my orgasm builds to a mind-numbing, all-consuming, going-to-scream-if-you-don't-cover-my-mouth ending.

His mouth crashes down onto mine as I start to shake. Over and over again, sparks of pleasure shoot through me and my orgasm becomes his and he's right there with me, coming hard and kissing me to the point of pain.

For every moan we stifle, we take it out on each other with our hands and our mouths and his hips grinding me into the leather couch. I'm sweating and breathing hard as I flutter my eyes open and find myself back in Matt's office.

At work.

In the middle of the day.

I stifle a laugh and turn my head to kiss his cheek. His face is still tucked in the crook of my neck and his eyes are closed.

He doesn't want to rejoin the world. I think I broke him.

I poke his chest and he grunts.

"You're suffocating me," I groan.

He rolls to the side and blinks his eyes open, but neither one of us make a move to get up. His hand reaches up to cup my chin and he pulls my face toward him so his lips can find mine again. His hand curves around my bare hip. Desire ignites inside of me like a match catching fire. He's insane. I'm insane. This *feeling* is insane. *Can you fall in love in weeks? In days? In minutes?* I have nothing to compare this to, so I decide the best option is to just ask Matt.

"Will you be honest with me about your feelings really quick?"

"Now?" he groans, stringing kisses down my neck. His hand is stroking the inside of my thigh. My stomach dips with anticipation and my eyes flutter closed. I spread my legs just a little.

"It's not ideal timing, I know, but I already started and half the battle is bringing up the subject in the first place." I conjure superhuman willpower and push him away so my neck is left bare and cold, and his hand moves back up to my hip. Just like that, round two gets pushed to the back burner. Boy, am I an idiot.

Matt props his head on his hand and stares down at me, amused when I expected him to be annoyed. "I'm all ears, but just to be clear, in the back of my mind, I'm thinking about what I'm going to do to you after this conversation is over."

I shiver at the thought. "Oh dear. Right, I'll hurry. Okay, so you were married once, right?"

"Yes. Once."

"So you know what love feels like?"

The tip of his mouth lifts and could I be more stupid?! This whole thing is transparent. I'm supposed to keep my cool and lock my feelings away until some distant time in the future when it's obvious he loves me too, and then—and ONLY THEN—should I be honest about how much I am head over heels for him.

"No!" I say quickly. "I'm not bringing that word up because I'm about to *declare* it...I was just hoping for some clarification."

"Okay," he replies, and I'm glad he sounds mildly intrigued, but unfortunately, I can't seem to figure out the best way to explain myself. Then a brilliant idea smacks me in the face.

I grin. "Okay, how about this? Let's play doctor and patient."

I don't miss the glimmer of mischief in his eyes.

"You have my full attention," he muses.

I laugh and press my hand to his chest to keep him at arm's length in case he gets any wild ideas. "No. Stay focused! I'm going to give you my symptoms and you're going to decide if what I feel for you is just lust or if, y'know, maybe—"

"You're in love?" he finishes for me.

My face burns.

My brows pinch together as I ask, "Does that scare you?"

His gaze holds mine, but he doesn't reply, and I hate how indiscernible his features are. He never hides his feelings from me. Not usually.

"This is stupid," I say, turning to stare up at the ceiling.

"Tell me your symptoms," he goads with a cheeky smirk.

I roll my eyes, but he kisses my neck and nudges me with his nose, like a dog begging for pets. "Tell me."

"All right, well, let's see…my stomach flips with excitement whenever you enter a room."

"Mmm, could be either."

"Right." I nod and continue, "Um, you really turn me on."

He laughs. "Either."

"I'm considering moving to another country with you."

He hums.

"I see a future with you—not in a let's-get-married-tomorrow sort of way, but more like wow I really admire and respect you as a person and think you'd make a great husband, a great dad."

He pulls back and frowns, really studying me. It's not exactly the reaction I was going for—more balloons and confetti, maybe a smile would have been nice—but at least he doesn't push me off the couch and make a quick getaway.

"Dad," he repeats slowly.

I frown as a thought pops into my mind, one that hadn't occurred to me until this moment. "Oh, god. You want kids, don't you? Please say yes because my heart can't take much more this week."

His brows soften and he nods, kissing my forehead, tugging me close. "Yes. I want kids."

"Okay good."

"A couple."

I grin. "Even better. So, do you have a diagnosis for me?"

"I should probably run a few more tests," he quips as his hand wanders across my back and over my butt. He squeezes twice. "But even without them, it's pretty clear what you've come down with."

"Oh yeah?" I lean my head back and smile up at him.

His other hand rests on my forehead like he's taking my temperature. He hisses under his breath. "Just as I suspected—you've got it bad."

I crack up. "Love, huh? Well then, what's my treatment plan?"

"Kissing," he says before laying one on me. "That should help some." Then he rolls up and over me so his body pins me to the couch. "Sex. Twice daily, or more as needed." His mouth is over mine as he speaks and I feel his smile against my lips.

I groan.

"Side effects may include elevated heart rate, sweating, feelings of euphoria."

"Matt. You're killing me."

He doesn't let up though. He's really enjoying this.

"If symptoms don't subside in four to six months, we might need to adjust our treatment plan."

I quirk a brow. "More sex?"

How original.

He grins and shakes his head, leaning back so he can really get a good look at me. "No, Bailey. Commitment. Marriage. Happily ever after."

My smile feels shaky. My insides are made of ooey-gooey mush.

"Happily ever after?" I ask, my voice coming out squeaky.

His face turns somber and he produces an Oscar-worthy frown. "I'm afraid it might be the only cure." Then he breaks character, grins, and lays another one on me. "Now how do we convince Josie to move to Costa Rica?"

EPILOGUE
BAILEY

TWO YEARS LATER

"CAN YOU HEAR it?" I ask impatiently.

Matt's mouth hitches in an amused half-smile as he glances up at me. "I can hear the sandwich you had for lunch working its way through your bowels."

"Charming."

His eyes widen. "Hold on. Shh, I have it."

My heart leaps into my throat and I reach for the stethoscope. "Let me hear! Let me hear!"

He shakes his head and his finger presses to his lips as he slowly pushes the diaphragm of his stethoscope a few millimeters to the left. I'm splayed out on my back on our bed with my shirt tugged up to my bra, trying and failing to lie still.

Matt's expression softens, a little spark flares in his eyes, and I know he's got it. He's listening to our baby's heartbeat. I've heard it a few times, but the moments in the doctor's office are always too fleeting and too clinical. My OBGYN is usually busy adjusting the settings on the ultrasound machine, checking the baby's vitals, printing photos. It's always over before I've really had a good listen, but now that I'm a little over four months pregnant, our baby should be big enough for us to hear the heartbeat at home, just like this.

Matt glances down at his watch and I know he's counting the beats per minute. He's checking the baby's heart rate and listening for any murmurs or abnormalities.

Even in this setting, he can't resist the urge to check up on his most precious patient: his son. He nods a few seconds later and I know everything is as it should be.

I release a deep breath—one I didn't realize I was holding—as Matt tugs the earpiece off. His other hand stays steady with the diaphragm in place. "Here, listen. He's moving a lot, but you should be able to hear it."

I place the earbuds in my ears as fast as possible, but I'm not quick enough. I can't hear a thing. *Wait! I hear—*

No. That's my bowel.

I frown and shake my head. Matt adjusts the diaphragm a smidge to the left.

"There?"

"No."

He adjusts it again and—there! I can hear it!

I grab his wrist to still his movements. Our eyes lock. My other hand flies to my mouth. There's no doubt about what I'm hearing. It's like a galloping horse echoing through the earpiece, the most distinct, awe-inspiring sound in the world: a tiny heart beating inside me.

"It's so fast," I say, amazed.

Tears collect in the corners of my eyes.

Matt nods. "I counted 152 beats per minute, and no murmurs."

I smile then lean my head back on my pillow and close my eyes, listening. I could stay here all day. At this stage, our little boy is still so small that most of the time I can't feel any sign of him at all. Listening to his steady heartbeat is a reassuring reminder that he's in there, hanging out right where he should be.

I feel Matt's hand flatten over my small bump and then he whispers something I can't quite hear. I wink one eye open and watch him as he brushes his hand lovingly back and forth across my skin, as if he's touching our little boy.

"Your mom is listening to your heart right now, so you have to hold still," he says. I smile and reach down to ruffle his hair. He presses a kiss to my bump and then glances up. "I've been thinking about what we should name him."

"Oh?" I tilt my head to the side and take out the earpiece. "Josie has quite an opinion on that. She presents me with new ideas every day. Half of them are just the names of characters from her books. The latest round included: Peeta, Cedric, and Dumbledore."

Matt smiles. "I'd like to name him Thomas."

My gut clenches. "After my father?"

"Yes. What do you think?"

"I love it," I say, my tone betraying how touched I am that he would suggest it. "But Josie will be so disappointed we aren't using one of her suggestions."

He laughs. "Why don't we let her pick the middle name?"

I groan. "The power will go straight to her head."

Just then a chorus of screams crashes through our closed bedroom door. Josie and four of her friends are having a sleepover to celebrate her birthday. It's been planned for weeks. She's been talking my ear off about it. I had a very specific list of items to purchase at the grocery store after work: popcorn, chips, soda, candy, and birthday cake. I snuck apples in the cart too and Josie shoved them to the back of the fridge to make more room for soda. They'll all need to go straight to the dentist first thing in the morning.

It's currently half past nine, and there's no end in sight. After making pizza and feeding them dinner, Matt and I decided to hole up in our bedroom in an effort to save ourselves and (our ears) from five very chatty, *very loud* high school girls. Since then, we've snuck out twice. The first time, Matt and I needed to steal more of their pizza. We found them sitting on their pallets in the living room prank calling boys from their grade. Hilarious. I might have had them pass me the phone so I could participate but would firmly deny that in a court of law.

The second time we ventured out, it was because they were all screaming bloody murder. Matt and I rushed out to make sure everyone's limbs were still intact. We found all five of them huddled around Josie's phone watching ghost videos on YouTube and trying to scare the crap out of each another. Matt and I watched one of the videos too. I pursed my lips and swatted my hand, tacking on a heartfelt "That is totally fake!", but to be honest, I'll be sleeping with the light on tonight and Matt will be on ghost duty.

Now, they're at it again. Their laughter and shouts have hit an all-time high.

The stethoscope is forgotten. I need to teach this little baby how to execute a stealth mission. I roll off the bed like a massive walrus dumping itself into the ocean then scurry to the door in time to hear one of them shout, "Did he seriously just text you 'hi' and nothing else?! What are you supposed to say to that?"

"Josie!" another one of them shouts. "He's the hottest boy in our grade! You have to reply!"

Matt stays on the bed, chiding me for eavesdropping. I shoo him with my hand and press my ear to the door for better acoustics. Where's a plastic cup when I need it?

Josie's social life is alive and well thanks to the small private school we found for her in Costa Rica. Most of the students are also expats. She goes to school with teenagers from all over the world and last I checked, she has three boys from three different countries head over heels in love with her. She's still more into books than ever, but I'm not sure how much longer that will last.

"Eh, I don't really want to lead him on," Josie replies. "You know the other day I asked him who his favorite literary character was and he couldn't name one! Not one!"

There's some mumbling and inaudible conversation. Most of it is drowned out because Matt has turned the TV on and cranked the volume to a deafening level to teach me a lesson. I hurry over to mute it. There's a skirmish with the remote, but I eventually wrench it free, opting to use a carefully timed fake contraction to distract him. I'm a proud little monster as I mute the TV and run back to the door. He groans, but this is important! This is teenage-girl gossip.

"Oh my gosh, wait—did Derek just text you too? Why do you even bother with him? He's a *total* nerd."

"I like him," Josie insists, sounding a little defensive. "We're friends."

"Why?! He doesn't hang out with any of the cool guys."

"So? Who cares? He's really funny, and I happen to think he's the cutest boy in our grade."

I pump my fist in the air. That's my girl.

Go for the nerd, Josie!

I turn, brush my hands together as if to say, *My job here is done*, and then stroll back to the bed.

"Happy with yourself?" Matt asks, looking adorable propped up against our headboard with his shirt off. He really should never wear clothes.

I grin. "Very."

I'm glad to see Josie seems to still have a good head on her shoulders, especially considering the whirlwind of the last two years. Moving to another country, starting a new school, adjusting to life with Matt, and now with this new baby on the way—I've kept her at the forefront of my thoughts, careful to make sure she's not totally overloaded with all the change.

We've worked hard to ensure she feels like part of our unit. When Matt was considering proposing to me, he took Josie with him to the jewelry store so she could help him pick out a ring. He later told me she tried to pick out the biggest stone they had (worth tens of millions) and he had to talk her into something a little more realistic, one that wouldn't cause back strain.

At our tiny wedding ceremony on the beach with close friends and family, Josie acted as flower girl, ring bearer, and maid of honor. If we'd allowed it, she would have been the officiant as well.

"I just got certified online! I think...I'm not sure. I had to enter your credit card information."

When Matt and I were first thinking of trying to conceive, Josie accidently found my stash of pregnancy tests in our bathroom cabinet. I was making dinner and she walked out, cradling the boxes in her arms, tears running down her face.

I freaked out, assuming the worst—that she was overwhelmed and upset we hadn't consulted her first—but then with a shuddering sob, she exclaimed, "OH MY GOD! I'm going to be an aunt!"

She didn't really care that I wasn't actually pregnant yet. To her, the possibility was just as exciting.

We've settled into life here easier than I thought we would. The clinic has taken off. Matt and I both spend our days there, continuing to train staff from all over Costa Rica and operating on patients three days a week. When the grant committee approached Matt and offered him the opportunity to stay on for another two years with full funding, we all jumped at the chance. We love our life here and even though we'll likely move back to the States when Josie goes off to college, we're all happy to be here now, growing as a family of three, soon to be four.

Another chorus of laughter rings out from our living room and Matt tugs me closer on the bed.

"You know we're not getting any sleep tonight, right?" I joke.

"Well, I guess there's only one thing we can do," he replies with a smirk.

I know immediately what he's suggesting.

"*No*. You're terrible. We said last time would be it. No more."

"C'mon," he says, nuzzling my neck. "You know you want to."

I smile and shake my head. "You're a terrible influence."

"You're the one who got me addicted."

It's true. This is all my fault.

He's already turning on the TV and navigating to Netflix. "C'mon, indulge your husband."

"Fine," I say, throwing my hands up in mock defeat.

Then we sit together, hip to hip, while the *Grey's Anatomy* theme song plays on our TV.

A few minutes later, he gestures to the screen. "Oh, c'mon! Those doctors would totally get caught."

He's talking about the surgeons currently getting it on in a storage closet.

I clear my throat. "Matt, *we* did that."

He narrows his gaze on me thoughtfully. "As I recall, we didn't actually kiss."

I roll my eyes. "Close enough."

He quirks a brow. "So you don't think there's a

difference between an almost kiss and the real thing?"

He starts to shift toward me. He has ideas brewing beneath that thick head of hair. There are teenage girls squealing with delight in the living room and I'm holding him at bay as he guides me down onto the bed. In seconds, I'm underneath him and he looks almost sinister from this angle, too intimidating for his own good.

He props a hand on either side of my head and cages me in against the blankets. I couldn't move if I tried.

"What are you doing?" I ask, voice shaky.

His smirk makes my stomach flutter. "Proving a point."

He bends his head and I arch up to meet him instinctively. We've done this a million times; my body knows just what to do—except he doesn't kiss me. His mouth barely skims mine and he's grinning like a fiend. I'm left...*wanting*.

Damn him.

"Tell me I'm right," he taunts. "Tell me they'd get caught."

"Ugh." I jerk my head away. "No! You're not allowed to critique the storyline and point out the inaccuracies the whole time. It's a TV show—just go with it."

He leans back, as if deeply insulted. "Pfft. I don't do that."

I narrow my eyes. "Are you kidding?"

He laughs and makes a move to roll off me, but I grip his shoulders and force him to stop.

"Um, excuse me—aren't you forgetting something?"

I pucker up and he rewards me with a heart-shattering kiss. Only after we've broken apart and I'm catching my breath does he think to ask, "By the way, I've been wondering—what would my *Grey's Anatomy* nickname be?"

"You already have one, remember? You're my very own Hotshot Doc."

He frowns. "But there has to be a 'Mc' in front of it."

"Okay then, how about Dr. McGivesHisPregnantWifeFootRubs?"

"Doesn't roll off the tongue."

"Okay...Dr. McPassesThePopcorn?"

"You see how that doesn't work, right? It has to be pithy."

I tap my chin. "Oh okay, yeah. I've got one now. Hear me out."

"All right."

"Are you listening?"

"Yeah."

"Dr. Mc..."

After a long pause, he finally asks, "You don't have one do you?"

"The good ones are already taken!"

He laughs and tugs me closer. "Okay, you're right. Let's just stick with Hotshot."

Find other R.S. Grey Books on Amazon!

Not So Nice Guy
Arrogant Devil
The Beau & the Belle
The Fortunate Ones
The Foxe & the Hound
Anything You Can Do
A Place in the Sun
The Summer Games: Out of Bounds
The Summer Games: Settling the Score
The Allure of Dean Harper
The Allure of Julian Lefray
The Design
The Duet
Scoring Wilder
Chasing Spring
With This Heart
Behind His Lens

Made in the USA
Middletown, DE
08 September 2025

17291240R00220